Prayer for the Blood Angel

*To: Martin
Enjoy!*

CHANTELLE ROBERTS

Copyright © 2014 Chantelle Roberts.

Author photo by Adele Roberts

All rights reserved. No part of this book may be reproduced, stored, or transmitted by any means—whether auditory, graphic, mechanical, or electronic—without written permission of both publisher and author, except in the case of brief excerpts used in critical articles and reviews. Unauthorized reproduction of any part of this work is illegal and is punishable by law.

ISBN: 978-1-4834-1021-0 (sc)
ISBN: 978-1-4834-1022-7 (hc)
ISBN: 978-1-4834-1020-3 (e)

Library of Congress Control Number: 2014905644

Because of the dynamic nature of the Internet, any web addresses or links contained in this book may have changed since publication and may no longer be valid. The views expressed in this work are solely those of the author and do not necessarily reflect the views of the publisher, and the publisher hereby disclaims any responsibility for them.

Any people depicted in stock imagery provided by Thinkstock are models, and such images are being used for illustrative purposes only.
Certain stock imagery © Thinkstock.

Printed in the UK by 4edge Limited

For the unmolded soul inside us all

Acknowledgements

I would like to thank the editorial and design team at Lulu Publishing Services. You have all been extremely patient, helpful and positive during the lengthy process that is publishing a novel.

I would like to give a special thank you to my editor, Clifford Dean. I enjoyed the shared moments where we laughed entirely at my expense. I appreciate all your hard work very much.

To my family, thank you for letting me get on with it in my own time and for giving me the opportunity to realize a dream. Thank you also for giving me raw material to work with when it came to the more colorful characters. I love you all.

Contents

Prologue xi

Chapter 1: Bethriam falls 1
Chapter 2: Daggers and darkness 24
Chapter 3: Prophesies 37
Chapter 4: The great divide 56
Chapter 5: Chosen paths 76
Chapter 6: Alliances 92
Chapter 7: Confrontations 124
Chapter 8: Dark days 156
Chapter 9: New magic 191
Chapter 10: Small victories 222
Chapter 11: Good intentions 251
Chapter 12: Progress 287
Chapter 13: The resistance 321
Chapter 14: Waiting 343
Chapter 15: The last day 377
Chapter 16: War 404
Chapter 17: Death 419
Chapter 18: Pestilence 432
Chapter 19: Famine 452
Chapter 20: Old magic 477

Epilogue 511

Prologue

He was right. Once all the nations had called their armies home, folded and packed away their war banners and buried their dead, they asked us; *how could you let it happen?*
    We had no real answer. "We are a young race" just didn't seem to cut it anymore. We have used that line too often now. The truth is that we allowed a relatively small group of people, to commit terrible and unspeakable crimes, as we have done so many times before.
    Most races have called us weak and afraid. Some have told us we need to learn to love ourselves so that we can rid our hearts of fear and lies. A few have decided that we will never cease to be cruel and base.
    I believe we are plagued by an innate ability to remain spiritually stunted; we can never seem to separate power from the ego, we fail to take responsibility because we are afraid of how much effort it will take, we continuously allow ignorance to play a role in our daily lives, we fashion ourselves free thinkers but we do not listen to each other and we are all so aware of our mortality that we forget we are alive right now.
    One day, it will be the undoing of our race.

*Effortless is the path that strays from love,
Sublime is the poison of fear*

Chapter 1
Bethriam falls

Something was tugging at her, and she paid it no heed.

'My lady!' Ramroth was desperately trying to pull her away from the window framing the slaughter beyond. 'There is still time,' he hissed through clenched teeth, at the effort of heaving her inert body toward him.

Wraiths were falling from the sky; thick and black, like acid rain upon the land. Dreya breath set flame to the atmosphere as their riders tried to defend the people down below. The talons and scales of many cruel, winged creatures glistened in the wake of the rising star and hummed through the ash-ridden air. The kuvuta were here. Demons banished had returned. This would be the end of her people, and bile stung the young queen's throat as the massacre played out.

A wraith, astride his black beast, circled before them. Its steed was clutching the lifeless body of a Bethrimian soldier in its claws, screeching wildly as others tried to tear pieces of the corpse away. Dark blood splattered against the glass, casting shadows of black tears on Arial's face. She shoved the old wizard away and retched violently across the floor, wiping her mouth with her silken cowl.

'Arial!' He had never before addressed her by her birth name but formality had been lost to desperation. 'We must leave *now*!'

She allowed herself to be dragged from the room, numb and unaware of her surroundings, down the stone passageways and spiral staircases she had grown up in. Memory kept her feet from tripping over the cobblestones and cracks that riddled the floors. Torches illuminated the flickering images of people trying to flee to any place of safety, their cries echoing off the cold walls like a nightmare. Twice Ramroth had to push hysterical mothers clutching infants away from the stoic Arial. They would only slow them down. No one else could be spared.

Finally they reached the corridor that led to the palace keep. It was quieter down here, and as Ramroth locked the heavy, wooden door behind them, there was a muted silence.

Ronan called out to her as he heard her dragging footsteps drawing closer to him, and Arial stirred from her paralysis. He had been afraid she would not come. He had smelled their stench just before they had entered Bethriam's atmosphere, and it had taken thirty strong men to hold him down as he had fought to reach his keeper. The alarm had sounded hours ago, but even then, it had been too late. He could feel her heart pounding in her chest, taste her bitter guilt for those she would leave behind while she was flown to safety. Fresh tears bit down in her eyes, and her feet faltered across the stone.

Ramroth, prepared as always, had kept behind the royal guard. They had eagerly volunteered to serve their homeland by joining the fight with the main hold but Ramroth had forbidden them to do so. He had told them that if they wanted to be of aid, they wouldn't waste their lives on a suicidal attempt to hold off the kuvuta until help came, but rather escort their standing monarch to safety. The magic slinger had looked murderous, rheumy eyes ablaze, aura humming an open invitation to any rider daring enough to challenge his word. Not one protested, but he doubted their obedience was for him. They were mounted and ready within the keep in mere minutes, and Ramroth had raced off to fetch the queen.

Arial burst out of the darkness through the granite entrance, the need to see her drey the only thing that kept her moving and armor clinked against scale as both man and beast knelt before their queen.

The keep was a colossal underground cavern large enough to house a hold of three hundred thousand dreya and their riders should the occasion arise. They were not a warring people, however, and Bethriam was home to an army of only one hundred thousand strong. There was a clean, underground spring in the cave, and fresh livestock was brought down twice daily. Black scorches upon the floor and thin wisps of smoke marked fires that had been hastily put out moments before. Large mounds of dung littered the floor and bats hung in enormous numbers from the high roof. The cavern dwarfed the small party still within it, all that would be left of Bethriam's army by noon.

Arial stepped forward, and her eyes met Ronan's. The warmth she found there gave her courage. She turned to face the warriors gathered before her.

'I thank you for your loyalty.' Her uneasy breathing filled the silent cavern as she tried to look these men in the eyes, knowing that their families would soon meet terrible deaths and they could not defend them because of her. One of the men stepped forward.

'My Queen, we share your sorrow and know you would gladly stay and fight with us but you cannot come to harm. We need your voice to warn others.' Arial bowed her head in admission; his words were true.

'You are all brave men,' she whispered. 'May your dreya die with you, many strong sons be born to replace you, and the daughters of the goddess lead you to her fields.' This was the finest blessing for a rider to receive and they bowed before her once again.

Ronan closed the gap between himself and his keeper in three short strides, the men still with bowed heads, and pressed his great snout against her, breathing heavily upon her chest. She stroked the leathery skin behind his ears gently and murmured encouraging words. She then mounted him with grace and ease, hitching her dress so that it fell around her hips in soft folds and pressed her thighs tightly around his muscular neck. She had never ridden Ronan with a saddle like other riders; she preferred to feel him beneath her, skin to scale. Ramroth hauled himself up clumsily and sat behind Arial, holding her around her waist.

Addressing the warriors from his elevated position he said, 'We engage nothing. We fly straight to Equa. Once we reach the planetary atmosphere and are within the safety of the High Council's realm, you will receive further instruction.'

Arial gave the signal, and in a single movement, twelve magnificent creatures and their riders rose into the air, making for a single aerial exit in the roof of the keep.

Tears and perspiration clung to Arial like morning dew, and as the rush of wings whipped the stale air around her face, she felt a part of her was being left down below in the cave, the shadows swallowing her up even as she flew toward the meager light. There was no radiance or fresh spring air to flood her senses, but she closed her eyes all the same and sucked in the last breath of Bethrimian air she would ever breathe. Savoring the taste and feel of it on her tongue, she prepared herself for what she was about to bear witness to.

*

Valador awoke with a start, an uneasy feeling in the pit of his stomach. He sat bolt upright, sweat-soaked and icy cold. It took him a couple of seconds to take in his surroundings and remember where he was, the ground hard and uncomfortable beneath him and his body aching with stiff joints and sore muscles. He tried to recall what had awakened him as he reached for his hip flask. He brought the bottle to his lips, breathing in the strong-smelling liquid and immediately thought better of it, rising groggily to his feet to drink from the stream nearby instead. Bending down, he drank deeply, refreshed by the cool water running down his parched throat. Valador stopped drinking, and the surface of the stream became still again, reflecting his face by the light of the moon. His hair had grown long and unkempt, his face was star-drenched and stony eyes stared back up at him. Twenty years of near solitude and just over one hundred years of life. Plenty of time to dwell upon the past, and he still failed to understand it. Banished from his homeland for high treason and branded a madman, he had been left to wander the Wild Worlds for longer than he cared to remember. The memory pulled painfully at his heart. He never wanted to be close to anyone or part of anything ever again. He wondered if his brethren felt the same, if they had suffered even half of the loss he had. The queen hadn't even looked him in the eye when she passed her judgment. Sometimes he wished she had sentenced him to death, rather than a lifetime of pain and desolation. He could see the look in her eyes even to this day. The last fleeting glance she had spared him; her troubled blue eyes seared his soul with doubt. He had always known they would have to talk about his position sooner or later, come up with some kind of plan to stem the flow of questions, but she had cast him out before he had even had a chance.

He sighed deeply, and his reflection shattered under his breath. Sometimes he felt as if his sorrow was the only thing that still made him a man and not some soulless shadow. He reached for his flask out of habit, took a generous swig, sauntered over to the dwindling embers of the fire, and emptied the rest over it. The fire hissed and sputtered back to life for a few seconds, illuminating the great beast that lay beside it. Valcan the mighty slept on, thin wisps of smoke curling hypnotically from his nostrils. Here lay the only thing alive that Valador still cared for, the only creature that had not betrayed him or left him alone to die. What was once the greatest of all the dreya now lay in a dusty clearing in the middle of the wilderness, Valador reflected sadly, with no glorious purpose, no fine blood line to lay claim to, and bound to a burnt out, sad and hung over keeper; a senseless waste.

Valcan was a rock drey, descended from the great Kylan himself. Valcan had chosen the young and ambitious warrior many years ago, and they had been summoned by the High Council in the Ivory Tower to lead the war against the darkness. They had been chosen from thousands of other crusaders for their superior combat skills, their impressive experience in battle, and for their flawless teamwork. Their bond was strong and together they made a formidable adversary to anyone brave enough to face them.

Rock dreya were bred large and powerful, covered from head to paw in tough leathery hide and armor like scales, double layered at the chest, which ranged in color from a brilliant bronze to a deep golden brown. Their fire came in massive mushrooms of impenetrable heat that acted like a shield to all who stood behind it, but an instantaneous death to anyone who stood before it. Valador, on the other hand, was of the ancient rider warlords. They were resilient and resourceful warriors, at home in the toughest of terrains, living for longer than was usual. That race had all but died out, their numbers spent in the wars of old. Valador often wondered if he was the last. Valador and Valcan. Warrior and war drey. They could wield fear into the hearts of even the bravest of brave. But as time passed, as it always does, their names slowly faded from reality into rumor, and now the dust covered the old records and erased them from time; the greatest figments of imagination to ever take flight in the skies of the Worlds. Valador chuckled despite himself. Valcan stretched his hind legs, and lazily scratched at the crusted mud on his belly. Valador envied his drey for his heat-retaining hide as he shivered under the cool of the dawn, fruitlessly trying to revive his meager fire. Suddenly he threw the stick he held into the surrounding shadows, his face twisted in anger. He sat alone in the wilderness fighting back tears as the images of his beautiful wife and daughter, the magnificent army he had once commanded, and his homeland, threatened to overwhelm him. He tried to calm himself, and closed his eyes against another day upon this lonely planet.

He was standing upon the Osgiliathian Mountains then, staring out at his army. His perfect art of war etched into the willing hearts of his soldiers. They would lay down their very souls for him, and for the Worlds. Valador could almost smell the sweet perfume of the woman that had stood beside him. Could almost hear the gurgles of the infant she held in her arms, and could still feel the warmth of her hand enclosed in his. The tears flowed unhindered now as Valcan came to sit beside him, unfurling his massive wing over his keeper's head to shelter him from the rain that now fell from the sky above.

*

'I know you do not wish to do this my lady, but I have explored all other options, and it seems this is the only door open to us,' Ramroth ventured gently since Arial's usual carefree demeanor was shattered. Just before they had flown up and out through the keep, she had felt Ronan pleading with her to shut her eyes and her mind to her surroundings until they had broken Bethriam's atmosphere, and left the horrors behind them. Arial was glad she had chosen not to heed his warning. The image of her beloved homeland swarming with black wings, and riddled with fire would stay imprinted upon her memory. She saw that image flash before her eyes even now, behind the safe walls of the High Council. It almost seemed as if she had dreamed it, standing before the massive arched doors that led to the council chamber. The cries of her people now just echoes in her broken heart. Her head was bowed as if in prayer, and she was hardly even listening to her ward; it had not been a long journey but a tiring one, and now her only thoughts were bent upon preventing anyone else sharing her grief.

Ramroth was watching his queen with growing unease. She had been reduced to but a shadow of her former self by the traumatic ordeal. Her skin had lost its youthful glow, and shadows of worry sat under her eyes. She spoke at last.

'They will do nothing but quail inside their Ivory Tower, even if they believe me, and watch the Worlds fall into the growing darkness. I understand that our choices are few, but to stand before this council of fools who care nothing for their people beyond what riches can be won, and who have long since forgotten their honor and their duty is surely madness.'

'We must try my lady. You hold sway over this council by birthright, and I believe you could make them allies to the people as they once were and if not, at least place a seed in their minds.' His words were gentle and persuasive, but Arial was still apprehensive. She stepped forward as the great ivory doors swung open, her invitation to enter.

'Nothing grows in the darkness Ramroth,' she said as she stepped inside, gown and golden hair rustling as she turned back to glare at him.

The doors shut tight behind her leaving the Adare' alone with his thoughts in the corridor. He didn't want to put her through this, but it would be far from a waste of their time if she could extract the information they needed. Ramroth knew that Arial spoke true and that the council would not listen, but he also knew that this was where he would find answers, no matter the question that was posed. He began nervously pacing, hoping he had done the right thing.

*

Arial's royal guard had made first contact with Equa ground in a clearing far from the looming Ivory Tower. The trees here were ancient. They stood like giant, ever-vigilant sentries, and trapped the heat beneath the thick canopy they created. The forest floor was a carpet of damp debris, all sounds seemed muted by age-old breath, and armor was stripped from sweating bodies.

A human emissary had ordered them to stay put, keep their dreya back, and to move no closer to the tower than they already were. The sheer height and majesty of the trees that surrounded them, in any case blocked out the sky-scraping stronghold that could be seen from almost every other vantage point, so Zach was pleased. The queen, however, had not taken so kindly to the news. She and Ronan were rarely ever separated, and she needed him now more than ever. This was what she had told Zach as he would not have a messenger speak directly to her. Her refusal to leave Ronan behind led to the terms being amended. In the end Zack had personally accompanied her to the tower with Ronan and Ramroth in tow.

The men were now sat on their haunches, huddled around their captain. Zach was a battle-hardened warrior fresh from the Coptic wars in delta nine. His reputation was fierce, and he effortlessly commanded attention and respect. He was a born leader, and a good man. But it had been hard for them all, witnessing their homeland become a butcher house. Even harder to fly away from it, knowing their loved ones were down below. Not much was said, not much *could* be said. They had simply waited for their captain to come back from escorting the queen, and speak words into their ears so that they could drown out the sounds in their heads, if only for a little while.

'When we arrived at the tower, we learnt that Ronan would be chained to the ground like a common dog,' Zach informed them in an uncharacteristically skittish tone, 'It seems the council has good reason to keep our dreya at bay and why they insisted on Ronan being bound.' He now dropped his voice even lower, and they all had to shuffle forward to catch his words, 'The only time I have seen that drey act the way he just did, was last night, when he smelt the devils coming. He only let himself be tied down by those bastards because she asked him to.'

The riders exchanged dark looks and curses under their breath at the lack of respect shown to their queen. 'We cannot fly back to Bethriam and leave Arial to the mercy of whatever dark force lurks here unseen...' but his words were cut short by a young soldier sitting close to the back of the group. Short, blonde hair and fiery, green eyes told of youth and aptitude untapped.

'But Captain! Survivors...' Owein began. Zach pierced him with a wrathful stare, and robbed Owein of his sentiments and courage. The rider dropped his gaze immediately, color flaring in his cheeks. Zach was on his feet now, his finger pointed skyward accusingly.

'Did you not see what we left behind?' he hissed, 'there will be no survivors, no one awaiting our return, and I will not leave our queen here with an old man and a chained drey as her only defense!' He walked a few paces away from the group, and turned his back on them. Zach stared hard at the ground between his sandaled feet, aware of the eyes of his loyal men on him. He had been wrong to speak so harshly to them. Many of them were too young to bear such great loss...they had lost everything. He turned to face them again, a pained expression on his face.

'Those of you that wish to return to Bethriam may of course do so. You are free to go even if it is simply to pay your last respects. I shall stay here, and guard one of the last pieces of my homeland that still draws breath.'

Lok stepped forward from the huddle of riders. He had served on Arial's royal guard since she had been crowned. He sported a nasty burn mark on his left forearm from restraining Ronan when Arial had cut her foot on a shard of glass two years ago. He had been luckier than one of the others who had stood in direct line of fire like a fool. Lok's eyebrow hair would still not grow. He was fiercely loyal, and had a good heart that had belonged to Arial ever since he had laid eyes upon her in their youth. It was he that had spoken in the keep back on their home planet when he had seen the guilt in her eyes. Now it pained him to offer to leave her but if he volunteered then the rest could stay and protect her.

'I will fly to Bethriam alone, and return with news. If there are any survivors, I will tell them to sit tight, and that help is on the way. The rest will stay here with you Captain, and guard our queen.' Zach slowly nodded his head in recognition of a good plan.

Lok belonged to Miko, a wind drey. Smaller than the others, capable of flying at high speeds that far surpassed her counterparts' limitations, and armed with the skill of almost completely translucent camouflage; the perfect scout.

'Do not let anyone see you leave or come back.' Zach warned. He did not want to draw any unnecessary attention to his men. He sensed that their presence was going all but unnoticed for now, and he wanted to keep it that way until he could figure out what the situation was. 'We will be waiting in a more secure area upon your return,' Zach said, dropping his formal tone and stepping closer to Lok, 'fly strong.' He clasped Lok on the shoulder and Lok smiled for the first time that day. He saluted and turned to mount his drey.

The waiting Miko had sensed his need to fly, and was ready and eager as ever to please her keeper. Her scales shone silvery grey, the star's rays dancing on them beautifully. As soon as he made contact to mount, she faded herself and her rider perfectly into their surroundings. Only a trained eye would spot them now. The only indication of their departure was the trees; their leaves all a flurry with the beating of her wings and the soft 'whuff' as her feet left the ground. Zach painstakingly followed their ascent while the others went to tend to their dreya. Miko was moving remarkably fast, and Zach marveled at the ability of a drey keen to impress. In less than a minute, the faint luminescent glow of her protective magic enveloping Lok with life giving air, and gravity for her own flight could only just be seen, as the pair broke atmosphere. A satisfied Zach left to join the rest of the men. They would now need to find a suitable base where they could keep the Ivory Tower under close scrutiny. First though, their dreya would need sustenance. Zach reached into his leather pouch, and drew out a silver whistle. Every captain carried one. Zach put the cool metal to his lips, and blew softly on it. The dreya immediately looked up, knowing what that sound meant, and the riders started to mount them without hesitation. They were all hungry, and the hunt had been declared.

*

Before Arial could take her place upon the throne of Bethriam, she had to be schooled in the art of inter-species politics. She had studied the High Council briefly in her tutelary period with Ramroth, and had not enjoyed it. The High Council had been formed only a few centuries ago, and as such, was relatively young in comparison to some of the older universal institutions.

The Worlds were inhabited by a multitude of different beings, but the peoples involved in politics and trade were classified as sentinel races. For the purposes of the council, six races were chosen to represent all others; races believed to be superior, higher sentinels. Their function was to act as peace enforcers amongst each other's nations, and in the beginning, they had been dubbed the Knights of Justice for their courageous efforts. The fatal flaw, however, lay in the reinstating of the chairs. It was only by birthright that a successor was named, and this was done with no concern as to who the person in question was. Arial and her people, along with many others, also believed in bloodlines, but an heir would be put through rigorous testing and endless tasks since childhood, to prove his or her competency. If the tests were not passed, another would be crowned, even if leadership was not a birthright. The council did not follow this law of ordainment, and simply placed the first born on the council to replace the predecessor. They had weakened over the years, becoming mere spectators of war. Roughly twenty year ago, the High Elves had declined to reinstate their seat, as had the drey keepers. The history books were vague at best on the topic, and she assumed that they had seen no point in sitting in on a dying council. Arial had, however, tried to uncover the lost past, much to Ramroth's intense displeasure, but to no avail. It was a mystery. Bearing all of this in mind, Arial stepped into the chamber, calling upon Ronan's energy to replenish her own. She would need all the help she could muster to awaken this sleeping giant.

The room was a cool white with a high domed roof supported by arched beams that ran along the ceiling. Six large and beautifully crafted stained glass windows broke the white of the walls. The array of colors and light filtering through them made the stories that told of the Choosing of Six come alive. A large slab of stone that was said to be a piece from the great moon of Lorain was the centerpiece of the room. The moon shone pale red all year round and was so large it could be seen from several planets, including her own. Myth told that it was home to a dead army who would never leave its bloodied rocks. The stone was perfectly triangular in shape, and six high-backed and intricately carved ivory chairs were placed, two respectively, along each side. The room provided a sheltered and refreshing atmosphere compared to the stifling heat outside, but Arial still felt claustrophobic. Her spirits lifted when she saw the familiar face of High Adare' Ethron with his long, silvery hair and sunken, poignant eyes. He did not return her smile, and she swept her gaze over the others instead, feeling a little out of place. She could put names to faces of three others purely by racial recognition. Falkhar, the Master malachi, sat two heads taller than the others. His hair was the shade of ebony, and his skin matched only the paleness of her own, but it was his strong cut, jutting jaw and clawed fingers that revealed his true nature. Not a beautiful people, she thought secretly, but alluring none the less. She knew that he could make himself attractive to her, and all others if he so wished, but he sat comfortably in his true form here. Just before the kill, the parasite within him would make his jaw stretch wider still, his claws unsheathe themselves, and his teeth protrude like so many fangs. Arial shuddered.

The woman on the malachi's left had hair like fire; skin the color of fertile soil, and large eyes that seemed too big for her delicate face. This was a wazimu, protector of the elements. Her name in common tongue was Cassandra. The language of her people was too old and complex to be mastered by any. The man with the ridiculous crown on his head must be one of the human kings, King Felias. More a spokesperson for his people than anything else, he looked laughable in his royal attire, dripping with jewels and cloaked in gold and silk. The seat that belonged to the Elves remained empty; a standing testimony to their stance on the doings of the council.

The seat that belonged to Arial's people was, to her great surprise, filled. This must be a new development since her last sweep of the council minutes had been two years ago. This new man had dark, wild hair and even darker, wilder eyes. There was an element about him that unsettled Arial, and he had not even looked up to acknowledge her presence. In fact, he looked bored and his mind seemed to be elsewhere. From his slouched posture and slight frame, she could tell he was human. Two Men of Adam on the council...how very interesting, she thought. How was she to gain the trust of a council that didn't even adhere to its own laws of equality? Or had times grown so harsh that desperate measures had been called upon? She highly doubted the ability of one man so great that laws could be rewritten to accommodate such things.

Felias had opened his mouth to speak, snapping Arial back to reality. Ramroth's words of warning from years ago when she was still his student, flashed through her mind. He had taught her that humans played politics with sharp minds and slippery tongues, better than any other. Anything they said had to be searched methodically for any hints of ulterior motives. The king broke the silence that blanketed the chamber with his deep, rumbling voice.

'Queen Arial, what a day this is that we are privileged enough to be graced by your presence.' He indeed meant these words, and would have been a blind fool not to. Arial was of noble drey keeper heritage and her beauty was surpassing of any description. Ronan's energy coursed through her spirit, her skin was flawless, glowing with youth, and her lips were full and pink. Her golden hair gleamed in the light that seemed to emanate from within, curling and cascading down to her curved waist. Her chiffon dress hugged her perfectly sculpted figure intimately, crystal blue eyes practically shining against the contrasting fair skin of her face. Around her was the glowing aura of strong dragon magic and she all but filled the room with it. She was a sight to behold, and had captured the rapt attention of everyone in the room. Everyone except the man she had distrusted from the instant she had laid eyes upon him. Arial smiled politely at the compliment and accepted the seat that was offered to her by the king.

'We extend our warmest welcome to you Queen Arial,' High Adare' Ethron spoke now, but his welcome held no warmth at all, only distant indifference as if she had never spent a whole year of her life by his side in final preparation for her crowning. She saw the second human shoot a glance at Ethron, and decided she would watch him more closely. King Felias seemed to sense the awkward atmosphere, and addressed Arial further;

'We were just discussing the great victory of your people in the recent Coptic battle. We give you our sincerest thanks for your personal contribution of fine warriors and our deepest gratitude for your aid in time of need.' Arial bowed her head graciously, and bit back the harsh reminder that it was her idea to send the riders to war in the first place. It was she who had held countless discussions with the kings and queens of other drey planets, pleading with them to join the failing war effort that raged on their frontiers. She knew that one day the kikubwa would be brave enough to bring the war to them, and by then their breeding season would have doubled their numbers. This "contribution of her fine warriors" had taken months of hard work, and the great victory that ensued had come at a high price. She alone had lost one thousand strong and a precious hold; one of her best scouting parties. Instead she said,

'No sacrifice is too great if it means the preservation of peace and justice.' This seemed to please the king of the humans.

'Well said my lady,' Master Falkhar said, a slight smile playing on his predatory lips. Arial considered his statement suspiciously. He looked like a cat enjoying the ultimate humiliation of his prey.

'However,' she continued, averting her gaze back to Felias with a tilt of her chin, 'I have come before this council to discuss more pressing matters than that of a band of rouge kikubwa playing up in distant deltas.' She decided to get straight to the point rather than let any of these people distract her from her mission with their political banter.

'Now now, Your Majesty, we have many hours to talk. Why, you have not even been introduced to the newest member of our council, Lord Soren,' King Felias interjected, indicating the man seated to his left. Felias was now smiling jovially and beaming at the beautiful lady seated opposite him.

'No,' Arial said, a little louder than she meant to, 'with all due respect King Felias, I did not come here to engage you in pleasantries and introductions.' The king's smile slowly faded with each word she spoke and she knew she was treading on thin ice with the easily offended monarch, but she ignored his sullen expression and continued, 'you must forgive me but we have little time to waste and I must be blunt.' She let her gaze sweep over the others. Falkhar's face was blank. The Man of Adam, Soren, hadn't even noticed her discourtesy, Ethron looked only mildly interested, and the wazimu was frowning at her slightly, her hair a fiery halo in the light of the setting star. Arial decided to concentrate her efforts on Cassandra instead. Perhaps woman-to-woman she would gain some ground.

She took a deep breath and said, 'I have come before your wise council to enquire in person as to why I had to leave Bethriam, and its entire population to the mercy, if there is such a thing,' she added, glancing at Felias darkly, 'of the kuvuta.'

Electric silence followed her brash statement, and her last word echoed off the walls ensuring that nobody could believe they had heard wrong. The human at Felias' side looked up for the first time. His eyes met hers. They were cold and calculating, almost with malicious intent. She stared back, matching his cool gaze with a violent determination not to be underestimated.

'Not one day ago in fact,' she elaborated, 'their foul beasts still feast on the flesh of my people,' she finished dramatically.

'Your planet was attacked?' Cassandra exclaimed in unmasked surprise. She was leaning forward in her seat as if she was straining to hear Arial properly. Arial paused for a moment, collecting her strength to speak of what had happened to her homeland.

'When an army attacks, its enemies have the ability to either fight back or hold them off until help arrives. My planet was not attacked… it was annihilated.' Her hands were shaking where they lay folded in her lap, but she gripped them together and steeled herself for the council's response.

Ethron fidgeted in his seat. Soren locked his fingers together on the table and shot the High Adare' a dangerous look. You could hear a pin drop in the silence that blanketed the chamber until Felias broke it.

'My ears must deceive me Queen Arial or your speech must be impaired.' Arial sighed inwardly as she had expected exactly this reaction. The kuvuta were a nasty problem from the past, to put it lightly, and nobody dared even utter their name for fear of a repeat of history, marked by blood and turmoil, let alone claim to have seen them since the dark era. 'The kuvuta have not been seen for many centuries,' he continued, 'and rightly so. They were banished from the universe upon pain of extermination, and pose no threat to our great Worlds.' Felias looked half amused, half outraged at the mere suggestion of kuvuta attacking planets on the doorstep of the council. A retort jumped to Arial's tongue, but again she bit it back for fear of worsening an already bad situation, and permanently damaging any hopes of cooperation from the council. Without them, her task would be daunting. She had neither the resources nor the authority to summon an army large enough to defeat this dark enemy.

'I assure you King Felias, however bad your hearing or my speech may be, my eyes did not deceive me nor the fear that stilled my heart at the sight of such atrocities.'

The human king sat back in his chair and regarded her with what seemed like unease.

'It is my understanding that you were accompanied on your flight from Bethriam by eleven members making up your royal guard and an Adare'. Where are they now?' Arial grew hot under the intensity of the malachi's stare and found herself stumbling over her answer to his obscure question.

'They have left, well, that is to say my ward waits for me and...' She was cut short by the wazimu;

'Of what relevance could that possibly be at this point Master Falkhar?' Her voice had an odd sound to it, like she had spoken from somewhere beneath the ground, yet it rang clearly in Arial's ears. 'If what this woman claims is true then the Worlds are in grave danger.' Arial had been right to center her plea on the world protector. Even though she cared not for the lives of the sentinel races, she would die before letting the wraiths consume a planet with all its biological riches. Their kind hadn't fought in millennia, being too precious a commodity, but to incur their wrath would be an unwise thing to do even for a kuvuta who deemed himself immortal. 'Furthermore,' Cassandra continued, 'none of my people have informed me of devastation on such a level which is even more worrying.' That struck Arial as odd too now that she thought of it. The wazimu guarded the Worlds ruthlessly and acted as sentries, reporting back to a single entity, and carrying out the Laws whenever occasion arose. The Men of Adam had been severely penalized for their near destruction of the planet Earth, and a wraith attack would not have gone unnoticed.

'Then we are at least in agreement that it is a strange thing that no other before now has reported such things.' Soren spoke at last, his tone an open challenge, his lips curled into a sneer. Felias leaned forward again, frowning deeply.

'It is my understanding that the wazimu are immune to physical changes around them, and are as such, indestructible. Surely the message of a large scale wraith attack would have reached our ears much sooner than now?'

Cassandra was growing impatient with the mortals that surrounded her, and frustrated with the tidings of the young woman. She was tired of trying to explain everything to these children.

'Felias, the Worlds are in a constant state of battle to ensure a balance is maintained. Wraiths are the Worlds' reaction to my kind. They work on the same physical plane as we do, and so we are not immune to their touch. Unfortunately, nothing is.'

The king didn't seem too pleased with this news. He hadn't been born to see the Dark Era, none in the room save Cassandra had, but he had read the history books, and the thought that not even the great and untouchable wazimu could survive the bloodthirsty tyranny of the kuvuta, made his heart quake. He couldn't let himself believe they were back. Luckily, another on the council seemed to share his sentiments, which made the lie more tangible.

'The truth, dear Cassandra, is that the kuvuta were banished from these very Worlds a long, long time ago, and have not been seen since, just as King Felias said,' Soren said impatiently, as if he found the idea of Worldly destruction a waste of his time.

Anger flushed red-hot in Arial's face.

'Do you suggest that I have fabricated this information Lord Soren?' She asked coolly, trying to control her temper, longing to release it among these councilmen. 'That I would come before this council and insult it with falsities?' He simply stared back at her without flinching. Now she directed her words to all that sat around the cold stone table. 'I must admit, it is a heavy truth to accept, but I expected a little more sympathy from those of you that can spare it.' She glanced at the motionless Falkhar. The only emotion he must feel, she thought, was cold-blooded hatred. With all his people had been subjected to, why should he care if those who had tried to control his kind for years were mindlessly slaughtered? Even if he had to suffer alongside them, at least he could revel in justice at its best.

She continued, 'over nine hundred thousand warriors and their families died yesterday. The soil still drinks from their blood, and you spit upon their brave deaths when you say that I lie.' Arial locked eyes with High Adare' Ethron who hadn't said a word for one who was so wise and eager to share knowledge. He made not a sound; he simply stared back at her then dropped his gaze in an uncomfortable manner, as if his former pupil's look was one of scrutiny instead of a quiet plea.

'That is indeed an unjust accusation my lady,' King Felias said, shaking his head like the befuddled old man that he was, 'we just seriously doubt the possibility that the wraiths have returned. My scouts scour the skies vigilantly day and night with keen technology, and no ionic wraith trails have been spotted in over two hundred centuries.' He said it matter of factly, in what was clearly meant to be comforting finality, smoothing down his bristling moustache repeatedly.

'What would a human know of such things?' Falkhar asked contemptuously, 'the *ichiji* wield dark magic that you cannot even begin to comprehend, and it far surpasses your feeble "technology".'

He had used the Osrillese word for the wraiths that meant *born of shadows,* and he was regarding Felias with an air of distaste and near revulsion that Arial found quite startling. The king's bulbous chest swelled with indignity, and probably fear, but Cassandra cut short his retort.

'Enough!' she thundered, her deep voice reverberating off the windows, 'we have heard the woman speak. We cannot doubt the words of one of the Six, but we have no proof save her first-hand account, and that we shall have to remedy before further counsel is held upon this matter.'

'Very well,' Felias said, regaining his composure before shooting the vampire a dirty look, 'Lord Soren, will you send a scouting hold to Bethriam?'

Arial nearly choked on the dry spit she was trying to swallow. Soren, a drey keeper? She had thought he was merely some human lord-ling. It could not be. He had none of the qualities that defined her race, and she refused to believe he was one of her own. Since when did her people reinstate their seat upon this pathetic council anyway, and on whose authority she wondered, looking at Soren in new light.

'No,' she whispered out loud.

'Excuse me?' Soren asked, leaning forward with eyebrows raised. Arial met his gaze evenly, despite her slip-up.

'No. Better to send a single scout,' she said carefully. Even if he were a keeper, and knew this to be the better tactical move, this would be a waste of her precious time. Scouting parties and more talks when they should be recruiting every able-bodied warrior from every corner of the Worlds at this very moment or better still…and this was what Arial's real angle of attack was... She had once snuck into Ramroth's private study, and had stumbled by pure chance, upon a fragment of burnt parchment that he had kept hidden between his endless volumes. It had been a miracle that she had ever found it. It held patchy information about a meeting the High Council had had roughly eighty years ago. It spoke of some way to ensure the safety and continuation of all the races *when,* not *should,* the kuvuta return.

A weapon was decided upon. Arial could hardly make out the strange language it was written in, and only understood parts of it. Scorch marks had defiled the rest. Now was her opportunity to ask, for she may never get another. Ramroth surely didn't believe that she would subject herself to the scrutiny of the council with nothing but a plea born of tragedy.

'Better yet, send your great weapon that this very council created not a century ago.' She said it with the never faltering belief that it was true, but now all eyes were on her, and even the wazimu looked confused. Arial looked to the pseudo drey keeper for his reaction, and it was when their eyes met that she saw it; just the faint flickering of a shadow across his eyes, darkening his features and the spirit that dwelt behind them. No one else seemed to notice, as they were all still staring at her, dumbfounded at her newest claim of some secret weapon that they evidently, knew nothing of.

She drew back from the imposter in fear. Was he possessed? Maybe it had just been a trick of the light. Perhaps he was just an arrogant man with no remorse. At least one of her misgivings was confirmed when Soren actually started laughing, and mockingly suggested;

'Perhaps you have come to the wrong council dear lady?'

Ethron laughed nervously, and Arial blushed. It was the High Adare' who had suggested it all those years ago, and Ramroth would never keep false documents. Why did Ethron not substantiate her claim? Soren sensed he had the upper hand, and continued speaking in that drawling manner that she had come to despise so quickly, 'my scouts are away on private business, but will be returning at first light in two days' time. I shall then need to give them time to rest and feed before I send them to Bethriam to chase this phantom. As far as your secret weapon theory goes, do you not perhaps need some rest yourself?'

'It is not rest that I need,' she replied heatedly, 'it is aid. And not when it bests suits the council, I need it now.'

'You came here for counsel and that much we have given you; we have heard your story, we just do not believe it, and you should be thankful for the great effort we have put into discussing your fictional claims.'

Arial's anger flared, but she would not allow this man to get the better of her;

'Please forgive me if I seemed ungrateful brave lord. I thank you for your words of wisdom, and for ensuring that I did not waste my time here under your just and fair considerations. It is good to see the council benefitting from your direct method of action before the slaughter continues.' The tyrant opposite her simply smiled as shadows flaunted themselves behind his eyes. Arial's stomach sank like lead as she realized she was alone.

Ethron sat watching their conversation with no obvious attempt to come to her rescue. Felias was still stung from Falkhar's comment, and showed no interest in anything other than staring angrily at the vampire. Falkhar himself sat as impassive as always, and the wazimu looked as though she was in a trance. Arial decided that it was time to leave. Something was happening that she could not yet grasp, and she didn't like it. Ronan's energy buzzed warnings in her ears that she could not understand. None of these people seemed to care at all and either none of them had studied the history of their own council or something very big had been covered up. She started to wonder how much danger she had placed herself in, and hoped she could make it out of the tower alive before she posed a further threat to Soren. The council was in any case a collection of fools, and it had been unwise to come here in the first place. They would toast to a minor victory, and bask in a glory that was not their own whilst the Worlds were swallowed by darkness too great to comprehend.

All these thoughts raced through her mind in the few short seconds after she had spoken, but that proved to be enough time for strong magic to gather around them without stirring a single atom. Maybe it had, but no one had noticed. Without the usual tingling sensation that accompanied the accumulation of magic or the barely audible crackling in the air as it struggled to accommodate the building energy, nobody knew what was happening, and nobody saw it coming.

Old magic, the type that Ramroth could only dream of wielding, and did not even dare to do as much, exploded within the space that the three walls enclosing the chamber held, with such force that it blew Arial's hair back in its wake. A spell powerful enough to mutate every particle of light within the room to a magnitude of one hundred times its primary strength was released. A light was borne, so blinding, that it penetrated Arial's every sense, and even with eyes tightly shut, she could not hide from it. It was only Ronan's strong protective shield that was able to save her from the full force of the raw energy. All rational thought and mobility was snatched from her. All that she could think of was escaping the magic that had rendered her helpless. Through the sound of impossibly heavy light, Arial could hear somebody calling out her name, and a small popping noise came from somewhere in front of her. Her confusion was temporarily eased when a gentle hand closed around her wrist. The intense light seemed to yield a little but came back in full force when the soothing touch withdrew sharply, releasing Arial from its protective charm.

Arial's mind was reaching out for the lost entity like an abandoned child. She could feel the ground beneath her now, and she was trying to sit up to find the comforting soul that had eased the pain of the spell, when the smell of death and rot assailed her. Strong enough to reach her through the light and press down upon her chest, stealing her breath clean away. As horrid as it was, it pierced the magical vortex and revived her for long enough to realize she was in serious trouble. The white light was slowly being replaced by swirling shadows, and her throat was gripped by a faceless menace. She could feel conscious thought slipping away from her, and the more she tried to fight it, to keep her mind open and clear as Ramroth had taught her, the weaker she became, and the more it hurt. She fell from the light into an impenetrable darkness, and just before all the lights around and within her winked out, she heard Ronan's desperate call, but it was too far away now to bring her back. That was the last that she remembered.

Chapter 2

Daggers and darkness

Two cloaked figures stood side by side in the black that was night. The air was cool, but not yet cold. A young couple walked past holding hands on their way home, blissfully unaware of the danger that lurked so nearby. The sharp sound of the woman's nervous laughter cut through the quiet, but they had both been aware of the soon-to-be lovers for a while. Their far-off footsteps had vibrated along the concrete, the musky scent of the male could be smelt from two blocks away, and the quickening heartbeat of the female reverberated through the air, sending out tiny little shock waves that bounced tantalizingly off their malachi ears.

It was always favorable to drink from an elevated heartbeat. Fear and seduction were primary weapons among their people. The blood always flowed sweeter, and more generously, when fueled by adrenaline or lust.

One of the night stalkers turned his head toward the sounds of the courting couple, but they would sleep soundly tonight, wrapped in their post-passionate embrace, for there was no possible way that the malachi would get away with it, and there were important matters at hand apparently.

'I am sending you tonight,' said the taller of the two, ignoring the prey that had just passed by with an ease the other could not fathom, 'we have no time to lose. If he finds out that we need her, he will try to bargain, and I have neither the time nor the energy.' He glanced at his wristwatch, 'the star will be setting there in a few hours. You will be at your strongest then, and you will need your strength.'

'How comforting,' remarked the second, absentmindedly. He still had his head cocked to one side, the better to hear the two people now two hundred feet away. His eyes were closed, better to picture how he longed to embrace them, and to feed. His blood surged through his veins, roaring in his ears. Consequence of action screamed protest above the need to drink, but it was soon drowned out. Without even needing to think, he had lurched forward, fangs bared and claws drawn. Snarling like a pack wolf with the anticipation of the hunt. He needed to quench his insatiable thirst and put out the fire that raged within.

His companion had foreseen his move, and grabbed both his arms, pulling them up behind his back. He hissed a warning in his ear. The blood hungering malachi went limp and whispered;

'Why did you bring me here?' The desperation in his usually proud voice was unsettling, but the one holding him was familiar with it in all his people these days. Gently, and slowly, he released him and replied;

'To remind you of how imperative this mission is, to remind you of what was taken from us, and most importantly, to remind you of what you are, and must be free to be. Take only the girl Damek; make sure she has the necklace with her.'

Damek relaxed his posture, and stood up straight, looking his master almost level in the eyes. He nodded once, and straightened his cloak, the color leaving his cheeks slowly.

'From what you have already told me, she will prove difficult without the others.'

'She will have no choice in the matter,' came the cool reply. Damek ran his long fingers through his hair, brow furrowed as he contemplated the words of his master.

'I'm a relic hunter, not a miracle maker. And no nursemaid either,' he added.

His master moved so quickly, he did not have a chance to react. He had him by the throat, and up against the wall in a heartbeat.

'Do not test me on this one Damek,' he hissed, his fingers closing around his captive's windpipe. Damek managed a sneer. 'Good. We have an understanding then.' He was gone before Damek's feet hit the ground.

He massaged his neck and spat on the ground at his feet. He was hungry and the blood banks were never far.

*

Miko was making good time and Lok was impressed. He found such joy in flying, and didn't even have to spur the young Miko on. Lok could feel the heat emanating off her perfectly formed muscles as she moved beneath him like water. He had lost his first drey to a rare respiratory disease some time ago, and his heart had been broken. Miko was her offspring, and had never bonded with a keeper. Without a keeper to comfort her, she had become even more withdrawn by the loss of her mother, but Miko had bonded to Lok when she was ready and it was the loss of both their greatest loves that had brought them together. It was an uncommon case but their bond was unique and strong.

They were nearly there now and as they sped through the air toward Bethriam, Lok noticed small meteor debris hurtling past his head at an alarming speed. He wasn't concerned for his safety since Miko's magic protected him; it was the velocity of their travel that disturbed him.

The strange, winged and leathery creatures that inhabited the black of space were also acting oddly, flapping in a panic-stricken manner like fish out of water. The rocks were going the same way as he and his drey instead of being left behind by the speed of their flight. Both were traveling with momentum instead of drifting aimlessly as they usually did. With each wing beat that drew them closer to his home planet, Lok became more and more worried. The urguls were in a frenzy now, madly flailing their wings as if they were being dragged against their will. Miko was paying no heed to the warning signs; she was wholly concentrated on the task at hand, and was simply flying too fast to feel the effect of the danger ahead. Lok, however, had seen the cause of the irregularity of his surroundings, and it took him a few seconds to fully register the enormity of it before he could rouse his drey to its presence. He frantically tugged at her mind in an effort to get her to look beyond, and stop before it was too late.

At first, she simply slowed at his call echoing in her mind. She arched her head in curiosity to look ahead. The realization and instinctual fear had her beating her wings backward with such strength, every stroke drained more energy than before. Now that she had slowed, and was no longer ahead of the force, she could feel her weight slowly being pulled toward it. It was like being stuck in quick sand with a current. Miko had never felt anything like it and fought madly against it.

Lok's heart was pounding against his ribs as he looked upon the place where Bethriam once was. Its shape was merely a deep, fathomless shadow etched against the black of space. The hole wasn't very big, but even as the pair fought against it, whole meteors were slowly being pulled into its field, rotating faster and faster. Lok, too, was fighting it, using all his energy to help his beloved drey in her desperate struggle.

Amidst the chaos, a glittering object caught his eye. It was the locket he had secretly hoped to find on his mission home, and miraculously it was sailing toward them, swirling ceaselessly in the void of gravity like a lost charm. He reached out with his hand to pluck it from the air, and they veered slightly to the left with his effort. One of Miko's hind paws got caught in a flux stream while she was kicking with it, and Lok watched in horror as the color drained from the scales; the sleek, sharp claws becoming long and haggard as his fingers curled around the precious chain. She pulled out seconds later, but even with her rejuvenating powers, most of the damage would be permanent.

However devastating the injury, it did little to slow the flight within her and, finally after what felt like an eternity, Lok felt the air around them lighten. They had managed to break free from the black hole's grasp. Miko did not pause to regain strength, she flew as if all the legions of hell were on her heels, and Lok lay flat against her back, water streaming from the corners of his eyes from the sheer speed, making no protest. He did not know how he would tell the others. All that they had once loved had been swallowed whole by the darkness.

*

Arial awoke cold and stiff, face down in damp straw. She still had the presence of mind to note the irony that this straw had probably come from her own land, given freely in tithe to the very same council whose prison she now lay in. Her acid thoughts were cut short when the putrid smell of mold and excrement hit her. She gagged. Arial lifted her head, to get away from the source, and it hung heavy with ache. She waited for her eyes to adjust to the near darkness and for the pain in her head to subside to a dull throb, before she pushed herself up into a sitting position.

Her back rested on cold, wet stone and she was almost sure she was underground from Ronan's shared gift of superior smell, but at the same time, she felt she wasn't. The light, the blinding energy and then the wraiths; the memory was disturbing and she shivered. Anger stopped the uncontrollable shaking that had taken hold, and it ceased just as quickly as it had started. She tried to concentrate on what had happened, wondered where the others were, and why the kuvuta had come. Had they followed her?

She was growing faint; the smell trapped within the small room was threatening to overwhelm her so she tried to focus on one object to stop the waves of nausea and nagging confusion. Arial sat like that for a long time, trying to unscramble her mind and regain control of her body, when she realized that the crumpled heap in the corner that she had been staring at was her ward.

Her heart skipped a beat when she recognized the embroidery on his cloak. The golden emblems were dulled with dirt, and the light was too dim to pick up the regal glint in his attire, but there was no mistaking her coat of arms that was spun with her own hair upon the back; the mark of the kept Adare'. She scrambled over to him on all fours, and bending over him whispered;

'Ramroth?' When he did not stir she shook him by the shoulder violently, fearing for the worst, and urgently hissed, 'wake up you old fool!'

The old man's grey eyelashes fluttered weakly and he tilted his head toward the voice, groggily opening his eyes.

'*Wraiths*,' he half murmured half spat. He tried to sit up.

'Be still! Rest a while,' she said, still holding him by the shoulders.

'I am sorry,' he muttered, gently pushing her away, 'I should not have brought you here. It was too dangerous.' Arial stared at her ward, again surprised by his strength, and angered by his words. Not caring for the state he was in she rose to her feet and pointed an accusing finger at him.

'So you knew not only that it would be pointless to come here, but that it would place my life in jeopardy too?' She did not wait for an answer, 'I demand to know what you know and why you felt it necessary to endanger me.' Her voice was cool and commanding, even though her hands were shaking.

Ramroth was listening with half an ear to Arial's demands. He was collecting his thoughts, calculating their odds of survival, possible means of escape, and wondering how best to answer his lady's questions. She would have to know, but not now. He would tell her the whole truth about her past, and his suspicions, once they were in a safe place away from prying eyes and ears. People in any case had a way of endangering themselves unwittingly, burdened with knowledge that they are not ready to have. He steadied himself and rose to meet her furious gaze.

'Before this conversation continues, you must understand that I had no clear indication of the threat here, and had I known, I would have never brought you to the tower. I sought only answers,' he added.

'What could *you* possibly need answers to!' she cried, 'there is an army of wraiths not two days away from here! If you needed to know if they were here too then surely you could have used another means!' Ramroth could see that she was angry and he would have to give her answers as it was the only thing that ever settled her temper, and the only time it ever raised its ugly head, was when she knew she was being denied them. He took a deep breath and said;

'Very well. First you must know that it was not I who created the lie to protect you. It was your mother. Secondly, your parents did not die in an accident. Your mother banished your father into exile shortly before she fled the realm. I doctored the records since you were bound to find them some day. You never questioned the information I gave to you, and therefore, never chose to speak of it. As is customary, no one spoke to you of it since you never asked.'

Arial opened her mouth to no doubt pose another question, but Ramroth held up his hand to silence her.

'Something terrible happened to your family that tore it apart and that is as much as I know. Your mother left you in my care with strict instructions to shield you from the truth for as long as I possibly could. I wish I could tell you why, that is precisely what I am trying to determine. Your mother was the bravest woman I have ever known, and I am certain that she would not put her family through the trauma she did if it were not for a just cause.'

He gently put his hands on her shoulders in an effort to ground and comfort her. Arial could not believe what she had just heard. Her entire past had been a fabrication, and her ward had lied without flinching, to her face. She was now staring at him with shock, the truth too fresh too stir anything else within her.

Ramroth let her go and moved toward the wall, his eyes misting over as he continued with his tale.

'Something happened that made her flee the land, and the people she loved, something she would not even confide in me about. She loved you and your father more than words could say, and I saw the look in her eyes when she banished him for his so-called madness, and gave you to me for what she said was your safety. I never once questioned her motives, believing them with every fiber of my being to be noble. I was her ward before I was yours, and she was placed on the throne of Bethriam when she married your father, with the blessing of every living soul on Bethriam.' He looked pointedly at her again before adding, 'she was a human.'

When Arial failed to reply he continued, 'I came here to uncover a tangled web of lies, and I needed you to do it. You are the missing link, I am almost sure of it.'

Arial bit back her tears and whispered;

'Please continue.'

Ramroth had turned his attention toward the wall, his manner aloof and indifferent as usual, as if nothing remarkable had been said at all. He was running his long, wizened fingers across it like he could feel something beneath it.

'Before she left,' he began, 'I was instructed to destroy certain documents kept here at the tower.'

'The weapon...' Arial breathed to herself, the fragment of parchment surfacing in her mind's eye. Why would her mother want the evidence to be destroyed?

Ramroth had been muttering under his breath, and now had his good ear pressed against the surface of the cold stone.

'I cannot tell you anymore as that too would be a lie, so hold your questions and tell me about the council.' His words were harsh and urgent but the reality of their circumstances came back in a rush and she did as she was bid. Without him, she knew she had little chance of escape. She took a deep breath and tried to push away thoughts of her lost family.

'I cannot recall much that I can imagine would be of use to you, save the behavior of one individual in particular. Soren; poses as a drey lord. Shadows of what might have been possession flickering in his eyes and such. He, most of all, opposed my claims.' Ramroth tensed up at this but she didn't want to press him further.

He was still inspecting the stone, grunting to himself occasionally, when suddenly he stepped back, pointing to a nondescript piece of the wall.

'This is where the vortex is the strongest. This must be the only exit.'

Arial had a thousand questions that she wanted Ramroth to answer, but the most pressing sprang to her lips first.

'Ramroth, why can I not feel Ronan?' She asked nervously as if she did not really wish to hear her ward's reply. All this talk of his was making her unsettled, and she feared for her drey above all other things. She had been anxious for some time now. Even when Ronan was far off hunting, she could still feel his spirit intertwined with hers. Now she felt like an empty shell.

Arial and Ronan had been bound together from the tender age of two, in sentient years. She had entered the nesting grounds of Bethriam merely as a spectator to the new hatchlings. The drey mother would let no one near until her hatchlings had seen three moons, and had learned how to use their powers to some extent. The young Ronan had chosen to bind to Arial the moment he had laid eyes upon her. It was extremely rare for two to bind at such a young age, but he had approached her without hesitation, despite her nervous disposition at the close proximity to an animal whose enormous power was evident to her even then. He had been floundering around his mother having been born only that morning, and had made his way toward the young girl. He had put on a fine show for her by spouting a plume of fire into the air; flower shaped sparks falling from it and landing on Arial. They did not burn; each left only a warm kiss upon her skin before vanishing. She had clapped her hands wildly and shrieked with laughter before flinging her arms around his neck, and exchanging the silent vow to love and protect till death parted them; an act that lay within every keeper's subconscious mind, and in the depths of their hearts, until they found their drey to give it to.

Ronan was a fire drey, and they usually choose keepers who were both strong spirited yet gentle in nature. The fire of such dreya is exceptional to witness. What some call a defect and others an advantage: stomachs with overactive phosphate glands, which result in an unstable amount of flame production. When these beasts throw fire, it can reach great distances at even greater volumes with pinpoint accuracy, if well trained. Close combat was not recommended because of their poorly developed scales and armor but a single fire drey could wipe out a battalion of men in mere seconds from a distance of over a hundred feet. Their metal-plate armor melted into flesh before their dead bodies hit the ground. They were fiercely protective of the keepers they chose and were a deadly adversary.

They had grown up together, almost been inseparable. She had even been riding him on his first flight. The ties between them were unusually strong because of the amount of time they had been bonded, and they were very advanced for their years. They could already read each other's thoughts far more clearly than most. This only happened in the third court by average standards, roughly thirty years. Ronan knew when Arial was crying after only ten. The worry etched upon her face at the profound concern for her drey softened Ramroth's heart.

He came towards her and took her hands in his.

'Have no fear my lady,' he said softly, 'you cannot feel Ronan because the strong magic surrounding us will not permit you. He has not been slain or taken far away. I seriously doubt his inability to fend for himself while you still live,' he said with a smile. 'This is, however, not good news for us,' he continued, 'we have no connection to the outside. We have no way of telling what our enemies' movements are.' He was standing next to the wall again, tracing his fingers over it once more, a forlorn expression on his face.

'Without Ronan, I feel weak,' Arial whispered, bowing her head into her hands, 'and for all your comfort, I still worry. What will happen to us? Will Soren kill us? If so, then why? It is sheer madness to stand down to the kuvuta! They need no allies and will leave none alive.'

'My worry,' Ramroth said, his voice straining, 'is for how much our adversary knows about you... enough to restrain your drey upon arrival and encase us with highly protective magic.'

'*My* worry is Soren,' Arial countered, 'what do you think he is?' Ramroth frowned and paused,

'He gives off some shadow that has not been seen in these Worlds yet...' He did not elaborate, he merely reverted back to his deep thoughts, and Arial knew the conversation was over.

She looked up toward the ceiling absent-mindedly, her thoughts on Ronan alone now, and a nagging worry in her stomach from Ramroth's dark words. An orb was hanging above her; the source of the eerie light cast over them. She knew from her studies in sorcery that it was an orb of sight. They were being watched. Arial thought of pointing this out to Ramroth, but realized that he would have noticed it the second he opened his eyes. Instead she said;

'I don't think Ronan has been harmed. That would have penetrated even this magic. Feeble it is compared to the magic of my soul bond with him.' Whilst she stood wondering what all Ramroth's words meant, how they were going to escape and chilling herself with thoughts of what would happen if they didn't, Ramroth was busy formulating a brilliant plan.

'My lady, you are a genius!' Arial stared at her ward who had surely gone mad with confinement already. 'We must inflict you with grievous pain and then your connection with Ronan will break through the magic that encases us,' he explained.

'Ramroth, I don't...' but he cut her off;

'I am not entirely sure of the physics behind it as no such attempt has ever been documented,' he continued, pacing up and down, one arm folded behind his back, the other stroking his bedraggled beard, 'but as I see it, the line, if you will, that binds him to you, should form a weak point in the vortex, crumbling the magic it makes contact with.' He was speaking more to himself than anything else now. 'It is pure genius!' he said, his eyes sparkling in the dim light, 'pure genius.'

*

The wazimu had used the raw energy that made up her core self to send a shockwave of blinding light throughout the chamber. It reflected off the walls, and bound itself to every particle within reach to increase ten-fold, in power and intensity.

Very clever, Falkhar thought, as he adjusted his perfectly evolved eyes to the extreme amount of light that now had to be filtered through his retina. A state of chaos had followed the surge of ancient magic, but Falkhar merely felt the deep itch within his bones in response to it. The shape-shifting pet that was slave to the imposter had transformed itself into a small bird with a popping sound borne from the heavy air it had to transform through. Falkhar supposed that it hoped to escape on wing but much to the malachi's amusement, it succeeded only in flying repeatedly into walls blinded by pain and confusion, squawking loudly and sending feathers flying. Falkhar caught it with lightning speed and, smashing the stained glass with his elbow, released the bird into the star set.

Cassandra had made good her unnoticed escape by distorting her essence into that which surrounded her. The ray of light, slightly brighter than those around it, floated majestically out through the window and away from the madness. Falkhar was surprised that she had finally realized what was happening but her kind did not need to be spared. *He* would be watching the destructive humans before long and all the others would perish.

Soren had made a hasty evacuation, and had taken the girl, aided by his personal body guard. Falkhar cursed her for her stupidity. Did she really know nothing of her true heritage? He would have liked to snatch her from where she had sat opposite him, with that childlike indignity spread across her face. It would have been so easy but Soren needed to be deceived for the Master malachi to succeed. He knew of the strength Soren had the potential to wield.

He strode calmly toward the great, arched doors and past the human king writhing on the floor in pure agony, his hands covering his smoldering eyes.

'Humans,' he sneered, as he ground the king's skull into the floor with the heel of his boot.

Chapter 3

Prophesies

Arial was less than impressed with her ward's plan, but if it meant their only chance of escape, then she would go through with it, if only to see Ronan again, and ensure that the kuvuta were stopped.

'How sure are you that this plan will work?' she asked nervously. Ramroth was already scanning the room for any object that could aid them.

'We need to pierce an artery which draws blood directly from your connection; your heart,' he said, ignoring her question. Arial drew a sharp breath involuntarily. She sank down to her knees, her hand flying to her neck. Her fingers touched cool metal; her chain, and she looked down. Upon her necklace hung a small, silver drey; the craftsmanship of this piece was nothing short of exquisite, and her royal jeweler had said it could be over five thousand years old. The scales were engraved in great detail, and it had two small diamonds, both with near perfect cut, for eyes. Her father, whom she barely remembered, had given it to her as a gift on the day that Ronan had chosen her. It was a symbol of her bloodline, and it was her most coveted possession. She noticed for the first time that its tail forked sharply, and she ran her fingers over the pointed ends while Ramroth watched her closely.

'You must be the one to do it my lady. When you were sworn into my care, I took a blood oath to never use any form of magic against you nor cause you any physical harm.'

'Very well,' Arial replied, sounding far braver than she felt, 'if it must be done then I would that it be by my own hand and none other.'

It was the custom of her people to only use violence against another upon the battlefield, and all were held to that sacred custom. Force - when it was necessary, but the hundreds of years spent evolving into a being with the ability to reason and compromise, was lost when a single hand was raised in fury rather than just cause. It would all be for naught if it were allowed in any place but the ground you fight for love and land on. The man, woman or child who used violence against one another, were cast out into the wilderness to live as the heathens they chose to mimic.

She raised the chain up and over her head, pulling it loose from the long strands of her tangled hair. Clutching the tiny drey tightly, she raised it to her beating pulse with trembling hands. Ramroth knelt down beside his queen in the rancid straw.

'There will be pain at first, and you will bleed heavily until we are safe enough to heal you.' He spoke his words softly, reassuringly, and took Arial's free hand in his once more. 'As soon as the vortex weakens, I will act swiftly to free us from this place. Ronan will come for you.' Ramroth could see the misgivings in Arial's eyes, but when she spoke, her voice held no trace of doubt or fear.

'I trust you,' she said with conviction, but she could see the serious flaws in his plan. She doubted the ability of even a strong Adare' and a fire drey pitted against the strength of the kuvuta. She decided to put her faith in Ramroth though, after all, what choice did she really have? He had never let her down before. *Until recently*, a small voice inside her added.

Ramroth's face came to her then, a mask of serenity and confidence as he watched her walk into a council that he had been suspicious of for years. She closed her eyes, pushing the image away, the tip of the dreya tail hovering above her quickening pulse. Do it quickly, she thought, Ronan will come.

*

Damek had been watching the Ivory Tower for what felt like hours now, trying to find a way in, a weak spot in the locked-down infrastructural security of the Worlds' representatives. Its solid white walls gleamed ominously in the moonlight; wraiths stood open guard at every entrance point now that the council had been dissolved, and humans patrolled the grounds with long swords and double-edged axes.

He checked his wristwatch; midnight. He was perched high up, on his haunches, in an ancient toulah tree. Its slender branches did not even give an inch of way beneath his poised and muscular frame, and its dense foliage provided him with cover as he stared down below.

From what he could see, they had gone to great measures to protect the imprisoned queen. She was obviously in the upper dungeons from the amount of air support up there. He had been told little about the woman he now sought though, and nothing about the relic she carried. And his research had yielded naught. All he had to go on were his master's riddles as usual, but he suspected it had something to do with the wraiths, and with the freedom of his people. He chose not to think upon it too much. That was not his job.

He scanned the tower once more and counted more *ichiji* than he cared to. He had had no prior experience with these creatures, and had been told little of what to expect. He was not afraid of any man or beast, but he had no idea what the wraiths full capabilities were, and he was not keen on finding out. Damek had survived doing what he did for so long because of his uncanny knack for sizing up his adversaries, and avoiding any unnecessary conflict with bigger and stronger things than he.

It was decided then; he would have to use the main gates if he wished to gain entry into the tower. It was his surest bet. Sneaking past a human sentry was the easiest thing to do. No race was as ill equipped to detect a malachi and no race bled as much by their hands. Up there, in the dungeons, greater challenges would await him. Probably some kuvuta, definitely the High Adare's protective magic, most likely wazimu spells seeping through every crack in the building; all very problematic, and not one of which Damek felt fully inclined to risk. Another looming problem would be that of a swift escape. He had been told the woman would have a ward and a drey in her service, but that he should take only her and return to Osrillia, as soon as their position was secure. A pity…the others would be useful if they were to escape fast and efficiently.

The still of concentration in his head was constantly being disturbed by something. He shut out his thoughts for a few moments, and it came to him. A faint and subtle presence carried by the breeze, an overwhelming feeling in his chest that he could not place. He tried to focus on the source and his eyes were drawn to the tower, the fifth level; the upper floor dungeons. It stood out from all the other stimuli his senses were capable of picking up, masking even the stench of the wraiths. He tore his gaze from the tower, and focused his undivided attention instead upon the humans guarding the doors.

*

As Arial plunged the dreya-charm tail into her neck, clutching her ward's clammy hands, several things happened at once. She felt, more than heard, a blood-curdling scream reverberate off the four walls surrounding her. It must have come from her own lips, she thought. Warm blood ran down her neck and chest. She felt Ronan's response to her pain as though a slack string tied to her very spirit had been pulled taught, and she heard what must have been the vortex of magic containing them rip open like a giant piece of fabric being violently torn.

Ramroth jumped to his feet the second the first drop of blood was shed, reaching the wall left of them in two short bounds. Arial followed him with her eyes, and immediately saw what he had raced to reach. The tear had revealed the white of the tower walls, and a small oval shaped window filtering moonlight through. A cool breeze played gently across her face. It was the only thing keeping her conscious.

Ramroth had stepped back with his side facing her, and she saw his eyes close, and the slight movement of his thin lips as he muttered an incantation under his breath. Standing a foot away from the wall, he thrust splayed hands forward, and as she watched, a crystalline bubble of light emerged from his palms. It traveled forward painstakingly slowly, rotating as it went. Arial could barely focus her eyes anymore, but she would fight the blackness for this; it was beautiful, shimmering hauntingly with shades of ochre emanating from within its depths.

She started to raise her hand to reach out and touch it, but was snatched from her trance by Ramroth's words drilling shrilly through her head.

'Don't! Don't!' he thundered, his eyes flying open wildly, the orb vibrating gently in a stationary position, threatening to extinguish from his lack of complete concentration. It was tantalizingly out of reach but the Adare's stern glare halted all her efforts to touch it.

'It seals the first break in physical fabric it comes into contact with, leaving it for hours as it is.' Understanding dawned upon her immediately, and she withdrew her hand as if stung. Ramroth closed his eyes again, and continued with his spell.

The bubble of light found the window, and stretched tightly across it. With a soft tinkle, the light was gone, and a stronger breeze swept the room, removing the stale dungeon smell, and rustling the straw where Arial lay.

The moon shone down upon the dreya queen, making her red blood shine grisly black against her paling skin, and removing the majesty of her beauty with its light. Ramroth stepped toward the window hesitantly.

'I thought we were underground. They fooled us. I need powerful amulets and charms for flight that I do not have with me.' His face was grave as he sought out Ronan down below, but he did not have to wait long to locate the dragon.

The silence that had been the sanctuary of the night air was broken by the sudden, high pitched and demented wails of wraiths. Ronan had obviously awoken to the renewed connection, and could feel the lifeblood of his soul mate ebbing. The wraiths were swarming around him, desperately trying to subdue him, and soon they would come to the source, the very cell Ramroth stood helplessly in. He was starting to panic now. He did not know, short of jumping or of Ronan hopefully breaking free, how they were going to escape in time.

In the midst of his frantic thoughts, and the screeches from the creatures below, the old ward heard a new sound; soft at first but growing louder. An almost inaudible whistling, like that of air letting something pass…something traveling very fast. Ramroth peered skeptically out of the window, dreading what new devilry this sound would bring.

Arial's head sank into the straw that littered the floor of their prison and felt no more.

Down below, Ronan had sensed Arial's loss of consciousness and was putting up a valiant fight against the bonds that held him, and the captors around him. Four figures lay burnt to ashes at his feet, and he was rearing up violently against the chains around his mighty chest. Even as Ramroth watched, captivated by the drey's power and obsessive will to get to his keeper, several kuvuta were caught in his fiery rebellion. They were instantly vaporized, their ashes swept away on the easterly wind as if they never were.

Then, before the ward could draw a breath, he felt something hurtle past him. His robes whipped around him in the wake of whatever had passed, and his ears sang as he made for the inert figure of his queen, spreading his arms protectively over her.

Someone spoke from the far side of the room. A cold and strong voice;

'Calm yourself magic slinger, I am no wraith.' Brilliantly green eyes gleamed in the darkness and when Damek stepped out of the shadows, Ramroth openly cringed.

'I take it you are not here on the hunt,' Ramroth said darkly to the night stalker.

'Keeper blood burns in the veins like a cosmic fire and stills the heart with its awesome power. Rule number three wizard,' the malachi replied.

'Then what does your kind have to do with this?'

'That is my master's affair, not mine.'

Ramroth simply stared at him, not knowing how to prevent the inevitable from happening.

'No time to chat,' Damek said stiffly, 'I came only for the girl.' He started striding toward the unconscious Arial, but before he could get there, Ramroth spoke;

'This *woman* is special. I cannot stop you from taking her, and I want her gone from this place in any case, however…' he began as he watched the malachi scoop Arial up easily into his strong arms, 'should any harm befall her, you will be relentlessly and mercilessly hunted till your death.' Damek could see the truth of these words in the old man's eyes. He nodded in acceptance. 'Also, she will prove difficult without her drey.'

Damek was gone from the room in an instant, just as the wraiths started to tear down the door. Ramroth acted quickly, concealing the exposed patch of reality on the wall, and hastily creating a hologramatic effigy of a sleeping Arial, all in a matter of seconds.

Three wraiths burst into the tiny room, and started sniffing wildly at the air. Ramroth knew they were simple creatures that knew only death and destruction. They had poor sensory systems at best, but he still held his breath, and his heart hammered in his chest, hoping they would not be able to smell his recent magic, and the faint sulphuric aroma it left behind. Mercifully, they slunk back through the door, seeming to be a solid wall, in a swirl of blackened smoke. The rift sealed itself neatly as the last of them slipped through.

The Adare' relaxed slightly and exhaled. They did not seem to have found anything significant, or so he hoped. Now his only concern was for Arial. Had she been rescued by the malachi or simply recaptured? There was no way of knowing and he slumped against the cold, stone wall, exhausted by his magical efforts, memories coming unbidden.

'Take her Ramroth. I fear for her life and the burden she bears...' The queen's face was streaked with tears and her hands shook violently, holding the child's head to her breast. *'My family is safe. They are lost to me and they are safe.'*

Ramroth let the memory fade again. This was all beyond him. He did not know if he still had a part to play or if he had somehow missed a piece of the puzzle. What would cause a woman to abandon all hope and rational thought? She would not tell him and ordered him only to make sure that Ethron gave him the documents to be destroyed but not read. She had accused her husband of insanity, given away her only child, and charged her ward with the child's life. It was then that Ramroth realized that no matter how many unanswered questions he had, no matter how many misgivings, his former queen had been everything to him, and now Arial had filled that void. He was responsible for her life, and he still had a purpose. He would have to find a way out or at least find a way to guarantee Arial's safety, and his every thought would be dedicated to that task from now on.

He shifted the hologram to the darkest corner, out of sight to lessen the weight of his heavy heart. He prayed that no one had been watching his ordeal through the seeing orb. If they had, the malachi had better be flying fast.

*

Cassandra was one of the first wazimu to come into being. When the Great Energy had begun to suffer under the influence of the many races, she spewed forth her life into tangible beings that could be used as emissaries for her. She gave them beauty and power unrivaled by any of her other creations, and sent them forth to enforce with words and deeds, which she could not. But since then the Worlds had changed and the wazimu had to adapt to political principles instead of using force as they used to. This was the only way to protect the Great Energy. So they joined councils, sat with kings and great leaders. They split their forces to guard each and every planet, their presence unseen.

Cassandra had been chosen to sit on the High Council and so it was that she was in the right place at the right time for the Voice to speak again. Cassandra had been listening intently to the drey maiden. She held much respect for the keepers who had always lived in harmony with the elements and the creatures around them. She had begun to grow uneasy at the woman's tale. The kuvuta were a very ancient race spawned from the Adare's old and dangerous magic which they had wielded unchecked. These kuvuta had only once dared a hostile takeover of the Worlds and had been stopped by a great sorcerer, Limneth, who had gained immortality and given it up in the face of the enemy to save the woman he loved and so all the people of the Worlds. The kuvuta had been vanquished and had fled, never to be seen again. Until now, if the woman before her spoke true.

They knew nothing of life and beauty, sought only to destroy. They had no souls; no understanding of mercy and the beasts they rode were no better. They breathed not flame, but noxious gases. Their saliva was deadly, and they were an immediate threat to any living thing. Such an enemy was worthy of note, and yet her people had not informed her of such things. Why had she heard no word? True, she and her people were not tuned in to the world of people, and could only comprehend physical entities if they concentrated on that plane, but the presence of a wraith would have reached them on some level at least. Unless they had all perished by the hands of the foul creatures...

The endless squabbling of the sentinels was clouding her mind. She could hardly hear herself think, and now the woman and the one they called Soren were engaged in a power struggle of words. It was then when she felt her ears drown out all sound. She became immobile, staring at their moving lips and hearing nothing. Soon, that also faded and once all was blank, like the fallen snow on a distant landscape, she heard the Voice.

It started to whisper in her ear, very softly at first, but Cassandra recognized it from ages long since passed; the voice of the Oracle. It was the sound of water beneath a mountain, the seed stirring in the ground, the millions of sounds all across the Worlds sewn into one. It delivered the words of an ancient prophecy. She could hear the silent thoughts of all those who held the secret safe, and the breathing of all those whose fate rested upon it. The words were uttered repeatedly until the urgency with which they were spoken became too much for her to bear. Finally they faded and Cassandra's reality was returned to her. She could once again hear the birds outside, the trees growing.

She had little time to act. She seized a ray of the fading light outside with her essence and magnified it one thousand fold. She did not even glance at the others for nothing else mattered. Only the woman. Only the dreya queen mattered now. She flung herself across the table, and grabbed her in the midst of the chaos, but the wraiths had come as she knew they would.

Cassandra cursed silently at her own stupidity. She had not made herself available to it and now it was too late. There was no other element at hand that she could wield. There were too many in any case and they were very strong. She could not compete, and could feel their evil drowning her from within like a giant, black ocean, its waves breaking upon her pure spirit. She had to let go and wait until opportunity presented itself.

She flew from the room and down to the woods below. The trees were dying; she could see it now, now that she no longer assumed it was impossible. Not the way all things are dying even as they draw breath, but the way a thing dies under suffocation, so slow it could go unnoticed until it was almost too late… here she would have to bide her time, watching and waiting.

*

Damek's original plan had been to use his perfected art of stealth to sneak past the human guards then dispose somehow of any wraiths lying in wait, use his various amulets against the powerful magic of the High Adare' and snatch the drey maiden from the clutches of the darkest force of evil ever known to cross the Worlds. That plan, he now realized, was a feeble and highly risky plan at best. Now that he saw the full might of the kuvuta army posted at the tower, he knew he would have never stood a chance against a full frontal assault. He had neither the skill nor the strength.

He had been sitting in his tree a few minutes ago, trying to remember all the fragments of information he had gathered on the wraiths over the centuries; trying to find a pattern that would expose a weakness. Then, the drey that he had been watching earlier had started to rear up, and roar in a wild frenzy. It strained against its bonds; apparently, with all the strength and vigor it could muster. Damek then smelt the distinct smell of freshly spilled virginal blood.

Kuvuta swarmed to the drey, trying to control the beast. He wished them luck. The fire-breathing creature was incinerating everything within a sixty-foot radius, and had started beating his powerful wings, snapping one of the chains that held him. The wraith and human guards were all so focused on the unfolding crisis that not one of them noticed the window that suddenly appeared on the fifth floor. A rift had been exposed. What wonderful luck indeed, Damek thought as he sped toward it. He knew it must be the sorcery of the trapped Adare' and hoped the girl was with him. Upon seeing the sealing orb stretched across the window he hurtled through without a second thought.

Now, with the girl in his arms, he wasn't making as good speed. She was badly wounded, and unconscious from lack of blood; dead weight. Under normal circumstances he would have been long gone but this was a mission, not a meal. He would have to find somewhere to rest soon, regain his strength, and try to help her before it was too late. Damek did not think his master intended her to be dead upon arrival and his last wish was to endure his intense displeasure.

He glanced back over his shoulder. His reduced speed had made him visible, and the wraiths were on his tail. They had mounted their monsters and were gaining on him. Damek tried to fly low to throw them off. He was lithe and flexible, but was finding it difficult to dodge the many trees and dense underbrush that blocked his path. He had hoped that the beasts would not be able to follow him as he dived deeper into the green coverage, yet every time he turned around, more of them had joined the hunt. Damek was not used to being the prey, and he had no intention of getting used to the idea. It seemed though, that they simply bent their physical form in ways that he could not, to overcome the obstacles.

Damek could feel his energy and will ebbing and just as he weaved his path once more, in a desperate attempt to gain the advantage, tapping into the last of his reserves as he did so; a great and deafening roaring assailed his ears. The noise was so powerful that it drowned out all others; the shrieking of the wraiths, the whistling of the wind, and his own ragged breathing.

He chanced another backward glance. His eyes grew wide at what he saw. It appeared to be a great river of flame raging through the air. A blazing furnace of all-consuming magical fire had joined the chase. Even as he watched, hypnotized by the flames, the kuvuta furthest behind were snared by the giant fire. It was as if they had been eaten alive. They writhed and twisted grotesquely as their spirit selves bubbled and tore open, the flames licking hungrily at the exposed and blackened flesh. Damek smiled to himself, glad to see that they could bleed.

Their cries of pain did little to break the sound of the monstrous fire that bore mercilessly down upon them. He slowed down, as the inferno grew closer. It was so beautiful. It looked like a drey now that he was near enough to feel the heat of it upon his face, but no dragon could do that, no matter how powerful. It moved swiftly against the wind, hunting down each wraith. It would open its fiery jaws, and encase them in a cage of red-hot death. He watched as the last wraith was consumed in this terrible way, disintegrating in a burst of ash and black smoke, its scream fading away into the night air long after its body had been taken.

Damek landed heavily on the ground to face the burning wall of flames the fire had now become. It had stopped just as he had, and now he could see that nothing else had perished in the massive onslaught of magic, nothing save the wraiths had even been singed. The wall was moving like a mirage, and shimmering with smoldering heat like a thousand fire sprites. He could feel the beads of sweat grow thick upon his brow while the trees around it remained untouched. He could not move. All he could do was stare into the fire.

A voice rumbled out of the blaze, and a face wreathed in flame, colossal as the fire from whence it came, erupted out of the wall. It towered above him, eyes like black coals stood out against the searing red. A wazimu, Damek thought. She must have harnessed the fire from the drey. Why aid them though? He did not have to wait long for an answer. The voice was as strong and commanding as the element of which it was made. It said;

'The woman you hold is part of an ancient prophecy that must be fulfilled. Fate has chosen you to take care of her.' Damek could hardly speak for the heat pulling through him. The wazimu's voice rang in his ears and reverberated through his body.

'Why me?' he asked with great difficulty. The fire raged stronger at his question and the voice roared;

'You would question Fate! You have very little time, she is leaving us...' the fire seemed to draw back a little, and the voice was steady once more. A few moments reprieve and then the face was growing closer once again;

'Watch over her, night stalker, and do not fail. She is precious to us all.' The flames grew hotter with every word spoken as if the message was to be burnt into him. Damek's eyes burned, and hot tears rolled down his face, evaporating before they could fall. Just when he thought he could take no more and that the eyes of the wazimu would bore through his immortal soul, the heat started to dissipate. The face slowly withdrew, and sank back into the furnace. 'She is precious to us all…'

The message faded into the night along with the fire, no trace was left of his overwhelming encounter save the knowledge of something too great to fully comprehend. Damek fell to his knees, shivering in the cold night air, humbled by his experience.

He lay Arial down gently on the forest floor. She held something loosely in the palm of her hand, glittering in the moonlight. The chain it was connected to was coiled around her slender wrist. He unwound it, and placed the small trinket around her neck, gently lifting her head as he did so, all too glad that it had not fallen in flight. It was going to be a long night. A child of the Great Energy had helped them escape probable death, and then spoken to him of fate and destiny. Wazimu told no lies, and meddled in nothing that was not of Worldly importance. Small wonder she had been so fiercely guarded, he thought. He knew his master had been hiding something.

He bent down to brush the hair from her face, removed his cloak, and wrapped her in it for warmth and protection. He had stolen it from a warrior king many decades ago and Damek knew everything of the things he stole. It had been woven by sorcerous Reichie Elves who had parted with their souls to create its magic. The king had hired the best assassins in all the Worlds to hunt them down one by one so that the secret of its making would be lost forever. It was invaluable and his most prized possession. He left it with her.

*

Soren felt the presence of the kuvuta behind him. It was a feeling that most would never have the need to get used to since as soon as they had registered the cool touch of death; they were already in its realm. Soren was comfortable with it; he had grown up with it. He was part of it.

'I thought the job was being done properly Esyago,' Soren said smoothly, his arms folded neatly across his chest.

'My lieutenants say they did not see them leave,' the wraith hissed in reply.

'Then why were they not intercepted before they got here? Surely you have not lost your Seers in battle?' Soren scoffed at the very idea. The Seers of the kuvuta were so genetically mutated that they had to be sealed off in quarantine permanently for fear of viral contamination on an essence level. Like gasses so toxic, the wraiths themselves could not even breathe it.

'They left with the breaking of dawn,' came the wraith's cool reply, 'our Seers were blind to their departure. They traveled fast, covering their ion-trails. Their beasts warned them and they had time to prepare.' Soren cocked his head slightly and asked;

'And you say it is too late?' this time with less contempt, more concern.

'Yes, an emissary has already been sent.' The kuvuta stood unmoving.

'Very well. We shall detain them at a later stage if I cannot sway what is left of the council. They have almost served their purpose in any case.' Soren turned to face the wraith that towered above him. 'Post guards outside the chamber,' he continued, 'and make sure they wear the amulets; I am told a wizard travels with her.'

'What of the others?' the wraith asked flatly.

'Leave them be,' Soren replied airily, waving his hand in a dismissive manner, 'they are but eleven riders against all we have gathered here.'

The kuvuta seemed to regard the man before him for a few seconds before saying;

'Underestimation will not serve us well here. They fight well and they do not run.' Soren slammed his fists down upon the wooden table he was standing before, the color rising dangerously in his face. He explained, through clenched teeth, as if to an unwitting child;

'If they try anything, we will crush them. They will wish they *had* run and hidden on their precious little planet.' He turned his back on the expressionless kuvuta. 'That is all. You may take your leave, Esyago.'

Just as the wraith made to exit, Soren turned his head around keeping his fists planted on the table. 'One last thing,' he said, 'how is my mother? I have not seen her in many moons.'

'Lady Mirkisha is well,' came the monotone reply, 'she waits for you.' The wraith was gone when Soren turned again.

'Come,' he said, speaking to the large animal that lay lazily stretched out on the carpet in front of the elaborate fireplace. It was an imitation of an animal now extinct, but documented in the ancient history of planet Earth; a mammal with orange fur like the last blaze of a setting star and black stripes like the face of a Nomad Elf in the Burnt Worlds. It yawned; exposing a long, pink tongue and glistening, white fangs the length of a man's outstretched hand. It was Riko's favorite form. By the time Riko was on his feet, the magnificent coat had been replaced by old, wrinkled skin and wispy white hair.

'High Adare' Ethron wears glasses Riko. You forget every time,' Soren remarked, shuffling through the papers on his desk impatiently.

*

Falkhar was in a hurry. The Six, or rather the Four since the High Elves and keepers had declined to reinstate, had been called to the council chamber. Normally he would be taking his time since matters affecting the Worlds held little value for him anymore. This meeting though, was of great importance indeed, and he would not miss a minute of it.

He walked briskly with his head cocked to one side, better to hear the one who accompanied him. A small creature that walked with a slight limp in his left leg, courtesy of the master who felt it necessary to use pain to remind him of his duty and loyalty, and to meet his own sadistic ends. He spoke to Falkhar in hushed tones, for Soren had ears everywhere, and his struggle to keep up with the malachi's pace made his breath come in wheezes.

'I was there when they spoke today. The general came this morning; he said they left with the break of dawn. They have arrived and the woman wears the necklace, just as you said. I checked.'

'Very good, I am most pleased,' The malachi said, never breaking his stride, eyes always ahead, 'and you say your master knows nothing of her true identity?'

'It is as you predicted. He is an arrogant hunter, never believing himself to be the prey.'

They reached the ivory doors and Falkhar did not even acknowledge the presence of the pseudo guards whilst his companion tried to conceal his shudder of disgust.

'You may return to Osrillia when this is all done, and await my arrival. Have everything prepared.' Now it was the malachi who spoke softly, so as not to let the wraiths hear. The little creature bowed and Falkhar turned on his heel sneering disdainfully, his magnificent cloak billowing around his muscular frame. He marched through the door and took his seat next to Soren's. High Adare' Ethron entered a few seconds after, grimacing slightly as he sat, his painful reminder. He touched his glasses again, just to reassure himself.

*

Soren was the last to join the council that morning. Riko was seated in High Adare' Ethron's place in full guise, and Cassandra and Felias were talking animatedly together. Soren took his place next to Falkhar, leaned over and said;

'Everything is still under control and will go according to plan. This woman's tale will be too far-fetched, you know that fear will still the others and our two great races will be safe. You will have your freedom.'

Falkhar curled his lips into what he hoped passed for a courteous smile.

This would do for Soren. Soon he would be rid of Falkhar and his parasitic kind. Cassandra had of course been told of nothing. She was not concerned with the peoples of the Worlds. It was her wretched race that had been worshiped by the pagans, had banished his people from their home planet so many centuries ago, forcing such strict regulations upon them. King Felias was a fool and did not follow the Religion. The magician had been taken care of long ago for he was extremely powerful, and while the vampires had no allies, all races were affiliated with the Adare', who wielded the blasphemous dark magic they all claimed to be the life blood of the Worlds. Falkhar, he had had to persuade and bargain with. He knew of the full might of the malachi nation and when the Master malachi had cornered him he knew that his lies would only earn him an early grave. It was no matter though; Falkhar would be eliminated with the rest of the vermin regardless. He, Soren, would become the savior of the Men of Adam, single handedly raise them to their rightful place, and with his black plague, destroy all other unholy creatures. The ivory doors swung open.

*

Damek hurried off into the undergrowth to find the plant that would save the young queen's life. He crept through the shadows without a sound, careful neither to stray too far nor get caught by a wraith, for fear of leaving the vulnerable woman alone and unprotected. He peaked his sense of smell, trying to discern the aroma of the color purple, and he adjusted his eyes to the pressing darkness of the forest. Now he saw only in shades of grey. He could pick up even the tiniest of movements around him. He skulked around the forest for a while like a hunter without prey, searching desperately for the regal holly. He found a rat scurrying across his path, and was so famished from his exertions, that he drained the blood from the tiny animal in one swift and highly illegal movement. He would pay someone off later when the blood tests betrayed him.

He found the flower soon after. It was being strangled by wild ivy, and was in poor condition. He thought of the woman lying as if in a deep sleep, and he thought of the time she had left. It would have to do. He followed her scent that had never left him, back to where he had lain her down. He knelt over her, grinding the purple petals between his teeth, and mixing his own potent salivary anesthetic into the mixture. He slowly applied the sticky substance to her wound. It tasted bitter, but did a fine job of masking the after-taste of the foul rat's blood. The plant was also doing well at healing the gaping hole in the woman's neck. It had started to close, and the blood flow had been stemmed. Her breathing had started to become more rhythmic and less shallow. She would be completely recovered by dawn.

He sat down beside her, watching her breathe. He tore his gaze away and busied himself with making a small, neat incision in his wrist with his teeth. She had lost much of her blood, and this was the only way to restore it. He knew it would burn but there would be no death in it for her. The drey bond that flowed through her veins was too strong, and would kill the veracious little parasite in minutes, before it had a chance to kill her. She would age as all races aged, she would not thirst for hemoglobin rich blood, she would be able to find a love to last and match her own, and she would die one day.

He cradled her head in his lap and lifted her chin up, letting his blood drip into her mouth. He watched as her pink tongue turned red and when he felt he had given enough, he laid her head against the soft ground once again, wiping clean with his knuckles what had trickled from the corners of her mouth. He chewed more petals and coated her healing wound evenly, and with less haste. It had been a while since he had played doctor to anyone. His own cut was already gone.

He sat with her for a while. Watching her breathing grow stronger, watching her eyelids flutter as the malachi blood raced through her, surging with energy and strength. All the while, he strained his ears against the noises of the forest, waiting for the sound of pursuit, but none came. He had a strong feeling that the wazimu had something to do with that. She could keep them hidden as long as they remained here, even if a kuvuta stood right beside them. That thought comforted him and gave him confidence enough to leave the woman, and soothe the ache in his stomach that the giving of his life force had created.

Chapter 4
The great divide

Arial awoke as the Equa star was rising. She was cold and a little damp. She tried to focus her thoughts and realized that she was lying on something soft; grass. She was outside. The morning dew clung to her, and she was surrounded by the sounds of many twittering birds, urging the star to rise faster with their song. She lay still, her eyes tightly shut, trying to remember why she was lying outside. As the memories came back to her, her hand reached up to touch her neck. Searing pain, darkness, nightmares of flying and...*fire*...and the fire had burned and pulsated through her veins with fury and wild passion. She tasted blood on her tongue and sat bolt upright, her lungs fighting for fresh air.

'You should not do that.'

Arial looked up, following the direction of the voice, and straight into the penetrating gaze of a night stalker. His eyes were deep, cool pools of malachite green, flecked with gold and framed by a heavy brow. His jaw jutted strongly and a sly grin completed his face. Through the foggy haze in her head, Arial was too confused to be afraid. It must have shown on her face for the malachi started laughing heartily at her, his shoulders shaking. Arial did her best to rearrange her facial features to look less idiotic and more assertive.

'Who are you and where am I? Where are my ward and my drey?' Arial demanded in the firmest voice she could muster, besides the throbbing in her head. She drew her knees to her chin, and tried to cover most of her bare legs with the white, chiffon skirt she wore. The stranger's eyes were roaming far too casually than she thought appropriate.

Damek had stopped laughing but still smirked at her.

'Don't bother,' he said smoothly, shaking his head. A look of pure outrage contorted upon the young dreya queen's face. 'I did not mean offense,' he said hurriedly, reacting to her emotions as habit would have, 'I did cover you with my cloak.'

In his mind, thoughts were racing. The wazimu had given him a task, but had done little to clarify the extent of his responsibility. He knew that she would not have come to him if it were a small matter, one that did not pertain to the entire universe for example. But no creature of dust and fire would save him from his master's wrath if he disobeyed him. He could not shoulder such a burden anyway. She was a heathen, nothing more. Queen of a race close to the Worlds with little or no technology and strange customs completely foreign to him. The energy child must have been mistaken, and he would hand her over as he was told. On the outside though, he smiled evenly and revealed nothing.

Arial found herself blushing slightly to her further discontent as she saw his cloak lying discarded by her side. She composed herself quickly and stared at him, levelly in the eyes, as she got to her feet.

'I am a Queen, one of the Six, and you will provide me with answers to my questions immediately.'

'Queen of what, pray tell?' Damek asked, picking his cloak up and brushing the dirt from it. Arial had no reply. The last minutes of her home-planet flashing through her mind for the hundredth time.

'Sorry to be the bearer of sore reminders but you are in fact, queen no longer, since you have nothing to rule over that is.' Despite her need to appear strong, tears of anger and grief welled up in Arial's eyes. Damek hardened his resolve. He was a man without pity and he had a job to do. 'Furthermore, my name is of no concern to you. You are in the forests of Equa, the home of our most esteemed High

Council,' he sneered sarcastically, 'from whom I recently rescued you. A narrow escape, yes, but at least I saw to it that your wound healed properly. I doubt it will scar.'

He decided to tell her nothing of the wazimu. If she had known that she was part of some great prophesy she would have been in hiding, not running around and straight into wraith territory too! The less she knew, the better, and the easier his task would be. Those who thought they were helpless did little to change the stakes.

'And my ward…my drey…?' her voice was breaking now, even as she tilted her chin in a show of misplaced defiance. Damek wavered. He was breaking what was left of her heart and he could see it in her eyes.

'We need to leave now.'

He was on his feet, throwing his cloak around his shoulders. Arial could feel anger welling up inside her chest like an inferno. She had no time for this, she needed to find Ramroth and Ronan and try to stop the wraiths herself since it seemed no one else held any value for life anymore.

'If you would,' he continued, holding out his arm for her. Arial stared at him incredulously.

'You cannot be serious?' she asked, 'surely you do not expect me to leave with you? I need to put an end to the massacre before some other planet falls prey to the kuvuta, and I will fly nowhere without my drey! So thank you for helping me escape but I have not been spared the wraiths to fall captive to the likes of you. Now I really must get back.'

She said it with such finality and made such a show of pretending to know in which direction the tower lay that Damek smiled a genuine smile, only to himself though. When he grabbed her by the arm and spun her around, his face was a mask of calm malice. He had pulled her so close to him that Arial could smell the blood on his breath. When he spoke, all the cadences in his voice that made him sound mortal had vanished. Only cold facts greeted her, delivered by a heartless captor, spoken as if the issues so close to her heart were mere trifles to him.

'Your drey is at the mercy of the kuvuta now, as is your ward. Their escape, if there will be one, shall be by their own doing, not ours. My orders are take you to my master and it will be easier for you if you cooperate.'

Arial glared at him, hating his every breath and hissed;

'My men walk this forest as we speak, and if I scream loud enough, they will come for me and slay you like the dog you are.'

'You scream loud enough, queen of a dead realm, and more than just your men will come. The wraiths seek out your beating heart. They will tear it from your chest while you watch,' he replied through clenched teeth, hoping she would not call his bluff, and shaking her to emphasize his point before releasing his grip and stepping back to extend his arm, more stiffly this time around.

'Why?' she breathed, hardly able to stay on her feet from pure lack of will. His face contorted with impatience, and there were neither tears, nor the haze of first light to mask what he was now.

His long clawed fingers flexed at his side, his jaw; strong and wide for the kill, his reinforced bones strung with strange muscles lending his every move an eerie grace. He was a pure blood malachi. No interbreeding had watered down his selfish blood. Arial knew she would never be able to run fast enough or hide from him. He was a relentless hunter, strong beyond comparison, and he had the ability of flight; all driven by the parasite that lived in his every cell. She could not scream, she could not flee, and she would not be able to save those she loved unaided. She would have to bide her time and plan an escape. She would see Ramroth and her drey again if it were the last thing she ever did.

She closed the space between them in two, small steps and put her arms around his neck, linking her fingers, blue eyes blazing in defiance.

'Thank you,' he said, surprised by her sudden movements, 'I am glad you chose not to fight me,' he said gently, sweeping her off her feet and into his arms. 'I will try to make this easy for you.'

'I am stronger than you think, *cheupe*,' she spat, using her own people's name for his race. It meant pale one, and all the while trying to keep her guard up. It was all an act on his part, and his kind were so good at placating those they meant to harm. In an instant, however, all her thoughts were swept away as the clouds came rushing toward her like a bad dream.

Only a few were able to cross the space between the Worlds space without the help of special crafts. Dreya were born with the natural ability and advanced riders are able to tap into that skill and remain unharmed. Kuvuta and wazimu simply did not have a physical entity to speak of and so, were unaffected by any space and time. Their physical forms used for interaction were a pure force of will. Malachi, however, cheated the system as it were. Long ago, they had found a way to stretch their essences, and compact them enough to slip through spatial realms so fast, that their physical selves have no time to be affected by pressure or lack of oxygen. Like most of their secrets though, it was guarded selfishly, passed down from generation to generation.

Arial recalled her first flight on the mighty neck of Ronan. Flying was an amazing experience in itself but leaving the atmospheric blanket of a planet was a religious awakening. The blue melted majestically into black, the stars blinked into visibility like the unveiling of precious jewels. The weightlessness and serenity was like nothing she had ever felt before. Her heart soared when she flew with Ronan, and it was to that feeling she clung, to try and make the pain go away.

She closed her eyes and buried her face into her new captor's chest, the feeling leaving her faster and faster. Tears streamed freely as her connection to Ronan pulled urgently at her heart. She could feel his confusion and hurt like it was her own. Her tears froze as they ascended with growing speed, higher and faster, until she felt her essence stretch till breaking point and then...silence. Hurtling through space at a speed where sound could not find them. They landed abruptly on wet ground. It was raining wherever they were now.

*

Zach was prodding the fire angrily with a stick. The men were all busy skinning and butchering the deer they had hunted earlier. The dreya had already eaten their fill, as was customary, and were lying silhouetted against the setting star like giant, breathing boulders.

The source of the captain's frustration was the ever-pending arrival of Lok and Miko. Zach had begun to worry some time ago and by now, his anxiety was so obvious that the others gave him a wide birth. He sat down from his hunkered position, gazing upward for the hundredth time that day and jumped to his feet as he spotted the telltale sign of Miko's magic unveiling within the atmosphere. He called to his riders and they responded immediately, dropping their knives, wiping the blood on their hands off on their chests and running toward their captain.

The wind whipped their hair back as Miko landed on the ground with a soft thud, removing her guise simultaneously. Zach's scout half stepped, half stumbled off her back and down her tail.

'Captain,' he said breathlessly, hunched over with both hands resting heavily on his thighs.

'Sit down man and get your breath back,' Zach instructed, steadying the exhausted rider. 'And bring that drey some water!' he barked.

Lok sat down on a rock with his head in his hands, still breathing deeply like he feared he would never taste air again. The other riders crowded around him uneasily, scared for the bad way he was in, while Llstar and Eiros fetched water for Miko.

'You pant like a dog that just rode his bitch,' Ionhar said in jest to try and lighten the darkening mood. The drey riders roared with laughter and Zach thumped Lok on the back, shaking his shoulder playfully. Lok waved him off and lifted his face. It was pale and grave. Beads of sweat clinging to his pasty skin. The others fell silent and waited for him to gather his words.

'What news Lok?' Owein probed when Lok failed to speak. Zach knelt down in front of his scout, concern on his weathered features;

'What of Bethriam rider?' he asked softly and slowly.

'Bethriam is no more,' came the strained reply. His voice shook with more than just exhaustion, but his lips seemed hardly to move at all. His hands trembled with the effort of staying upright and Zach took them in his own. This seemed to steady Lok, and his eyes finally met Zach's;

'That is why we took so long. Miko had little strength left after we battled to free ourselves from it.' Zach turned his gaze to the drey and saw that she was almost as spent and shaken as her rider.

'Free yourselves from what?' he asked, turning his attention back to Lok.

'The kuvuta,' Lok answered, 'they took it all. The darkness took it all. It's all gone now.' His head sank back down again.

'The darkness?' Cahan asked, his brow furrowed. No one moved nor uttered a word. A voice spoke up from behind them;

'A black hole, the beast in the heavens.' It was Llstar who spoke. He was older than the other riders. His hair was greying around his temples, his face scarred with burn marks, and his hands calloused with many years of dreya handling. He sat on his haunches next to Miko, the drey taking deep gulps of water from the hide bucket he had brought her. He was fingering the aged scales upon her foot and shaking his head sadly;

'It sucks all things through its blackened, gaping mouth with endless hunger. It is never satisfied. It lives for many years and devours anything and everything around it.'

The warriors became increasingly unsettled with every word he spoke. All of them had logged space time with their dreya, and had been warned of such things, but none had ever witnessed one and it had been commonly accepted that it was a myth designed to scare them into obedience out there.

'The kuvuta have not the power to conjure one though, Llstar? It is a mathematical anomaly, not some magician's trick, or a piece of dark magic able to be summoned at will,' Zach said, hoping he was right but knowing in his heart that Lok would tell no lie.

'I am not telling you why or how,' Llstar retorted, his voice pitched higher as he stood up, 'I merely give a name to Lok's ramblings!' he added angrily, gesturing to the broken rider with a sweep of his gnarled hand.

Zach dismissed the old drey keeper's tone and the whisperings of the other men. If what Lok said was true, and if Llstar's interpretation was correct, then all had truly been lost. The scout was still shaking and Zach barked an order for someone to bring him fresh water too.

He stood up and walked away from where Lok sat. He felt as if he was walking through a twilight zone, like he was not a part of all that was happening around him. Everything played out in slow motion as he walked through the mayhem. Men shouting and fetching water, talking in whispers to one another, glancing around skittishly. Others crowded around Lok trying to get the full account of what he had seen. The dreya had raised their heads, craning their necks toward the source of the commotion, some feeling their rider's confusion.

Zach walked through the chaos until the sounds of the guard faded. He stood under a canopy of giant, age-old trees, the smell of wood and water not seeming real anymore. He listened to the faint rustle of the leaves as the evening breeze swept through the forest, the sweet smell of wild flowers borne upon that same wind. The evening star winked down at him as it did every night but Zach knew that the heavens would never be the same again, for wherever he was now, he could never again look up and know that home was out there.

*

Valcan tore hungrily at the flesh of the large animal he had helped capture. It was his and Valador's favorite game to hunt. An enormous stone-grey beast with two giant, white tusks that curled up and out toward the heavens. Clever and patient, strong and unyielding. It was difficult to bring down but well worth the effort.

Riders through the ages had developed many different ways to chase and kill this ancient Earth creature. One could ride on drey back, low and swift, to cut its hamstrings with a sword and run it down, or use a silver arrow to pierce it just above its large ear. It would drop to the ground eventually no matter what the technique, and send tremors across the plain. Ambush was another method, though less popular, since the dreya did all the work and the grace was taken out of the hunt. Valador and Valcan had found a way to bring the creature down alone and in a dignified manner.

Three hours earlier, they had come across the herd. Valador had counted one hundred large moving east toward the watering hole. Together, they had picked out the one they wanted. As a rule; no females with babies, carrying or nursing, and no big breeding males. Fair game was the sick, the old and the young reaching sexual maturity, even if it did mean less chase. This herd was thick with them, but one in particular stood out; a boisterous youngster with the beginnings of only one impressive tusk, and a nasty demeanor. The herd would not mourn too long for a trouble causer.

The hunters glided just behind the ridge of the mountain overlooking the grassland, and positioned themselves downwind from the mass of moving grey. They settled behind a rocky outcrop, Valcan's hide blending in perfectly. He lidded his eyes against the glare of the new star, and fixed them upon the chosen prey.

Valador crept down the leeward side and closer to the herd. He rested for a short while with his back against a fleshy thorn tree and picked their target out in the throng. It was only when he felt the tree he was using as cover begin to shudder, that he realized one of the creatures was almost on top of him. It was withered and old, eyesight made even worse by age but it still had the strength of twenty men. The flat of its immense head was pressed against the trunk of Valador's tree and the animal was leaning upon it with all its weight. Valador stepped back swiftly as he heard the tree creaking and groaning under the great force. He lay down to reduce his visible presence and then rolled out of the way just in time for the tree to crash to the ground where he had been lying seconds before. He held his breath under the foliage knowing that if he moved, and the beast saw him, he was a dead man. It moved laboriously closer, reaching out with its long, snake-like trunk to eat the top most leaves now on the ground. It snorted loudly and dust and mucous rained down on Valador's face. He made not a sound, and moved not an inch, until the creature had eaten his fill and moved on to join the others. He released his breath deeply and continued to scramble down the rocky hill, following the old one.

He had been lucky. If he had been discovered, he would have been tossed into the air, and trampled until his bones meshed with the sand. A terrible and brutal death, but it was this fierce protection that he most admired about his prey, and it was for this very reason that they had to be isolated if they were to be brought down.

The ancient animal trudged toward Valador's young bull, leading the rider straight to him. Valador had named him Bluff. For such a young animal in such a large herd, he acted like the head-honcho. He was trying to court one of the older females when the rider snuck up behind him.

At first, he was cautiously sniffing her rear, poking her underbelly and playfully flicking her with his trunk. She tolerated his childlike advances, but when he made his first attempt to mount her from behind when she was not looking, she trumpeted loudly in alarm and outrage, batting him across the head with a mighty thump from her trunk and trotting away indignantly. The old male shuffled by as if he had seen that play out a hundred times before. Bluff was left standing in a cloud of dust the female had kicked up, staring after her hopefully.

Valador was in awe of these creatures who, just like dreya, mourned their dead, treasured their young, and interacted with each other in ways he could only guess at. For a moment he was saddened at the thought of killing one of these magnificent creatures but then his stomach rumbled softly and he could feel Valcan urging him on. One such mammal yielded enough meat to feed a small hold of maybe four at one sitting, dreya included. If dried and salted properly, it could feed him and Valcan for five days. The fat not only tasted good when cooked but also made the finest saddle and weaponry grease. Some native tribes also used it as a repellant for a certain insect that drew blood from the skin, infecting the victim with a deadly fever. It was also smeared along the inside of the ears to prevent another bug from crawling inside and laying its larvae. Valuable, needless to say. Valador used the giant teeth, when they were available, to carve fine scabbards for his handcrafted swords and knives and beautiful stirrups and handles for his seat upon Valcan. He thought mainly of the meat though. He had not eaten in three days and perhaps that was the cause of his strange dreams and restless nights. He doubted that, but a full stomach could only be beaten by a warm woman in your bed, and Valador was sure he would not receive that this night.

The hunger and the thrill of the chase made him inch closer still. He snaked his way through the tall, yellow grass on stomach and elbows. He was close enough now to see the long, dark lashes and the amber eyes that dwelt beneath them. They were glazed over in absent thought as the bull chewed lazily on the round, yellow fruits it had collected from the ground at its feet.

Valador drew his hand blade silently from his hip. The fat from his previous kill glistened on the blade and it made not a sound as it sliced through the air and nicked the unsuspecting animal on its right flank. Now the creature's eyes lost their misty and faraway look as the pain Valador had inflicted registered. At first, they depicted pain and confusion, then anger and finally, when the drey keeper jumped out from behind the long grass that camouflaged him, exposing himself and waving his arms frantically in the air - the small, beady eyes became focused and seared Valador with an unrivaled intensity.

The rider was already backtracking fast to where his drey lay in wait as Bluff started to lumber toward him. Valador's heart was beating wildly at the thought of imminent death mere moments behind him, the adrenaline alone kept his weary and hungry limbs going. He could hear the giant ears flapping, feel the heavy thud of the ground as it shook beneath the creature's feet, and the mad trumpeting was so loud; Valador thought it would shatter his skull.

He was making a mad dash uphill, over loose rocks and slippery rubble, trying to stay on his feet and dodge the thorny bushes that tore painfully at his skin. He could not falter. By the time he had reached Valcan's hiding place, his legs felt like lead stumps, and his breathing came in shallow, ragged gasps. Bluff had very nearly closed the gap between them and in another few, long strides, would have been upon him with blazing fury.

Valador streaked past his drey, sending the signal with what little breath he had left. In an instant, Valcan reared up from his hidden position, spreading his great, leathery wings to an impressive span. He threw back his horned head and roared to the skies above. The trees shook and the leaves upon them trembled in the wake of the power of his call. He did not throw flame, as was customary in the traditional ambush, used to trap the prey in a ring of fire. His display was merely meant to distract the creature, and slow it from a full on charge to a cautious trot.

Valcan beat his wings furiously, kicking up great, billowing clouds of dust high into the air, thick as an autumn fog. He then took off; flying to the place he and his keeper had first observed the herd.

Bluff had now stopped in his tracks, confused by what he just seen and heard, and the dust that now obscured his sight. Valador had used the time given to him by his drey to catch his breath and steady his nerves. He retrieved his silver sword he had left lying at the base of the tree he stood beneath, wrapped in soft leather. He took a deep breath and prepared for battle.

He stepped out of the swirling haze of fine yellow mist that separated hunter from hunter, to face the raging giant. His sword hung at his side as he strode toward Bluff. The animal had spotted him now, but stood still as he considered the small figure before him. Valador came to a halt and raised his sword so that now, the shining shaft of metal was the only thing that stood between him and death, as it had so many times before. It glinted challengingly in the daylight, reflecting in the rider's eyes. Bluff accepted wordlessly, without hesitation and charged at the man before him. Valador stood ready, breathing steadily and increasing his grip on the ivory hilt.

The creature was upon him now, mad eyes gleaming, dust clouds rolling behind him. Valador had closed his mind to everything around him save his prey and the task at hand. He could smell the sweet, honey smell of the young bull, his every move echoed in the rider's mind. The gap closed. Valador's footwork was perfect, his form; flawless. His aim was precise and the fatal blow, delivered with such force as befitting his enormous adversary; faultless.

As Bluff lowered his head for the charge, Valador side-stepped and leaned all his weight into the thrust that sent his sword deep into the creature's throat, pulling hard and out again for the retrieve. He had seen it done in the arenas of the naizhan gladiators. It was an art. He had perfected it.

Bluff stumbled a few paces on; the sand being painted red with the blood that already coated Valador's straining arms. He turned his great head toward Valador, and blinked slowly before falling to his knees. He was dead before his head touched the ground.

Valador stepped toward the mighty creature and knelt beside it. Whilst saying an ancient prayer to the children of the goddess, Keeper of Souls, he cut the creature's heart out of its chest, holding it high above his head as he uttered the final words. The prayer was for peace and safe passage for the soul, and that retribution would not fall upon him for taking its life, as this life would give to his own. He buried the heart at the foot of the tree where he had first left his sword. He called to Valcan and together they stripped the carcass bare.

Once Valador had finished packing the meat, tusks, bones and fat onto his drey's back, the star was already casting an orange glow across the horizon. Valador began to pile white pebbles above the place where Bluff's heart lay and when he had finished, Valcan threw flame and heated them until they burned red-hot. The herd would now know where to come mourn their fallen member.

The two hunters returned to camp, weary with hunger and fatigue, but with hearts soaring at their success. Later, their eyelids heavy with sleep and their bellies full to bursting point, Valador thought - a good day, a good hunt. Perhaps he would sleep soundly this night.

*

Adonica could not stand the cold. The way its icy fingers tugged at her flesh. The warm body of her master that lay beside her was comfort enough, but the fire was burning low, and dawn was approaching. She pulled back the satin sheets that enveloped her and stood up to stoke the fire. The bearskin rug tickled her feet as she walked across her bedchamber to fetch her gown. It was black silk, embroided with red roses. It was a gift from Falkhar and she treasured it more than she let him know. Another silly token from a man she loved. It was true, she was the only one he took to his bed by day, and one of the few he hunted illegally with by night, but their liaison remained a secret.

The fire was blazing now and he stirred in her bed but did not wake. She sat by the window and stared out at her world. She could not remember how she had come to be so alone. Soon though, she thought secretly, there would be no hiding. Something stirred inside her and she had yet to build the courage to speak of it...

'I need you to do something for me.' It was Falkhar; he was standing behind her with his hands resting gently on her neck. Even after so many years, she still marveled at how quickly and silently he was able to move.

'That depends,' she answered softly, 'on what's in it for me,' she teased. He moved his hands down her neckline and slowly peeled the gown away that covered her naked chest. Running his fingers up and down the curves of her breasts, he lowered his head and whispered softly in her ear.

*

The rain was falling heavy and thick. Damek ran with Arial in his arms to a nearby over-hanging rock, mud spattering against his boots and cloak. He put her down on her feet and realized that his chosen shelter did little to protect them from the sheets of icy water that fell from the sky. The rain pounded on the stone above them and not on their eardrums though, so at least they could hear one another speak.

'You look terrible,' he said, once he had finished shaking the mud from his shoes.

'You brought me all the way out here to tell me that?' she asked, incredulity and anger shining through her eyes.

Damek was, of course, doing what he did best; lying. She stood before him, soaking-wet and mud-flecked, her dress a dull pink color in places from the diluted bloodstains, and completely transparent in others. It clung to her body like a second skin. Her hair was frizzed and had plastered itself to any surface it could find. The rain snaked down her skin and her blue eyes matched the color of the water-drenched sky. She was the most beautiful thing he had seen in a long, long time.

'I must apologize for my behavior before...I am sure you can appreciate the fact that I needed to remove you from the realm of the High Council as a matter of urgency. I have brought you to the planet Avril instead,' he said, a gentle smile on his lips, 'it is surrounded by the purest water in the Worlds but cannot be used for drinking as it contains microorganisms poisonous to all foreign beings, hence its uninhabited splendor.' He spread his arms and gazed skyward, mostly to give himself a distraction.

'We have a saying where I come from *cheupe*; "the beauty of the lion's mane is lost on the lamb".'

'Since you needed to bathe, I thought you might like it.' His voice had risen and he seemed genuinely crestfallen. Arial's heart almost softened but her composure remained solid as she reminded herself whom she was dealing with. She knew she was not food for this man but he would try to lull her into complacency before handing her over to his master none the less.

Damek admired her self-control. A lesser woman would have crumbled by now, but he could tell that it would take more than flattery to gain her trust and cooperation. He planned his next angle of attack whilst they walked to the nearest stream.

The rain had eased up into a soft drizzle and the native birds were singing their hypnotic songs in the treetops surrounding them. They reached the edge of the river and Arial started to take her sandals off, leaning against a thick tree trunk for balance. Damek was lost in thought.

'You aren't planning on watching are you?' Arial asked him, half laughing.

'Of course not,' he sneered, stalking off into the greenery. Arial merely shook her head at the night stalker.

Damek was now genuinely annoyed. He needed to focus. He did not know whose wrath he feared more; his master's or the children of the Energy. He would be hunted to his death if he did not bring the woman to Osrillia. He would be cast from the realm of men if he transgressed the wazimu. Damek sighed angrily; she had not even told him what the prophesy was; let alone his role therein. He knew it involved at least keeping the dragon lady safe. His master, he was almost sure, had no one's safety in mind unless it directly affected his own. It was a toss-up, a gamble, and his life was at stake.

Despite his precarious position, he stood on the Forgotten Planet, the pitter-patter of the rain all around him, wondering what drew him to her so. He stepped toward the wall of creepers that blocked the stream from view and peered through the undergrowth. She was only visible from the waist up. The arch of her back and the delicate line of her spine were sparkling with droplets of water. She had her hair slung over one shoulder and was washing the other, fine hands caressing soft skin. Damek blinked twice and quickly averted his gaze. An unnecessary complication.

Arial had slipped back into her white, chiffon dress and had discarded her sandals. She was watching the water sprites, *zimun*, playing amongst themselves in the river, smiling to herself. It was a rare sight to behold. She turned her head when she noticed Damek's arrival and frowned quizzically at his facial expression. He wiped the worried look off his face. He too stared at the nymphs at play, their lithe figures dancing in the water as they splashed around, their laughter part of the stream as it flowed by. They were blissfully unaware of the two standing beside them, and gradually moved away with the current they were made of.

'Thank you for rescuing me,' she said after a while. The rain had let up a little and the star was out. Her voice was pitched low as if she was afraid of sounding weak. 'My name is Arial, if you did not already know. The kuvuta destroyed my home planet yesterday. I came to the High Council for help, although I should have known better,' she added snidely, 'and now I have lost my ward and my drey and am captive to a *cheupe*.'

'Yes,' Damek replied evenly, nodding.

'Answer me this,' she turned and asked, 'why am I so sought after all of a sudden? First the council decides to imprison me and now the malachi have need of whatever it is I have to offer.' Damek considered her question for a moment, wondering how best to answer;

'It was not the council that ordered your arrest, it was Soren.'

'Ramroth suspected as much, but why me and why now? I do not understand how my warning could have angered him so, unless he has somehow sided with the foul beasts.' Her voice was almost pleading and Damek could understand her confusion and hunger for knowledge.

'I cannot tell you anything you do not already know. You are safe though,' he added reassuringly. Arial sighed deeply, not comforted at all but frustrated and exhausted.

'No one will give me answers!' she cried. 'I am stripped of everything I have ever known and loved and I am unable to find an ally, a grain of sanity! Do what you will with a queen of nothing but know this; I do not need your protection.'

Damek felt taken aback. She really had no idea how important she was, or at least how important the wazimu and his master thought she was, and she spoke true when she said she had lost much. Was it not security that she sought? She would need all the brave faces she could summon to fool herself through what lay ahead if the Energy child spoke true. They *all* would if the kuvuta were left to run unchecked.

'We must go to Osrillia now. Every second spent here is a second wasted,' he said, deciding to drop all attempts at gaining her trust. Arial flinched at his reaction;

'Have you lived for so long, and been so alone, that your heart has shriveled to nothing?' she whispered. He glared at her, his eyes alight with anger;

'Do not presume you know anything about me,' he spat. Arial shook her head sadly;

'No *cheupe*, I see your walls. And I mourn for you and your cold heart. It seems all I am made of is sorrow and regret but you have grieved more than I, burden more guilt than I, and yet you have none to spare.'

'If it is pity you seek then you have come to the wrong man.'

'If it is pity you believe I seek then you are even more far gone than I thought,' she replied softly, 'I have no need of your false emotions and charms. There is nothing you have to offer that I would value save the basic empathy one being has for another.' Damek was silent for a while...

'I do not need to explain myself to you.'

It was Arial's turn to nod in acknowledgment;

'True.'

Damek leveled his gaze once again and tried to fathom what she was thinking and what it was that she wanted from him. It had been so long since anyone had expected anything of value from him. The things he wanted and felt had been suppressed for longer than he cared to remember.

'I am just doing my job,' he said, a little harder than he intended to, 'you are making that difficult.' Arial scoffed but he could see the humor in the lines around her eyes.

'Do not expect an apology malachi, I am the one that needs consoling remember.' He curled one half of his mouth into a smile.

'Damek. My name is Damek.'

*

There was not a breath of wind that stirred the blue cloaks of the Religion soldiers, but the cold of the dawn cut right through their poorly copied skin armor. The small party stood before a face-brick house near the eastern woodlands of Metacheyene. It was the home of a High Elvin duke and his wife, a human woman of high political standing. Her name was Nyvera and she was with child. The couple worked tirelessly on inter-racial cooperation between warring Elvin tribes in the south and had helped to build orphanages for the affected children of the wars.

The leader stepped forward and turned to address his men;

'An example will be set here tonight.' He looked at each soldier in turn, his hands folded neatly behind his back. 'We do our duty in the name of the one god,' he continued, his hand now raised to the sky above, 'and we gladly spill heathen blood.'

Nyvera was busy in the kitchen and did not hear the soldiers enter her home. When she heard the soft whistle of a knife being drawn behind her, it was already pressed against her throat. She could think only of the unborn child in her womb and her husband in the room next door. The man walked her through the kitchen door, and toward the fire in the living room where her love, Yourr, sat restrained by three cloaked men.

'Who are you and what do you want with us?' she asked. Her voice was thick with raw fear.

'We are soldiers of Religion and you have displeased god by having relations with one not of your own but of the unclean and godless.'

Nyvera could not believe what was happening. She lived in a free land!

'Your crime is punishable by death and the creature you chose to sacrifice your soul for, dies too. The deformity you carry is not fit to witness the light of the Worlds.'

Nyvera was now sobbing uncontrollably. Yourr was calm and still. He raised his head to speak;

'You may do as you please on your own planets, carry out the massacres of innocent people and fill the minds of many with your poison, but how dare you bring your beliefs into my home.'

'Innocent!' the soldier next to him spat, 'you befoul our fine race with your seed, you displease the one god with your very existence and you worship false idols. You will watch this traitor die and then you will follow.' He gestured to Nyvera with his long sword, raising her chin with the tip as her tears wet the blade.

Yourr could see that that these men were beyond reason or mercy. They truly believed that they alone were to inhabit the Worlds and that killing was what their god wanted. Yourr now looked into the eyes of his wife. The woman he loved regardless of creed but because they believed in the same things. He smiled at her and his eyes told her that it would be alright. He then looked to the human holding the long sword;

'I will die with love in my heart. You will die with hatred in yours and it is fear that drives your blade, not your religion. I pray your god has pity on you for I will not need pity from mine.'

The first score was through her belly; red-hot blood drenched her quavering legs as she was held standing by the neck. She dropped to the floor when the vice hold was released and stabbed through her broken heart. Yourr watched as her blood seeped into her beautiful, blonde hair. Brown eyes wide with disbelief, hands clutching her stomach. That was the last image he would ever see. His throat was cut and justice in the eyes of the Religion was done. The star rose red that day.

Chapter 5

Chosen paths

When Zach finally returned to camp, the men were all sitting around the fire, looking somber and lost in thought. A gloomy atmosphere filled the clearing as each one sat silently, chewing on grilled meat.

Zach stood just outside the circle of flickering light that the fire cast, wondering what he was going to say to them, wondering how their queen was faring. They had heard nothing, and had not been able to move close enough to the tower without arousing suspicion.

Llstar had turned his head away from the others and was staring straight at the shadow that concealed the captain. He sat away from his fellow riders and had not touched his food. The two stared at each other for some time before Llstar rose without a sound and made his way toward Zach.

'Captain?' he asked quietly, once he had joined Zach in the darkness that hid him from his men.

'What would you have me say to them Llstar?' Zach asked, 'that we are all doomed, and that the shadow will grow until we are all of us consumed and forgotten?'

Llstar was not paying attention though. As far as Zach could tell he was in fact ignoring him flat, a strange and wistful look upon his old face;

'I dreamed a dream of this night,' the old rider said as if he knew Zach was about to speak again. 'Though I dreamed it long ago, I remember now.' Zach was starting to worry for the man's sanity when he suddenly gripped him by the shoulder in desperate urgency and hissed, 'We must go now. Follow me.' Zach had an impulse to pull away but he did not. With a backward glance at the others, he followed the keeper into the forest.

Deeper and deeper into the shadows and silence they traveled but still Llstar walked on.

'Where are you taking me rider?' the captain asked, after what felt like an age of walking in silence. Llstar stopped dead in his tracks and said,

'You will speak of this to no one.'

'Well unless you plan to carry out some illicit fantasy of yours with me all the way out here in the forest, then there really is nothing to speak of,' Zack replied irritably. He did not like the rider's tone and he grew restless.

'We go to see the Oracle,' Llstar hissed. Now it was Zach who froze where he stood.

'The Oracle? Here? But how? Why?' he stammered like a bewildered child. Llstar ignored his questions;

'We are nearly there. These are the trees and this is the sound,' Llstar said, reaching out with his fingers as if he was trying to grasp something that was not there.

Like a blind man he walked on. Zach hurried after him and soon the sound of rushing water reached his ears. They stepped out of the trees and onto the banks of a small waterfall. It was bathed in bright moonlight, and Zach could make out the form of a naked woman down below, floating on her back in the stiller water of the rock pools. Her skin was the color of amber, her hair; thick and black like liquid shadow.

'Come,' Llstar said, pulling Zach out of his spell bound state. He trotted down to where she lay, water rippling over her skin in translucent sheets.

'I do not understand,' Zach said, his voice shaking in reverence. The Oracle was a mythical creature. She was only ever spoken of in hushed whispers, and was said to speak of things yet to come, and only to those whose duty it was to change the course of these things that had already happened. Of all the failed attempts to see around time, she was the only one who could. Many did not believe she existed. No direct account of her had ever been recorded. An anomaly, a scientific mystery, an intangible creature and yet there she lay. Real as the ground Zach walked on, real as the adrenaline that pumped through his veins for he knew it was her, would have known it if he had seen her by accident with no forewarning. Something came from within her…no; all things seemed to draw into her.

When they approached her, she rose and floated across the water toward them. Her eyes were like black holes burnt into her lovely face and now Zach could see the markings that covered her breasts and stomach, down to her navel, more clearly. It looked like a map scotched into her skin. When she reached land, her feet did not touch the grass. Her toes merely skimmed the blades as she glided to where they stood. Zach was not sure if he should speak or even move. So scarred but so beautiful was she.

'Great Guardian, I have brought him to you as you asked.' Llstar's voice was strong and confident in the face of such awesome power, but when she turned to face Zach, and he stared into those empty eyes, he did not know if he had voice left himself. When she spoke, her lips did not move. The words were inside the keeper's head.

'Do not be afraid warrior,' she said. It sounded like the voices of all the people he had loved and all those he had lost. Zach closed his eyes. He answered her, by pure intuition, in thought alone;

'Fear is all that I have become.' There was silence for a while but he kept his eyes tightly shut.

'You are a good man Zach, which is why I have chosen you. You are to find Valador.'

At this, his eyes flew open. They were no longer at the waterfall. He was in a place he had never before seen. It was not within a building or in the forest or any other place of Worldly description.

Misty, white light surrounded him and he could not see very far through it. He was alone now and he was even more afraid.

He stood quite still, straining his eyes to try see through the fog. He could make out shadows moving beyond the mist, faint voices calling out to him too. He took a couple of steps closer and the voices grew louder. He walked forward faster now, the voices crying out to him, some sounding desperate and in pain. He began to run toward them, groping in the mist as Llstar had done before him. Just when he thought he was getting closer, the crying grew further away until he was running in circles like a blind man, faster and faster, getting more and more frantic in his efforts. Fayre games playing tricks with his mind... Now they were all around him; faceless shadows swirling in the mist just beyond his reach, calling his name, calling for help until he cried out in frustration;

'WHAT MUST I DO!' His head in his hands, he fell to his knees.

Once the echo of his own voice had faded, he heard that the other cries had disappeared with it. He lifted his head and saw that the shadows in the fog were gone. A lone figure walked toward him. The Oracle. She knelt down in front of him and took his hands into her own. Zach could do nothing but stare into those endless eyes.

'Do not be afraid,' she said again. This time her lips moved to form the words and Zach was overcome with the feeling that he should smother them with his own. He drew back as if the thought was a poisonous snake. Her hand now cradled the nape of his neck and she smiled as she drew him closer to her. He could feel her spirit all around him and he was powerless to stop the need that overwhelmed him. Once he had accepted the urge, his heart stopped hammering, his knees stopped shaking beneath him and all his fears melted away in the Oracle's ethereal embrace.

His mind was clear when their lips touched, warmth flowed throughout his body, and he relaxed even more. She was pushing him down now till he sat leaning back with the power of her kiss. She wrapped her slender legs around his waist and the warrior rose up instinctively to meet her. She broke the soothing kiss and placed his hands around her hips. Zach was by now, consumed by what was to come, and ached with desire, but only stared back at her as if in a trance.

'*Do not look away,*' she said softly. Then, she lowered herself down onto him, squeezing his waist tightly with her thighs. Zach wanted to throw his head back and scream with wondrous sensation but he dared not disobey the Oracle and so he kept his eyes locked on hers, his lips trembling, and a hot sweat breaking out on his brow.

As she mercifully started to rock back and forth, slowly at first, he could feel everything else around them melt away. His only reality was what was happening between them. It was as if he had become the sensation he was experiencing and he was made of nothing else. She started to rock harder and faster and Zach thought he was going to die right there in her arms, like he was falling into her. Her eyes became all he could see and as the feeling escalated and finally peaked, he cried out uncontrollably, breaking the eye contact and could see only vast, dark emptiness.

Before he could think or move; he was flying. Soaring through space and time with the eyes of the Oracle. He was everything in all the Worlds, every small grain of sand, every mighty mountain. He was the wind and the water, the winter and the summer. He saw himself as a small child on his home planet. He saw the young man he once was riding his drey, and making love for the first time to a pretty woman late at night in the planet keep. He saw himself then as a rider, readying for his first battle, and the blood splatters on his face from his first kill. He saw the faces of all the men and beasts he had ever slain. He saw his queen being borne from the tower of the council by a creature with mighty black wings, he saw the faces of the council men melt away into masks of black shadow, and he saw all the armies of the Worlds amassing beneath figures both light and dark. Then he saw his wife and children standing before him, as beautiful as spring's first day. He started to weep, and his tears became a river which he followed to the sea. He stood there, on the isle of his soul, the Oracle standing beside him on the soft sand. She took his hand in hers and whispered softly into his ear,

'*All you have seen and done in your lifetime and all that has been and will be have led you to answer this call. You must find Valador and stop the growing darkness.*' Her lips brushed against his neck and he shivered.

'*What if I fail?*'

The ocean suddenly pulled back and away from him, with a deafening rushing sound, and its emptiness was filled with the sorrow and fear of millions of people from all corners of the Worlds. Forests burned, lakes turned to tar and black rain fell from the skies. Thousands and thousands lay dead and bloodied before him, the kuvuta's beasts feasting upon their rotting corpses, the empty eyes of their Seers burning a hole through his soul. Zach was the father who had lost a son, the woman who had lost a lover, and the child who had lost a mother. He could feel each one's pain and was filled with it until he could feel his heart aching to die, until he *was* the perished Worlds and the bloodstained soil. Then a black hole appeared; hungry and unyielding in its form. More joined it until together; they spanned half of everything the endless spans of space had to offer. They grew and grew and consumed every last piece of space fabric.

All was dark now and cold. The silence pressed hard upon Zach's ears and his essence. A great loneliness filled him and his soul ached with grief.

'*You cannot fail.*' Her voice echoed across the vast nothingness in reply, '*I will show you where to find him.*' The planets and all their living things were spewed from the blackness in sped up reverse time and Zach was hurtled to a planet long since forgotten.

A rider and his drey sat beneath a tree in deep slumber and the rider was awoken from his nightly dreams by the captain's presence as Zach's mind struggled to reach out and remember this place. Just as quickly, he was pulled back to the present and he could feel his body again, pressed tightly to the Oracle's.

He was staring into her eyes once more, shaking and drenched in cold sweat. He breathed in deeply as if it was his first breath. He felt born again, vulnerable and naked there in her embrace. He buried his head into her chest like a child, not wanting to see anymore. His muscular frame racked with great sobs, and she held him close, whispering gently in his ear.

After a long while, he became calm again and when he opened his eyes, he was stood outside the camp once more. Llstar was at his side. There was few moments' silence. The night was holding its breath for Zach.

'What will you tell the men Captain?' Llstar asked. The two warriors stood like that for a while. The question hung in the air and Zach breathed it in deeply. He looked upon the sleeping riders and their dreya. He looked to the mighty trees that surrounded them and the stars above them. He savored the sweet smelling air and soil and the sound of a sleeping planet like he had never done before. He said,

'I will tell them that there is hope and at first light, we ride to find it.'

*

Riko had been summoned to Soren's office. He had been supervising the replacement of the drey's snapped chain and he had a long way to walk and to reflect. Riko had voiced his many concerns over and over again, but had been told only that events had to unfold naturally, and that all would be well. He had been forbidden to interfere and had simply been reassured that fate had a plan.

'But is it not fate that you know of these things and have the power to intervene?' He had asked. The reply was merely;

'I also know the sun will rise tomorrow; it does not need my intervention.'

He was more comforted by the fact that this would be the last time he would ever have to visit Soren. He knocked on the door and waited for the irate voice on the other side to grant him entry;

'Come in,' came the clipped reply, 'close the door behind you.'

Riko did not really see the need for secrecy anymore. The council was dissolved. He was not brave enough to point this out, however.

'Riko, I don't care if half the damned army was burnt to a cinder. I want you to find me the woman. I need the person who took her alive, and I want to know why they did it. I need to know what this "weapon" is.'

'We are working on that as you speak, Lord Soren. All our efforts are bent upon it and soon we will know her importance,' Riko lied calmly, to soothe the angry half-breed that stood fuming before him.

'If it is connected to our great matter I need to know, do you understand?' He was obviously trying to remain in control, but his face turned a terrible shade of red, and his hands were shaking.

Riko walked over to the bookshelf to fetch Soren's medication; tiny blue marble-shaped tablets in a glass container.

'This is *my* holy war and *no* man will stop my cleansing. I will smite down the unclean and serve their blood up to the one true god.' He grabbed the vial from the shape-shifter and swallowed two of the pills before sitting down heavily on his leather chair. He ran his fingers over his elf-skin bible and smiled. He was feeling better already.

'I will see what the progress is your Lordship, and if none has been made, I shall see to it that something is done,' Riko said, as he started to back slowly out of the room.

Soren scared him. His form was human but every now and then, the wraith in him could be seen. His voice or his mannerisms would give it away. Now, it was his eyes, and the sadistic smile on his face. He was dangerous and he was strong and his religion only served to feed his insanity.

Riko was half-way out the door when Soren called out to him;

'Let the guards know I want to fetch the magic slinger personally. The riders are to be found and executed, the beasts to be cut up and divided amongst my army.'

Riko's skin crawled at the look upon Soren's face.

'Yes Master,' Riko lied again, bowing ever so slightly. Soren's lips curled into a cruel sneer.

'You aren't going to leave right away are you Riko?' His question was no more a question than it was a polite invitation and Riko shuffled forward like an obedient dog. Soren moved in front of his desk and leaned against it, hands gripping the edges, till the knuckles were white with strain.

Riko stood before him and let his dress fall to the floor in one, clean, theatrical movement. Soren's eyes glinted as he took in Riko's young and supple body. She was young. Not very…but enough.

'Turn around,' he said quietly, stirring the air with his finger. Riko did as she was told without question, just as he had taught her. The marks his fingernails had left flaunted themselves across her pale skin and the bruises had flowered so beautifully.

*

Mirkisha sat on the cold, wooden benches of the church, fiddling with the silver cross she wore around her neck. Her beautiful, raven hair was streaked with grey, and her skin no longer shone with youth. Her eyes, however, had not lost their glow.

Today she was more troubled than was usual. She had not seen her son in two moons and she was worried about his recent behavior. The Lord Kuvuta did not let her see the boy often but she could read him like a book; there had been something brewing behind his furrowed brow when last they met and she would ask him about it when next she saw him.

The choir had stopped singing their hymns and were slowly filtering out through the church doors when Mirkisha felt a chill run down the length of her spine. The air stilled and cooled around her and she drew her shawl closer.

'When can I see him?' she asked, knowing whom it was that walked toward her. She saw him first in the corner of her eye, and then the candles sputtered and died as the wraith passed them by.

'I still do not understand this faith of yours.' He spoke calmly and articulately, ignoring her question as though she had never spoken. He was one of the few who had mastered the language of the Worlds, Udaranese, and spoke with no trace of the guttural hiss that stained his own mother tongue.

'You wouldn't. You have no soul, no compassion.'

'I let you live, did I not?'

She remained silent and stared straight ahead, not wanting to lay eyes upon the beast that had cost her her happiness and her family. A price she was paying every day in her solitude. She almost scoffed at his idea of "letting her live".

'Would you rather I had not?' he pressed, leaning into her line of sight, clawed hands clasped behind his back in a business-like manner as he poked at her soul. Meeting his cold stare at last she asked,

'When can I see him again?'

'He is on his way,' Lord Nagesh said, straightening up and walking towards the altar. He ran his blackened hands across it curiously as he said, 'he has news for you that I think you will enjoy. He is eager to serve his races and your god faithfully.'

Mirkisha stared at him more intently now.

'What do you mean?' she asked suspiciously. He was gazing upward, at the glass cross on the roof. It was dusk and the stars were starting to blink into life. Mirkisha could feel her anger well inside her chest at his blatant arrogance and indifference.

'If you are using him I will find out and you will be sorry. He is my son...' her words were cut short by the wraith. Within seconds, he was inches from her face, black eyes staring, foul breath reeking. He grabbed her by the jaw and pulled her face closer to his;

'He is *my* son. You use your maternal sway and you will die at my hand. Do you think I ripped him out from between your legs for nothing?' A single tear ran down Mirkisha's cheek and the emotion burned the wraith enough for him to let her go.

He turned his back on her, a cue for her to leave. She breathed a silent breath of relief. Every second spent with the monstrosity was more than she could bear. She hated him for what he had done to her but she loved her son fiercely and all that kept her going was the thought that if she were gone, he would have only his father and that she could not allow.

She exited the church through the back and followed the cobbled pathway to her cottage. Her moonflowers were in full bloom and she could not wait to show her son. She worried what his news was though. He was easily influenced, emotionally unstable and if molded by the wrong hands, could be very dangerous.

Even on this distant planet, rumors still reached one's ears of some enemy force growing. No one believed such things anymore though. There had been too many wars and too many enemies to still care. But Nagesh's words echoed in her mind and she was afraid. She could feel that something was happening. All she could do was pray that her son had no hand in it. She had always been afraid that a day would come when Soren chose the wrong side…

It was some time after the Fifth World War that the humans discovered that they were truly not alone in the universe. Fear and panic had gripped every nation, races for arms and rebel uprisings as the elves came to make contact. Dictatorships rose and fell; civil wars broke out between those for peace and those against. The Black Years. The aliens had left them then. Disappeared into the black of space like sad ghosts. The people continued to riot; they flocked to churches as the 'age of apocalypse' was upon them; the end of the World, the coming of which ever savior you chose to believe in.

Out of the suffering and the madness, a leader rose. He guided the humans through a spiritual revolution and most were united under a single flag of faith for the first time in human history. He stopped the energy raids and the water poisoning, that had left millions destitute, and on the brink of death. Contact was made with other alien species who were not so different from them and fear was driven from the hearts of many. A time of prosperity and peace followed. Trade lines were opened and new technology enhanced the capabilities of the human race.

Mirkisha had been part of the first generation to grow up in a mixed-race schooling system brought about to promote interracial cooperation and foster a notion of equality. She had gone on to become an interpreter for the drey keepers, on a political front, and lived on a planet far from her home. It was there on that foreign land amongst the strange new people and their fire breathing beasts that she found happiness, could see the face of god everywhere and met the brave young captain who stole her heart.

Then news came of a new order. A cult at first had now grown into a widespread fanatical religion. They preached of an old god who had created them alone and spoke not of any others. One of the many 'written' religions that her people had suffered at the hands of throughout ancient Earth history. Fear once again corrupted the people and soon, the government was overthrown by the dogmatic indoctrinators who called themselves the Religion. They had a set of laws that resulted in horrifying bloodshed. All who had ties with the 'unclean' were to be punished. They did not get very far with their genocide however. The High Council intervened. It was a mess but in the end, the humans could not bomb every planet in the universe.

The Five signed a dictated peace treaty and the humans were asked to join the council in the hope of restoring the peace instead of becoming eternal enemies. All races were to stop the manufacture of nuclear bombs and explosive weaponry. The humans were assigned five planets, much like their planet of origin, Earth, and their energy intake was ruthlessly monitored by the wazimu.

The Men of Adam, as they had been dubbed, did not ever let go of the grudge that was planted by the Treaty of Earth. Not only were they to submit to those who had not been created by the hands of their god, but also now their souls would never find eternal peace until they wiped the uncrowned from the skies…or so their leaders told them. This lunacy gave people food for their uneducated hearts and ensured that the Religion maintained its foothold, for the council could not curb their religious practices, only the results thereof.

At times, Mirkisha was not proud of her people. They could be so noble but chose rather to be selfish and blind; to remain a third grade sentinel race.

As she thought about the past 200 years and what it all meant to her now, the face of her husband and her first born child swam before her eyes. Not a day went by that she did not think of them. He had told her one night, as she nursed the suckling infant, that she need not be afraid of the darkness spreading. He told her of his army. That memory was fading now. She no longer believed.

*

The wraiths that had first searched Ramroth's cell had been fooled by his sorcery, but when Soren, flanked by five of his kuvuta burst into the tiny room, the Adare' knew his luck had finally run out.

'Old man magic,' Soren sneered, as he waved his hand through the hologram of Arial. 'Bind him and release the vortex.' His voice was full of venom and his eyes were dark storm clouds.

Two wraiths glided toward Ramroth and bound his only weapons behind his back. Once the magic was released, the walls became ivory colored, and the door and window were revealed.

Soren saw the wizard's eyes flicker over the exit points. 'Oh you aren't going anywhere magic slinger. You are to be sent for processing.'

'And what, pray tell, do you think my mind will yield?' The eyes of his captor narrowed at his words;

'You will tell me everything or you will beg for death before the end.' The wraith in him shrouded his human anger with black mist and Ramroth stepped back so it would not touch him, white eyebrows raised.

'Do not underestimate me demon,' Soren said quietly, searching the wizard's placid face for traces of guilt and smiling. 'Take him,' he said, stalking out of the room, 'and pass no fire or water on your way.' He slammed the door shut behind him, leaving Ramroth alone with the looming kuvuta.

They took him by each arm and leg. He made no protest. He was more use to Arial alive than dead. They marched down corridor after corridor, down winding stairwells and through heavily bolted doors. They were in the lower levels now and Ramroth could hear the distant screams of prisoners all around him. He felt nauseous. He prayed they had not upgraded their memory extraction devices. One could never really block the pain but he had taught himself how to deflect the probe and even throw them off the scent with false memory projections. It had taken many painful months but it was a skill well worth mastering. Ramroth had become lackadaisical in his old age though and technology developed fast.

They walked through an unmarked door and stopped. A human in a long, white lab coat was busy with buttons and screens at the far end of the room.

'Do not let his feet touch the floor, he wears no shoes,' the human said, snapping on black, rubber gloves and translucent goggles. Ramroth assumed he spoke of the urine and vomit excreted by creatures of magic before him. If his bare skin touched it, he would be able to channel that power, and use it against them. The human was well schooled.

The wraiths held him upright and aloft as they carried him to the chair. Ramroth cursed himself as he looked upon the contraption. It was far in advance to any of the contraptions he had mastered and he had not had the forethought to learn its weakness. He hoped the malachi had hidden his lady well for within the hour they would have learnt enough to perhaps piece together the story he himself could not even tell.

They lay him down on the large, reclining chair. There were thick, steel straps attached to it for one's arms, legs, head and neck. A large projector screen was mounted on the wall to his right and all around him were counters of flashing lights and switches. A bright beam of electronic light was fixed upon the chair and shone directly into his eyes. Rough, clawed hands secured him and the smell of death overwhelmed him.

'Thank you, you may leave,' came the voice of the processor who would be working with him. Ramroth heard the door close and a chair wheeled across the room. The human face leaned over him with an injection needle in hand.

'Listen to me wizard; I hold no magic within my blood. You will also not be able to channel this light, as it is entirely artificial. You will benefit in no way should you choose to struggle, it will only compound the duration and pain.'

Ramroth almost smiled at this. The good doctor had obviously never had to go through this procedure before. It was like having your brain filled with hundreds of tiny spiders, scurrying about, invading every inch of your most private thoughts. They crawled through your very memories and when they found something valuable, they clawed at it like drowning rats, and then the real discomfort began; a blinding pain so sincere in its reality that all other thoughts and processes failed. If attached for long enough, you could die. Your body simply shut down in system-overload, killed itself to stop the pain.

Thoughts raced non-stop through the Adare's mind as the doctor injected him. He needed to think of a loophole in the system. He needed to think fast.

*

Ronan was frustrated. The creatures around him smelt of all things dead and he could feel their evil intent like a sticky substance at the back of his throat. Once he killed them with his fire, more just took their places.

Now they had him tied down, snout to the ground, with metal chains that burnt his scales. Seers fixing him with their weakening gazes. He lay in pain, his heart struggling to find his soul mate. She had left him and she was with another but he could not tell why or where. He knew she had been in great pain a few hours ago and that was when he had broken his promise to be still and patient. He was confused, but he knew he had to find her, without him she was defenseless and alone.

Now, as he struggled to concentrate on his dying connection with her, something was tapping at his mind. He tried to wave it away, but it was ever persistent, growing louder and more demanding.

He was in a strange place, surrounded by evil and he was reluctant to open up. After a while though, he gave in, knowing that it would not cease until he did. An image of the old man, the one of magic, swam into focus. Ronan did not let go since this was the man whom he knew his maiden trusted and held counsel with. He was trying to say something. His lips moved around the words faster and more urgently every time he had to repeat himself.

Ronan could not understand the tongue but the man's energy spoke of fear and urgency and if he was in peril, then his keeper must be too.

The image disappeared and Ronan could not find it again. His feeling of unease was now growing stronger with every second that passed. True panic set in when he realized he could no longer feel his maiden. He reared up and struggled desperately against the chains that held him down, his efforts becoming more and more frantic as the bonds seared him and his emptiness grew. The wraiths had started to take notice of him again and were closing in once more. He could barely breath for the stench they emitted, his mind was becoming clouded and he needed to focus.

He lay suddenly very still and the wraiths backed off a little. He relaxed every muscle in his strong body and concentrated on clearing his mind. His only thought was composed of pure instinct - find his keeper. He started to gather every last ounce of energy and draw it inward so it could form as one purpose. His every inch of being bent upon it, every thought within him perfectly channeled, he rose up and in one graceful movement; broke the heavy chains with power of mind and need of soul. He spread his red, leathery wings and took flight.

Chapter 6

Alliances

Two men were seated opposite one another in a dimly lit hall. A large expanse of glass table separated them and a woman sat on the right-hand side of each. There was silence for a while as the two parties sized each other up.

The High Elves and the Drows had called a truce in light of recent events. It was not that they waged war against one another but together, they were a formidable force, and others might take example from their lead. For this day, ancient rivalries were set aside in preparation for a new age.

A door to the side of the hall opened, and a serving girl shuffled in holding four fine cut glasses and a jug atop a silver tray. Water would be served as was customary, to cleanse the drinkers' tongues of lies.

The taller and darker skinned of the two men lowered his golden haired head in prayer and said,

'May the Energy guide us and make a bounty of us all.' They raised their glasses and drank.

'May It take our souls gently and may It grow many forests upon our battlegrounds,' the fair-skinned and dark-haired Drow added, and they drank again, draining the cups and placing them down on the tabletop.

As soon as the last glass was collected and the serving girl was gone, the Drow said,

'So, Altair, we come to decide on the rules of unity.'

The woman next to him placed her hand on his thigh. A tall and proud woman, with full lips and a long, pale face framed by charcoal curls.

Altair smiled broadly, the skin around his bright eyes crinkling and replied;

'We will accommodate you in any way necessary, my dear Carden. You need but ask and you and yours shall receive.'

Carden gently inclined his head in thanks and looked up again.

'So, we have already decided then that we shall merge here at the city of Rmeid?' It was Carden's wife who spoke. Elvira was an outspoken woman and she defended the heritage of the Drows religiously. Carden knew she was opposed to the truce for the great battle, and he had tried to explain that it was for the best.

'Why, naturally Elvira. We here are best suited for it. It is a geographical matter as far as space and supplies are concerned, and a logistical one too since our Alvar is simply too great to be moved.' Delwyn was the High Elf Maiden, wife to Altair. Deep blue eyes on a coffee complexion, and flowing hair as white as the tides that ravaged the coasts of Emara, created a beauty difficult to match.

Elvira narrowed her large eyes slightly. Carden placed his hand over hers under the table and squeezed tightly. She put a smile on her features that paled in comparison to Delwyn's and said with difficulty,

'You are of course right. We thank you for your hospitality.' Carden was pleased that she caused no fuss. He returned Altair's smile and continued their conversation now that their wives had established hierarchy.

'I will need twelve temples for my people and we bring an Alvar of twelve hundred thousand. Most have wives and children,' he said.

'We will yield the west wing of the palace for your royal needs, as well as three garden temples also to the west. The adjacent fields will serve the Alvar. The lake holds the other temples and we will set twelve aside for your people. There are numerous wells in the fields and we will erect temporary housing. I will have my hand maidens ensure any other needs are seen to,' Delwyn replied. 'Carrick, our High Elf General, will set up military training grounds for your troops. This will be sufficient?'

Carden was pleased, his handsome features gracious as he said, 'Your Highness is most kind. We hope this will be the beginning of a fruitful alliance between the High Elves and the Drows.'

'It is strange how war be the force that bring us together,' Altair said, sitting back comfortably in his seat, 'perhaps it is only in the face of the true enemy that we see our enemies as friends.'

Elvira released her hold on her husband's thigh and flicked her dark hair over her shoulder;

'Perhaps it is just the *business* of war that keeps us from slitting one another's throats in the night and not the promise of allegiance.' Her voice was icy and Carden stiffened beside her. But Altair was quick to fill the silence;

'Come my dear. Let us depart of all this talk. I for one could do with a proper drink and perhaps our children could join us.' He knew he had no head for such things and tired of them easily anyway. Elvira would be better subdued in his knowing hands. Delwyn and Carden would decide on the details and all would be well.

He led the reluctant Lady Elvira out of the side door by the arm and quietly closed the door behind them. They walked in silence for a while. Elvira's curls rustling against her silken gown, her slippers making barely a sound on the wooden flooring. She wore a grim expression, which grew even darker when she saw the cheery look on Altair's face.

'Are you not going to ask me why I am so against the alliance?' she asked, stopping under the arched entrance to the gardens.

'No,' he answered, smiling brightly at her. He did not stop walking and Elvira had to hurry to catch up.

The sun shone brightly on the little streams that weaved around the royal gardens and the trees swayed gently with the breeze. Children's laughter reached their ears and eventually, Altair stopped walking. He sat under a willow and picked up a stick to prod the water with. Elvira stood beside him. She watched his child-like behavior with contempt.

'It does not matter,' he said at length. Elvira stared down at him, hands folded neatly in front of her.

'What doesn't?'

'What you think, what I think, what we think we want, and what we think is important.' He put the stick down and looked up to meet her cold gaze. 'Do you know why I am here?' he asked her. When she did not answer he said, 'not because I am of noble birth or because I am a strong leader. I am here because the people love me and the people love me because I am not selfish. I put their needs ahead of my own and I care for them like they were my own children. Most of all, I am here because I do not want to be.' The Drow mistress frowned slightly but his words seemed to make sense to her for she sat down and kept her eyes locked on his. Altair placed his hand upon hers and said, 'We do what is best for our people. We try to anyway.' He released his grip on her and he looked sad. 'In the grand scheme of things, my dear, nothing *really* matters.'

As Elvira contemplated this, her thoughts were interrupted by the sound of running feet and shouts of glee.

'Father, father!' It was Altair's youngest, Vanora. Her hair was snow-white like her mother's and her eyes held the same blue luster of her father's. She would be fourteen this fall; two years shy of her Forth and was to be betrothed to Carden's eldest, Kieran.

'What is it darling?' Altair scooped her up into his arms, his bright smile back in place.

'Alarico has caught a hawk and he says once he has trained it, he will give it to me for my birthday!' The words were out in a rush and her cheeks were flushed. Altair laughed heartily and Elvira found herself wishing her lord were as kind to his children.

'We shall see, Vanora.' The girl's smile faded and now Elvira could see Delwyn's temper in that young face. 'This is Queen Elvira, she will be staying with us for a while,' Altair said. Vanora put on a polite expression and held out her hand.

'Pleased to meet you,' she said, shaking Elvira's hand with all the vigor a little girl with only an older brother to play with has. Elvira felt a smile spread on her features as she saw the innocence in the girl's eyes and thought of her own children.

'If Alarico trains the bird well and when we release it, he comes back to you, then you may keep him in the gardens,' Altair said, fixing his daughter with a promising stare. Vanora lit up again and hurried away excitedly.

'It will be his first hawk,' the High Elf Lord said, cupping his hands around his knees. He was quiet again and apparently lost in thought as the waters swirled beneath his bare feet.

'I can see my questions will have to wait till later, old friend,' Elvira said. Her tone was gentler now.

'Yes, all will be answered in time. Now is the time to eat and be merry…before the storm comes and all that we hold dear perishes.' Elvira had never heard Altair speak so grimly before.

'Unless, that is, we can all learn to work together,' she said, hope betraying her seemingly casual air.

'Unless indeed,' he answered, fixing a place far away with a stern glare.

*

Ramroth's only hope was to try and use the system against itself. Always the best last resort in his humble opinion. He would have to find and seize an opportunity to send a message to the only ally he had left. It may be his last hope, he thought grimly. He now understood the gravity of the situation. Soren was in league with the kuvuta and Ramroth suppressed a shudder.

As the computers around him hummed into life, and the doctor started to flick switches and type commands in, the metallic headpiece came down slowly over the Adare's face. It looked like a mask of cruel design, built for purpose and not for comfort. He could see the tiny needles on either side that would insert themselves into his temples, extracting his memories with powerful shock waves. They would also excrete a liquid substance into his brain, commonly known as truth serum, except Ramroth had never been exposed to this foreign type before.

As the serum coursed through his cells, it would open up his mind, and prevent him from using any form of internal telepathy to shield himself. The dosage would be strong and Ramroth would use it to send a message to Ronan. He hoped his plan would work. The nanos in the liquid truth might not be programmed to counter external telepathy, but he would have mere seconds before they found the unusual brain activity, and shut the message down.

As soon as he felt the pin pricks on his skin and the nanos scurrying through his thoughts, he opened up and sought the creature down below. He could not speak with their tongue, but he repeated his message, over and over again, until the words failed to make sense even to himself.

When Ronan finally relented and unfolded his essence, Ramroth could already feel his mind slowly failing, and his pain was making it hard to concentrate. He let go after a few precious seconds and prayed his urgency would somehow be relayed to Ronan.

The ward lay in agony, memories reeling through his mind, tears rolling down his wrinkled face and he thought of Arial as everything faded to black.

*

The drey queen stepped closer, ready for flight. Her body was tense, and her breathing was shallow. Despite the lighter mood between them, she was angry. And upset. His heart went out to her.

Damek had always been taught that the keepers were barbarians, evolutionary subordinates. They lived with very little technology and had strange customs very different to his own. In fact, he had been taught that most races were inferior to his own, and by the way the woman practically flinched each time he touched her, he realized that perhaps all the peoples had been conditioned such. Her jaw was small and delicate. He could hear and feel the difference in lung capacity and muscle formation from the blood flow and body heat. It was not only these physical differences that intrigued him but also this woman had great depth of soul and her essence was stronger than any other he had encountered. The spirit she shared gave her strength exceeding his own, which sprung from a place unknown to him. She was made pure from her bond.

Arial's lips had broken into a smirk.

'Why do you always frown?' she asked, 'except of course when you are trying to charm your way to some end.' Arial suspected that she had at last overstepped the boundary. She could already imagine his strong features contorting into a sneer, but he simply smiled.

'Come now.' He said it gently and Arial closed the gap between them. She draped her arms around his shoulders, the lopsided grin still on her face. Damek scooped her up and gazed upward, desperately trying to ignore the warmth of her body.

Arial prepared herself for the terrible transition through space, but her thoughts no longer dwelt on Ronan and Ramroth constantly. Suddenly, the air was pressing hard against her ears and lungs, the absence of ground beneath her feet was exhilarating and Damek was holding her tighter. The trip seemed to be over far too soon.

He was still holding her close when they landed on Osrillia, the only malachi stronghold planet in all the Worlds. A planet rarely visited by anyone not of malachi heritage but one that Arial had always wanted to see. The technological advances here were astounding but this was no digital world. It was a cultural mecca, a haven for the arts, and a masterful fusion of old and new. The architecture was unique and of genius design. They surrounded themselves with grandeur; their cities sprawled like giant, granite creatures, unfurling their beautiful wings. Exquisite marble statues lined the main streets, the story of their ancestors carved into life. Great domes of light, needle-like buildings that raked the clouds above, arches of iridescent color, a multitude of textures and materials woven together to form a perfect visual feast.

'Welcome to my humble home,' Damek beamed as he gently put Arial down and gestured to the malachi capital, Decimus. Arial could only gaze in wonder at the mega city that lay before her. Triple walls protected it and Arial could see the local militia that patrolled them day and night. 'What do you think?' he asked, pleased with her initial reaction.

'I don't know what to say,' she said breathlessly, 'It's so marvelous.' Arial could only stare in awe, her mind struggling to take in the pure splendor of it all.

Damek's grin broadened as he looked at her. She embodied something. Something as pure and powerful as the first star rise he had ever witnessed many years ago. Damek did not think he would ever see something like that again but there she stood, only a few feet away, shedding more light on his heart than that bright dawn ever did. He wished he could capture the moment and return whenever he wished, but he could not, and the realization of why he had brought her here dawned suddenly and harshly upon him. No, he thought, he would not let harm befall her. Not only for the word he had given her ward nor even for the one he gave the wazimu, but for the promise he now made to himself.

*

'Repeat that hotel 1, the signal on this god-damned planet is... can you hear me!' Corbin was sitting in the rogue's vehicle, the Eye runner. Cadeyrn was busy working on the Typhoon. Cadeyrn slid out from under the armor-plated tank, glistening with sweat and grease. Corbin slammed the radio piece fiercely against the black box it was attached to a few times and then threw the whole contraption out of the buggy. Cadeyrn snapped off his goggles and hauled his enormous frame to where his captain sat, head in hands, dark and messy hair splayed through his rough fingers.

'What did headquarters have to say?' the big man ventured gently. His voice was deep but soothing, not commanding. Corbin wondered what he had sounded like booming out orders as a Religion general. He sighed and confessed,

'Couldn't hear much. Difficult to work with this shit equipment we have out here but it sounds like they have advanced into elvin territory and a general warning is being sent out.'

'Which delta? Maybe someone is close enough to help or at least speak to the locals?' Ex-general Cadeyrn looked concerned and his massive, muscled arm rested upon the roof of the Eye runner, dwarfing the man who sat in his shadow.

'Romeo's signal is out, no one has heard from them in days. The planets being raided are in Delta Four so we can't do a damn thing. Headquarters are having difficulty organizing everyone since our satellite was taken out. So they are pretty much on their own...as well as us...and everybody else for that matter...'

'The other crews will be okay, we haven't survived this long without some serious skill and luck. And never underestimate an elf, my friend,' Cadeyrn said, smiling and slapping Corbin on the shoulder.

Corbin looked up at the sound of echoed barks as Ahlf and Conan came bounding over the dunes. Corbin shaded his eyes against the glare of the angry sun that shone down on Omihana, one of the Forgotten Planets.

Corbin and his team had been sent there by the Rogue Headquarters in order to try and find one of the missing crews. They had been unsuccessful thus far, their misfortunes starting with the solar flare that plummeted their ship, the Paladin, into a crash landing, wounding their pilot. His other three team members were unharmed but this wasteland of a planet did nothing to better their situation. It was giant territory primarily, *kikubwa* – big nomads with tiny brains and a natural distrust of anything smaller or smarter than themselves. The climate was hostile and arid. Water was a scarce commodity, and with the ship taking so long to repair, the supplies were running thin.

Corbin's stomach growled a reminder of their situation but it went unheard as he saw the lithe figure of Eira appear on the horizon. She had taken the dire wolves out to hunt. The pack leader, Ahlf, was his. She leapt into the buggy and on top of Corbin with the strength of five men but Corbin was used to it and wrestled the bitch to the sandy ground, glad for the blood around her muzzle - at least someone had eaten this day.

Eira appeared at his side soon after and smiled at the play. Her hound, Conan, was only half the size of Ahlf but full of the same energy, and soon it was yelps and growls amid flying dust, as Corbin tried to take them both on. Ahlf let him win, naturally, and licked his face happily as she lay pinned beneath him.

'Careful Ahlf, envy doesn't become me,' Eira said, a smile playing at the corners of her lips. Corbin stood up and grabbed her around the waist, pulling her down into the sand with him and the wolves.

'Good hunt?' he asked.

'The game here is wise from the giants, but Conan brought one doe down. I'll ask Cadeyrn to cook, he has more skill than I.' The big mechanic laughed heartily, patting his belly as he shuffled away, leaving the two in peace.

'I was worried about you.' Corbin brushed a stray strand of red hair away from her freckled face as he spoke, 'you were gone for hours.'

'This place has slim pickings. It is a desert in case you hadn't noticed. Besides, I had these two with me.' She ruffled the silky, white hair of Conan and he grumbled with pleasure.

'Well, with any luck,' Corbin said, sitting up, 'Cadeyrn will have salvaged the parts we need for the Paladin from the Typhoon and we can be out of here by sun up tomorrow. I can't get through to headquarters but it looks bad. We need to get back.' The tension had settled between his brows again.

'We have only been here a week, perhaps we should look some more?' One of Eira's close friends had been on the Foxtrot crew, and she was desperate to find any survivors, but her question held more resignation than hope. They had already searched well outside the last known location radius and when Corbin made a decision, he rarely ever changed it.

'This place makes me nervous, Eira. I don't like having the crew out here.' His voice was laced with the pain of previous decisions and she decided not to press him further.

The dire wolves suddenly lifted their heads and perked up their ears. They could smell Lowell, Raul's hound, and they raced up and over the dunes to find him. The Rogues had been using dire wolves ever since their break from the Religion. They were big, they were loyal and they guarded human life fiercely.

The sun was setting and Eira hugged her body to Corbin for warmth in the desert dusk. Soon, the three wolves had returned with Nyx and Raul on their tails. Raul's left leg was healing well and his limp was only slight now. The pilot's sleek, blonde hair remained plastered back on his handsome head, despite the winds that blew constantly. Nyx reached for his sister and hugged her tightly.

'Did you get the food, woman?' Raul growled, a sly smile on his smooth face.

'Yes. Did you manage to stay off your arse for more than a minute today?'

'Ha!' he barked, 'I managed to do more than that! I managed to find a solid reason to get the fuck off this planet… tonight,' he added. Corbin looked to Nyx;

'It's true,' he said, 'we found something.'

'Crew from the Fox?' Eira asked hopefully but Corbin knew what Nyx had not yet said. The news was not good. His eyes said it all. They were dark and his long, reddish hair that hung before them could not hide it. True, he never brought good news but that was because he no longer believed in it. In his world there was his sister, his revenge and everything else faded into grey.

'Come, brother,' Corbin said, leading his scout away from the other two who were too busy exchanging trivial insults to notice them leave. He led him to the Typhoon and tapped Cadeyrn on his thigh. Cadeyrn slid out from under the tank again and stared quizzically at the two figures now framed by the moon. He turned his headlamp off and sat up.

'Time to cook?' he asked.

'Not exactly. More like time to tuck tail and run, if you were so inclined,' Nyx replied, casting a glance at Corbin.

'Tell us what you found,' Corbin said, sitting down next to Cadeyrn.

'Well, I have some footage here,' he said, reaching into one of his many pockets inside his military issue trench coat, 'Raul says that a picture is worth a thousand words.' He smiled grimly and handed them the image recorder. They hit the play button. The bright image projected by the screen illuminated the expressions nicely on their faces. First there was curiosity, then intrigue, followed by shock and finally, two perfect masks of anger and disgust. Cadeyrn swore loudly and handed the device back to Nyx.

It was a well-documented fact that although giants were fiercely territorial and dangerous hand-to-hand adversaries, the females were natural nurturers. They would take in just about anything if it were young enough to suckle and needed care. Once, a giantess had been seen raising three abandoned dire wolf pups, with all the care of an overzealous mother.

The giantess in the footage had apparently found a human baby. Corbin's stomach turned, as the images played through his mind, still fresh from a few moments ago. She was propped up against a tree; all limbs removed and made to form a cross on the ground beside her. The amount of blood on the sand was astonishing. The human infant lay against her tummy. A single stroke through the neck had left the child's head hanging on limply by a few ounces of flesh and skin. Neither man spoke for a while.

'We can't figure out why they killed the infant. Why not just take it with them?' Nyx asked. Corbin shook his head;

'You should know better than to ask. They probably thought the child was already contaminated in some way and that it was better off dead.' Nyx nodded.

'Yeah well, every once in a while, it's hard to remember that they can't possibly be human beings and you try to find reason in the madness.'

'That means that they are here?' Cadeyrn asked, 'how far away did you find the giantess and the baby?' Nyx shrugged his shoulders;

''Bout twelve miles from here.'

'Shit,' the mechanic said.

'There is more,' Nyx cautioned, 'we found this near the scene.' He held up shiny dog tags, encrusted with dried blood. Corbin reached up and took the necklace from him. "Fox" was engraved into the metal on one and the name "Amada" on the other.

'The blood is not giant, it's human,' Nyx sighed, 'we have no reason to stay any longer.'

Corbin threw the tags back to the scout and looked down. He was quiet for a while.

'Give that to Eira please…Amada was pregnant when last we saw her…don't show her the tape.' His words were heavy, his shoulders slumped, 'we cannot light a fire and eat tonight, we work on the ship and we leave in three hours under cover of night. Place the wolves on guard.'

Corbin got to his feet and started picking up tools. Cadeyrn handed him a pair of goggles and a flashlight. Nyx hesitated for a moment and said,

'We could stay, we could fight.' His hands were clenched into fists and Corbin knew that Nyx unleashed was an ugly sight. Hatred drove him, kept his heart beating and his blade hand fast. He had once been cornered, and had slaughtered six special operative Religion soldiers in under a minute.

'I am a killer no more brother, we are outnumbered and probably out resourced.' Nyx knew he had gone too far asking this of his captain. For the respect he held for Corbin, he left the plea, and strode into the darkness without another word.

*

Zach moved out of the shadows and stood by the dying embers of the small, night fire. He heard a bowstring stretch somewhere in the darkness behind him, and then heard the tension slowly release as the armed rider on watch realized he was taking aim at his captain.

'My apologies, Captain.' It was Delano; a promising young warrior, keeper to an impressive female rock drey and looking more and more like Cahan, his older brother, every day. He walked toward Zach and hesitated before saying, 'We were worried. You were gone for some time. The men put me on watch since the dreya were starting to become restless. Ealunan joined me, she cannot sleep.'

Zach nodded, stroking Ealunan on the soft part of her snout around her nostrils. Everybody knew Delano was the sharpest ears and eyes. He and his drey could spot danger a mile away.

'What have you picked up?' Zach asked him.

'I smell rot in the air but I cannot be sure enough to wake the others.' Delano was aware that his disguised question had not been answered, and did not press the issue further.

'Rouse them now,' Zach said, gesturing to the sleeping riders, slumped against their dreya for warmth and protection.

'But Captain, it...'

'Do it,' Zach commanded. Delano slung his bow over his shoulder and shook each man awake with the help of Llstar. Zach gave them time to wash their faces and awaken properly before he called them all together.

Llstar now sat directly to Zach's right and no longer away from the others. The dreya were unusually still.

'Things have happened here that were beyond our power to control. Our queen has been taken from the tower and the council has been infiltrated by our enemies.' There were sharp intakes of breath and furious mutterings at this outrage, before Zach stilled them with his palm in the air. 'My path has been chosen for me. I must leave this place and I must also leave my queen, whom I swore to protect, in fate's hands. This task is not an easy one, but it is far greater than just our sovereign and our people. I go to find salvation for the Worlds and I want you all to think hard upon it. You are free to fly from here and seek haven wherever you can. If you fly with Llstar and I, no guarantees may be placed on your lives.'

The riders were silent for a few measured breaths. Kai then stood to speak;

'You are our Captain. We tread where you tread, we fly where you fly, we fight where you fight. This is our decision.'

Zach stared very hard at each of his men in turn. This hold that he had handpicked was nigh irreplaceable, and he was grateful that he did not have to face his task alone, but he did not want any of his men to feel that they had nowhere else to go. There were a few kin planets not four days flight away. He knew it and they knew it. If they chose to come with him, then they would be doing so under his command, and of their own free will. They all met his gaze solemnly and answered with a single nod.

'Very well. Owein, you have been schooled in the geography of the Worlds. Come with me.' The fair-haired and sharp-tongued rider stepped forward, his Plato accent rich on his tongue as he asked,

'What can I do?' Zach put his arm around the scholar's shoulders and steered him away from the group.

'I had a dream you see,'

'I understand, Captain. Tell me what you saw.'

Zach omitted no detail in his explanation of the strange planet, and even drew some sketches in the sand at their feet. Soon they had a destination, but had no time to explain to the others. They had been so engrossed in the task at hand that they had not had the presence of mind to notice the eerie silence that filled the forest behind them. Before, there had been the sound of whispers, men packing their belongings, sharpening swords and dreya breathing. Now, there was nothing. Suddenly the fire was out, and Zach could not see his own hand before his face for lack of the moon's full light, and the complete darkness that surrounded them. A light breeze blew and the smell of rotting corpses filled Zach's nostrils.

'Kuvuta,' Owein whispered.

'Hush!' Zach hissed to the rider he knew sat beside him, but only for the warmth his body gave off in the cold night air.

A twig snapped to the right of them and Zach tensed his every muscle. He cursed his own stupidity for leaving his long sword by the fire. His only weapon was the stick he held in his hand, and what good would that do if he needed to do more than make scribbles in the ground? Something grabbed his hand and he had to fight the urge to cry out in alarm but he was spared the effort when that same hand clasped itself around his mouth.

'It's me.' Zach could only just make out the outline of Delano's spiked hair.

Delano pulled Zach's hand toward him, palm up, and began to write the special code on it for times when no words could be spoken. He said that he counted fifty kuvuta in all and wanted to know what Zach wanted to do. He added that there were five standing about ten feet off from their current position. Zach relayed the first part of the message to Owein who immediately seized up with fear as he realized how much danger they were in.

Zach asked Delano where the others were and Delano replied that he had left them with Kai in charge by the river with all the dreya. All were accounted for. He also said that they had no beasts with them, no Seers either. No accounting for stupidity, he added. Zach could trust Delano alone to make light of such a precarious situation, but the information was good news in a sea of bad.

The seconds were ticking by as Zach made quick calculations and Delano was urgently tapping away that the wraiths were coming closer.

Go to the river and tell the others to be ready, Zach spelled out on Owien's hand. Owein scuttled away into the night as quietly as he could, hand gripped around the comforting cool of his scabbard, hoping he would not bump into anything he needed to use the weapon encased inside it on.

When Zach was sure Owein had gone, he stood up, pulling Delano's sword from his hip and standing at the ready.

'Guide me, Delano!' he roared at the invisible enemies.

'LEFT!' Delano cried, almost immediately. Zach raised the sword and swung down hard left, feeling the flesh of the wraith cleave beneath the steel, and the cold blood that sprinkled his face. There was a scream of pain followed by the cries of fury that filled the air around the captain. 'BEHIND YOU!'

He could only just make out the yells amid the screeching of enemy voices. He spun and thrust forward with all his might, twisting and pulling out once he heard the death rattle of the kuvuta on his sword. Soon he did not need the rider's guidance. He could feel the evil around him and although the stench of it threatened to subdue him, his aim remained true and as the last kuvuta fell to the ground, Delano was at his side, pulling him to safety.

Zach ran blindly through the woods, Delano his only eyes. Then, he could make out the glitter of the water in the river, and the black forms of the dreya that broke it. Karo, Zach's water drey, was with him in the blink of an eye. Zach could smell her familiar stench and was immediately comforted by it. He mounted her and shouted,

'NOW KARO!' The drey needed no more encouragement than that. She belched forth a plume of fire, and the scene before them was lit up. Wraiths were everywhere. Some were in the trees, directly above where they had been sleeping, many were now coming out of the surrounding undergrowth, but most had been caught in the deadly fire. They were clawing at their searing flesh and falling into the river to appease the pain but it would do them no good. Water dreya fire was a sticky substance and could be quenched by no form of liquid.

'WE RIDE!' Zach roared and the drey keepers rose into the air amid a flurry of dust, water and wings. Soon, the ground was far beneath them and the air was rushing past them.

'I am glad we are to be gone from that planet!' Cahan cried above the rush of wind in their ears, 'it was crawling with wraiths and starting to smell like Llstar's old man shite!'

Roars of agreeing laughter and relief greeted his jest as they flew beyond the clouds, and to the safety of the open space beyond, made brave by their lucky escape and eager for the journey ahead.

*

Soren was sitting in his office, staring out at the mountains beyond, thinking. He wondered about his quest and he wondered about his beliefs. He was a half-breed. His pure and holy human blood was tainted by some creature not of his god's making, and not meant to ever feel his love, but he had made good of his curse. He would bring about the purification of the Worlds in his god's name. Surely that would redeem him the sins of his forbearers? But most of all, he wondered who the woman was.

It was a question that rang in his head, an image that seemed so tangible yet one he could not place. He feared she was an important link, a demon that had come to ruin his salvation. He wondered about the weapon she had spoken of...

'My lord.'

'What?' Soren was not in the mood for interruptions.

'The wizard has been processed,' the wraith said flatly, 'the results are difficult to decipher.' Soren spun around and snarled,

'Which room?'

*

The wizard was lying motionless in the chair, each temple sporting a tiny drop of blood. Soren fought the urge to dispose of him right there and then with a dagger through his heart. He hated mages. He needed him though; processing could only yield so much. If it were important information, the questions such as "why" and "where" would have to be extracted too. Soren decided he would oversee the torture personally. It would give him great joy to watch this heathen suffer. He tore his gaze away from the old man and turned his attention instead to the blank screen at the far end of the room.

'Show me,' he said.

The only other person in the room was the doctor and his focus was on Soren's face. As the images flashed by, he could only guess at what they meant to the councilman, for not a muscle in his face moved. The doctor was about to ask a question when a wraith glided in through the closed door. He was still getting used to this and flinched a little at the smell and cold.

'The drey has escaped,' it said, 'as well as the woman's guard. This morning under cover of dark.'

Soren's eyes narrowed and he fumbled in his pocket for a few moments before bringing out a glass vial. He uncorked it and shook out four pills. He swallowed them all at once. He was hanging on to his last shred of patience when he said,

'Follow the drey; it will lead you to the woman. Kill her immediately...in fact...kill everyone in her company. Except her captor. Bring that vampire back to me alive. Leave the riders; they will be dealt with when the time comes.' He paused, wondering if he needed the wizard still. 'Do not dispose of the magic slinger just yet. Clean up this mess.' He gestured to the urine on the tiled floor with a look of disgust, 'I will return to speak to him myself.'

He left the room without another word, and made his way down the many corridors and passageways. He exited through the main doors of the tower, glanced at the broken chains of the escapee dragon that lay snaked across the ground, and made for his private spacecraft, the Justice. It didn't need to be hidden anymore as his drey keeper pretense no longer needed to be kept up. The stolen dragons would be slaughtered and fed to his kuvuta army's beasts.

He hissed a command to the wraith that stood by the Justice in the ancient language of the Shadow and the boarding strip was dropped. He walked aboard and the door closed behind him, the airlock sucking shut and the engines humming into life.

The visit to his mother could be delayed no longer. It would be less pleasant than he had initially hoped for. He sat quietly in his suede seat as the take-off process was initiated. He swallowed two more pills and hurled the empty bottle as hard as he could away from him, the vial shattering against the wall, and showering the floor with tiny pieces of glass.

He would learn the truth and the truth would set him free. Free from the vice grip of fear in his stomach that plagued him every day, the fear of damnation, of burning for all eternity in a fiery pit of doom. These images of searing flesh and cries of pain echoed in his chemically laced mind as he massaged his stomach gently and laid his head back, falling into a fitful, drug induced slumber.

*

'It is said that no star ever shines here,' Arial said, 'that the only light comes from artificial particles in the air.' Damek laughed lightly.

'You were well schooled,' he remarked, 'it is true, an old tradition actually. We inhabited this planet for its unique solar position. When the only star here is supposed to shed its light, another planet, much larger than ours, blocks the rays partially. The ancients had not yet discovered the UV resistance drugs we have today but we like it like this. We prefer the night and some are permanent night stalkers, choosing to hunt the old-fashioned way. Well,' he reflected, 'not anymore.'

Arial realized that a raw nerve had been hit. Humans used to live there too, she remembered. And the malachi used to be worshiped as gods, but that had all changed.

They were walking along a cobbled road and had passed several of his kind on the way. They were a strange race. Their skin was fair and their eyes were a piercing array of strange greens, made so because of the way the light reflected off their powerful lenses. They had prominent jaw muscles and long, clawed fingers. They were all tall and walked proudly, dressed in fabrics that moved around their bodies like water. They glanced curiously at her as she walked by, but she never once felt threatened or under scrutiny. She sympathized with them more than anything else. For years they had been monitored and regulated regarding their feeding habits. Subject to constricting laws and controversy in all matters political and financial but they had persevered, and been unhindered in their evolution by the judgment of others.

Their planet too, was strange. It seemed a world of black and white but stark color slashed at the senses every now and again. A flower growing by the side of the road, so richly pink it seemed there could be no other shade to match it. A stained glass window of such dazzling composition that she had to look away. The artificial light lent such an extraordinary atmosphere to the place that it felt she dwelt within another's dream.

'So, you have blood banks now? Or are you still permitted to visit designated areas to hunt?' Arial ventured after her eyes had drunk their fill of the peculiar scenery. Damek frowned.

'It is odd to talk of such things with you.' Arial simply shrugged and he smiled in return. 'The rules have changed once again. We may not even drink from the criminals anymore nor keep those who wish to give without dying. We may not hunt; we may not drink from any living vessel.'

Arial felt his grief, sprung from being denied the right to eat as any other wishes to.

'I drink from a plastic bag. The blood gets cold quickly and leaves a strange taste.' He laughed a cold laugh and added, 'sometimes I wonder if they are poisoning us.'

'For what it's worth, my kind are not on the council that prohibits you and yours, and I moved many a vote elsewhere to permit the drinking where you harm no innocent or take from what is freely given,' Arial said softly. He was quiet for a while.

'I know we are not popular, but we are not evil. Yes, I would prefer to hunt,' he said carefully, trying to gauge her reaction, 'but to diminish us to such a humiliating level is an extremity. I thank you for your vote though,' he smiled, a smile of understanding. Arial seemed impassive so he continued.

'Why do you say your kind have no place on the council? My master spoke often of the drey keeper, Soren, however contemptuous his referrals were.'

Arial frowned deeply and shook her head.

'No. He is no keeper. He is in league with the kuvuta and I am all the way out here, powerless to stop them all.'

Damek considered her accusation for a while. He was still trying to figure out exactly what Falkhar wanted with this woman. Neither his master nor the wazimu had told him anything that he could base an informed decision on. The wazimu had only implied a 'destiny' and he knew she was obviously of great importance, enough for an Energy child to try burn a message into him. Was she as important as he thought? He could hardly convince himself that she had nothing to do with the arrival of the wraiths and that too weighed down in Damek's mind. He had been born just after the Age of Chaos but had been told enough stories to never want to witness a repeat. What if she held the answer? Then she really was precious to them all! If that were the case then surely his master would do her no harm?

An ancient prophesy.

Well, there were enough of those around to confuse just about anybody with anybody else, but was it the one prophesy that he suspected?

Take only the girl Damek; make sure she has the necklace with her.

He pondered the relics he had procured for his master over the past few years. He had been sent alone to buy drey breath on the black market from a dangerous thief and goblin.

I'll even wrap it in a fireproof silk casing for you, we don't want you burning those pretty fingers of yours do we now?

It was an expensive item and a dodgy task to close the deal. Damek disliked anyone who would bargain in the blood of another for a material item. He hated having to be a mercenary as well as a relic hunter. Then there was the more recent item, stolen from witches living in the heart of a mountain.

Bring me the twilight crystal; do not wake the witches who dwell in that cave Damek. When you get outside, open the crystal and close your eyes.

He could still see the look on his master's face as he issued that warning. Damek had done research, as usual, and found that these women held the power to turn any life they laid eyes on into stone. They had stored their precious souls in the crystal should any of them befall death. Then, he had bargained with the Drows for water from their black forest.

Excellent choice, malachi. This water will cleanse the blood from the throat you cut seven years ago.

The Drow had been suggesting he use it for blood raids. Damek had told him to hand the water over unless he wanted his blood to be the freshest spilled.

The last item he had collected for his master before his latest mission was a mirror. He had acquired it from a wizard who wanted to be rid of it, and would accept no payment for it. The only information his search had yielded was that it could be used for soul-stealing rituals.

Arial cast a sideways glance at Damek. His brow was furrowed and he ignored the greeting from a fellow malachi as he walked past, so lost in thought was he.

'Damek?' she asked.

Drey breath, black water, a twilight crystal, a soul stealing mirror.

'Damek, I do not know my way around this place, and you are not concentrating on the road.'

Drey breath for a drey maiden, black water for a cleansing ritual, a twilight crystal capable of holding souls, a mirror for stealing them...

'Arial!' he shouted suddenly, 'where did you get that necklace from?'

Arial got such a fright from his sudden response that she jumped back instinctively, holding the tiny, metallic drey effigy in her hand. 'Do you always hold that when you are afraid?' he asked, more gently this time.

'Yes,' she answered, looking down, 'I suppose I do, though I never noticed it until now.'

'And who gave it to you? Was it someone who cared for you greatly? Did they give it to you on a special day, say your birthday perhaps?' Arial was taken aback by his sudden interest in her necklace and her history. She answered him anyway for fear of another outburst;

'My father, he gave it to me on the day that Ronan chose me.'

'And your ward never told you what it was?' he pressed.

'Well it's a family heirloom. I have never asked!' she said, exasperatedly. Damek grabbed her by the arm and pulled her behind the closest looming statue. Arial started at his strength and speed and she nearly tripped over her own feet. When he drew her close to him, and she could feel his hardened frame beneath her hands, she could barely even breathe.

He was looking at her with the same searing intensity that Falkhar had subjected her to in the council chamber except the Master malachi's gaze had been cold, Damek's eyes glittered with fear. When he spoke, his voice was no more than a whisper;

'You really do not know do you?' he asked. Arial felt irritation spark inside her.

'I have told you before; I have no idea what part I have to play in this whole foul affair,' she hissed, 'what are you babbling on about? Earlier you refused to speak to me about it, now you ask me strange questions and practically scoff at my ignorance!' Damek shook her by the arms roughly and said,

'Now is not the time for child-like behavior. I have figured it out! I knew just as much as you, perhaps a little more and I had my suspicions, but now I know for sure and now I am truly afraid and I truly believe.'

Arial refused to be intimidated by his words and shook him off forcibly.

'What! What have you figured out? Why are you afraid?' Damek fell to his knees. Arial stepped back in complete shock.

'You are the beginning and the end. Arial, you are the One Prophesy and I know it now for certain.'

Arial took his words in and felt them settle heavily around her heart. The One Prophesy. She could feel her mind coiling around this fact, could feel it taking root as if she had always known. When she did not respond, Damek asked,

'Do you not understand the gravity of your situation? I do not know what Falkhar will do with you!' Arial stood frozen for a few brief moments and Damek could see she was battling to come to terms with the turn of events, and the consequences that they had on her life. He was about to utter some feeble words of encouragement but he was cut short. She knelt down on the soft grass before him, a plain expression on her face.

'If...you speak true...then surely your master cares enough for the fate of his own people to let no harm come to me.' Damek looked at the drey queen with ill-concealed perplexity. She was so devoid of all things evil that she was almost incapable of seeing it hidden in others.

'You do not understand! Falkhar is a bitter man. He will seek to find a way to bring circumstances under his direct control. A *cleansing*. On his own terms as it were.' His words came slowly and he sounded exhausted as he spoke them. He could not bring himself to tell her that he thought Falkhar would steal her very soul to achieve his goals.

'Do not worry yourself about these things. Fate will work hard against my demise. For collectively we must survive. This is the way of the Worlds,' she replied, her resolve hardening visibly with each word she spoke. Damek was amazed that she could accept such news so calmly; embrace her destiny unflinchingly, believe that she could sway death with words and reason alone.

He closed his eyes once more, wishing he were someplace else. He was trying to suppress the riot of emotions within and did not notice her stand up and step closer. Only when her scent filled his nostrils did he look up, startled to find her standing so near. Her tongue darted out to moisten her lips and she took a deep breath before she spoke again.

'You need not be afraid.' She spoke softly, cupping his hands in hers. Her voice sounded so foreign but soothed his troubled mind none the less. He stood up and embraced her tightly, this queen of dragons who had so completely and selflessly accepted her duty.

'You are so brave,' he whispered.

'And now you must be too,' she replied, angling her face so that she could look into his eyes. He looked hurt and afraid.

'I know.'

*

The old Adare's mind was stirring, like the dormant seed at the coming of spring. He was beginning to hear things now; footsteps echoing far away and voices trailing off into the distance.

He knew the nausea would soon come in irrepressible waves. The nanos will have left a splitting headache, and it would take his body many hours to recover, and that was because he knew how to cope. Others would have been left in a coma-like haze for days.

Someone was singing. The voice was enchanting, like a spell was being murmured on the high winds. It was the voice of someone young except centuries old...and it took not more than a couple of seconds for his trained mind to recognize the song. A song of magic long since passed. It was as if a hammer had been brought down upon his mind, clearing the fog and releasing him from the serum's foul grasp.

From an inert old man with urine drying on his legs, harmless and dulled of sense, his eyes suddenly flew open, and he grabbed the girl by the wrist with such force, that he felt her bones might break.

The girl was startled but she did not scream. Ramroth fixed his eyes upon her. She did not look away and he was grateful. He could feel it now, the magic coursing through his tired veins. It filled him and replenished him, and gave him the power he needed. In a burst of magical energy, he broke free from the constraints of the chair and sat up, releasing his hold on the frightened girl. He threw up all over the floor.

She fell to the ground and lost consciousness for a few moments. When she awoke, the old man was on his feet, staring down at her with brilliant eyes and a quizzical look.

'Who are you?' he asked her. His voice was perhaps a little too harsh. She put her hand to her forehead and sat up slowly.

'You are not supposed to be awake,' she mumbled, 'and you are definitely not supposed to be out of the chair. When he comes back, I will be in so much trouble,' she moaned. Ramroth could see that she was in distress and drained from the power he had stolen. He kneeled down beside her and gently asked instead,

'What is your name?'

'Mary,' she answered, after slight hesitation, milky brown eyes still a little out of focus.

'Mary, I need you to lead me to a safer place. Somewhere where there is water.' She looked afraid at first but then she said,

'Alright, I will take you to my chambers, but then you must take me with you when you leave. If you do not, I will tell him about you and he will not let you leave.' Ramroth was amused by her bargaining but agreed, for the time being.

He helped her to her feet and paused at the door. He decided to create a barrier orb to help them. It would not stop another from passing through, but it would let them know someone was there. He sent it out, through the wall and down the corridor, at least twenty feet ahead.

'You are a magic slinger?' Mary asked in wonder, looking at the aged man before her with awe.

'My dear, you are an *Adare'* too.' He winked and smiled at her look of even further amazement. 'But now, you must be silent. You will stay behind me and guide me with as little sound as possible. Do you understand?' Mary nodded her head and Ramroth slowly opened the door.

He stepped tentatively into the corridor and felt for his orb. No one was coming. They inched their way down the passageway, ears strained for any foreign sounds. They made it down two flights of stairs before Ramroth felt his orb vibrate.

'How much further?' he asked the girl, in barely even a whisper.

'One more level down and three more corridors,' she replied, mimicking his near inaudible words. Ramroth pushed her up against the wall and stood facing her.

'Do not move, do not breath,' he mouthed. He then threw his cloak around himself so that it covered her too. The fabric was so thin that she could see right through it. She was very afraid now. Something was vibrating violently in the air, reverberating through her rib cage and she could hear that someone was fast approaching. Heavy, armored footsteps, and the clink of metal on metal.

Three human soldiers came into sight around the nearest corner. They were looking straight at them; Mary was even holding eye contact with one. They were big men and she had to fight the urge to run or to scream out, but fear had stuck her tongue to the roof of her mouth and her feet to the ground.

Ramroth sensed the girl's unease and clasped his hand over her mouth, stifling any sound she wished to make and any breath she wished to breathe too loudly. Her body was trembling against him as the soldiers walked by, magic pulsating through her as if trying to find a weak spot and burst forth but only when Ramroth could feel his orb no more, did he dare remove his hold on her.

'How did they not see us?' she asked, as soon as her lips could move again, 'they had to be blind not to see us!'

Ramroth started tiptoeing down the passageway once more, ignoring her temporarily and relieved to feel her energy had pulled back. He was curious as to the source.

'People never see what they do not wish to see or do not know is there,' he replied simply after a while, 'and a little bit of magic usually goes a long way.'

They walked down the last flight of stairs before he spoke again; 'knowledge has nothing to do with magic though, only fear. There are Adare' who build their lives around knowledge and yet they are afraid. There are some who know very little and yet they are brave. Conquer your fears and you will master your abilities.' He suddenly pushed open the door and shoved her inside. 'Water,' he said gruffly, as he slumped down onto her bed. She immediately fetched a large glass and filled it, handing it to him, and being careful not to make physical contact with him again.

She sat down on the floor opposite him with her legs crossed, watching him gulp down the water, looking at him expectantly all the while. When he had finished, he placed the glass unceremoniously on the floor and asked her,

'What?'

'You said I was a wizard.'

'An Adare',' he corrected, 'we use our own name, not the many others that were given to us. Magic flows in your blood Mary, or rather, the ability to wield it. You could have obtained this gift by any number of means but that is not important. What is important is that you are *able*. Why? Well I can only imagine that the Worlds see fit to grant you power and that is all there is to it.' He said it with such finality that Mary felt she would look a fool if she asked him anything else, like she was just supposed to understand.

'I do not understand,' she said, 'and I feel like I should, like it's important somehow.' Ramroth frowned down at her.

'The only thing you need to understand, which I am sure you do, is that we need to remove ourselves from this place before we are killed or worse, processed again.' He made to lie down. He was exhausted and did not feel like inane conversation at this point. He was afraid for the amount of information he had yielded. He wondered who else was now in danger.

'So you will take me with you then?' she asked, rising to her knees as if in plea, 'and perhaps teach me to use my powers?' Ramroth sighed.

'I cannot very well leave you here now can I. As for your powers, surely by now you have used them to some degree before?' It was not really a question but when she did not reply, he propped himself up on one elbow and looked at her questioningly.

'Once before,' she said, in answer to his gaze. She looked down and seemed unwilling to elaborate. Ramroth sensed her guilt, usually seen in adolescents who perform magic for the first time without prior instruction. 'Why are you so clean all of a sudden?' she asked, 'was it the water you drank? A spell?'

'Do not change the subject,' Ramroth said, 'always finish what you start.' To his complete shock, the young girl stood up and peeled off the straps of her dress, letting it fall to the floor around her ankles. Large purple bruises covered her naked body, bite marks and deep cuts that resembled scratches were also visible along her thighs and small breasts.

'Who did this to you?' Ramroth breathed, completely shocked and unable to stop himself from staring openly at the wounds.

'He comes late at night.' She spoke softly; the fragility of her statement moved his heart.

'Who is he?' Ramroth asked gently. He did not want to frighten her into silence.

'Lord Soren. He looks like a human, but when he comes to me alone, he looks like a shadow and when he is near, I cannot breathe and his eyes…his eyes are like the night except they are white.' Ramroth inwardly contorted with rage at the monstrosity that called himself a man of god and not only wished to overthrow the Worlds in his stupidity but would also seek to do such grotesque harm to a young girl. On the outside, however, Ramroth seemed calm and nonthreatening.

'Did you perform magic on him?' he probed, 'one night when he came to you perhaps?' She looked down, her hair falling in front of her face and covering her tears.

'Yes. It was a mistake. I was so angry! It was like someone had grabbed him and flung him into the opposite wall. He did not move for a long time.'

Ramroth was silent for a while. It was quite a confession to take in; also, she had more power than he guessed. She had summoned something that not even the most powerful Adare' he knew could, because it was not a taught trade, or something you built on. Natural, raw talent. A true gift. 'Did I do the wrong thing?' she asked timidly.

Ramroth stood up and walked toward her. He placed his cloak around her bare shoulders and hugged her to himself. Now that he knew where to look for the point source, he could feel it. She was a Tarayelo. A rare type of magic resided in her and she was very powerful, able to summon ancient, winged creatures at her will with the aid of neither spells nor relics. The angels of Umanok guarded her. It was their song he had heard in the processing room. They sprung from certain emotions - love, extreme serenity and anger. She had only been able to summon them once because of her perpetual state of fear and now guilt. Ramroth was impressed. He had never met one before.

He let her go and bent down so as to be eye-level with her and he said,

'For now, we rest. Later we will leave this place, and with your help, we will be able to fly far away from here.' She smiled in response. He took her hand and led her carefully to her bed.

'Please don't leave me,' she said, her voice threatening to break.

'I will watch you sleep, do not fear and always remember,' he said, 'you have a special ability and you may use it. Be responsible with it though. Most importantly, you must never be afraid of it.' He was an instructor after all so he gave her the best advice he could. He had no level of experience with regard to her kind, and to a degree, he feared for her. She was still young and powerful magic could consume her essence if she did not learn to bend it to her will. He looked down at her firmly but kindly. 'And do not use it on me,' he added, winking at her before she fell into the first deep sleep she had had in many months. Tears of rapture sprung to his eyes when he saw the dream shadows of giant, feathered wings enfold her body as her eyes fluttered shut. He gladly fulfilled his promise and watched her sleep.

Chapter 7
Confrontations

The cab driver was not impressed. It was two in the morning and he had been hauled off the streets on "official Religion business" and away from his actual business that made it possible for him to provide for his family. His nicotine gum was finished, his soft-drink was flat and warm and he hated driving these important church people around. No talk, no smiles. All long, blue-black robes, solemn faces, like they had some noble but terrible secret, and the marks...the marks were the worst. Forehead and the tops of each hand scrubbed red raw, almost scar-like in their intensity.

They crawled all over Owase, his home planet, enforcing strange laws and leering at all those who did not follow. It was the last thing they all needed, what with the already thinning atmosphere and water supply troubles, but he dare not voice these thoughts. He was but one man against an entire secular state. A state that was involved, it was rumored, in mass genocides on far away planets.

He glanced into his rear view mirror and at his fare. Dark hair and dark eyes, like clouds never stopped passing behind them. Slightly hooked nose, average build, shaking ever so slightly and the acrid smell of sweat clinging to him. The driver could spot a drug user from a mile away. Working his job, anyone could. He never let them in, no money and always with the sweating. He hadn't had a choice in the matter, however, and this one had paid him double up front to halve the time. He looked down at the neatly folded and newly printed bills lying on the passenger seat, the Supreme Archbishop's face staring up at him grimly, and he pressed his foot down harder on the accelerator.

The streets were quieter now. Three o'clock curfew was approaching. He remembered a time when curfews were something your parents gave you, not the government.

The smooth highway that led away from the airport wound itself into smaller and smaller roads until the tar eventually gave way to gravel, and they were in the city outskirts. Finally, Fallshore came into view, a village perched on the edge of a massive man-made lake. The town's little church was his fare's destination. It stood at the top of the only hill that served as the town center, and was one of the few places that still preached the Old Faith.

It sat hunched like a beggar in the night, cold and silent. The driver wondered what business the holy man had here this evening and decided he would rather not know. He pulled up alongside the wall of the church, pressed a button that opened the left rear door, and was relieved when the man climbed out, closing the door behind him. Not a word, not a smile.

*

Soren was relieved to be out of the cab. He had asked for someone reliable, bribable and silent. The man had driven fast and had asked nothing, but had kept looking at him more often than he felt comfortable with. Kept staring at his forehead and hands like they were something disgusting. It did not matter. Let him stare. He was proud of them, had not been able to perform the cleansing for a long time because of his drey keeper pretense. Maybe he would make it compulsory, and then no one would ogle him and his brethren; the real followers.

He walked briskly down the road once the cab had gone, passing the church gate and heading south. He did not like using the graveyard pathway to his mother's house, and would instead walk all the way around to the southernmost boundary, where there was a part of the wall that was lower than the rest, and easier to climb over. He hated walking among the dead. The ancient trees creaking in the wind, the leaves rustling around the age-old tombstones. The night noises of the crickets and the owls, all emphasizing the silence of the deceased. The peace and the silence. He envied those rotting corpses, resented them even.

He hopped over the wall and could see his mother's cottage, nestled snugly in the garden she tended lovingly, religiously. His mother was so stubborn, refused to fully embrace the new Religion. Choosing instead to cling to the Old Faith that was slowly dying like a leper in the golden city. Shunned to the far corners and given a wide berth. He let her have her church, let her keep her Faith. All those who attended her sermons were closely monitored, but no trouble had come of it yet, and it kept her happy, kept her busy.

The only light was coming from the kitchen and a faint glow from the living room. He shifted form and glided silently through the wooden front door, over the shaggy carpets that covered the tiles of the living room, past the fire, crackling away merrily in the grate, and into the kitchen, where Mirkisha was standing with her back to him, staring out the window, waiting for his arrival. She was smoking a long, thin cigarette, ashtray filled with water and floral air freshener at the ready.

'You know what I think of that habit.'

Mirkisha started and dropped her half smoked cigarette onto the floor, her free hand clamped against her heart, her mouth a small "O" of surprise. Soren expelled his wraith cloaking and walked toward her, black mist spiraling outward in a radius around his feet.

'I have missed you so much,' she said, finding her voice. Old memories being brought back from the past like a knife to the heart. 'And *you* know how I feel about taking your father's form under my roof, Soren,' she added, arms outstretched for her second child. They embraced and held each other tightly. They stood like that for some time but when she made to release, he would not let go.

'Something to drink?' she asked, after a long while of being held by her son. No reply. He held on to her as tight as ever, bunches of her woolen wrap clenched between his fists. She was silent and a little afraid. He had always been unpredictable, unstable. Finally;

'I learnt of something today.' It was more a question than anything else and Mirkisha answered,

'Then why don't we go to the sitting room where it is warmer and you can tell me all about it.' Also, more a question. She did not want to upset him more than she feared he already was. Slowly and reluctantly, he released his grip on his mother and locked his eyes upon hers.

'And you will tell me the truth.' His hands were on her shoulders now, long fingers caressing the skin around her fragile neck. She was shaking when he let go and turned his back on her, walking toward the door, more black smoke swirling around him, all the way up to his chest. She forced herself to follow him, one trembling foot in front of the other, dread building inside. Did he know? And if so, how? What would he do?

When she stepped inside the lounge, he was seated in her armchair, but had moved it far away from the fire, the warmth. His legs were crossed and his arms lay down along the sides of the chair. She sat down opposite him, quiet as a lamb. He waited until he could see the silence was consuming her before he said,

'I have your old ward.'

Mirkisha tried to breathe, tried to fight back the tears that already brimmed and threatened to fall. All she had fought so hard to protect and all she had sacrificed and this was how god repaid her. More silence. She felt actively nauseous. 'So, you have been hiding things from me?' he asked. When she did not reply he gripped the edges of his seat and leaned forward, whispering menacingly, 'answer me.'

Mirkisha nodded once, tears falling onto her folded hands in her lap. Soren leaned back again. 'I have a sister?' he asked, 'what is her name? Is it Arial? She spoke of some *weapon*. What do you know of this mother?' Mirkisha was silent once more. She was so afraid of what the monster that sat before her would do to those she loved.

His patience wore thinner with each second that ticked by and he screamed, 'TELL ME!' Red-faced and furious, 'tell me where you have hidden the half-breed! You helped her escape didn't you? You and those god-forsaken vampires that I trusted!' Mirkisha jerked back and more tears splashed down her pale cheeks. 'And the records? What of those? The ones you had your wizard destroy, what were you hiding from us mother?'

Mirkisha kept her silent vigil. She would tell him nothing, even if it meant her death. 'If you do not tell me, I will choke the words out of you myself and perhaps even then you will lie so I will turn to your precious spell-throwing demon when I am done with you,' he spat. Mirkisha let her head drop, lips physically sealed shut, salty water seeping through trying to part them. Soren got to his feet but she did not cringe in fear nor try to protect herself. She sat as still as stone while the storm grew before her. He placed his claws on the back of the chair she sat on, leaning over her and breathing his poisonous breath in her face. 'It matters not.' He stood back, calmer now. 'I built an army.'

This at last caused her to look up at the thing she had created. 'A black plague summoned to do the bidding of our true god and purge the Worlds of the filth not created by his hands.'

'You cannot,' Mirkisha whispered, 'this is not what I taught you.' Soren's smug features melted into a scowl and Mirkisha could only stare at the creature her son had become. Could not believe the words he spoke and the pride with which he spoke them. He was going to bring back the kuvuta. Not some plague to wield or the will of any god to be unleashed. They would destroy everything. As she stared into the eyes of evil, a memory came to her. Not the memory she thought those eyes would provoke; it was hope that filled her heart then.

My Blood Angels fare well. Never fear the shadows again.

Valador's words sang through her ears, as clearly as the day they had been spoken to her and suddenly she believed. She was smiling.

He snarled at her and she smiled broader still.

'You *will* fail,' was all that she said, the certainty of her words shining in her eyes.

Soren's face contorted into a mask of utter cruelty and she knew that her day had come. The darkness inside her son leapt forth.

*

Elvira did not like the heat of her High Elf brethren's planet. Emara was almost always hot and if the sun wasn't beating down, it was raining. She missed the cold snow of Efetla, the six months of darkness, the deep caverns that she called home. She missed the gentle kisses of her fur cloaks and the sound of worn leather bending around her body as she moved. Her milky skin would turn dark in this climate, her lush hair become bleached and dry. She missed Deephaven with its pine-tree smell above ground and far away sounds of trickling water below, but most of all, she realized, she missed the Drow her husband used to be.

Another meeting had been called that afternoon. This time, both royal families, their advisors, generals and public record keepers, in their entirety, had been invited. Carden had already spoken to her about what she was, and was not, allowed to say. She felt like a child again. At least her brother, Ather, would be there to support her if she felt very strongly about anything, and would provide a buffer against the constant passive aggression of her husband.

It had all started a few months ago with distant rumors of war and now they were here with their ancient rivals, taking orders and sharing shelter. It did not sit well with her, but Carden had said that the past was not profitable for their people, and the only way to move forward was to take a leap of faith. He was so busy with political trysts and the forging of new alliances, that she was afraid he would forget their past, what had set them apart and who they were.

There came a knock at the door which disturbed her thoughts, followed by her own younger face.

'Mother?' the girl asked.

'Yes Mirian?' Elvira noticed the grey strands in her daughter's hair and was about to reprimand her when she remembered that she had celebrated her Forth last year and as such, was entitled to do as she pleased. The Drow queen wished that Mirian would rather focus her attentions on finding a suitable husband, and perhaps hunting or artistry skills, instead of dabbling in magic. It was the only thing that she and her advisor really came to loggerheads about. She had seen what it had done to him. Duncan was only twelve years her senior but he struggled to retain the Energy as well as others, which made him look old beyond his years. His features were shadowed, his hair had been leached of all color by the magic he practiced and only his alarmingly attentive eyes gave life to his face.

'Sorry, but father sent me to ask you to please not be late.' Elvira tried not to let her temper get the better of her.

'Alright,' she said, rather stiffly, 'let us go now and be early instead.' She dabbed her glistening brow with a cotton kerchief and followed Mirian to the great hall.

People were slowly filtering through the low, arched doors, mostly High Elves but she spotted a few Drows, nodding in recognition, noticing more and more the minority her people were. She made a beeline for Ather, Mirian's already curving figure parting the way for her. She suited the new airy attire, a fresher look. She seemed more comfortable than her mother. Excited even, at the prospect of new people and new surroundings.

Carden joined them a few moments later followed by Duncan and General Braenden. In this room, Elvira could see just how different their people were in appearance alone. All tall, but the Drows were stockier, had fair skin and an array of different greens and browns in their eyes. The High Elves were tanned and dark, with light colored hair, blues and greys in their eyes, longer fingers, sharper ears. She could hardly believe that they had sprung from the same gene pool all those millennia ago.

'Are you well?' Ather asked. Elvira realized she was openly staring at the High Elves around her, scrutiny in her eyes.

'I'll be fine, just need to adjust to my husband's new games.' Ather laughed quietly and they shared a smile. Carden leaned toward his wife and asked,

'Where is Kieran?' Elvira sighed inwardly. Their eldest child was difficult to control at best and apparently, one of her new duties since their arrival on this planet was to monitor his exact location at all times.

'He will be here,' she answered coolly. Sure enough, at the last minute, Kieran walked through the doors and holding Vanora's hand non-the-less. Many heads turned to watch as he escorted her to her father's table before joining his own family. An innocent act but Elvira stiffened. Carden had mentioned the betrothal he hoped for, but had not brought it up again at his wife's reaction. Vanora was still a young High Elf maiden, delicate and childish in her ways, where Kieran was tall and already stood proud like his father. Elvira knew he would make a fine Drow King.

She would speak with him later though. For now, she settled for a warning look shot directly at him as he sauntered over to their table after shaking hands with Alarico, exchanging a few quiet words as they did so, that she could not make out over the din. Carden managed to send his son an approving nod whilst casting nervous glances at his only daughter, who was sitting in intense conversation with Duncan.

Once everyone had settled down and the chatter had subsided, Delwyn got to her feet;

'Welcome and thank you to everyone for attending today's meeting. This will be the first of many and we hope not to keep you for too long. Carden will address you all on the general outline and purpose for this gathering, Altair will elaborate and your questions will be taken afterward. Today we drink to all wise men come before us, may their Energy be ours.' She sat down again, once everyone had drained their glasses.

Short and sweet, thought Elvira, very diplomatic too; let the Drows have a little say and all will be well? Carden had gotten to his feet now, speaking in his low, quiet voice and Elvira could see the people straining to hear.

'Thank you, Delwyn, for your hospitality and for the opportunity for our two great peoples to meet and work together.' Scattered and polite applause halted by his upheld hand. 'We know that there is to be a great war,' he continued, 'our sources have already confirmed that the army grows in strength and numbers and we have decided to join forces as together, we stand more of a chance. We all know of the merciless intentions of the kuvuta, and we are here today to decide on the terms of temporary cohabitation, so that all will feel comfortable.' Carden did not emphasize the word "temporary" as Elvira would have, another small stone in her shoe. 'The last time they came, our forefathers suffered devastating losses until the head of the snake was smote down, and the enemy was forced back. We hope to gain a faster victory this time around and dispense of them for longer or perhaps for good. These are the things promised to me by our High Elvin brothers and sisters, and today we will share ideas on how this shall be achieved.'

The Drows had a group of record keepers called the Seven Quills. They attended all royal meetings and drafted letters for the people so that all could stay informed about political matters. They were rich men and had no families. As such, they could not be bribed nor threatened into false information. The High Elves had a different system. Their kingdom was divided up into states and each state elected a Warden whose duty it was to take the people's grievances back to the royal council and bring back any news that was discussed between them all. In cases like this, each region elected one warden to speak for many. They merely listened and nodded, speaking when it was their turn. It was a trust-based operation that had never failed.

Altair gave the Seven Quills some time to finish writing before he rose to speak his turn. A long pause as he carefully swept his gaze over the audience, trying to gauge the feelings behind the demure expressions. He picked up curiosity, doubt and a little fear but no animosity and he hoped his words would not change that. He waited some more; he needed quiet for what he had to say. It was of the utmost importance that his message was not misinterpreted or misheard.

Delwyn squeezed his hand tightly once for encouragement, then released it so he could say what he needed to say. He cleared his throat and began;

'My dear Drows and High Elves. I thank you for listening to boring talk on this glorious sun-blessed day, I know you would much prefer to be with your families but I beg you to listen carefully all the same.' A few smiles but they soon died under his intense gaze. 'I invited our Drow brothers and sisters here for the purpose of war and for the purpose of peace. They came without question and for that, I am grateful. But I am sure they, and the rest of you, would appreciate a little clarity.' Nodding heads and whispered comments followed. Altair took a deep breath and Delwyn's heart fluttered, she hoped for the best.

'Our spies have come to us with grave news.' Everyone leaned forward, wondering what could be worse than the promise of wraith-wreaked havoc. 'Firstly, the kuvuta are not working alone. They have procured the aid of the humans, who's fall from grace comes at a time of great weakness within their ranks. We know they have taken on a dangerous type of spirituality and once again feel the need to be alone. They were easy prey so we cannot blame them too much. However, they stand with the enemy and slay our kinsman as we speak for so-called crimes against their god.' Altair inclined his head a little here, in memory of a friend slain in his home, along with his pregnant wife not one week ago. 'They now seek the help of the wraiths to complete what they started so many years ago,' he continued.

People were now shaking their heads and talking angrily amongst one another. The humans had once again proven their naïvety and destructive nature. Altair waited patiently for the outbursts to subside, he knew this news would not be taken well but now it was time for them all to face the reality and calm themselves in preparation for what was yet to come.

'There is more,' he said, and immediate silence greeted him. 'In the time that the wraiths have had in hiding, their numbers have grown exponentially and what we see here now is not half of what they have gathered. This is the honest truth. They have an army that will dwarf our two Alvars combined like the tree dwarfs the blade of grass.' Altair looked at the many faces of disbelief before him and his heart went out to the people. 'As Carden said, the last time they came, it was no small thing. This time will be even worse and we are fools to believe that we will live through the hammer strike that will fall.'

People were on their feet now, demanding to know what was being done and why the Drows had been called if they were all to die anyway. The Drow royal family was a sight to behold. Duncan was holding Mirian, Carden looked stumped, Elvira was enraged and Kieran looked mildly frightened for the first time in his life. Braenden and Ather were deep in conversation and the Seven Quills could not write fast enough. Wardens were shouting and it was chaos all round. Fear was covered with denial and denial was sheltered by rage.

Altair did not yell for silence, he did not try to calm the storm; he simply let it ride out until no one had anything new to shout about anymore. The humans had been blamed, the royal families, the gods themselves; but soon there was a disturbed quiet as they realized the High Elf Lord was not yet finished and that they were.

'I had a vision,' was all he said. Delwyn looked up at her husband with unfeigned surprise and a little anger. Elvira shot to her feet and said,

'Oh please, Altair. We don't need this rubbish. This is completely ridiculous and you are nothing but an old man with nonsense in your head. I will...'

'You will what, Elvira?' Altair cut in. 'What will you do? Will you run back to your white world and believe you will be safe? Will you try to take on the darkness alone? Will you blame me for the truth? What will you do?'

His words were heavy and Elvira sat down with the weight of them. 'Despair is not the answer,' he continued, hands planted firmly on the wooden table in front of him. 'I did not bring you here to tell you that death waits for you, all creatures of the Worlds know that already. I brought you here to inform you of the reality we all face, that there is still hope and to tell you of my vision.' Everyone was in a state of shock and had no choice but to listen to him. 'I saw two waters meeting,' he began.

Elvira half rolled her eyes but everyone else in the hall was silent. Altair was a respected High Elf Lord, he never lied and his gift of foresight had a reputation for bearing truths. Delwyn was frowning slightly but did not interrupt.

'The one tide was black and viscous, as vast as the skies that surround our World. The other, clearer and thin like water. A cupped handful at most. As the dark tide surged forward to meet the other - the clear tide had become an ocean and the darkness was consumed.'

The Warden from Falconmoor stood to speak. When Altair nodded his head he asked,

'What does that mean? That if we all stand together we will indeed defeat the wraiths?'

'Yes, Warden, it does,' was Altair's reply.

One of the Quills stood now, not waiting for permission he said,

'But you have just told us that our numbers will be too small even if we unite.' Altair was quiet for a while and then he said,

'We are not the only creatures who inhabit the Worlds, many other lives are at stake and many other armies are amassing.'

'Do you mean to imply that *all* will stand together? That is madness!' The Drow did not look impressed and the others shared his sentiments.

'Even if all the Worlds decide to amalgamate their forces, it would be an impossible task. Too many flags. Too many generals.' Another Warden had voiced his opinion.

There was much conversation now, furrowed brows and grumbling. Altair held up his hands and said,

'That is my vision and whether you choose to accept it or not, the fact remains that we must still fight, as must everyone else.' The people were not happy but it was true. Sit around and wait to die, or prepare for battle and wait to die. Altair sat down and waited for more questions but none came. Delwyn stood again; it was her turn to speak.

'Please settle down, there are things we must decide upon.' Her voice was stern and soon the planning was underway.

A grim atmosphere settled over the hall as the High Elves and the Drows decided upon civil rule and cohabitation. Each race would stick to their own laws and everyone would live separately in order for that to work. One of the Wardens suggested that the Drows make home the caves that ran along the mountains that his village stood in the shadow of. The colder forests of Agrum and Utorea would also be utilized for Drow living space. Energy temples would be erected far away from the High Elves so as to avoid conflict. The warriors would be shown by the common folk how to live off the land, for when the war came, supplies would run low.

The Wardens were all very concerned about the safety of their villages and the Drow general, Braenden, suggested setting up safety drills to be practiced every day. Braenden and Carrick, the High Elf Warrior, decided to have a separate meeting to discuss and outline possibly merging their two very different military tactics. In the meantime, night and day watches were to be set up and civilians to be taught general safety guidelines. Temporary hospitals would be built in preparation for the coming war and food would be shared. General consensus was reached within a few short hours.

At the end, everyone was tired and grumpy. It was hot and they had not yet eaten. The Quills were jotting down notes by now and the Wardens were growing listless. Altair did not want to adjourn the meeting, he wanted to round it up and send everyone home with something to think upon;

'We need to remember that in these grave times it is especially important that we learn to work together and forge understanding and helpfulness within our ranks. The time for petty squabbles and selfishness are over. Please try, above all, to remain hopeful and trust in your own ability.'

The Drows and High Elves got up and made straight for the doors. The fresh air outside beckoned to them, as did the promise of food and cool water.

'Why did you not tell them of the Blood Angels?' Delwyn looked, if possible, even less happy than Elvira when she pulled her husband to one side, 'I thought we had agreed that the people needed to know, to have some kind of solid piece of hope. Perhaps then, this meeting would have been a success, instead of a grim reminder of death drawing nearer.' Her eyes flashed anger and hurt and Altair held her by the arms while he said,

'No, it is better this way, my dear Delwyn. You want all the facts but you ignore the truths.'

'I have no time for this Altair...'

'Just hear me out,' he said calmly, applying only the slightest bit more pressure as she made to free herself from his hold, 'the meeting went well. The people were working together and coming up with ideas, bonds were made, not broken. If I had told them of the weapon, they would have had need to neither be strong nor find strength in one another. It is only in times of trial that we see our greatest successes and the Blood Angels are no sure bet, the people need to be prepared for the worst.' Delwyn wanted to argue, but once again, her husband was too wise and instead she smiled warmly, her icy composure melting as she admitted her fault and praised the leadership qualities that she did not have.

Carden did not want to speak with his wife, he wanted to talk to Delwyn. When she saw him coming closer she excused herself, squeezing her husband's hand tightly.

'That was interesting,' Carden remarked as he and Delwyn met halfway. Delwyn did not want to lose his trust; he was the only way in to political partnership with the Drow family, the only one interested in the future and potential benefits of merging.

'I…' she started but he grinned and she stopped.

'We would have come even if we knew all we know now. It was wise for you to save the worst for last, not for my sake, but for the others. We are here now and I look forward to the "meeting of the waters".' He did not sound sarcastic and his tone was friendlier than it had been before, reassuring instead of a little reproachful.

'Why do you seem so pleased?' Delwyn asked, confused by this Drow she hardly knew but now had to work in close proximity with.

'I trust in Altair, he is a fine leader, I trust in you, you are a fine negotiator,' he said slyly, 'but above all, I trust in my own people and their ability to survive. The kuvuta will not be the undoing of us. We are too strong.' And for once, Delwyn appreciated the blatant arrogance of the Drows.

*

They had been walking side by side for some time now, down the long and winding paths that led deeper and deeper into Decimus. Arial was too busy taking in her surroundings, and trying to stop her mind from lingering too long on what she had learned, to be interested in small talk and Damek was once again, deep in thought. They neared another bend in the path when he slowed down a little and cast her a sideways glance.

'I have been very selfish,' he said. Arial kept her eyes down. 'I have not even asked if you are alright or attempted to apologize for this whole mess.' She smiled, head bent, grateful for the slower pace and replied,

'You need not apologize. If it were not for you, I would still be locked away in that tower. At least I can converse with a malachi master, a wraith knows nothing of reason or mercy, and Soren seems no better,' she paused, 'and…I will be alright. It is much to take in but it gives me strength somehow and a sense that I *can* stop this madness for it is what I was born to do.'

'I did not ever think of it that way,' Damek said in reply, 'you are very wise…and very brave.' Arial did not like the way he kept repeating that but said nothing. Damek had stopped and it took Arial a few steps lost in contemplation to notice. She turned around questioningly and he was grinning and pointing to the house he stood before. Dark stone and varnished, cherry wood broken by blue stained windows and overgrown with ivy.

Damek walked up the steps without waiting for Arial and swung the heavy, iron knocker back and forth a few times.

'Where are we?' she asked lightly, feeling anxious.

'Adonika. She will know what Falkhar is up to. She never leaves his side.' He smiled reassuringly as they both waited for someone to answer.

When the owner of the house opened the door, eyes lighting up at the sight of Damek, Arial felt something else. Damek rushed across the threshold, sweeping the violet haired beauty off her feet and into a deep hug. They parted long enough for him to plant a tender kiss upon her crimson lips before embracing her again.

Arial stood outside on the steps leading to the front door like a forgotten guest, waiting to be invited in. For a moment, it looked as if Damek had indeed completely forgotten about her before he wheeled around, last minute, and motioned for her to come inside.

Once they were all standing in the entrance hall Damek said,

'Arial, this is Adonica.' Arial extended her hand politely if not a little reluctantly and felt the cool grip of Adonica's long, elegant fingers envelop her own. The malachi lady was beautiful, tall and graceful. Amethyst tinged eyes and high set cheekbones.

'I was not expecting you Damek, even less a visitor,' Adonica said. So Damek was no visitor in her home, Arial thought a little hotly. Adonica looked at Arial when she said, 'You are both more than welcome though.'

'I am sorry for the sudden intrusion but I feared to send a message ahead and I needed to talk to you.' Damek's beaming smile had been replaced by a look of concern and worry lines crossed his brow.

'You never intrude,' Adonica smiled, worsening the feeling in the pit of Arial's stomach, and when Damek wove his arm around Adonica's waist, Arial thought she would visibly cringe with distaste.

'We really need to talk,' he repeated in his new somber tone.

'Oh, sounds terribly serious,' the malachi lady cooed, winking at Arial. Her girlish attitude did not fit her sinister image and it made Arial feel uncomfortable.

'It is,' Damek replied, not happy with the light manner of Adonica either. He released the woman's waist and turned to Arial and asked, 'Is there somewhere she can wait for a little while?' Arial tried not to redden with embarrassment at the way Damek was treating her all of a sudden. Words of protest evaded her as Adonica moved to her side. She draped one arm over Arial's shoulder as if they had known each other for years and pouted.

'He can be so rude.' She steered Arial away from Damek and into the adjoining room.

The room was softly lit by the light shining through the wide bay windows and a pleasant breeze was filtering through. A general atmosphere of relaxation filled the area. Much needed, Arial thought.

The grate was empty on this warm day. Neither stifling heat nor stale air hung in the open space and Arial felt strangely consoled in here. The awkwardness in the entrance hall was forgotten as she gave in and sank down into the nearest seat that Adonica had steered her to. Adonica smiled down at her but the familiarity of it did not ease the image at all. Arial made to stand again but Adonica sat down beside her, hand lightly on her arm.

A figure appeared at the open door.

'Olai, please be so kind as to prepare some food for our guest, and wine, yes, some fresh wine. You must be thirsty,' she said, reaching over to stroke Arial's chin with hands that now felt warmer and more welcoming, 'not to mention starved and scared half to death.' She smiled kindly, lips sealed this time, and Arial felt at last that someone understood the turmoil she was going through, related to her, sympathized and was willing to listen. She did not speak though; Adonica's voice was like a soft lullaby carried on the sweet winds of home and she felt no need to interrupt. 'It is not every day that my brother brings a pretty maiden to my home.' Arial relaxed even more if it were possible, her brother...and she had called her pretty. 'Do not worry, I'll get this whole affair sorted out and you can just sit here, enjoy your food and wine and we will be back before you know it.' Adonica was very close to her now but the proximity felt more comfortable than intrusive and her breath smelt sweet, like the fresh wine she had sent for.

Arial closed her eyes and when she opened them again, the manservant Olai, was busy setting down her tray of refreshments. The fresh bite wounds in his neck and the drip he pulled along with him did not even make her look twice. He bowed and left and Arial greedily snatched up the tray wondering when last she had eaten. Adonica had vanished and the door closed behind Olai with a click.

She stuffed her face hungrily. Dried figs, fresh bread, cheese and honey. The wine too, was so delicious, and Arial settled deeper into her cozy chair, enjoying the breeze and the sounds of life outside.

Then Ramroth was in her mind... *"Let no one and nothing ever lull your senses, they are your best defense system."*

Arial sat bolt upright. The wine now tasted sour on her tongue, the room felt hot and she wondered how she could have succumbed. Perhaps Adonica *had* just wanted her to feel welcome but Arial paced around the room, chastising herself none the less. She could not afford to be careless.

She scanned her surroundings more closely now. There were three doors leading to and from the room. The one she had come through, the one Olai had brought her food and drink through and another, on the opposite side of the room.

She walked toward it, curled her fingers around the polished handles and pulled down. Not locked, as she had expected. She pushed the door open a little at first, just enough to peek inside. A library. Not enormous but big enough for a mere personal book collection to be ruled out, very simple in its design too. Very old volumes lined all four walls, right up to the roof of the circular room, with a single rolling ladder to reach the top and two tables, pushed together in the center, for reading. The air was a little close and the only light came from a lamp on one of the desks, the trapped dust illuminated by the shaft of artificial light.

Arial stepped inside but left the door open. She hung back to listen for any sounds of approaching feet or voices and when she was satisfied, started to look around.

She had always loved books, had spent entire days and nights locked away in Ramroth's private store. She browsed only the titles at first. Some very intriguing reads. It seemed that Adonica was into her history of magic and the study of the races. Whole sections dedicated to one specific time period for a single species, and sets of encyclopedias devoted to the development of Chaos magic alone. She became braver and pulled out one or two, taken back to her childhood days where even if she could not understand the text, she was pouring over the pictures, transfixed by the images of enchantments and peoples of the Worlds locked in battles. She was careful to place them back where she had found them and soon her attention shifted to the table and the scripts that lay open there.

She sat down on the single chair, ready to find out what the Adonica's current interests were. There were a few loose pages on ancient malachi prophecies. They were written by self-proclaimed "foreseers", very vague, and Arial soon lost interest. Next in line was a large book on her own people. It contained detailed family trees and royal stations. The bits on culture and lifestyle were not very accurate and she scoffed at some of the things that people assumed.

She pushed the book to one side and pulled the next one closer. It was a volume on drey species, their appearance, abilities and so forth. Again, rather inaccurate but Arial's heart nearly stopped when she turned the page to find a crude sketch of a male fire drey. She ached for Ronan once again and felt cold tears trickle down her hot cheeks.

She slammed the book shut, anger flooding her system at the cruelty of their separation. Her wrath was soon to be replaced by the shock of even more unexpected recognition. Beneath the "Guide to Fire Beasts" was a document that she knew well. It was written in the official blue ink of the malachi instead of the red that her people used, but it held the same High Council seal, and the same information as far as she could tell. The document was also written in the same hand, though not in ancient human tongue; in malachi dialect. She was a little better schooled in this language since it was still in widespread use, she was not as fluent in it as say Jayla of the High Elves or Udaranese, but she could make out more of it than before since this document was still whole.

It had been written quite long ago, as she knew, and had been signed and agreed upon by all members. High Adare' Ethron, King Ferguson of the humans, High Elf Altair, Brianna representing what she assumed was the wazimu; Uasail of the drey keepers and Master Falkhar of the malachi…how interesting. The man she was to see had indeed known of what she spoke; which could explain why he had taken such a keen interest in her. And Ethron! How could he have left her to such a fate when he had the power and sense to intervene? She wondered once more. She read on, the words and phrases she understood jumping out at her and the message becoming clearer.

Arial looked up from the parchment and stared off into the distance. She had hoped that this was true, ever since the day her Bethriam had died but now she wished it so even more. How was she supposed to be the cure alone? What was she, one woman, supposed to do to protect all the Worlds against one of the most formidable foes to ever breach the boundaries of the Universes? If this weapon existed, then she would not be alone in her task, but how to wield it or find it? She realized that she had to get out of there. She could not risk an encounter with the Master malachi for if he wished her ill then all would be lost.

Just as she made to stand up, the feel of warm breath on her neck interrupted her thoughts and intentions. It made the hairs on her skin prickle and a small sweat break out on her brow. She was not sure what to say, if anything she could say would excuse her prying. She just looked up and into the eyes of the malachi but could not read the emotion behind them.

Adonica straightened and walked toward the books lining her walls, her back to Arial, hands delicately stoking the spines of her books. Her hair flowed like a violet river down her back and Arial could see a smile tugging at the corner of her lips as she half turned her head. Arial lowered her gaze again and she saw things that she had not noticed before. Scripts on magic. Dark magic and dark relics that were not meant to be found. There were images of people roiling in pain as their souls were ripped from their bodies, men begging for mercy as their blood turned to stone inside their veins. Cold fear gripped Arial and loosened her stomach. Did these people truly mean her harm? And not the kind any blade can wield - a different kind, a kind that Ramroth had exposed her to if only to put the fear in her.

The door opened and Damek cleared his throat awkwardly. When Arial looked up he was surprised to see her terrified expression and knelt down where she sat.

'Do not be afraid. We have spoken,' he began gently, 'and I have decided it is safe to go to Falkhar.' Arial's eyes were wide with fear and she shook her head, opening her mouth to speak. But Adonica's ice cold hands on her shoulders stole her breath. She looked back to the table but the images had been covered. They were too fast for her, she lamented privately. On the outside though, her resolve hardened. She would not let the *cheupe* have her without a fight.

'You are being deceived,' she said to Damek, 'your master means to do me harm and I cannot allow that to happen.' She could almost feel Adonica smiling behind her and she knew that if she could not convince Damek then all would be lost.

'I understand your fear Arial, you have been made to suffer much but we only wish to aid you!' Adonica reassured her, 'Falkhar desires to keep you safe, safe from the wraiths and the others who would plot against you.' She too knelt down and smiled the sweetest smile Arial had ever seen. Arial scowled.

'You are being deceived!' she implored, ignoring Adonica and leaning in toward Damek, her last hope for survival.

He frowned and ran his fingers through his hair. Adonica caught his hand and held it in hers.

'Brother, I have never lied to you. I have loved you since the day you were born.' They held one another's gazes and Arial could feel the centuries that flowed between them, could feel the love they bore one another and it frightened her. She had thought for a few precious minutes that she could compete, make him believe her over Adonica, but she had been a fool. How could she compete with a bond of blood, a sibling affection that had been nurtured and treasured for hundreds of years? There could be no greater love and no greater trust. She was alone.

*

The riders had landed it seemed, in relative safety. After a quick look around, they decided that it was a good place to stop and rest at. The night's previous events had left them in need of nourishment and somewhere to lay out a better plan.

'I remember this place vaguely,' Owein said, fingering a strange pod that hung heavily from its branch, 'I believe it is the planet Mira, but little is known of it.'

Zach nodded. He was glad to have Owein on the team.

'The men must all keep a sharp eye out. We will make camp here, Cahan and Delano can go find game in the evening when the dreya can see better. You and I will begin to plot a proper course whilst the others rest up and prepare to spend the night.'

'I will inform the men,' Owein replied, striding over to his fellow riders and leaving Zach alone with his thoughts. *Find Valador.* And then what? Tell him that the Worlds are standing on the brink of destruction and that he must do something about it? Zach almost laughed out loud, but he knew that the Oracle would not have sent him for naught.

Zach went to lie down beside his drey, exhausted from his stay on High Council ground. Karo was a lot less disturbed here, on this lush planet, than she had been on Equa. The humidity bore her well, unlike the fire dreya of Cahan and Eiros.

'Thank you,' Zach whispered to her and the drey looked down at him. Zach felt comfort in her gaze, knowing that there was nothing great or small that she would not do for him. Just as Zach had drifted off to sleep, she looked up. Her sudden movement awoke him and he lifted his head to follow the direction of Karo's gaze but could see nothing and soon, the drey lay down her head and neck to curl around her keeper. Zach shrugged it off. It was probably nothing. Karo would have made a fuss if it was, and with those thoughts he fell into a light slumber.

He awoke with the feeling that something was amiss. He looked over to the others but they were all sleeping. The dreya were looking ahead though, all of them, and in the same direction Karo had. Zach got to his feet quickly, eyes darting around for his weapon. Karo got to her feet and stood half in front of Zach in a protective gesture, but Zach could feel no sense of threat coming from her. He stopped moving and stared into the undergrowth that surrounded them.

Light brown skin flashed through the gaps in the leaves and Zach tensed up.

'Awake!' He half whispered, half shouted to the men. Every rider responded and Cahan took up his battle-axe. He was a mountain of a man, his body riddled with the scars of his over-zealous drey and his bulk was a great comfort to have placed in the corner of your eye in troubling times.

'What is it, Captain?' Kai breathed.

'Hush! I thought I saw something,' Zach replied. The dreya too, were up, but their scales were not raised and they seemed not to be as perturbed as their keepers. Zach felt very uneasy at this but he kept his eyes locked dead ahead and soon the nameless fear came into line of sight. Zach could only count two and Delano verified this.

'Only one is armed,' he added, 'and lightly at that.'

'Perhaps they mean us no harm?' Kai asked. Zach was not going to take any chances and he snatched up his sword but told the others to hold position and leave their arms until he gave the command.

The two figures were walking slowly toward them; half crouched in a near submissive gesture. As they brushed aside the last of the jungle vines and broad-leaved ferns, Zach could see that they were small in stature and wore only loincloths, better suited for the climate. Bands of what looked like woven hair were tied around their foreheads and their scalps were shaved bald, in stark contrast to the riders' long hair. They wore no armor and one was armed with a curved piece of wood that made Zach wonder if it was either completely useless or deadly in the right hands.

'Peace.' The foremost man had spoken. His hands were in the air, more like a motion to stay back than surrender. Zach glanced over his shoulder.

'It seems they are not afraid of us but believe we should be of them,' Cahan remarked, his huge shoulders rocking with silent laughter.

The two strangers did not move and seemed no less wary of them than before. Eleven men larger than they and eleven great creatures and they seemed unperturbed.

'Peace,' Zach echoed and they relaxed their posture. The one behind shoved his wooden toy into the back of his loincloth and the other stepped forward toward Zach.

'Argos,' he said pointing to his chest, 'Brokk,' he continued, pointing to the man behind him. Zach smiled but it was not returned.

'Zach,' he said instead, his finger on his heart. The man nodded and said,

'You follow. We go to Valwald.' It was not a request and Zach felt that these two strangers had no place to be commanding him and his men to do anything. His stance became aggressive and he was just about to argue the issue with the back that was now turned to him, when he felt an urgent tug at his sleeve. It was Owein.

'What is it rider? I am in no mood to take orders from this man.'

'That is no man,' the young keeper said, 'that is a warsaur warrior and I need not tell you it is best we do as he asks.'

Zach was no fool and he had been educated before he joined the army. The warsaur were a tribal people who had a fearsome reputation for being the hardiest warriors in history. They numbered not many, only a few thousand, and not much was known of them. Apparently, they lived on Mira. Zach almost laughed at the irony of relative safety as he recalled the things that he had been taught about these people.

Initiation included young men willingly lying down so that his peers may hammer long, steel nails through the soles of his feet. The blood spilled between friends, for everyone had his turn, was supposed to be a blood bond. The soldier was then to stand and run. If he could stay ahead or out of sight of relentless pursuit for three days and three nights, he was fit to become a warrior. The nails stayed in his feet as a reminder. Zach glanced down for the first time and he saw them; silver fangs protruding out of hardened flesh. The warsaur man walked as if they had never been there.

Anyone caught in their territory without due cause or anyone suspected of doing them harm was given three choices; they could die by the executioner's hand; a spear through the base of the neck from behind whilst on your knees. This was the preferred method of dealing with intruders. They could try run and hide too. They were even given two hours head start but it was said that none made it past the third hour. The last option was to go through the initiation process; thereby incorporating themselves into the tribe if they made it, and after three years, they could choose a wife. The warsaur did this to ensure that they gained more worthy warriors and that these men contributed to the gene pool.

Zach did not wish to go through any of these ordeals. He could not afford to waste time. They had the dreya but he feared even still for their chances of survival, for the warsaur were legendary and no one had dared challenge them and lived to tell the tale.

The warsaur, Argos, had stopped and turned to see what the delay was.

'War,' he said in an urgent tone, pointing to the skies, 'talk.' He turned and walked on again.

'I think you are right, Kai. I think they just want to talk,' Zach said, never taking his eyes off the warrior. 'We will go with them but if anything goes wrong, just fly.' Kai nodded.

He looked back at his riders and hoped he was not leading them to a terrible fate, but the way that the dreya had reacted to the strangers now reassured him. They were not under threat.

Zach moved forward and all followed. They walked in silence for about an hour, through the hot and sticky jungle with its strange plants and flowers. The warsaur put up an unremitting pace, navigating their way through the impossibly thick flora like they knew some secret of the Great Energy that alluded the riders. But the men were strong and well trained; nobody lagged or fell behind.

Their dreya saw fit to fly overhead and he looked up every once in a while for encouragement. He could see their serpentine forms gliding above the canopy, their wings skimming the tree tops sending multi colored birds flying and squawking in all directions and in this way, the warsaur knew of their imminent arrival and were all standing at the ready for the coming of the strangers.

*

High ground, he needed to get to high ground.

By now, Rassev's breathing had become labored, and his feet were starting to stumble clumsily where he would have usually been sure-footed. He was almost certain he was being followed. Perhaps it was just fatigue and dehydration but the sound of bare feet slapping against hard ground never seemed to leave him for long, and he was hearing other things too. It was like something in the forest was mimicking the sound of his heartbeat.

All he needed to do was get to high ground. From there he would be able to assess his surroundings, try work things out; a psychological achievement would be won.

Sweat was dripping from the end of his nose now, running into his eyes from his forehead and blurring his sight. The visions of his last moments with the wizard were clear enough though, and Rassev was sure that that was where it had all gone wrong.

He paused, straining his ears over the noise of his own haggard breathing. The pitter-patter of feet had stopped but he knew that as soon as he made to move again, they would continue. He started forward, feeling for the metal piece he had tucked into the back of his pants. He did not pull it out though, a madman in the middle of nowhere brandishing a gun at no one in particular. What would his superiors think? In fact, what were they doing right now? Looking for him? They had better be, he thought angrily. It was their fault. They had taken his amulet, said it would open the wizard up to him and he would yield more information that way, and now look.

He had only been out there for a few hours but he dreaded nightfall. Perhaps it was not a hostile place but Rassev was not feeling optimistic. He realized he was running again and forced himself to slow down. He was losing vital fluids by the bucket-load and he did not know why his feet felt the urge to go faster while his body was screaming at them to stop.

Rassev could hear something now…the sound of water. He struggled on for a few minutes and sure enough, he came to a stream. Not wide or deep enough to cause him a detour but fresh and swift enough to drink from. He did not have a water tester with him that could measure the chemical composition and parasitic content but he was *so* thirsty. Acid could burn his throat and worms could infest his bowels for all he cared. He fell to his knees and plunged his face into the cool liquid, not even bothering to scoop it into his hands to drink. He resurfaced, gasping for air.

Now he scooped and threw the precious fluid all over his neck and face. His movements were feverish and maddened when watched from a distance but they soon slowed. He looked confused, was frowning now despite the look of pure elation that had donned his features moments before.

Rassev could smell a familiar scent, could taste something in the back of his throat. It reminded him of the torture chambers he worked in as an interrogator. At first, he thought he was imagining it, but now the tang of metal in his throat and nose was becoming stronger. Blood? He looked at his hands…clean. Perhaps the water contained too much iron? No, he thought, brushing off the water on his pants. He could smell blood, not just taste iron in his mouth. He started to feel dizzy. He rubbed his eyes with the back of balled fists like a child and looked up. The leaves of the trees were turning red, right before his very eyes. The whole landscape looked like it was gradually bleeding out, slowly oozing out its hidden life force until the crimson droplets grew thick, and threatened to fall to the ground.

Rassev rubbed his eyes again, trying to erase the image but he ceased when he felt the stickiness on his own face. He looked down only to see blood on his hands. The river ran red too and his whole front was covered in the blood that he had drank and walked in and washed himself with. He had already sunk ankle-deep into the bleeding ground and he let out a cry that would have weakened the resolve of death himself. He put his hands on his head, not knowing what else to do with them and stood screaming like a man possessed. He fell to his knees, pulling out his gun and firing it wildly in all directions screaming,

'YOU BASTARDS! WHAT HAVE YOU DONE TO ME YOU FUCKING BASTARDS!' choking on the thick blood in the back of his throat. Over and above his own yells of dismay and utter despair, he heard the sound of laughter…It mocked his world of chaos and psychosis, chuckled at his nightmare and all the while it grew closer. His cries died down and he swiveled his head wildly about him, trying to locate the source. It seemed as if it were part of the blood, all around and covering everything. He flung his empty firearm ferociously into the trees in a last-ditch effort to stop the insanity and to his amazement, the laughter stopped. For a few seconds, there was nothing but silence and blood, and Rassev actually wished that the laughing would continue…he would feel less alone.

Toireann was standing about twenty paces from the man kneeling on the ground. He was smiling. By the time Rassev realized there was something behind him, it was too late. He turned slowly, there on the ground, not feeling man enough to stand or strong enough for that matter. Toireann was a frightening creature to behold without the current situation to enhance his effect. He stood taller than most men, taller than a High Elf even, and seemed oddly thin and flexible in strange places, like a spider. His black skin seemed to pull all light in instead of reflect it, making him seem denser and less penetrable than an ordinary being. He had white eyes and large black pools for pupils, thin lips framing a broad line of razor sharp teeth. He was hairless as far as Rassev could guess, his bald head like some giant, dark egg laid by a demon. Rassev had never seen anything as terrifying in his entire life and he had seen a lot.

Words were lost on the human kneeling on the gravel river bed that Toireann could see properly. He considered lifting the illusion but decided against it. Yes, the human was now unarmed but it would be better for him to be petrified beyond comprehension as he was now, and the Adare' enjoyed his palpable discomfort immensely.

'What have you done with High Adare' Ethron?' Toireann's voice sounded like distant thunder rolling across the hills, far away and then too close for comfort and Rassev did not reply at once, he merely sat there, blinking like a fool, lips trembling and hands shaking. The apparition before him said nothing and it made Rassev all the more uncomfortable. He had the feeling that this creature was otherworldly, his silence and apparent patience made him seem grotesque.

Toireann was no longer smiling but he still bared his teeth, like a man about to bite into something. Rassev found his voice at last as his mind started to work things out.

'If you are a wizard, then all of this is highly illegal.' Rassev got to his feet and the spell broke, the illusion shifted and fell away, revealing sunlight filtering through the trees and clear water flowing behind him. Greenery once more, normality, but the figure remained.

'I can have you arrested for this,' the human said, chin lifted in arrogance. Toireann's face grew darker and he narrowed his eyes. He lifted a long, spindly-fingered hand before his face, spread the digits out in Rassev's direction and pulled his hand into a fist. Rassev saw the transparent effigies coming for him, and made to dodge them, but he was in the wizard's grasp now and as sure as the mage had a balled fist, Rassev could feel giant fingers around his torso, gripping tight enough to hurt but not enough to break his bones. Toireann pulled his fist closer to his face and Rassev was flying through the air toward him, stopping short, feet dangling inches from the ground, about two feet away from the Adare'.

'I am the beginning of a new era, human,' Toireann said softly.

'You cannot kill me!' Rassev managed, his voice now pitched higher with fear.

'You are afraid of death?' the wizard taunted softly, 'there are far worse things I could do that you should fear.'

Toireann was smiling again and this close, Rassev's heart beat all the faster. He had markings on his face that Rassev could see now, strange tattooed swirls, curling around his terrible eyes and all the way down his neck and shoulders. He was a cleya of Lar.

Toireann picked up the faint change in facial expression that no mortal could, the dawn of realization for this poor man and grinned.

Rassev felt his resolve dissipate completely. The drums were calling, though distantly still. The drums that he had failed to recognize before. He was only a man, was he not? How had fate decided to deal so harshly with him and overlook all others?

'We...we can work something out!' the human's voice climbed higher still with every desperate word he spoke and now, as his eyes flitted around him, instinctively looking for some way out, he could see the people between the trees. A bare snatch of flesh here, a marked face there and all the while, the war drums beat louder, matching the thrum of his frantic heart. Toireann laughed again, he seemed genuinely amused.

'The old man sent you here for *me*; I can *smell* him on you...' Rassev had been drawn in even closer, should have been able to see his reflection in the mage's eyes, but he couldn't. Sweat drenched his back and his mind flashed back to all the things he had done to the wizard they needed information from, all the things that he had witnessed being done and he prayed, almost out loud, that this cleya wizard could not read minds as well.

Toireann began sniffing the air around Rassev and Rassev could not wipe the imagery from his mind. Perhaps the immortal man could smell his thoughts! Rassev was weeping uncontrollably now.

'Most of all, you smell like fear,' Toireann breathed, 'you stink of it yet you know nothing about it, only how to inflict it,' he spat. Rassev cringed against the harsh but true words and lifted his hands to his face as Toireann's lips brushed his ear. The dying thunder whispered, 'I'll show you real fear.'

*

Lucio bent down to brush the lost strand of hair from Mirkisha's cold face. He had always been able to see things that others could not, sense things where others felt nothing, and he had smelt her death before he had even opened the door.

All the fine features of her face were black, her home was in ruins and her tongue had been ripped out. He stood up and surveyed the scene around him. He touched the walls, the floor, and the scattered debris but found nothing, just an aftertaste of malice that stung the back of his throat.

People often asked him if god spoke to him. He thought of the answer he always gave them as he knelt over the dead woman he had come to cherish.

'God speaks to us all, every minute of every day and in everything we see, do, hear, feel and...say.' He said it out loud, bending down to kiss her for the last time.

Mirkisha had once confided in him that she had a secret, one so important that she would die before she would let it pass her lips. This was it then, Lucio thought as her pain and sorrow flooded through his body. In that kiss, he saw everything, all that her words over the years had failed to relay and his heart was made heavy. He was with her the night Lord Nagesh had come to her and planted his seed inside her. He bore her wretched grief when she saw his face where death's kind face should have been. He could feel her realize the beast's plan and he was by her side the day she let go of her family for the good of the Worlds, the greater pain that assailed her when she bore forth the abomination within her womb that she grew to love...and fear. He saw the army, the multitudes that would sacrifice their souls to beat back the darkness. He felt someone coming.

Magic; as intangible to him as what life after death held. But he could feel it. An aura like honey in milk...strands of bending fluid, strong and rich. A wizard was coming. Lucio did not turn to face the doorway that was now occupied. The figure within it was breathing hard; aged fingers clutching at the frame as if it were the last remnants of something beautiful. The figure was weeping.

Chapter 8

Dark days

The whip fell again, and again harder, and faster until Soren lost count. He could feel the blood trickling down his back now and he released his hold on his mouthpiece a little. The blood calmed him.

Her breathing was steady behind him and he could imagine the way her crimson lips were curled into a semi-smile but her eyes were still focused, focused on his bleeding flesh, wringing from him all she could. And soon it was over. Cold, dark eyes flashed their satisfaction as he turned and felt with the tips of his fingers at the red welts that had risen.

Sirena was already packing away her instruments and Soren felt duped in his pleasure. Did she not also delight in her part of cleansing him? Was it not her idea?

'Don't give me that face Soren, it doesn't suit you. Velasco needs me as much as you do.' She glanced at him as she donned her midnight blue Religion robes. 'Don't get blood on my sheets.' A rare smile stealing her usually stern expression away. She disappeared behind the doorway and Soren was left alone.

She was the only one who could get away with treating him with such impertinent indifference. She was a great prophetess and she was his wife. She had led them all to greatness and had a thirst for unclean blood that almost surpassed his own. Ambitious, cruel and beautiful Sirena.

He was looking forward to the meeting tonight, he was anxious to hear how their campaign was faring, and was keen to listen to his associates speak of their conquests. He quickly bathed, reveling in the image of his blood swirling down into the drain and prepared for the gathering of the Religion.

The Religion's strong-hold was Terrius, his home planet, and they had built many fine cathedrals there, but the finest was built in Daemoa, the Religion's capital. Carved from stone and supported by steel, the massive building contained seventeen churches and housed the forty Supreme Cardinals of the Religion. The walls, both inside and out, were engraved with hundreds of scenes from the holy script and he had missed gazing upon the many faces of the one true god. He had been on Equa for mere months but it had seemed like an eternity. Now, he was back among the true and faithful, cleansed of the wicked he had had to endure at the council. Wizards, children of Energy that followed no god as well as parasite ridden vampires and various other forms of vile creation.

He arrived at the Sixth house of god and made his way to the front. Sirena and the Supreme Archbishop were standing on either side of the altar and Soren took his seat amongst the others. Two colossal chandeliers gave light to the domed hall; they made the stone faces of the savior alive with their dancing flames. A choir was singing somewhere and the chanting soothed his racing heart.

'Brother Soren?' A man to his left asked, 'we have not seen you in many moons. On what business were you away?' Soren smiled and replied,

'All will be revealed in time.' The days he had spent on Equa flashed through his mind; the screams of the processed that had filled the nights and the pride he had felt watching his plague grow strong. He smiled and turned his attention back to the front.

The Supreme Archbishop took a step forward. There was silence now as he opened the black, leather bound book he held. Velasco was all that Soren one day hoped to be. His hair hung over his shoulders and his beard was kept at one year's growth at all times. Hazel eyes, like an autumn storm, and a small but commanding voice that penetrated the soul of the listener.

'Ulomah 3 verse 5: "You must always keep what is clean away from what is unclean. Do not become tainted by unclean things..." This is what we have been striving to do brothers.' Velasco's arms were open in welcoming and everyone had hands pressed to their lips in silent prayer. 'We have built an empire of clean things and we have forbidden the unclean to taint our sacred souls... but alas! It is not enough,' he looked down upon his closest followers gravely and they all stared back expectantly. 'Xadehl 15 verse 8: "They do not take rest from mocking the one true god; they do not stop mocking his believers. The wrath he has will rise against the non-believers and there will be no cure".' There was silence as they all took in his message.

'When will this wrath be raised great leader?' Someone from the back had risen to his feet to ask the question that everyone wanted to know. This was Sirena's cue; she swept forward like a giant carrion crow and seized the moment;

'Our foreign campaign goes well, brothers! We smite down many each day.' There was enthusiastic applause and Sirena reveled in the moment. 'It goes so well,' she continued, 'that our great General Midas, cannot even be among you today. But,' she cautioned, 'we suffer still...' Bated breath awaited the reason for ongoing suffering. 'How many holy soldiers and how many long years will it take to complete such a task? How many souls will wait for how long, until we have done what has been written?' No reply, blank faces. Velasco stepped forward again to join the gesticulating prophetess.

'Meberai 2 verse 1: "There will be a great black plague and it will wipe the unclean from before the face of the holy one, for they have refused him and refused his messengers".'

Sirena raised her arms up to the ceiling and rolled her eyes back in her head. Everyone gasped quietly and waited for her to speak, for she spoke his words true, and channeled his life force through her own so that his people may know what it was he wished. She had converted half the known world with her power and now, she would deliver unto them a message straight from god;

'My people! My faithful followers! I asked you to build an army and destroy that which flaunted itself soulless and unclean in my realm and you have done well. I now tell you that reward for your hard work will come. I send a black plague and you will all be safe from it. Only the unclean will suffer! It has been foretold!'

Sirena fell to the floor in a useless heap and several young Religion students rushed to her aid. They dabbed water to her brow and fanned her flushed face. Velasco carried on without her as if he saw such holy things every day.

'Uniib 8 verse 4 tells us that only those who believe will be saved, those who do not believe will be damned. Thrown into the fiery pit for all eternity.' Someone near Soren found his voice and asked,

'How can we help, great leader? How can we serve?' Soren was amazed at the power that Sirena and Velasco held between them. They all knew that they alone were god's chosen race, but this was genocide on a Worldly scale, and people were not hesitating to ask how they could help, holding on to an unwavering belief in the face of such enormities.

'For now, dear brothers, you will preach of this in your churches and you will tell the people of the foretold beginning. Our support wavers. The people start to doubt when we try to do what is meant to be done. We need a swift remedy and to tell the people of its coming now, will only secure our numbers when the deed is done.'

Soren grinned at his cunning. Sirena had recovered and was on her feet, pale and dizzied but her voice had lost none of its previous conviction;

'Do not question what was said here today, only believe its truth and go to the people with a clear message; his will be done and we are the only ones.'

Once the prayers had been said and they had all received Velasco's blessing individually, leaning forward to touch the vessel of the one, they quietly left. None lingered, all were intent upon their task.

Soren waited till last, wondering all the while about the woman, the drey lady, his sister. Should he tell Sirena that somewhere out there a woman *might* be responsible for the wielding of some weapon to be used against them? And why did he suspect this? Because of a series of coincidences? He could not explain his hunch. Perhaps he was just paranoid. No weapon was great enough to defeat the black plague. His wraiths would find her and kill her and all would be well. Even if she was from the planet of origin, even if she was sprung by the vampires. Falkhar could have her if he felt she was so important.

'Soren?' Sirena's voice pierced his thoughts and he found himself looking into her eyes. They were alone now, with Velasco.

'Yes?'

Sirena concealed her irritation and turned to Velasco;

'He has had a grueling time so long among the unclean,' she explained gently. Velasco nodded solemnly.

'I understand. Now, you must rest. We all have much to look forward to. You must tell me if you hear of anything else from our savior, you are the only contact we have with the darkness. We shall all be forever grateful. Be strong.' He too left them, and walked toward the door to join the others.

Sirena turned her attention to her husband and when Velasco was safely out of earshot she hissed,

'Do you not know how to control yourself? You had shadows crawling all over your eyes when he came to us and you seek to keep your identity hidden from his scrutiny and punishment!' Soren started, he was not aware of how deep in thought he had been.

Only Sirena knew of his wraith father, only she did not judge him and only she could keep him safe. When he had first told her, she had hardly been able to contain her excitement. She had told him that he was the key to the undoing of the unclean, but that he must never tell another soul, or he would be condemned and useless to her. And so they had created a separate identity for the wraith that would only speak with him. This was how he gained his reputation and station.

When he made no reply her features softened and she put her arms around him. He winced a little but she ignored him.

'Tell me of the High Adare' and how our plague goes.'

'Three planets have fallen and the army grows. It will take but a fortnight to fulfill our holy task.' Sirena smiled and Soren loved to see her so pleased. No, he would not tell her of the woman and what her ward had shown him, he would deal with it himself.

'The wizard, Ethron, yielded nothing. After he told me that he knew of a force that would stop me, we had him taken for processing, but no amount of might could penetrate him. We even lost someone to him and now his mind is so scrambled, it is doubtful that we will ever find out if his words held meaning.' Sirena did not look surprised;

'Wizard demons have ways that we will never understand and perhaps it is better that way.'

'There is more,' Soren cautioned, 'he speaks of "blood angels" in his sleep and we cannot figure out what that means.' Sirena frowned.

'Like you said, his mind is scrambled, pay him no heed.' Soren nodded his head at her sage advice but could not shake the feeling that he had missed something.

His comm. device bleeped and the message came through that the drey's trail had been lost, that the riders had escaped and about forty kuvuta lay dead and smoldering in the river. The old anger resurfaced. It felt good.

*

As Zach entered the giant, straw-woven gates to the inner city, he spotted a few humans, some doirya and even a few pirates. New recruits. The people of Valwald were huddled around the sand path that led to the chieftain's hut. Most were just curious onlookers, some wanted to greet these elusive fire tamers, and a few just wanted to see the dreya themselves. All the men bore the nailed feet and all the women were throwing flowers in a gesture of greeting and welcome. They were a strong people, not an ounce of fat on any of them. Fine, chiseled bodies and large, staring eyes. Snatches of deep flute music accompanied by war chants could be heard, but mainly just the sounds of everyday living greeted them.

Zach and his men followed Argos and Brokk demurely up the pathway, trying not to get too involved with the locals. They finally reached the hut of the Chief Warsaur. Two burly doirya and a human flanked its entrance. The doirya were a tree-dwelling race with long, muscled arms and small legs. A hairless tail aided balance and was also used as a sensory organ.

They parted spears without a word when Argos raised his palm. Inside, hundreds of candles burned, and incense clogged the small space with a cloying sweetness. Despite the light of flame, the chieftain sat in darkness, apparently deep in conversation with another. It seemed that the riders would have to wait their turn.

Kai shifted his weight nervously and tried to catch his captain's eye. He was not comfortable with the situation. Zach could feel the young man's distress and knew he was far more accustomed to being the crew with the upper hand. He did nothing to console him. Kai would have to learn to deal with diplomatic situations and Zach decided he would introduce him as his second in command to see how he handled the pressure.

The barely audible mumbling from beyond the light stopped and a figure emerged. He had the mark of the Adare' on his forearm; a symbol rarely seen but in this heat, Ailfryd could not bear to sweat it out in his heavy robes.

He walked straight toward the weakest looking of the group and swiftly took him by the hand in an introductory embrace that the humans used; a good tool, for the hands yielded much.

Kern was taken aback but training held him fast and he returned the strange gesture, not letting go of the wizard before he did.

Drey keepers, Ailfryd thought, he could have guessed as much. On an important journey. This young rider had seen much for his age and held great respect for his leader. Ailfryd pulled the man closer and whispered in his ear;

'You will need even greater faith in Zach before the end.' Before Kern could reply, the magic slinger was gone, the flap of the tent closing behind him.

'I apologize for Ailfryd.' The voice came from the back of the dwelling.

'You may go now,' said a man standing to the right. He gestured in the direction of the voice and they all followed Zach.

Cushions were scattered on the floor but no candles lit the hot darkness here. The chieftain's outline could be seen but not much else. He was a large man, also finely built like all his people.

'The Adare' is a High Elvin representative but he has none of their formal niceties.' He chuckled to himself as the riders settled down on the floor.

'I am Zach, the Captain of this party and this is Kai,' he gestured to the young rider, and Kai stepped forward, bowing slightly before taking his seat next to Zach. 'What do you want with us?' Zach asked. He had no time for formalities either.

'You use my soil and my water and now you ask what I want. I like that,' the chief muttered softly, chuckling to himself again. 'My name is Thorr and I want what everybody wants; answers.'

Zach pulled at his leather, neck armor and Kai spoke for him;

'We meant no harm or discourtesy. We used your planet as a stop-off point. We are on an important quest and we cannot be stalled for long.' There was a quiet and Zach was afraid Kai might have indeed offended Thorr. After a lengthy and uncomfortable silence, the warsaur spoke again;

'We are not a well-known people. I am one of very few among us that can speak the tongue of the Worlds and we like it that way. Left alone, we have made a happy home, and our planet prospers, but now we hear of black wars and vile beasts that will span the Worlds and who, I am told, we cannot hope to fight alone and who can never be joined to us and accustomed to our ways. This disturbs us for it can mean only two things: death or the preservation of life. To define life would be to encompass all things on the outside, not just what we have here.' He paused and Zach drew a deep breath before saying,

'We have seen of what you have only heard. They will spare no one.'

Thorr nodded his head solemnly.

'I have been given a choice,' he explained, 'the elvin friend who spoke with me told me that the elves are amassing and call upon all races to aid them in their fight for the preservation of life. I think this a noble thing to do but cannot uproot my entire army for naught. We here believe in the truth of seeing and not in the truth of foreign words but I see the pain in your eyes when you speak your foreign words and so I have seen the truth that I needed.'

Kai spoke again now;

'It would be wise to join forces with the elves but how will you get there? It is many, many leagues away from here. The elvin realm will not be reached by force of will.' Thorr smiled and leaned forward so that half his face was now bathed in the soft lighting. His grin was toothless, but his features were still fine cut, as of a young man, and a massive scar reached from his forehead down to his cheek and through the scar peered a milky white and unseeing eye.

'Do not underestimate us, young warrior. We have many allies and we could leave at first light if I give word.' He leaned back again, the toothless grin swallowed by the shadows. 'I thank you for your honesty, riders, and I tell you that we mean you no harm as you meant us none. Tonight we will feast the coming departure and you will join us.' His tone brooked no argument and under the circumstances, Zach thought it better to accept his invitation.

They filed out of the hut one by one and were told they could see to their dreya, hunt in the forests and walk freely, for the feast would only begin when the star set.

The dreya were enjoying the vast amount of attention being given to them by the local inhabitants and some, like Kai's Valeo and Owein's Tuan, were putting on fire displays and flexing their leathery wings for all to see and touch.

'Do we stay for the feast?' Owein asked, 'It would be a cultural sin to decline. Besides, I do not believe you will be able to persuade the men otherwise.' He did not mean disrespect but Zach seemed anxious to leave and looked irritated by the riders' enthusiasm. Delano had his tongue down what Zach could only guess was a very pretty prostitute's throat and his hands half-way up her gypsy skirts. Cahan was getting bare fist fighting lessons from a group of warsaur children and Karo was giving rides to the chief's commanders who were jostling one another for better places in line.

'Yes,' Zach said, recovering his senses, 'we will stay and leave later.' He knew it was important for the men to be happy and they deserved a little merriment after what they had been through.

The feast seemed just what they needed. The food was plentiful and fresh. The people were friendly. The music was upbeat and the dancing that accompanied the hypnotic beat was infectious. When they had eaten their fill and gyrated themselves to near exhaustion, the royal guard sat down near one of the fires.

'Did you kiss your sweet star good night?' Cahan asked Delano, jabbing him in the ribs with his elbow.

'Syrita is her name and we shall kiss until the star rises!' Delano shouted over his shoulder. The woman, Syrita, winked and danced with added vigor.

'Do not look so sad, Owein, some women like a man that speaks more than she...' Ionhar broke down into laughter at his lie, and Owein shook his head, smiling shyly all the same. Broad grins were abundant as the men jested with one another and a renewed sense of the Worlds and what they were fighting for refreshed their spirits.

Zach knelt down in front of the seated men once they had quietened down and began the prayer for the evening. There were the customary recitals that they all knew from childhood but they were merely guidelines. One could add and re-create as one went along, to suit the occasion and mood. It was encouraged and it was better that way for each time you prayed, the words would mean something, not borne from repetition but from the heart. This was Zach's prayer;

'We have broken bread together on this day and many days before, we have watched the unseen threats for each other this night and many nights before, and we will fight together tomorrow as we have done before and will do many times more. Though the stars fade and the shadow falls, we will be for each other, as we have been for each other, till we can be for each other no more.'

*

Till we can be for each other no more…

The words of the old prayer whispered through Valador's tired mind. It had been two days since the snake had bitten him and he had neither the strength nor the will to go find the plant that would speed up the healing process. It was taking his body longer this time to regenerate, the tissue longer to mesh and push out the poison.

When the Six had decided upon their great solution at the High Council, Valador had eagerly volunteered for the position of General. An army that could not die! He had been so young and naïve back then. It was probably a good thing that his beloved wife, Mirkisha, had banished him from Bethriam. She would be old now and he was still… no he was not young anymore. But he would live until he fought the darkness with his long-lost comrades. Until he could be for them no more, he would live.

He could feel the shadows grow longer as the wraiths crept closer but perhaps it was all in his mind and they would never come. The council had not taught him how to deal with immortality. And the only ones who knew how kept it a secret. The malachi steeled their hearts, the cleya fed their souls with blood and fire and the elves ended it when they felt the need. He could not go to any of them though; he could not go to anyone. He was an outcast in his own life. Guarding a secret that guarded him.

He wondered how the others were faring and where they were hiding their timeless existences. If he were to find out for certain that the great enemy had returned, he would have to call them all together. The thought chilled him. To see his own kind again and to be a leader among many again. The Blood Angels would have need of him though, and he was not sure if he was ready. He was an old man. Not physically but spiritually. His grief and regret had fossilized him, paralyzed his mind.

He inspected his wound again. It was getting worse. He could smell the rot. The festering wound oozed puss and grew purple. Maybe he was no longer immune to death? Maybe someone else more worthy had taken his place and he did not yet know it? He knew nothing of the outside world. He knew only of his pain.

You are going to have to help yourself Valador. I will take you to the herb.

'Thank you, Valcan. I nearly lost myself again.'

I know.

*

Ramroth was tired. The spell that had cleansed and revitalized him was only temporary. He had found half a loaf of bread hidden away in Mary's room but that had been a while ago. He had stayed awake to watch over her seemingly fragile, sleeping form for a few hours now, but it was time for her to awaken. He needed answers; he needed to ask her to take him to Ethron and he needed to do it before anyone realized he was missing. He could feel the faint presence of the ancient Adare' stirring somewhere, but he would be protected, and Ramroth would not be able to succeed in his task alone. Could he ask her help though? She was just a young girl. He stood up from his cross-legged position on the concrete floor and turned to her bed. She was not there.

'I will take you to him.'

Ramroth spun one eighty toward the sound of her lilting voice. She was standing in the corner; waiting patiently for him. Her body language did not indicate that she was aware of the frightening effect she had had on her guest, in fact, her body language suggested very little, like she was dreaming and unaware.

'If you are able...' he cautioned. She made no reply, she simply walked over to him and took his hand, as if that was all he needed, and she opened the door without concern.

'But...' he protested.

'Shh.' She had her small finger pressed tightly to her lips and Ramroth heard it, the faint rustling beneath her whispered command. The slight footsteps that never really fell, not in this time and not in this place. They were just ahead of them now, rounding the corner and traveling fast. The Umanok were on the move.

'How far is it?' he asked. She only gripped his hand tighter in reply and he realized that she wasn't really with him and that she needed to concentrate, so he kept his mouth shut and his questions to himself. He wondered what would happen if they came upon a wraith, he wondered how he was going to escape and he wondered about Ethron. Wondered what *they* had reduced him to.

They wound their way along many corridors and went up five flights of stairs, his prospects of escape becoming bleaker every time they climbed. Mary sped up and Ramroth was just beginning to come to the last of his willingness when she stopped, pressing her hand against his chest, pinning him to the wall. After a few heartbeats she pulled him slowly forward by his cloak and around the last corner.

Two human sentries guarded the door to Ethron's cell. They were heavily armed with illegal hand-held cannons, plus they were draped with charms and amulets. He and Mary stood there like painted targets, Ramroth's face paralyzed with fear. He was out of time to use his cloak but Mary made no move to fend off the coming attack. Soon, he found out why.

It all happened very fast. Just as the humans came rushing toward them, cocking their fire arms, they were stopped dead in their tracks. Ramroth saw the Umanok only momentarily as they crossed over onto his plane. Hard, muscled and huge feather-covered bodies gripped each man by the neck, snapping the bone and sinew that held the head in place with frightening ease. A brush of feathers across his face, warm blood sprinkling his cheek and then they were gone.

'Where are the bodies?' Ramroth managed to ask, after wiping the fresh blood away with his sleeve. Mary merely shrugged and replied,

'They are hungry.'

They stood in front of the door for what felt like an eternity. He was unable to speak or move after what he had witnessed.

'The best is yet to come,' she smiled at him, as if reading his thoughts were amusing. He frowned at her and was about to ask, when he felt the rush, before he could even see it. Strong arms wrapped themselves around him and spun him through the door with such speed and grace that he hardly knew what was happening. He saw the creature's eyes then, in that moment of their embrace. Glowing red coals in a snow-white mask of down feathers. They flashed past him as he was released, sent spinning through the absence of a solid door on their plane and crashing into the room on his.

Once he had retained his sense of balance and where he was, he saw the old man he loved strapped to a soiled chair in the center of the dark room. Rats were nibbling at his feet and he was unconscious.

Ramroth rushed toward him, kicking the brazen rodents away. He knelt down and tried to undo the restraints that held one of the most wise and respected Adare' down like a criminal.

'Don't bother.' Ramroth stopped his efforts and raised the old man's head. Dead eyes. Had he imagined the voice? He waved his hand in front of Ethron's face. Nothing.

'Ethron, can you hear me? I need you to hear me,' he said, loudly and slowly, so that the scrambled mind could have time to string the words together. There was no reply; only blank staring eyes answered him and Ramroth knew he would have to use the last of his strength for this. He grabbed Ethron by the sides of his head and channeled his essence into his withered spirit. One second... two... three... and Ramroth was falling...then an explosion in his head like firecrackers had been set off inside his skull. Ethron's essence had replied with a force that sent Ramroth flying into the opposite wall.

He looked up and the old Adare' was struggling against his straps, eyes darting about, neck strained taught as he pulled and fought.

'Stay still, save your energy,' Ramroth said, palm outstretched, as he walked slowly toward the maddened mage.

'They took me!' Ethron said wildly. Ramroth knelt before him again and locked his gaze onto the crazy eyes of the High Adare'. They settled on his with an unnerving intensity. 'They do not know anything.' He was smiling now, a mad grin that exposed yellow, crooked teeth.

'I do not know anything either!' Ramroth replied in frustration, 'you must tell me what the Blood Angels are and how it is used! You must tell me if it has anything to do with Arial.' Ramroth was desperate. He was unsure whether or not Ethron's senses were still awake and if he would get any of the answers he needed, and had banked so heavily upon the old man to give him. He had no idea the man would be so far gone.

Silence…and then…sanity. Ethron's eyes grew sad and he calmly replied,

'It was my idea. Make an immortal army and place the task of defending us against the enemy on them. Who would fight? Uasail said his people would do it. A worthy leader who could call them together at any time and without anybody knowing. Hundreds of thousands of them, all willing to lay down their lives and the lives of their dreya for us. The Blood Angels. Our angels.' It was then that Ramroth lost him again. Lost him to the dark recesses of his vast mind. His eyes glazed over and lost focus once more but Ramroth was not done and he shook Ethron violently.

'And what of Arial?' he asked, desperately. The last seconds of clarity and Ethron's last words;

'The fire maiden, Arial, yes. She holds the key…' and he was gone. A shrill scream pierced the air, borne from Ethron's lips as if in pain from releasing a terrible secret. He struggled uncontrollably in his chair, urine running down his leg, hands shaking and sweat-bedraggled hair snaking down his pinched shoulders. A soft hand on Ramroth's shoulders as tears collected in his eyes.

'They are coming.' She still sounded peaceful but there was an edge to her voice that he had not heard before.

'You cared for him?' he asked, looking up at her with a glistening face. The screams of Ethron had now subsided into wretched sobs. She nodded slowly. She was sad now and Ramroth could feel her power ebbing.

'We must leave,' he said suddenly, and that seemed to bring her back.

'Alright,' she answered quietly.

He stood up and they turned to the still shut door but Ramroth could feel something wrong. No, not wrong, just different. He put his finger on it just in time, pulling Mary away from the door and shielding her with his own body. The door crackled and flared with green flame and burst open, clean off its magical hinges, stopping short before the once-more docile Ethron and hovering in the air before it fell to the ground in a heap of blackened ash, emerald sparks flying. Toireann, thought Ramroth. His raw power had never learnt the patience of immortal magic and it seared with a passion that threatened to overwhelm the very foundations that held it fast. Ramroth turned his head and there he was, framed in the smoking doorway, bald and clawed like a giant bat from hell. Ramroth was relieved.

Toireann ran over to Ethron and took the old man's hands that he had been raised by, and wept silently. Ramroth gave him a moment before demanding,

'How did you get here, how did you even know he was here?' Toireann sneered and replied,

'The human told me soon enough. Sang like a bird and I flew like one to get here.' His voice broke at the last and he looked down again.

'So you can fly?' Ramroth asked, a real ray of light beginning to shine.

'Not far and not with you.'

Well planned, once again, Ramroth thought dully.

'I will send you,' the little voice spoke up. Toireann looked up and walked over to Mary, taking hold of her face in his spindly hands and holding it up for inspection.

'A Tarayelo, Ramroth. Too young and too strong,' he smiled, 'I like her already.' If Mary was surprised by Toireann's uncouth behavior, she showed no sign of it.

'We must go now,' she said urgently. She strode out the door, two wizards in tow and out onto the balcony that stood adjacent to Ethron's cell.

Ramroth's mouth hung open as he looked upon what faced them. The swarms had doused the blazing noon star, those down below crawled over each other to climb the tower like so many snakes. Ramroth felt weak then and he knew Toireann held no power over these beings, this army. It was the fragile looking creature who stood calmly at their sides, which all their hopes of life rested on. Ramroth thought back to when the Umanok had held him and the white face of death beyond had stared at him, the massive wings, the powerful form and the preternatural aura. This little girl had the power. Small and demure, she could unleash seven legions of hell.

'I am not afraid anymore,' she said. Her eyes never left the hundreds of kuvuta, waiting for the trio to make a move. 'I cannot go with you though.' The truth of the sacrifice brought fresh tears to Ramroth's eyes and he knelt down to embrace the girl that would lay down her life without thought for them. 'I will not die, Ramroth. They will take me with them,' she whispered softly into his ear.

'Thank you,' was all he could manage. He knew that such a feat would take her essence to the end of its capabilities and she would perish in some way or another. He felt the wings wrap around him nevertheless, and he did not struggle against it. Toireann knew better too and soon, they were flying, higher and higher, the beating wings sounding like the distant, rhythmic heartbeat of a sleeping giant in their ears.

There was not even a fight that day. She channeled her power, closed her eyes and the grey-white winged mist sprung forward, decimating the shadow like a shockwave of redemption. Every wraith fell, every one of them died and Mary was taken away to be with her angels until time stretched into oblivion.

*

Corbin and Cadeyrn were sitting in the cockpit of the Typhoon busy with a last minute systems check before they would be on their way. Corbin was anxious. They were a well-trained crew with much experience behind them as a team, and as individuals, but he was not interested in confrontation. He wanted to get them home safely this time, all of them. If they were captured, it would not necessarily mean death. Cadeyrn was an ex-Religion general. This did not mean that he had been relieved of duty, but that he had chosen to step down after two years "honor" and to add insult to injury, he had also chosen to join the Rogues in their struggle against the Religion militia and the havoc they wreaked on foreign soil. He always said that others should not have to pay for the wickedness and stupidity of a race not their own. They would come for Cadeyrn and they would torture the rest for information. Corbin knew of their ways. He had been a Religion executioner, and by the time the captured came to him, it was almost already over. At least in their eyes it was. No life left to take save the beating of their brave hearts. Two hundred lives he had taken and two hundred thousand tears he had cried.

He and his crew had been working together for six years, five months and fifteen days. Eira had been his wife for three of those years and he had watched the blood run from many a Religion soldier in that time. Killing them did not help him though, could not redeem his soul, could not make him forget nor ease the pain. But every time he put one of those bastards down, he knew a life somewhere out there had been saved. Someone could live out their dreams and hopes for a while longer, free from persecution and judgment.

'Right, all we need now is a working GPS,' Cadeyrn said, leaning back in his chair, massive hands behind his shaved head.

'We better start praying that it still works,' Corbin said, throwing his friend a dark glance.

'Ha! Don't look at me; you're the one who takes it out on bits of tech!' They were laughing now, as Nyx and Eira walked into the cabin.

'Here,' Nyx said, handing Cadeyrn the device, 'it should be in working order and then we can stop messing about and get the hell out of here.' It was his turn to throw dirty looks at his two snickering superiors.

'We're just going to go pack the last of the things up and then we'll be back with Raul and the wolves.' Eira kissed Corbin lightly on the forehead before taking her brother's hand and exiting the Typhoon.

Cadeyrn busied himself with wiring and pliers while Corbin frowned and fidgeted.

'I can't wait to be home,' Cadeyrn said. 'It's terrible, what happened to the other team, but at least we can let their families know,' he added.

'Are you winning?'

'Just give me sec,' the big man replied, fiddling with the last of the wiring, 'there, we are officially on line.' The little screen blinked into life and zoned in on their location. *"Omihana, desert planet in Delta Two. Little life support with a rainfall of one inch in the rainy season and surface temperatures exceeding forty degrees Celsius in the dry season. Viable terrestrial activity. Caution to sand storms.* The machine monotoned.

'Well thank you very much,' Corbin said dryly to the computer, 'anything else?' he asked his mechanic. Cadeyrn held a button in and leaned forward;

'Computer, give me a field radius.' It took a few seconds for the device to comply.

'You really want to know what's out here with us?' Corbin muttered.

'Better safe than sorry.' Cadeyrn shrugged.

Corbin sat bolt upright suddenly and Cadeyrn looked at him quizzically, if not a little fearfully.

'What?' he asked. Corbin was silent for a few seconds longer before he relaxed a little in his seat and said,

'Nothing. I thought I heard something but it's probably nothing.' Cadeyrn was not convinced and Corbin did not look so either. While Corbin sat straining his ears against the coming dawn, Cadeyrn was busy shaking the GPS. It was giving a reading, but not one that he wanted, so he thought that by maybe roughing it up a little, it would change its mind, but the little red dots were not going away.

'Corbin...' he said slowly, 'I think we have a situation.' Corbin leaned over with an irritated look upon his face but when he saw the moving blips on the monitor he jumped to his feet and ran for the door.

'What do you want me to do?' Cadeyrn shouted after him.

'Stay here, start the engines. I have to get Eira!' And he was gone, into the night, and Cadeyrn was left alone to watch the ever-nearing dots, each representing a Religion soldier. He counted thirteen all in all. He switched the GPS off and laid it down on the switchboard. They had come for him at last and the people he loved would pay for his choices as dearly as he.

Corbin was running blindly through the darkness, charging over the dunes to get to the wolves. He had tied them up earlier because he wanted to leave without a hitch when they were ready. He did not want to go looking for stray animals playing in the ever-changing sands. He could hear them now. The first barks indicating danger approaching, the growl of its closer proximity and the last dying efforts, voiced in a series of broken yelps. This was the sound that spurred Corbin on. He and his team had raised the giant dire wolves and he loved them all dearly. They were loyal and fierce and had been an enormous asset to them. He felt personally responsible for their lives and a piece would be missing from him if they were taken.

His feet were kicking up dust and his eyes were streaming with the effort but he knew it was too late. He got to the sticks in the sand just in time to watch Ahlf die. Conan and Lowell were already down. Half strangled, half bloodied and limp on the sand. Corbin stopped in his tracks, eyes on the man who had Ahlf in his arms.

"Bit stupid isn't it?' the soldier said, wolf blood dripping down his navy blue sleeves, 'leaving them out here all tied up and waiting. Easy pickings...' He smiled and then Corbin was knocked out cold, before he could say a word. A heavy blow to the head from behind and it was lights out.

When he awoke, he was face down in the Typhoon. The cold floor was joined by the cold muzzle of a rifle to his head.

'Easy now,' came the voice of the wolf killer, 'don't go doing anything you'll regret.' A lazy accent but a big gun. Corbin managed to turn his head and take in his surroundings. Cadeyrn and Eira had been tied up and gagged, back to back, seated on the floor. Nyx was in a protective force field that muted the captive; a nasty cut on his forehead was bleeding into his right eye. Corbin looked up at his guard and, fixing him with a glare, rose into a sitting position, hands behind his head.

There were six soldiers in the cabin. All were heavily armed with cannons or rifles but four were even worse off than Nyx. One had a broken arm and two were nursing various small knife nicks that had gone a little too deep for comfort. One was dead. Pooled blood lay around his head. Nyx's knife was in embedded in his eye. Corbin's eyes met Nyx's and the red headed dare devil smiled.

'So you think it's funny?' Corbin's guard asked, 'this man here,' he continued, pointing at Nyx, 'should be put down!' Corbin could only grin broadly in response. At least something had been accomplished.

'What are you waiting for?' Corbin growled through his smirk of satisfaction.

'We are awaiting Captain's orders like good little soldiers, unlike you lot, running around for the other team. The scum!' he spat. Corbin shook his head, brainwashed like all the rest. 'You think you're so clever,' wolf killer said, sitting on his haunches to be eye-level with Corbin. 'I bet you didn't think leaving your little doggies tied up was clever.' Corbin glared back at the insult, trying not to bite the bait. Wolf killer could see the restraint, had learnt how to recognize it in his victims. 'What about her?' he asked, smiling cheekily and nodding in Eira's direction. Her eyes grew wide with fear and Corbin's facial features contorted in reply. 'We've hit the jackpot boys,' the soldier said. The others looked up, rearing at the sport of blood and revenge. 'You take one of ours,' wolf killer said, 'and we'll take one of yours, if you know what I mean.' He winked and Corbin tried to make a mad scramble across the floor to get to his wife, but enough firepower to blow a hole the size of his fist through his head stood in his way.

'Don't touch her!' Corbin shouted desperately. They all started laughing and the soldier with the broken arm removed Eira's gag, stoking her face leisurely as he did so. Nyx could not be heard behind his ectoblastic wall, but he beat his fists against it with all his might, as if that would drive them away.

'Please,' Eira mumbled, 'please don't.'

'Oh, I love it when they beg,' another said, moving in to grab a handful of her flaming hair. Her pleas, and the protests from Cadeyrn and Corbin, as well as the taunting laughter from the four soldiers were all cut short by the booming voice of General Midas.

'What the HELL is going on here!?' he roared. His hand was on the hilt of his long sword, his favorite weapon. He was known to savor the look of death in the eyes of his victims and never spared them with the bullet. The four soldiers stood to attention and wolf killer stepped forward;

'General, we have captured the traitors and killed the wolves. We are entitled to the spoils of war.' General Midas considered the assembly before him. His eyes fixed upon Cadeyrn once he had taken in the rest.

'Well well, General Cadeyrn, we meet at last.' He said, smiling broadly, ignoring his own men. One of the soldiers removed Cadeyrn's gag so he could speak when spoken to.

'I know you,' Cadeyrn replied, glaring at Midas with contempt, 'I recommended your removal from office. You showed signs of mental instability.' Midas frowned deeply.

'I suppose they felt I was best for the job because of it then, for I now wear your badge and the job I've done far surpasses your own efforts.' He said proudly.

'What a wonderful resume for the Devil, Midas,' came Cadeyrn's reply, 'you think I *wanted* to do a good job? You think I *envy* you? Then you are truly insane.'

'YOU ARE THE INSANE ONE!' Midas cried out, spittle flying into Cadeyrn's face, 'we have been charged with god's duty! It is an honor!' Cadeyrn simply shook his head as Corbin had done. There would be no reasoning with these men.

Midas did not get a chance to retort. He was so distracted by the ex-general that he had not been watching the others. The leader, Corbin, the executioner, he had a strange look in his eyes. Midas had almost missed it but he caught it just in time. Corbin's eyes should have been on his wife, on his wing-man, on the soldiers that surrounded him, dashing about wildly for the exits, any of these would have passed for normal but no. He was staring straight over Midas' shoulder and into the darkness beyond. Not normal and almost guilty he looked when he realized his captor had been watching him. That split second of guilt was all he needed. Midas spun around just in time to grab the arm holding the knife destined for his throat, twist it around and have the assailant on his knees before him.

'What are you here for!' he barked at his men, 'you will let a traitor dog slay me?' He flung Raul to the ground and wolf killer ran to tie him up with the help of two of the wounded. 'Who is this worm?' Midas asked.

'His name is Raul. Worked as an assassin for us about six years ago. He disappeared and we heard nothing until we infiltrated headquarters,' broken arm informed his leader.

'So you knew he would be here!' Midas yelled out, 'and you did not think to capture him too?' He lurched forward and grabbed the man by his broken arm, twisting and squeezing, daring the soldier to cry out in pain or protest.

'We could not find him, General,' came the barely audible reply. Midas let go and broken arm fell to the floor in a heap, trying not to clutch at his heavily damaged limb. Everyone was quiet now; the soldiers kept silent for fear of their leader and the Rogues did not care to provoke him either. Now there truly was no hope. Time left to them would be determined by the mad general and how long he wished to toy with them.

'You are all fools,' he said, 'you run around trying to save the damned and in doing so damn yourselves. You think you can defeat us, but we are far too powerful, and soon we will have an army that will bring the black plague to you and the abominations you try to protect.' Corbin glanced at Cadeyrn but he looked just as confused as Corbin felt. A black plague? What new madness was this? 'Whilst you have been sitting here on this desert planet, we have found your headquarters and thus, found all the rats scampering behind our backs and we have all but exterminated you. Well done, "Rogues", what a fine job you have done.' He smiled sarcastically at the group and clapped his hands. He leaned in closer to Corbin and continued with his mockery, 'We have slain so many, watched so many worthless, blasphemous dogs die. It has been such an honor. Our god will be pleased.' His breath was foul and Corbin turned his head. His eyes fell on Eira. She was not weeping, nor did she look afraid. She was so brave. He felt powerless in the face of what was to come but his doomed thoughts were interrupted by the slow drawl of Raul.

He was smirking, enjoying the opportunity to laugh at death;

'Excuse me, I wouldn't wrestle with angels on the matter but doesn't it say something about free will and all that in your holy book?' Midas spun around to glare at the intrusion on his monologue. 'Just a thought,' Raul added, shrugging his shoulders.

'You mock our Religion?' Midas hissed through clenched teeth.

'No, I mock you,' Raul replied calmly, frowning as he spoke as if he thought that would be obvious, 'but perhaps your methods of religious interpretation could do with a comic review too.' Boldly said, striking at the heart of it and turning decades of undercover mayhem and murder into a simple fact. 'You cannot possibly believe that religion is a perfectly good excuse to be really crappy to everybody else. We are all ants and you just want to be an ant with a bigger stick.'

Midas had had enough and in one long stride he had Raul by the hair and his long sword was drawn.

'Do it,' the assassin hissed, 'put me out of my misery that I do not have to live another minute and see what my own people are stupid enough to believe.' The light tone was gone from his voice. His words were laced with pain and anger, guilt and grief the like of which Corbin recognized as a reflection of every sane human left to watch on, as their people in power raped the Worlds, and lied about its glory. Those were his last words. His teammates watched on, helpless, as steel met flesh and Raul's lifeless body fell to the floor with a thud, followed shortly by his head. Midas was breathing hard as he looked up to face the others.

'He lies,' he said, half to himself. He stared down at Raul for a while, no one spoke a word but Eira had finally cracked and Corbin had to listen to her soft sobs while he looked upon the staring eyes of his trusted friend. Too big a mouth but alas, the truth would out, and sometimes you had to die in order to say it. When he looked up again, Midas had an even more hateful gleam in his eyes if it were possible. The general said to his men with blazing eyes square on Corbin's, 'Take her outside and do as you will.'

*

'Is it star set now?' Arial asked softly, looking sideways at the malachi that led her to her fate.

'Why do you ask?' he said, frowning at her as though she irritated him. Arial stopped in her tracks and when he spun around to face her questioningly, more irritation sparking in his eyes, she stared fiercely back at him.

'Because my kind prays only when the sky darkens and all I have now is prayer!' She did not shout but her anger rose in her cheeks and Damek took a deep breath; walking towards the woman he had sworn to protect.

'You do not need your prayers Arial, I will keep you safe. Adonica has told me...'

'She has told you nothing!' Arial interrupted, 'I know more than you do, I have seen more than you have and these people mean me harm!'

'*These people?*' Damek asked, raising his eyebrow, 'these people are *my* people and Adonica is my sister, she would never lie to me.' Arial did not know how to win this battle. Her face sank into sadness and her shoulders slumped.

'You will not hear what I have to say for fear of what it means. Those things you feared will come true and it will be too late,' she said to the floor. Damek softened his stance and reached out to the queen. He drew her in close and held her but she hung limp in his arms and would not return the embrace. 'I am loath to give up but perhaps this is the path I must walk. I can do nothing.' And that was the truth of it for her. Alone on a hostile planet, her only chance of escape had withered away in vampire's library.

Damek stroked her fair hair and whispered softly in her ear. She heard not a word and resigned herself to be half dragged along by the hand to the great stone steps of the city main. She spared an upward glance to take in the enormity of the structure and wished she could race to the top and fly far away with Ronan. Damek gently jerked her hand forward and the spell was broken.

She climbed the stairs purposefully, one by one. She would not look broken and defeated to these people, she would be strong and she would not yield when the time came. Be focused, she told herself. Magic is a whisper of will made real. Make your will stronger!

Their footsteps echoed in the lonely, vast entrance hall and Arial stared on at the polished walls, gleaming with florescent light. It stung her eyes after the gentle luminosity of the outside. Glass cases lined the walls, filled with ancient scrolls. They walked together toward the steel and glass desk at the far end, and Damek greeted the seated woman.

'Brother Damek, how nice to see you.' It seemed that all the maidens were fair here and Arial could not tear her eyes away from their calm but dangerous beauty. She found herself thinking that if she were a man, she would gladly offer up her neck for this woman. 'Master Falkhar awaits.' Damek nodded curtly and led Arial through a sliding door.

More silence met them in the corridor, more bright light. Damek took her hand again for comfort but Arial felt only trepidation. They rounded a corner to find two more malachi, dressed similarly to Damek. He seemed happy to see them and walked over to embrace them each in turn. Necks were clasped and smiles were shared. A few whispered words were exchanged and once again, Arial felt lost and alone. Damek stepped back to her and said,

'This is Tariq and Quinn, they will escort you to where you need to be and I will go see Falkhar.' He sounded confident enough but when Arial's eyes pleaded silently with his he added, 'They are good friends, and you will be in the best of hands.' He gave her a gentle squeeze and kissed her lightly on the cheek. His lips lingered for longer than was necessary and when Arial opened her eyes, he was gone. Just the flash of his black cloak around the corner marked his departure.

The one called Tariq was tall and slender. He had sandy colored hair and kind eyes. His face was alert and intelligent and he smiled with his lips closed.

'I am told you are a Queen?' he asked, offering her an arm. She took it after a slight hesitation. Quinn was meaner looking. An older malachi with a scarred face and a solemn air about him. Tariq must have exchanged some kind of words with him because he tried to arrange his face into a more placid expression. 'We will be taking you to the chamber where you will have audience with our master. Do not be afraid,' Tariq said, after she made no attempt to converse with him.

'For it will do you no good,' Quinn added.

*

Damek found Falkhar waiting for him on the podium. It overlooked the great hall where all important matters took place. The last time it had been used was for the execution of a traitor, and the ill omen still seemed to hang over the massive dais.

Hands clasped neatly behind his back, Falkhar did not turn to look at Damek when he came to stand beside him.

'You seem different,' Falkhar said, as they both stood staring down.

'It has been a long journey.' Damek replied wearily. The walls gave off cold and no comfort for him. This was where he would learn the truth. Falkhar grinned.

'No, you seem…*different.*'

Damek had no reply.

Falkhar took a deep breath before saying,

'You know why we are here.'

It was more a question than a statement and Damek had the feeling that he was supposed to know the answer.

'I know it has nothing to do with relic hunting if that's what you mean.' Damek spoke in a measured tone, wary for a trap.

'Yes, you are correct.'

Damek turned to his master, his father, with a furrowed brow and a question in his eyes. Falkhar matched his gaze and asked him another question,

'Do you know why I sent you? Because you are gentler than the others and you would do the best job in placating a young and beautiful queen? Am I right?'

Damek frowned slightly.

'Yes, I did my job as you asked me to,' he said in a measured tone.

'I also knew that you are the smartest of them all which would be my biggest downfall had I not also known you are the most hopeful and trusting,' Falkhar elaborated.

This did not sound good to Damek.

'You mean to say you betrayed that trust?' he ventured.

'No, I merely used it to my advantage and to the advantage of our people.'

Damek was growing impatient…

'Are you trying to tell me I did well or are you trying to tell me that I am a fool?' he asked heatedly.

Falkhar chuckled and put his arm around his son's shoulders.

'Both,' Falkhar replied, 'but perhaps I am wrong. Perhaps you knew all along and were not fool enough to be honest with yourself.'

The cold seeped into Damek's stomach as he realized he had indeed done just that. He had been afraid and had lied for the sake of trust in his people and in his father. Hopeful that they were not the monsters everyone painted them as.

'Why did you make me do it if you knew I would have a problem with it then?' he asked angrily, shoving his father's hand from his shoulders and glaring at him.

'You needed to play your part Damek!' Falkhar said, raising his voice, 'you needed to learn how to sacrifice for the greater good!'

Damek's hands were shaking. He balled them into fists to stop the tremors and spoke again;

'You intend to harness the One Prophesy? To what end?'

Falkhar broke into a self-satisfied smile and said,

'We will be free again. I *need* to be free again.'

Damek could hardly believe his ears. He planned to use the darkness to obliterate the Worlds and he planned to use Arial to stop it short of his own people and their prey. The dull witted humans under Soren's leadership obviously had a similar plan, but they did not have the Arial. They were going to foolishly rely on the kuvuta. Damek wished them luck.

'You are more selfish than I imagined.' Damek hissed.

'*I'm* selfish?' Falkhar exclaimed, two long-nailed index fingers pointed at his chest, 'they have been selfish!' he yelled, now pointing at some faceless assailant, 'they have taken away our right to life, they run around slaughtering all those who oppose them and we may not even hunt! And they expect us to do nothing?' He shook his head. 'They are the selfish ones,' he finished.

'And you want the Worlds to burn with them,' Damek said, flat toned and incredulous.

'They had their part to play too,' Falkhar countered, waving his hand dismissively. He was back to staring at the pulpit again, intent and focused.

Damek looked on in awe at the beast he called father.

'So that is it then? Kill them all, all who would speak against you, just like the Men of Adam?' Falkhar sneered in response;

'They do not merely speak against me; they smother out my existence and call it fair play. This is not a time for the meek, son.' Now it was Damek's turn to shake his head. His father really meant to go through with this and the full weight of that realization did not dawn upon him until he heard the distant shriek. The cry of fear sprung from a woman's lips.

'You will do her harm!' Damek exclaimed, grabbing a fistful of Falkhar's robes, fear in his eyes.

He watched on as they brought her into the hall. She was unconscious and her frail form was now carried by one of his father's men, to the altar that was being dragged into the center of the room. They laid her out as others started to bring in the very items that he had collected unbeknownst. His mouth hung open and his fist still clutched his father's clothes.

'Love and trust are but tools for the wise,' Falkhar explained sympathetically as he watched Damek's face, watching the girl. 'Be glad instead that I saved you this pain. Love is not real, it is our destroyer.'

Falkhar was upset that his son had let it come to this and he was not sure why Damek had fallen so quickly to one so strange, but he knew that look when he saw it, had recognized it the moment he felt Damek behind him.

'No,' Damek breathed, 'love is real.' And he knew it to be so when he looked upon her face. His heart was tearing in two. He could not leave her to this fate not only because he saw the stupidity of his father's plan and the wasted life it would yield, but also because he had felt something so briefly, however small, and he would not let it die with her. 'It is real,' he repeated, 'and it has made me so too.' Falkhar grabbed him by the collar and shook him out of his trance.

'It is an evil witch that seduces our heart to feel *love* and then takes it away only to leave you a shell of your former self. Look at Kaleo!'

Damek remembered the day that his Shadow Brother had fallen in love with a woman not of their own, remembered the day when he confided in Damek of his plans to leave with her and shun the malachi ways. He remembered the day that Kaleo had returned, a broken man. Looking at him was like looking at a ghost. His mortal wife had died of disease and he had lived on, untouched by the fierce parasite that protected him. His soul had died with her and that was of whom Falkhar spoke now.

'Do not mistake love for pity,' Falkhar said, more gently now, as he released Damek and planted his feet back on the floor, 'we are powerful creatures and we see weakness everywhere. Perhaps you seek to protect that weakness in her, but I will not let your need to shelter the feeble destroy you, nor stand in the way of our greatness, our freedom. Remember what I let you feel the last time we were together...'

Falkhar held Damek by the chin and guided his head to the side. Damek's dull eyes grew life when they clapped upon a live human, sedated and slumped against the wall. 'He will awake soon, and you can feed,' Falkhar promised.

'How…?' Damek started but Falkhar placed a long finger over his lips to hush him.

'He is a gift from your sister, a bid for pardon.'

Damek could smell the blood in the living veins, feel it rushing through his ears as if it were his own. A mad and wild hunger tore through him and all thoughts of betrayal and anger, fear, and even love fled before the enslaved desire.

'No,' he managed faintly, 'we have been made weak.'

'Yes my son, we have been made weak, and soon we shall be strong again. We shall feed when we wish to feed, we shall hunt when we wish to hunt and we shall take back what is rightfully ours. I want you to imagine what it would feel like to not be starved for all eternity. We shall be weak no more.'

The powerful words sang through Damek's mind, feeding his need, and he could almost taste the sweet, fresh blood on his lips. His full strength would return with just one mouthful. The endless strength that he was built for possessing, but could only gain from the beating heart of a man. They had been holding him back; the Worlds had been suppressing his might and his right.

'Yes,' he whispered, gazing lovingly at the sleeping figure, 'we shall be weak no more.'

*

Ramroth felt soft grass and welcoming, hard ground beneath his feet long after he had smelled it. There was a promise of rain in the air too, mingled with the musky aroma of the wings that had borne him to this place. He was placed lightly on the surface of wherever he was, the sound of those beating wings all around him, loud and rhythmic and frightening. He waited for the sounds to fade away, time to appreciate only the sound, as he would probably never hear it again, before he opened his eyes at last.

The last thing he remembered seeing was Mary. The Tarayelo girl that had saved his life by giving her own. The soft whispers that were her last words would remain with him forever, the gentle touch of her small hand.

'She is better off where she is now,' Toireann said abruptly, one hand on Ramroth's numb shoulder, 'it is not natural for her to be here, she belongs with them.'

'She did not have to die,' Ramroth said, trying to keep the calm in his voice.

'She did not die, you fool,' Toireann said impatiently.

'You should have been better prepared!' Ramroth yelled, 'yet you stumbled in there blindly thinking only of yourself and not even! You would have died, and all to see an old man once more. I would have thought you had grown beyond that by now.' Ramroth's words were meant to cut deep but Toireann remained still in the face of Ramroth's torment and replied,

'Yes, I was there to see an old man one last time and that is what sets me apart from the rest of you. I think with my heart first. My immortality will never dull my senses. You were there also, what made you so much better prepared than I? You were going to use the girl, just as we did, but when I came, you hoped you could spare her your own selfishness.'

Ramroth looked away from the cleya and surveyed his surroundings having nothing to say in reply. They were standing in a meadow, rolling hills of jade colored grass lay in every direction. The sky was an angry smudge of steel-grey emptiness. Four tall pillars of crudely carved stone where pointing toward the heavens not five paces away, but there was naught else to be seen.

'We are very far from home my friend,' Toireann said gravely, 'this is Aoracea, the resting place of the last Tarayelo before their Umanok were sent beyond. Here, we give thanks and then we fly. You are too hard on yourself, Ramroth. You were not selfish; you were wise to use the resources available to you. She was there for a reason. I doubt any of those wraiths still draw breath! At least not in our world,' he said grimly. Ramroth blinked at Toireann a few times before saying,

'So you do still have liquid left?'

'Yes,' Toireann nodded, 'enough for us both and yes, I do mourn the young girl's *passing*. But we all have a purpose. Use her gift well.'

Ramroth said nothing. He sat down cross-legged on the grass in silence, thinking upon all he had come to learn, all that Ethron had told him.

'I am sorry,' he said at length to the young cleya, 'I have too much on my mind and I was wrong to speak harshly to you.' Toireann stood as still as ever.

'You all have too much on your minds and that is why nothing of import ever gets done.' Ramroth stared up at this insolent apprentice of Ethron's who had graced their presence for ten years now. He was fiery and dangerous and insulting to boot.

'What are you speaking of now?' Ramroth asked haughtily.

'Of what else is there to speak?' Toireann asked incredulously, 'did you not see the shadow just a minute ago? That is what we must think on, that is what we must do something about instead of sitting around in our grand halls, debating magic and the doings of other creatures.'

'What do you think I have been doing?' Ramroth said heatedly, 'I have literally lost the only chance we have, I think, and what do you intend us Adare' to do anyway?' Toireann was clearly fuming and when he answered he had his face almost pressed up against Ramroth's.

'You think? You think too much! Go and find out. If there is a way, go and find it! I will call the Elders and we will do anything and all that we can to aid the Worlds, as we should have been doing for the past three lifetimes. We are so much more powerful than we allow ourselves to be but it is time. Time to wield the only force that will stop the shadow!'

He was upright again, gesticulating like a lunatic. Ramroth could not help but smile. This lunatic of a cleya was indeed probably one of the best things to happen to the Adare' for a long time. He had the right idea of it, neither losing himself in his art nor his immortal life. Many a man had squandered both these gifts but this one wanted to use them wisely, even if he did not seem so wise all the time. He would not let him know it though…

'Very well, madman, I will go my way and you will go yours. Try to keep the Elders placated enough to remain seated until I come with news,' Ramroth conceded. He then stood up and made to clasp hands with the cleya.

'No, I will shake them out of their slumber and they will be kept on their toes until you arrive.' Toireann paused and then said, 'Then we will do something about it!' His finger was pointing toward the heavens and his eyes looked even wilder that before. Ramroth smiled again, despite everything.

'Very well, do as you please. You always do anyway,' he shrugged.

Toireann swept away Ramroth's hand and embraced him instead.

'Ethron spoke well of you,' he said, handing Ramroth a vial of amber liquid and a gem stone that was so perfectly cut and grown that it seemed almost invisible.

'Thank you,' Ramroth said as he doused his fingers with the potion and swallowed the gem, 'he...spoke of you too,' he winked. 'Give thanks for me as well, I must leave now if I am to succeed,' he said, nodding his head in the direction of the stones.

'I promise, but bring back good news, old man,' Toireann warned, arms folded across his chest as Ramroth spread his fingers to create a porthole, slipping through just in time to see Toireann kneeling at the pillars. A man of his word at least. The immortal who risked his life every day. Ramroth was not glad he was an Adare' but he was glad he was on their side.

Chapter 9

New magic

Mirian's hands were shaking a little. She still needed to learn how to control the power that surged through them, and the pre-magic hum that made her fingers unsteady. Like being able to hold a powerful snake steady, dense muscles coiling with the promised strike.

This was how Dunkan had trained her but this exercise had a lot more to do with mind, not strength.

'Close your eyes,' Dunkan instructed. He stood behind her, hands resting lightly on her shoulders, 'Breathe.'

She took a deep breath and reached out mentally for the water just beneath her fingertips, trying to feel the cool power of it and grasp it.

Mirian could feel the approaching footsteps even before the keenest of ears would be able to hear them. When she was performing magic, she was far more in tune to the elements. The way the torch was alive with warm fire moving through the air, the echoes in the stone of one foot placed before another. Her eyes flew open but her hands were still;

'Someone is coming.'

Dunkan swirled around her in his bearskin cloak, strode toward the mouth of the cave and shouted down the tunnel,

'Guards! I thought I told you to let no one pass!' He stood framed in the tunnel's dark mouth, waiting, but instead of the apologetic voice of one of his posted sentries, he was greeted by the smiling face of Kieran. The torchlight illuminated his features, making his grin lopsided and rearranging his usual good looks into something almost frightening.

'Come now, Dunkan. Surely you do not expect your loyal men to deny access to the Drow Prince.' Dunkan only sneered in return. He could not see very far into the darkness that swallowed the stone behind the circle of light but shadows cast darker marks than the people they belonged to and Dunkan could make out that Kieran was not alone. The advisor also had an inkling of who the girl was. Her stature and presence spoke volumes of her unseen face.

'Not only are you foolhardy enough to bring yourself down here, but you have the gall to bring an unwelcome guest. Have you turned spy little Prince? You openly mock our practices and even go so far as to humiliate your sister in public for her courage to take up such a challenging art.'

Kieran only smiled wider at this. He moved closer to Dunkan and draped a long arm across his shoulders. He ignored the stiffness he was presented with and used his words to placate the old man;

'My dear Dunkan, you of *all* people should understand the importance of public appearance. My father, he feels the need to move forward and leaves things behind as he charges gallantly ahead, and my mother, well, she just does not believe the fall is worth the risk.' He stroked Dunkan's wrinkled cheek at his last words and stared deeply into the man's eyes as if searching for something intangible beyond them.

'I had no idea that was how you felt,' Dunkan managed.

Kieran laughed.

'We all have our secret interests and this happens to be chief on my list.' He gestured at his sister, and the table she stood before, and the firelight arced over the dark room.

The invisible figure then stepped bravely forward. A young and pretty face made pale by the cold. She said,

'My father says that there is enough magic in every day and that we need not create more.' Vanora was not frightened, she was curious, and Dunkan picked up on it like a bloodhound. All former suspicions erased, he dropped to his knees before Altair's youngest child and spoke softly to her like she was a prized pupil;

'Child, magic cannot be created or destroyed and yes, there is enough of it. Enough for everybody! It is our privilege to be able to wield it, nay, our duty. It was placed here for *us*.'

Vanora furrowed her brow and Kieran smiled to himself.

'But father says people will only use it for evil because power conquers all good will.'

'No no,' Dunkan said gently, 'not all people are black-hearted but just as a sword is raised in the name of the corrupt, so can magic be. What if those who spoke for good had no sword?' Vanora's face opened a little and she replied,

'So we need to have magic too, for when evil raises arms against us. For defense,' she added.

'Yes, and no,' the old man said, standing up and holding Vanora's face in his hands, 'magic is so much more than just a weapon. It is life and it is death, it is everything and it is nothing.'

The princess looked confused so Dunkan said, 'I will show you.' That seemed to please her and Kieran led her to the stone benches that Dunkan motioned to.

He sat down beside her, close enough to give her slight frame some heat, and clasped her hand in his. She looked at him, excitement dancing in her eyes.

'Thank you for trusting me enough to come,' he whispered into her bejeweled ear.

'I enjoy spending time with you and I would never be able to see this if it were not for you.' Her words were sincere and Kieran was swept over with a tide of warmth. He knew that magic would soon be an outlawed practice among his people and knew that if he did not do something, it would be another lost opportunity. He had been jealous of his sister for a long while but had bided his time. He did not wish to seem overeager or weak, lest the clever Dunkan take advantage of him. There was place for no one's ambitions but his own, so he had waited until he could bring another. Someone who would steal Dunkan's attention and cloak his own intent. He needed to know the full potential of this magic and how it could be used to his advantage. He had chosen Vanora because of her obvious purity that would appeal to the teacher in Dunkan, and because she was to be his queen. They needed to be of one mind if they were to rule well together, he needed her on his side. This would be the experience that bound her to him and so he settled down to see how it would all play out.

'Brother,' came Mirian's crystal bell of a voice, 'pleased as I am that you came, please put out the fire. I am working with water tonight.'

As Kieran was doing as he was bid, Dunkan was moving around the cavern.

'She still needs to learn how to separate one element from another. The fire will draw her abilities since it is the more alluring of the two, but she needs to understand the water first,' he explained.

The Drows usually used natural fire to light their caverns as it gave warmth as well as illumination. Dunkan was busy with small lanterns along the walls, but they looked odd in their design, not at all like the holo-fire that Kieran was used to seeing on this new planet. It seemed even pseudo fire would draw her attention.

'Battery-operated light. Artificial. From the humans,' Dunkan muttered as the darkness was devoured by the eerie light. He resumed his position behind Mirian and she closed her eyes once more at the reassuring feel of his powerful hands on her shoulders. Kieran and Vanora drew a collective breath as they waited.

Mirian channeled her energy, focused her thoughts and reached out. Her hands were steady, her nerves taught, but Dunkan was patient and well pleased with her progress. He stepped back and away from her to allow her spirit all the space it needed as it attempted to touch the liquid. All was still.

Vanora felt the tingles down her arms and across her face before Kieran did. It felt like an invisible spider web had caught upon her exposed flesh, tiny strands that could not be located or cast off. She started to brush off the transparent assailant but Kieran took hold of her hands and whispered,

'It is just the magic unfolding. It will soon be gone.'

Vanora craned her neck to see better into the bowl of water that Mirian's hands hovered over. Small but steady ripples were flowing outward like tiny stones were continually being dropped into it. Suddenly, and quite majestically, small forms started to rise from the bowl. They were butterflies, Vanora saw. Water butterflies, dancing slowly around each other above the water they were born from.

Mirian's eyes squeezed tighter shut still, and her fingers flexed in the direction of her brother and the High Elf princess. The butterflies started to drift toward them, slowly flapping their wings and sailing across the room, like they were part of some strange ballet.

Vanora's delighted smile was enchanting and Kieran could not help but grin himself. Dunkan watched the young girl also, as she tried to reach out to touch one. Her fingertips brushed through one of the butterflies whilst another landed on her cheek.

Vanora had expected them to be cold, but the barely tangible touch was warm and not entirely unpleasant.

Kieran could feel his excitement building. He knew his sister had a flair for the dramatic and this was just a small taste of what she probably had in mind. The butterflies fell to the floor like small waterfalls and lay in puddles at their feet. Dunkan stepped forward again and whispered something inaudible into Mirian's ear without making physical contact with her. She drew in her fingers ever so slightly and the puddles began to merge into one as if they were alive. Once every drop had been collected, a perfect liquid sphere began to rise from the floor. It rotated slowly on its own axis toward Mirian. She was busy stretching her fingers again and as she did, the sphere grew in diameter until it was wafer thin and about three feet wide. It hung in the air over the bowl just before her face.

Vanora simply stared ahead at the beauty of it but Kieran was picking up the finer details. The watery orb was not reflecting anything but Mirian. No light, no other figures, not even the darkness was absorbed. Mirian's face was the only image portrayed upon its surface.

The orb began to vibrate and give off a low humming sound like a swarm of bees not far off. It grew and shrank in intervals with alarming speed and as suddenly as it had all began, the sphere abruptly dropped back into the bowl. Not a drop was spilled and Dunkan wore a smug expression.

'What is going to happen now?' Vanora asked, tearing her gaze away from the bowl to look imploringly at her escort.

'I do not know,' he whispered in return.

'Hush!' came the voice of Dunkan. They both sat quietly again, waiting.

Kieran was not sure if Vanora could feel it but he dared not ask. Pressure was building in the room, low vibrations emanating through the stone and the air around them. It was a massive power build-up and Kieran could barely contain himself. Just as he thought his ears would pop, it happened. A jet of water erupted from the bowl with a mighty force that blew his hair back. It gushed upward and arced out as it touched the ceiling, traveling across the roof above them sticking to the surface like wild fire. Vanora stifled a scream at the sheer sound of the gushing water and the cold air that stung her face. Kieran drew her to him and held her close. The water was flowing down the walls now and the only reminder they had to ground them to reality was the stone floor beneath their feet. The small bowl seemed to hold an endless supply of water because Kieran did not see any of it returning there. It simply seemed to be seeping into the space where wall met floor but kept coming in a smooth and steady tide. Vanora stood up on the bench and inched her hand forward to feel the water. As soon as her hand made contact, she pulled back. It was icy cold and painful to touch.

Mirian balled her hands into fists and opened her eyes. Kieran was taken aback a little. The water behind him and from all directions of the room was pulled toward her with such force that it had no time to find a way around the other people standing in the room, it simply rushed through their very beings with fingers of ice. Kieran was still holding Vanora and she now clutched him with a need he was unfamiliar with. She was shaking with cold and shock but he was too stunned himself to offer her words of solace. The water was pouring back into the bowl, volumes and volumes of it as if it had an endless chasm to occupy. That was not what held Kieran's gaze though, it was his sister. Her arms were parted and her fingers splayed, she was completely focused on the task at hand, an aura of visible power hung around her like a mirage and her eyes were the color of fresh coal. Black and staring, vividly terrifying.

The last of the water sucked into the vessel and as it did, Mirian fell to the floor in a crumpled heap. Kieran jumped up to help her but Dunkan was there first.

'She just needs rest,' he said, as he scooped her fragile and limp form into his arms. He took her to the nearest bench and laid her down. Her eyes fluttered vaguely but she was utterly spent.

'Will she be alright?' Vanora asked. Kieran looked to Dunkan who nodded solemnly.

'She is very tired; she just needs time to recover.'

'Is she hurt though?' Vanora's worries would not be calmed so easily. She looked down at Mirian, beads of sweat clung to her forehead and she was as pale as a ghost.

'No child, she is well trained.'

When Dunkan smiled, Vanora seemed to relax and she sat down next to Mirian, stroking the damp hair away from her face.

'That was truly remarkable,' said Kieran, 'how long has she been practicing?'

'Long enough,' Dunkan said darkly. He was replacing the battery lanterns for holo-flame ones and the natural light that swept over the cave was less unnerving, creating an atmosphere where they could all feel at ease.

'She is my only student and I dedicate all my time to her,' he continued, 'she will soon be capable of great things and if Altair speaks true, and I know he does, then the enemy will soon be upon us. I can only hope that she will be ready.'

'What good will one magician wielding a little bit of half learned magic be anyway?' Kieran asked, frowning.

'She is no mere magician, Kieran. They are people who shun their own and take up the art that is taught to them. Mirian is a Drow Sorceress and a powerful one at that. The magic she learns is unique to her and her alone. This war will be a long and hard fought one. No single battle will quell the wraiths so in time, she will be fit to face them.' Dunkan spoke slowly so that Kieran would stay on track. His mind had a knack for wondering but for once, he seemed interested enough to concentrate. 'As for what good magic will do, well, wraiths can *only* be killed by magic. This comes in the form of pure magic or drey fire as we know it, as well as steel forged with this same fire. The magic all other beings wield; tainted or channeled magic - can also be used. An arrow not dipped in charmed liquid will fly straight through them and a normal blade will pass without a mark, since they function on a different physical plane, but magic knows no boundaries and if we are to defeat them, we will need as much of it as we can get. All warriors will wield it on their blades and all creatures great and small capable of harnessing it will be needed.'

'Father is wrong then, about magic,' Vanora remarked.

Kieran smiled.

*

Everything seemed to happen in slow motion around him and yet it all happened too fast.

They were dragging Eira out of the Typhoon by her feet and her head thudded noisily against the steel stairs as they pulled her down and out into the cruel night, her screams of protest muffled by the bloodied cloth shoved half-way down her throat. She did not turn to look at anybody.

Raul's spilled blood was inching its way across the floor, closer to Corbin's feet with every slow second that ticked by, and he could move back no more. Corbin could hardly move or speak from the intensity of the pain and disbelief that flooded his system. They had never prepared them for anything like this. All the people running the wars always drilled into your head that defeat was not an option and so - never trained you for the pain. The realization that someone you had spent every waking hour with, someone who's life you had sworn to protect, lay dead at your feet. They never trained you how to deal with the fact that they would take a woman crew member and do with her as they pleased while you sit helpless. The blood and the screams - they never train you for that.

All Cadeyrn was doing was staring at Midas as if he were the very devil himself.

'I would ask you why you are doing this but I know there can be no explanation that I could accept for this madness.' His words were heavy and Corbin was surprised he could find a voice to speak to them with at all.

'I like watching you suffer,' Midas sneered. He sat down on his haunches in front of the two Rogues and cast a look over his shoulder at Nyx. The man had lost his mind. Blood was trickling down the inside of his confinement net from the effort of trying to claw his way through it. Midas turned now to the entrance of the ship and called out,

'Do not keep her gagged; I want them all to hear it.' The look in Nyx's eyes was un-paralleled. They had taken his sister from him once before, when they had ransacked their parent's house and slain them before his very eyes before separating him from Eira, sending him to the military and her to a Religion school. He had been sixteen at the time and it took him only four months of agonizing training to be able to take down ten of them, break free from the compound, cross two hundred miles of barren country with hounds on his heels, and rescue her. He had almost been too late. Their reformation programme was very efficient, especially with the young. They had fled to the safety of the Faith who had given them refuge and raised them.

Now they were taking her from him again and Corbin saw his own pain reflected in the madman's eyes as he screamed silently into the air and struggled like a caged animal.

Corbin could not find it within him to steel himself for what was to come. He had failed her, he had failed everyone. Shock blanketed him with its false sense of familiarity and he was numb. He knew that it would not last long though. All he could do was close his eyes and wait...wait for her screams to reach a zenith until he became her pain and humiliation and would probably die of a broken heart. A welcome release.

After a time though, he opened his eyes again. Perhaps he was dead already for no screams had come. Perhaps he had been spared the pain? Only the heavy breathing of general Midas greeted him. Nyx had stopped struggling and Cadeyrn was still staring the general down.

Midas was on his feet now, making toward the door to see what was keeping the men. He stood in the frame of the entrance, frozen. He strode toward the cockpit, wanting to turn on the outside lights. He unclipped his gun from its holster and Corbin wondered what would make him do such a thing. Before the general's finger could press down on the button, a great light came from outside the Typhoon. Fire, Corbin thought as he watched the scene from the open hatchway reveal itself in the dazzling flame. The soldiers lay slain upon the ground, the sand eating the blood from their severed limbs. Eira was not among the dead and Corbin saw the first glimmers of hope.

Midas roared his outrage and half flung himself at the door, pistol drawn and at the ready but what met him, made him drop it clanging to the ground as if some part of his subconscious knew that there was no way it could help him know. A massive, snake like head blocked the exit. Golden scales covered it, massive horns helmed it and two fierce eyes gave it sight. Large tendrils of blackened smoke curled from the creature's nostrils. The thing itself smelt like fire and Corbin could actually feel the heat coming from its body, smell the blood upon its breath.

'Dragons,' Cadeyrn whispered under his breath.

Midas' eyes grew wide with untold fear as the thing made guttural sounds that resonated throughout the body of metal they sat in. It came from deep within its chest and rattled Corbin's ribs with its strength.

'Activate your bio suit!' Cadeyrn cried. Corbin did not need to be told twice and he fumbled clumsily with his bound hands until he found the release mechanism on his belt. The technology was stolen from the elves. A perfectly fitted suit of armor that was fire, arrow and bulletproof in its strongest parts - the ones that covered your head and torso. It wrapped itself around you like some living thing but it was painful and unpleasant because it knitted itself into your flesh, and prolonged usage resulted in migraines and loss of limb mobility. They had not perfected the art as the elves had, but now it would have to do.

Corbin embraced the pain and even welcomed it as he saw what Midas had to endure. He was assaulted by fire so hot, that it melted the very skin off his body, and boiled the red rivers of blood that ran from his veins. His face was a contorted mask of horror. He uttered not one sound.

Corbin was burning up inside his suit though too; he could feel the blisters forming, the pain cleaving his thoughts away. He could feel the heat as if he wore no armor but soon it was all over. Cold and dark once more.

*

'Cahan, withdraw!' Zach commanded. The rider pulled back on the reins and his drey withdrew its bulky head from the Typhoon.

'Kai, go inside with Eiros and bring out anything alive.' Zach smirked at his own words and they all chuckled along. Cahan's drey was fierce; the biggest in the hold and no one survived his fire.

Kai stepped inside with his companion. The steel they walked on was hot but all it did was warm their feet through their dragon hide boots.

'Karo,' Zach called out, and the water drey lowered her head from outside and blew cool air into the vessel. The black smoke cleared and it was less hot, easier to breathe and to see. Kai stepped forward and over the melted heaps that had once been men.

'We have three dead,' he called out before scanning the rest of the small ship. A glowing blue net was suspended in the air at the far end. Kai walked toward it and saw a man huddled in the corner. His eyes were closed and he was rocking back and forth like a child, clutching stubs of bleeding fingers and singing something to himself. Kai could not hear the words, could only see his cracked lips moving in song.... or perhaps prayer? 'The device must have protected him,' Kai said as Eiros moved to his side to stare at the man. 'He is also human, probably one of the captured. Can you shut this down?' he asked Eiros, placing his hands on the laser lines, cool to the touch as if Abiro's fire had never been there.

'I can try,' the rider replied and hunkered down to find a switch or something of the same kind. The only one in the hold with any sort of hands-on technological experience.

Kai turned and looked around some more. Melted plastic, sizzling pieces of equipment and two men lying side by side on the floor. They looked like reptiles in their strange armor. Kai smiled as he saw vestiges of elvin technology wielded by inept human hands and minds.

'I wonder if they survived?' he asked Eiros as he stared down at the immobile figures.

'In any event, we will need our swords to cut through that cage, and probably the armor too,' Eiros replied, getting up and going outside to retrieve his blade.

Kai bent down to look at the men more closely. Only their eyes were visible through the visors and they were closed, but the eyelids of one moved, the smaller built of the two. They flickered but stayed sealed. He cocked his head to one side to hear if there was anything to be heard and realized that he was speaking. Muttering the same thing over and over. Eira. A name? He followed Eiros outside and went over to the woman they had saved.

She lay curled up in a fetal position and had refused any attempts to help her or give her water. Lok was watching her.

'Eira?' Kai asked. She looked up. The first response they had had from her. 'So that is your name. We have found three men inside. They bear the same symbol as you do on their breastplates. Do we save them?' Her eyes grew wide with fear and she said in a voice as small as the whisper of the grasses;

'Yes, they are good men.'

Kai nodded at Lok.

'Miko,' Lok called and the drey moved toward the woman, lying down beside her and folding her gently into her wings. Eira made no protest.

'What happened here?' Kai asked, once he had seen her relax in the embrace of Lok's drey. No reply.

Kai stood up and walked toward Zach, leaving Lok alone with her so that he might get a response from her. The other riders were busy carrying out the three surviving humans from the ship. Strong magical blades had cut through any attempt the humans had made to keep anyone out. The one they had found in the cage had the same look of the woman, Eira. He groaned out load as they placed him on the sand, tears stained his face and he still clutched his badly damaged fingers.

'Seems he wished to claw himself out,' Eiros remarked, holding Nyx's fingers up for inspection.

'Nyx!' Eira cried, leaping from the drey and toward her brother. His eyes flew open at the sound of her voice and as the two embraced, words were lost to them and they just sat there, saying each other's names, holding on to one another as if they would never let go again.

Zach smiled; it was a good thing to save a life, an even better thing to give it back.

'What of the others?' he asked, 'how badly are they burnt?' The two armored men had been stripped and covered with special blankets woven of wild herbs and drey saliva. Delano peeled back a part of the covering and replied,

'Not too badly. They will make it.'

Zach grunted. He was not happy that they had gone ahead and made a furnace of the ship and injured two innocent men, but he had not been willing to take any chances at that stage. Nevertheless, only those he meant dead had died and he smiled in satisfaction as his riders heaped the bodies up. The count was at thirteen and all had been taken with ease, too busy reveling in victory and enjoying the spoils.

Once Eira had finished clinging on to Nyx, she crawled over to her husband. He was out cold and wounded, but when she placed her hand upon his cheek, he weakly opened his eyes before succumbing to the body's natural sleep of healing. Cadeyrn seemed okay too and Eira could hardly believe their good luck.

'There was another,' she said, looking up into the wild faces of the warriors, 'though he was already dead.'

The leader shook his head.

'These were all we found. These three men and three wolves further down. I am sorry,' he added. Eira shook her head;

'No, don't be sorry. You did all you could.'

Zach bent down and took her hands in his, pulling her to her feet. He stood two heads taller than her and she was no short woman. His hair was tangled and woven with clay pieces. His beard was unkempt and his face was hardened from the light of day and wind. He had kind eyes though, gentle for one so large and strong. Scaly armor covered his torso and moved with his body and the dragons that surrounded her were an even greater sight to behold.

The others were busy lighting fires around the dead wolves and muttering what she guessed were prayers beneath their breaths.

'We know what a creature means to a man,' Zach said, following her gaze, 'those men we will leave for the hungry.' He gestured to the pile of blue-cloaked humans in the sand. 'My name is Zach, come, let us sit.'

He walked Eira over to one of the fires that had been lit and offered her water from a flask, which she now gladly accepted. The liquid ran down her parched throat and seemed to wash her muffled screams away with its cool fingers. Zach was staring into the dancing flames now and Eira was unsure of what to say, but he spoke up first and she contented herself just listening, knowing that those she loved were being cared for and that she was safe.

'I am the Captain of Her Majesty's Royal Guard. Our queen was taken from us and now we are sent on a mission to find the only one who can help us.'

'Help get her back?' Eira asked.

'In part perhaps...'

'What's the other part?' Eira was saddened by his tone and wary of what the answer to her question might be.

'Something far more important. A black plague threatens the safety of every living thing in the Worlds. They destroyed our home planet and we need to find a great warrior to help save the people from the shadow.'

'I am so sorry about your home,' Eira said quietly. When Zach made no reply she decided to change the subject, 'I thought you cut the hands off the men you defeat, so the gods may not reach out and take them to the afterlife from the grave. Those are the legends I have heard,' she added. Zach frowned.

'That is not for us to decide, who gets taken and who gets left behind. No man is fit to judge another to such a fate. We leave such things to the gods,' he smiled.

One of Zach's men, the one they called Kai, came to fetch him. 'Please excuse me,' he said, following his rider into the sands.

Eira got up and went to be with Nyx, Corbin and Cadeyrn. She began helping the two men already caring for them. She bandaged her brother's fingers after one of the dragon men had smeared a strong smelling paste on them and helped re-apply the saliva to Cadeyrn and Corbin's bindings as they needed to stay wet. All the while she wondered about what Zach had said, about the black plague. Was this just a tribal squabble blown out of proportion in simple minds or was it as he said it was; a universal threat? And if so, what was it? Midas had said something about a plague too and she shuddered to think what the Religion had in their clutches that could destroy entire planets.

Zach came back to her when he was done with his men and said,

'Your ship has been badly damaged by the fire. You will have to send for help or come with us.' Eira could not judge by his tone how pleased he was with this news.

'I'm not sure if there is anyone left to send for,' she replied cautiously. Zach was quiet for a moment, his fingers stroking his bearded jaw line.

'How well do you fight?' he asked.

'We are Rogue soldiers. We have been trained by the Faith and have been in the field for many years. We can fight. We can build. We can scout.'

'Very well,' the captain said, 'you will come with us.' Eira was dumbfounded for a while but could ask Zach no questions for he had already stalked off.

One of the men helping her with the bindings grinned. He was a handsome man, younger than Zach.

'Delano,' he said in answer to her open stare, and she assumed this was his name. 'Do not worry. These men will be up and healed in a few hours and you will get to ride a dragon.' He winked and Eira grinned broadly in reply.

She looked down at Corbin. He had third degree burns all over his body but he was healing before her very eyes. He looked better now than he had a few minutes ago.

'Thank you,' she said at last.

'It is good training for the battles that lie ahead.' Delano had an easy manner about him and Eira felt welcome around him.

'You should be thanking me, brother!' Cahan roared, 'you were about to be food for the worms if I had not saved your hide!' The two were laughing now and the others had gathered round to tell of their victory over the human soldiers.

'One cannot be too proud of taking an unarmed life, but the one who deemed it fit to urinate on the dead dogs...I came from the front and stopped his stream with my blade. The look on his face will keep me laughing long into the night.'

Eira did not know whether to be appalled or thrilled. The ones who had taken her outside had been slaughtered first and the others, stalking the perimeter, had been made fast work of. The dragon men seemed very pleased with their kills. She watched as they displayed their sword skills against one another for her entertainment. Cahan slapped Lok on the arse with the side of his blade and everyone roared with laughter as he rolled in the dust, rubbing his backside. Eira smiled to herself and said a prayer then, to give thanks that they had been saved when all had seemed lost. Warriors had dropped from the very skies and rescued them from certain death. She gave thanks for a miracle.

*

The blood swept through his veins like a river of mercy. It filled every inch of his longing and his essence screamed out with pure elation, as power coursed back into his body. Power Damek had not felt for a hundred years. The true power of the parasite in his own blood. His fangs sunk deeper into the young man's neck as he stroked his hair with the touch of a lover.

He held the body close to him, long after it was drained, savoring the warmth of the man he held. He listened to the heartbeat ebb as his grew stronger. It thumped in his ears like a war drum and made him weep. He placed the body on the floor at his knees and licked the last drops of precious blood from his engorged lips. He was aware of every being within a twenty-mile radius; their feelings, their scent and their beating hearts. Most beat slowly. The hearts of malachi denied the true blood. Only two others beat with the same velocity and intensity of his. One belonged to the drey queen down below. The other belonged to Kaleo. Damek was puzzled by this but waited patiently for his Shadow Brother to come to him.

'Should I give you time to calm down?' Kaleo asked. He was on the other side of the door and down the passageway but Damek could hear him whispering the question inside his mind as if he stood beside him. He did not answer.

He stood up, flexing his rejuvenated muscles and savoring the taste of a fresh meal. He walked over to the ledge. Falkhar had asked him not to watch. To go out and enjoy his renewed energy. To find a warm woman to spend a few hours with. To be safe in the knowledge that soon, all would be right and Damek could have this whenever he wanted.

He did not need to look over to see what was happening. He could see it from his angle as clear as if he were standing right next to them. He moved his essence closer whilst arching his neck and staring upward at the ceiling. He was so close he could smell the beads of sweat that ran down Arial's face, taste the salt of her tears in the air. His heart was torn in two. He could not bear to see her like this but could not bear to live the life he had been forced to live. Was this the only way? Her eyes were wide and seemed to be staring right at him. Silent pleas bore through him from that foreign face he had come to cherish.

Do not worry dear brother; she will come to no real harm. Falkhar wishes only to ask something of her. It is for the good of us all. Appease her, all will be well.

Ask for her soul or take it? Damek thought angrily. This is not the way he had wanted it. Placated by his sister, bribed with blood by his father. How strong his need was that he was willing to let Falkhar go through with this, willing to lie to himself and to her about the truth. No, he could not throw away the chance to be free just to give a mortal back to the random chaos of life that it may be taken in another way and to no purpose. Her soul would go to the liberation of an entire race. If she knew how it felt to live a half-life, then she would give it gladly.

'Do you really feel that you live a half-life?' A hand was on his shoulder now. Kaleo. 'One free race does not tip the scales of all those who will perish.' Again, Damek made no attempt to reply. 'They all betrayed you, all except for her.'

'How is it you come to know so much?' Damek asked angrily, sarcastically.

'I live a whole life. You dwell on what you fail to achieve rather than what is already yours.'

Damek was busy listening to the breathing of the woman below. Small gasps of fear and anxiety. A tear fell to the floor and echoed in his heart.

'You are a shell of what you once were. You have forgotten of what you speak. We have all gone too long without true blood.' Damek whispered in reply to Kaleo's accusations.

'I know this. I wish to tell the Worlds that I care for the lives I took no more than a lion cares for an antelope but I do not let *it* rule me.' Damek seemed to consider this for a while before asking,

'Is her life worth the one feed I was sold to?' He already knew the answer Kaelo was going to give him, and he yelled out in frustration, 'but this is not just for me! This is for the good of our people! And it is not just this feed I was sold to, it is the promise of thousands more...' he trailed off. Kaleo was silent for a moment before he replied,

'Our people will be fighting the good fight for many years to come, with or without the help of the drey queen. Have no fear of that. This woman, however, has a greater part to play than just us.'

'So challenge Falkhar to play my part in giving deliverance unto the Worlds?' Damek did not seem convinced.

'Deliverance unto yourself too,' Kaelo said quietly. Damek whirled around to face his companion;

'Do not speak to me of such things!' he hissed, 'I have no part to play in this!' Kaleo shook his head and Damek could hear the words once more;

Watch over her night stalker and do not fail. She is precious to us all.

'No, I do not have to do this,' he said, teeth clenched and hands over his ears.

Kaleo anticipated the attack but gave in to it. Damek launched himself at his Shadow Brother, leaping as a cat does with claws out, and balanced as keen as a midnight lynx. As soon as his feet had left the stone floor, his fingers were around Kaleo's neck. His eyes were blazing with all the fear and guilt that was locked inside his heart and it pained Kaleo to see him so.

Kaleo's hands were clenched around Damek's wrists but he made no effort to release the maddened creature's grip on him. He simply stared back into the blackened pools of his adrenaline-infused eyes.

Damek's anger abated as he became aware of what he was doing and he slowly loosened his hold. He let his arms hang limply at his side whilst Kaleo massaged his bruised muscles. He would forgive Damek, for if he had truly meant harm, then Kaleo's neck would have been snapped the instant he gripped it. A mere bruising was but a tenth of what Kaleo knew Damek must be feeling.

Damek turned back toward the altar where Arial lay. Falkhar was busy with the rites and the mirror had been raised. His knuckles turned white on the banister as he endured her silent wish to die well.

'I know not what is right and what is real any longer,' he cursed, his own tears joining Arial's on the floor below, 'I am sorry, I do you wrong.'

'The first time I laid eyes upon Isha, I knew all I needed to know. Let no man tell you that what I did destroyed me. It gave me life. It gave me real life. You can argue *anything* either way! So how is anything ever right? Do what you need to do, for no one will ever do it for you.'

Damek felt weak at the knees. His head swam with his recent kill and the love he bore the lady down below. Images of the night that he had saved her came flooding back to him. He could still feel the heat from the wazimu, the weight of Arial in his arms. This image was marred by Falkhar's face, calculating eyes, hypnotic words and empty promises. Yet, he had always been there for Damek and offered him, as well as every other, what they all yearned for, what any creature yearns for - freedom. But did she not offer him the very same?

'What will it be old friend?' Kaleo was still standing behind him, every muscle in his body relaxed and a lazy smile on his face.

'It seems you already know what I will do.' Damek smiled. Kaleo shrugged and returned the smile;

'Sometimes you need a little push.'

Damek turned to look his Shadow Brother in the eyes and for the first time since Kaleo had lost Isha, Damek saw them with his malachi eyes. He saw no emptiness, no loss of soul. He saw only the great knowledge of sorrow and loss. The only emotions that are able to give hope, joy and peace; for without them, everything was nothing.

'What did it feel like...loving?' Damek asked, averting his gaze. Kaleo smiled again and took him by the hand;

'Let me give you that push and you will know.'

*

Ramroth's aged legs could not keep up with his need. He squeezed his eyes tightly shut and when he opened them, he was seeing the elemental plane, so that he could see if he was too late. The ground he ran across showed its true age now, the trees around him sang and breathed with life. And when he looked up at the house he saw them; the wazimu were busy with their cleansing rights and Ramroth began to weep as he realized how little work they would have to do for the great woman who had died.

Every time a mortal soul passed through the Worlds, marks were left upon the elements they came into contact with most. The stone in their houses, the paths they walked and the greenery they tended. Pieces of their souls were left imprinted upon these things and the wazimu came after to ensure that no smear of evil or harm had been left behind. What they found, they cleaned for fear of contamination.

Long ago, the humans had been left unchecked on their blue planet in the far corner of the Worlds and malevolent traces had been left to fester like wounds, until they became tangible to the living. Mirkisha's pure spirit had left only the marks of sorrow and loneliness that pulled painfully at Ramroth's heart and was reflected in the faces of the guardians as they worked.

He reached her front door, seeing once more with mortal eyes, for he could look no longer upon the pain she had endured in her last moments. He flung the door open and stood framed in the doorway, puffing and panting from his efforts, tears streaming down his old face as he looked upon his queen. His gaze next fell upon the one who was standing over her body. Ramroth asked no questions nor looked more than once.

Lucio could just make out the translucent fingers reach out in a flat-handed spread as they came rushing toward him mercilessly. He was pinned against the far wall by invisible forces but said not a word in protest against the wizard.

Ramroth fell beside the body of Mirkisha and his face shone with tears as he held her hand with all the care and devotion of a lover while with the other, he held the man who had surely had a hand in this, flat and firm against the wall.

Mirkisha had written to him only once, forbidding him to seek her out but telling him where she was and that she was safe. She had repeated her plea for him to watch over her first born, to see her safely into womanhood and to keep all his other promises. As he had read the letter over and over again, an image of her as she had been in her youth became fixed in his mind, but time had ravaged her as much as her ordeal. He lowered his head until it touched hers and he sighed heavily. Not only had he lost her, he had also lost her child and lost his faith somewhere along the way.

Whilst he sat there, feeling like eternity would trap him in that death embrace, he felt warmth enfold his outspread fingers. It felt as if someone was holding his hand. He snapped his head up, ready for a fight, wondering how the assailant had escaped. The man was still pinned up against the wall, still as a statue, eyes closed and head bowed.

'What magic is this?' Ramroth breathed. The man simply smiled in reply.

Ramroth slowly let go of him and drew a finger across the palm of his hand, staring in disbelief while the feeling grew stronger as the man walked closer. Five paces away and the heat spread, like a body was pressed against him in an embrace. Ramroth was on his knees, looking up at this stranger in awe.

Lucio drew level with the broken wizard and laid a hand upon his shoulder. Ramroth was silent with wonder as the heat squeezed him and enfolded itself around him.

'You must be Ramroth.'

'And you must be Lucio. She spoke of you in her letter to me,' Ramroth replied. Lucio inclined his head and smiled sadly. Ramroth sighed again and wiped the tears from his face. Then he laughed and stood up. 'I cry so much these days and seem to do little else! She said you are a man of great faith and that she trusted you. I, however, cannot even be trusted to do what I swore to do – keep her daughter safe...'

Lucio looked up sharply.

'Does she still live?'

Ramroth raised his eyebrows.

'How much do you know?' he asked.

'We will bury her first, in her beloved garden, and then we will talk.'

Ramroth nodded his head in assent. They set to work folding her body neatly in a white linen sheet. Ramroth walked outside to create the grave where she would lie forever. He moved the ground with his hands. He could have swept it away with a simple gesture and a single thought but he grabbed a shovel instead, toiling like any other. He felt he owed her that at least, to put his sweat into one last deed for her.

He thought back upon the day he had stolen into the High Council Records House with the help of Ethron, to destroy the council's copy of the Decree, burn Valador's birth papers, and retrace all evidence of their marriage. Mirkisha had been so afraid of something. She had refused to tell Ramroth why she had had Valador banished from his home, why she had relinquished the crown and fled her family.

"The darkness is growing" was all she had said.

He tossed the last of the dirt over his aching shoulder and leant heavily on the spade, his head well below the surface of the ground. What could have caused her to fear for the Worlds so much as to commit sedition and abandon all she loved?

'You make fast work of such a heavy task,' Lucio remarked from above him. He was smiling down at Ramroth's handy work. 'I have cleaned the house inside as best I can. I will bring her out now.' His face disappeared and Ramroth was left alone once more.

'Would that I had made such fast work of finding Arial and solving this riddle,' he said to no one in particular. Ramroth knew only that the document that Mirkisha had asked him to destroy was about some great weapon. The Blood Angels. Something about *immortality.* That was all that was left after Ethron had snatched the paper and set fire to it. Ethron had asked no questions and had even seemed eager to help Ramroth with his strange and forbidden task. Why would Mirkisha wish the knowledge of such a powerful weapon erased? And why would she flee, send Valador away...perhaps Valador had something to do with the documents. That made enough sense since his banishment coincided with the theft. Did she send him away to keep the secret even safer? Perhaps that was it. Send him to a place where no man could be found nor reached; the dark recesses of a broken heart. Did she know something that no one else did?

He knew that the council was corrupt. He had learnt as much from the High Elves. Whispers of shadows had confirmed themselves when he and Arial had been captured and Arial had spoken of this Soren. The kuvuta were back, that much was undeniable, and the human imposter had something to do with it. The most important question of all still rang in his mind and it was Ethron's voice that kept fighting for confirmation. *"The fire maiden holds the key".*

The star beat down upon his back and his robe clung to his skin like a wet rag. His head ached with unanswered questions and he longed to speak to Mirkisha one last time. He had watched her grow from a happy child to a sad woman and he wished only to make it all right.

The two of them lowered her body down into its final resting place and filled the grave in. Ramroth could feel the wazimu watching them work for a while before they left the scene. It was an eerie feeling. Lucio said a short prayer and held on to Ramroth's hand when he was done. Eyes closed and head bowed once more. Ramroth was not a pious man but he did believe. He had no choice. He had seen too much. They were both silent for a long while, each burdened with their own grief.

Ramroth thought better of breaking the silence and went down on one knee instead. He dug deep inside his pockets and found what he was looking for. He pulled out a seed the size of his thumbnail and placed it an inch deep into the freshly turned soil. The star had almost set now, casting a pink glow across the horizon, topped with deep, velvet blue. He spread his hands over the seed and recited the incantation for growth.

As Lucio watched, a tree began to take form before his very eyes, as if the seasons had been sped up a hundred fold. From sapling to small oak it grew in less than a minute.

'It is for her child, so that she may know where to find her mother and know that in her death, she must now find strength to live on. It is custom.'

'Arial thinks her mother is already dead does she not?' Lucio asked softly.

'She will have to endure the death of a mother twice in one life time.' Ramroth's words were heavy. He would have to find Arial and when he did, he would have to speak only the truth to her. It would be hard.

'Plant another,' Lucio said.

'Why?' came Ramroth's reply.

'One child, one tree, right?' Lucio said, eyes staring dead ahead.

'Right.'

'Wrong. Mirkisha had two children.' Now he looked down at the wizard who was still kneeling in the dirt. He held two fingers up so that Ramroth could not claim he had not heard properly. His eyes showed confusion in the fading light but there was no time. 'He has even been kind enough to send an emissary,' he added.

Ramroth merely thought it was the death beneath him that he could smell but at Lucio's words it became clear that the stench was far fouler than that of a day-old corpse. He did not have to look up to know that a wraith approached. He got to his feet quickly;

'I do not understand!'

'No time now friend.' Lucio smiled as if he were not afraid and that bolstered Ramroth a little. His face set, he cast a protective but temporary spell around the grave and pulled out his short staff. 'Do you plan to beat death over the head with that?' Lucio asked, laughter sparkling in his eyes.

'A religious man with a sense of humor?' Ramroth raised an eyebrow.

'No, a man of faith,' he replied, holding his finger up in a mock-stern gesture.

'Brace yourself,' came Ramroth's reply.

They could hear the hiss of the wraith coming from deep within its chest, the hiss that would be for most, the last thing they would hear, but Ramroth was prepared as always and he slammed the end of his staff into the ground with such force that the wraith paused.

He stared at the pair with dark and calculating eyes and a blank expression. When nothing happened he started to advance again.

The staff quivered in the wizard's hand but Lucio had no idea of what was to happen and he wondered if they would make it out of this fix alive.

Ramroth kept his grip steady even though the power he held fast threatened to throw the staff clean out of his hands. He had to wait till the very last second, channel every ounce of essence he could find in the ground and focus it upon the kuvuta.

It happened in slow motion for Lucio. Like it was in the moments before a car accident. Time slowed and built up, every molecule in the air advancing toward the coming impact with excruciating sluggishness until finally, they met, and the world exploded with the effort. He heard Ramroth shouting at him to get down from some place that sounded far away to his ears. The mage had lifted his staff and brought it up so that the tip was raised way above his head. Lucio took in the expression on his face, the contortion of complete concentration. Then his eyes were drawn to the tip of the staff.

What Lucio at first believed to be wisps of smoke was growing in magnitude. It soon became a small dark cloud, like a swarm of bees overhead. The swarm grew and emanated a strange sound, like that of millions of tiny teeth gnashing against each other in millions of tiny mouths. It started to move toward the wraith, a singular movement at the slightest flick of the wizard's wrist. It flew straight over Lucio's head and all other sounds were drowned out by the grinding and snapping.

'Not it...they,' Lucio breathed as one of the tiny figures flew low and broke away from the throng. It flew past his face, sticking out its little tongue in an ironically funny gesture, before it made a beeline for the target.

The kuvuta had little time to react as they descended upon him. He was half hidden by the cloud in mere seconds, falling to his knees in pain Lucio could only guess at. He wondered why the creature did not scream but the swarm shifted momentarily and his face was exposed. Half the flesh had already been eaten away and strips of dangling meat hung off his cheek bones only to be cleared away as he watched. The wraith's mouth was open in a silent scream. They were inside his mouth, down his throat; the kuvuta would perish in silence. He fell to the floor, barely able to support himself any longer. The creatures made quick work of him, seemed to drag him into the ground from whence they came.

As fast as it all started, it was over, the noise had stopped and the only sound left was that of the wizard's heavy breathing. Lucio looked up at him with an odd look of surprise on his features.

'Paido,' Ramroth explained, 'they live underground and feed off all evil buried there. The wazimu use them for their cleansing rituals but I learnt how to summon them some years ago. Quite tricky and it does not always work.' His smile was a little sheepish but Lucio had swept him into an embrace;

'Thank you,' he said, 'we live to see another day because of you and your magic bugs,' he laughed.

'There are not enough willing paido in the Worlds to help us against this shadow,' Ramroth countered, 'we must find somewhere safe. I need to call in on the Adare', I need to find Queen Arial who is the only hope the Worlds have left, if I am not mistaken, and I doubt I am. And we need to talk.' He looked meaningfully at the priest. Lucio nodded his head.

'Come,' he said.

*

Soren was standing in the decimated doorway. Blood stains marked the sentry posts but no bodies had been found. The frame of the cell's entrance still glowed faintly green from the magic that had destroyed it. No fragments could be found from the door either.

Soren had been told by the human detective that Chaos magic took with what it destroyed and warped the essence to build on itself, and that it was a dangerous and volatile kind of sorcery.

'Aptly named then,' Soren had hissed sarcastically.

Ethron was dead. The battle had finally been won between mind and body and Soren was furious. 'They would not have come all this fucking way to have a last visit! They wiped out half the fucking guard!' He had roared when his team had suggested that he had nothing to fear. 'They came here to get the information we could not…that YOU could not!'

His mood was foul as he stalked around the body of the dead High Adare'. 'Clean this shit up and bring me my Seers. I want this woman found, I want the people responsible found and I want those in charge of guarding Ethron executed immediately!' People scurried from him as if he was the plague. Each eager to keep their lives, let alone their jobs. No one brave enough to point out that those guarding him were already dead.

When he was alone, he sighed deeply. Sirena would be very disappointed. He had lost the girl, the drey, both the wizards and he still didn't know what was afoot. There was movement and scheming just beneath a surface he could not scratch and it was driving him insane.

He walked over to the chair and gripped his hands against the armrest. He felt his anger suffuse within him and excite the wraith inside. That part of him surged forward, up and through him, fed by his rage. It burst forth out of his skin, a dark cloud of kuvuta essence that pulled itself toward the dead Ethron, clawing at his staring face and screaming an echo of Soren's frustration. It was drawn back in the moment he turned around to face his father.

Lord Nagesh, dark and menacing as ever. Great leader of the kuvuta.

'The one who bore you is dead,' he said in a voice as cold as the stone that surrounded them. Soren flinched;

'Yes, I know,' he replied.

'You are beginning to lose sight of your task,' his father droned, 'we are invincible, we have destroyed the planet of origin in your prophesies and there is no army that can face us.'

'The planet you *believe* to be the origin,' Soren corrected him, 'you know not for sure, you only hope. I believe I have the name for it, this weapon, if it be real; Blood Angels. It was the only thing this madman would say.' He kicked Ethron hard on the leg and the old man slumped lower in his chains and straps. 'I need to trace down these people and find out for sure before we make our move. The girl could mean something…the wizards could be up to something.'

'She is your sister.' Soren looked up, shocked that his father had known. 'I believe Mirkisha saved her when she knew she could not stave me off.' Soren stormed up to Lord Nagesh, shaking with fury;

'Yes, thank you! This much I know! My point is proven then – why go to such lengths to protect her daughter if she was not worth something! The woman spoke of some weapon the council had created even when her own planet and army with it had been destroyed!'

Nagesh's face was impassive as he looked on at Soren's outburst, watched his wraith essence fighting for surface control.

'We have destroyed her army. She can do nothing and she is of no importance. You will leave this place to me, go back to the humans and initiate the battle plan.' Nagesh's tone was flat and unwavering. He saw only in two dimensions, life and death. Nothing in between mattered to him or his people. He wanted his war and he wanted it now. Soren was left unsatisfied.

'Why would my mother try to hide her from us? She would tell me nothing of her. Why would someone see fit to free her from us? She must mean something! We are missing a piece here, I can feel it…' Nagesh grabbed his son by his neck and the babbling stopped.

'Meaning is nothing, pieces are nothing. We are everything and everything else is dust.' He let go and stalked out the door.

Soren always felt a little queasy after his father touched him, tainted somehow, like the touch of death had spared him and it was wrong, it defied the laws of the Worlds. For a moment he imagined how his mother must have felt and he shuddered. The moment passed and was replaced by the weight of all the questions that he had no answers for.

Someone was hurrying down the corridor toward him, he could feel it. He turned to face the doorway and one of the chambermaids appeared. She looked a little worried but not for herself.

'Beg pardon my lord, but I have searched everywhere for Mary... she is simply gone.'

The pieces fell immediately into place for Soren. The magical girl had freed the wizard and helped him find Ethron before she had left her final farewell gift; the destruction of a thousand troops. She was strong, he had felt it that one night and many other nights but he had never known just how strong. He was almost sure that this was her work. He remembered the way she had looked at him each time he had sampled her soft and young flesh. Biding her time no doubt.

He roared out in anguished frustration. His kuvuta side leapt forth gladly and snapped the neck of the woman with an ease that surprised even him. He tore at the walls, long scratch marks that used to grace her skin. He succumbed to the power inside of him and took flight, down the winding corridors and out into the sky.

His form had become fully fused with his inner wraith DNA and he would never be the same again. The pills he took to control it would be of no use to him now. His eyes stared blankly ahead and his limbs were swirling black effigies of their former selves. He burned with a need to destroy and consume. He needed to see Sirena; he needed to know it was all going to be alright. How was he going to face the holy brothers like this? The change was happening fast though and soon he was struggling to remember why he had been afraid. He could almost feel the pain he had caused others, could feel the eyes of god watching him with distaste. He flew to his home, flew from himself, flew from the guilt and elation that fought one another inside his twisted mind. He flew from Equa, from the place where the legions of hell would pour.

Chapter 10

Small victories

Corbin was dreaming, or at least he hoped he was. He was standing upon a raised platform erected in the city square; wood creaked beneath his sandaled feet and the hood he wore scratched at his face. It was cold; his breath came in waves of mist that must have made him look even more monstrous.

He could see the crowd before him. Hundreds of faces swarmed before his eyes, all eager to see the guilty fall.

One of the Religion Brothers stepped forward from behind Corbin. He held up his hands to silence the crowd and slowly, the excited hum of the captive audience ebbed.

'People of Daemoa! Today is a day of retribution!' The crowd roared its approval and Corbin could feel the bile rise in his throat. They knew not even what they were shouting for. The sheep that the human race could so easily become stood bleating before their self-proclaimed shepherd.

The brother smiled, crooked and yellowing teeth beneath eyes that glittered with insanity.

'Today we bring before you the impure…the non-believers…the blasphemers…the damned!' Between each false phrase, the crowd erupted like some cruel play was being performed, each knowing their thespian part. 'These sinners reject the one true god and therefore reject the right given to them by him to live!' More applause, as if every one of them standing down there had the right to pass judgment or give that power to another being as naïve as themselves. Corbin's executioner's mask hid his ashamed face. His cheeks burned and his heart pumped lead-like blood through his body, each beat more painful than the last. 'Bring forth the first perpetrator!'

Corbin drowned out the sound of the merciless crowd below with the sound of his own heavy breathing. He tried not to look the brother in the eye for fear of wielding the heavy axe he held straight through the man's skull.

An old man came into view. He wore a pair of stained and ragged pants, his bony shoulders exposed. He was bloody and bruised, all his fingers were broken and his left eye had been removed. He stumbled forward like a lamb to the slaughter and knelt down before Corbin. He neither looked up nor uttered a word. His head rested on the executioner's block as if he was finally to sleep.

'This man has confessed to high treason!' the brother screeched, 'he has had carnal knowledge of a number of impure races and will therefore be punished here and in the life to come!' People shouted abuse, threw whatever they had brought with them and spat on the platform.

The man said nothing and his eye was closed. Corbin took two steps forward and swung the heavy axe up and over his head. He paused and then brought it down with a heavy 'THUNK' of metal on flesh and wood. Corbin always tried to keep his eyes open right until the very last minute. The last thing he wanted to do was to botch a job due to his own guilt. He wondered where the days of "green dream" had gone. He supposed it was not enough to condemn a man to death; you had to see the blood spill with your own eyes to prove something.

Tumulus roars greeted the rolling head that fell into the bucket at the bottom of the platform. Corbin took a deep breath and stepped back again.

'Next!' shouted the brother amidst the cries for more. A young woman walked up. The tanned skin of a laborer, face hardened by her long days in the sun and tatty, bleached hair. They worked on the genetic food farms, doing the work for less than it would cost a machine to do. Her face was dirty and tears had carved out two perfect lines down her cheeks.

'This woman refused to offer up her food for our god as sacrifice and in doing so has brought his wrath down upon her!' The brother pointed his finger at her, his face livid and his eyes bulging. The woman rushed forward and yelled,

'It was food for my family! *My* sheep to keep and eat! I had made my sacrifice and the Religion guards wanted it for themselves!' Her voice was strained and fearful, desperate. Again, Corbin wondered what had ever happened to simply going to church or saying your prayers in bed at night. The brother took an exaggerated intake of breath and screamed,

'Blasphemy!' His call was taken up and echoed a hundred times over.

'Cut off her head!' some blood-drunk member of the crowd called.

She was forced onto her knees by two Religion soldiers. Her shoulders shook and her hair waved feebly in the wind. Corbin cut her head off too. A few more like this were brought forward in quick succession, each claiming to be innocent, some begging for mercy. All died by his hand.

The seventh perpetrator was a young man in his early twenties. He bore the mark of the Religion on his forehead; the scrubbed scarring. He marched onto the platform like it was his very own stage and stared the crowd down into silence. His look was grim for one so young and his brow was furrowed but there was sadness in his eyes.

'We are all equal!' He said, loud enough for all to hear, 'we are all love!'

'Guards!' the brother called out, sensing something coming. Two men rushed forward but the man could not be silenced or contained.

'Do not let them tell you any different, do not let them build a cage of fear for you!' He was being dragged down to the block but his voice still rang out clear and true. One soldier tried to silence him with a chain-mail gloved hand but the ex-Religion Brother bit down hard, and the soldier leapt back in pain. The young man looked up and smiled through a mouth of broken and bloodied teeth and gums.

He said; 'Deliver my soul from the sword, save me from the lion's mouth, hide your face from my sins but smite down my enemies for they do not speak peace but they devise deceitful words against those who are quiet in the land.' He spoke now to his god, not to the people.

The soldiers forced his head down...

'For you are my shepherd and though I walk with shadow, I fear not -' and those were his last words. The remaining soldier had put the point of his sword through his neck, severing the spinal cord and the words that had been uttered. He had quoted the old Faith which was punishable by immediate death. Corbin's job had been done for him. The crowd was silent. All remembering the words from childhood, when the world was still and good and light.

More or less twenty more souls passed beneath Corbin's axe thereafter, but the people had lost their love for the spectacle. Despite all the efforts of the brother to rile them up once again, the damage had been done. Corbin carried out his job to the cool sound of silence, punctured by the occasional mad voice of the brother as he announced the victims. His mask was wet with sweat, his muscles ached and his heart was numb. Or so he thought...

A boy of no more than ten years of age had been led onto the platform. The crowd moaned with displeasure and a riot was near. The threat of it hung thick in the cold air. The boy had wet the front of his trousers and looked so pitiful that it was painful to watch him. He was to be killed for defying the direct command of an officer to give over the location of his older sister.

Corbin's legs had turned to lead and his mouth stung with acid. He looked up and saw the faces of his people, his race. Religion had made a monster out of them all but faith still gave them hope, made them humble. The only reason he did what he had done that day, was because he had seen that faith in those hundreds of eyes. Faith in someone to do the right thing. He had cast off his mask, thrown it down upon the crudely carved wood he stood on, blood stained hands and pale white face. He had stared at the people down below and then fled. The people had cheered for him then. Given their voices to the cry for life instead of death.

They ran after him, the Religion, they tracked him like a dog. But he ran day and night until he could run no more. The cheers of the people spurred him on, the last echo of their renewed faith in man. That day and all the days before that had made him vengeful. His hatred had made him careless.

He had been found lying face down, broken and desolate in the forest. Lucio's face had smiled down at him like the light of the sun. They had taken him in and seen the anger within him like all the other broken castaways and runaways. They had warned him but he had not listened. The cold wind stung his face even now, as he dreamt it, like it did that night.

They had been sent into Delta Fourteen to break up a band of Religion soldiers who were terrorizing the local Hapais. A tribe of humanoids who led an atheist and pastoral existence out in the old lands.

When Corbin and his group had bunked down for the night after five days of solid tracking, Raul had seen a fire in the distance. They followed it on a hunch and came across a burning village. Unlike the smoldering remains they had seen etched into the landscape for a full week, here the people were still alive. Mothers and their children being fed to the hungry flames, men being executed outside their homes.

Nyx and Cadeyrn had urged Corbin against a full on attack. The soldiers outnumbered them by at least three-to-one and were armed to the teeth, still drunk on bloodlust and cheap wine from the looted farmers' stocks. They had told him it would be better to wait until they were off-guard and the fires had died down so they could launch a surprise attack. Corbin had wondered what had ever happened to a good, old fashioned sniper rifle. Meg had grabbed on to his hand, pleading with him to ignore the cries, asking him to do the impossible. He had refused them all and led the open attack.

Every soldier died that night and most by Corbin's blade. Forty souls were saved but twenty more were lost to the blaze and blade. Meg was among that number. She had been cut off from the rest and hacked down in a frenzy of desperation from those of the Religion who still drew breath. It was the first time Corbin had ever seen Raul cry. He had held on to her limp body until the sun crept up over the horizon. It rose like a beacon of hope for the Hapais but Raul had never been the same again.

Corbin felt the guilt tear through his heart again, still fresh after three long years. He held onto it like a jealous lover even though Eira scolded him so for it. He watched Meg die again, watched her lover die in the same way, felt the heat of the fires, the ash falling like rain from the sky and his eyes flew open, unable to bear the images burnt into the darkness of dreams.

*

Lok was alerted to the cries first. He jumped up, dropped his sword and made his way hastily over to the wounded human captain. Delano followed him, wondering how well the human would react to the current situation.

Corbin sat bolt upright, every inch of him burned like fire and he struggled to keep his eyes open. He tore the bandages from his face and was greeted by even greater pain as his skin met the air. He held his hands before his face, fighting the urge to touch himself, fingers shaking and blistered. He opened his mouth to scream again and his lips tore, sending blood trickling down his chin.

'Please calm yourself!' Lok had reached him and knelt down in an attempt to help the man reapply his bandages and avoid more damage. Corbin's face was a mask of horror. He was alive but by the way he felt; barely. A man sat before him. Young, dressed in boiled leather, shaggy fair hair and a concerned frown upon his weathered features. Another stood behind him, taller and stockier, dark, not so welcoming in his first impression.

'Do not just stand there! Fetch Zach!' the fairer one shouted impatiently. Delano did not move, his arms folded across his chest. Lok shook his head at Delano's stubborn protectiveness.

'Do you know where you are?' he asked Corbin gently. Corbin slowly shook his head and tried to swallow the putrid spittle in his mouth. It made an audible path down his throat and he opened his mouth to speak;

'Where...others?'

Lok looked up at Delano and the slightly older rider pointed to a space about two feet away from Corbin. It was not a mound of grass and sand in the middle of the desert. It was the bulky frame of Cadeyrn wrapped in the same material he had been. A low moan escaped Corbin's lips as he realized Cadeyrn must be dead. Raul's death came back to him in the same instant and the last look he saw upon his wife's face.

Lok frowned slightly and tried to make eye contact with the deranged man.

'I believe they wrap their dead or cover them if you will for a while before burning or burying them.' Owein had joined the party. 'I think he believes his friend is dead.'

Lok nodded and said in a low and unobtrusive voice,

'That one there is not dead.' He said it kindly but the reaction was far from one of relief.

Corbin looked up at these strange people. They were lying to him, they were so calm, they seemed half amused in the face of his suffering. He yanked himself up and onto his feet in one swift motion that vibrated through his broken body like a flash of lightning pain. He turned to face the one with his arms crossed and swung viscously with his fist. He felt skin tear off his knuckles as he connected with the man's jaw.

Delano took a step back and ran with the punch. His arms were still folded but he stood further away from the human now, as did the other two.

'Are you happier now?' he asked, a slight glow forming on his lower jaw. No retribution, no anger. Corbin stared blankly at them all, swaying slightly on his feet.

'Did you have to stay for that?' Lok asked Delano.

'Rather me than you,' he mocked as he grabbed Lok playfully by the jaw, 'your face is too pretty.'

The one Corbin had hit was walking away; the other two were watching him closely.

'Where are my friends!' Corbin roared at the impassive faces. The one with chalky blonde hair and shocking green eyes backed away slightly, he had clever eyes. The short one stepped forward. Stupid move, thought Corbin, but he did not lash out.

'There is much you must learn but you are safe and your friend lives. There is another, a woman...' He did not get to finish his sentence for Corbin let out another moan, half-way between pain and liberation.

Eira had heard the commotion and had come running from the water's edge to see her husband. The others had warned her that he was badly burnt but that the plants and drey saliva in the dressings would heal him completely. Nothing prepared her for him though.

She broke through the crowd of spectators and ran toward the figure she was sure was Corbin. His hair had only half grown back and his skin was pink and blistered. His lips were torn, his eyes were nearly swollen closed and he could barely stand. He moaned deep in his throat again. She walked slower as she neared him; saw the full extent of the damage. She lightly brushed past Owein and placed herself beside Lok, his frozen blue eyes looking intently at her.

'He is...' she put her hand upon his arm and he nodded, turning his back on the humans and leading Owein away, happy to be relieved of duty.

The sight of the man she loved broke her heart. She cupped his cheek in her hand so gently that it could have been the wings of an angel.

'Are...we safe...here? You...hurt?' were the first things he croaked to her. She smiled at him and now his heart broke. He moved to hold her close to him but the pain in his body made it almost impossible.

'It's okay,' she said, laying him down in the shade of the desert tree, his head resting on her lap. 'These people saved us, the soldiers are dead.'

Corbin felt a wave of anxiety wash away from him to be replaced by the extreme need to rest. He was a little confused still and his head swam but Eira was alright, he felt sure that Cadeyrn was too, and his brain was too tired to think of anything else. He heard footsteps approaching his little oasis of peace beneath the tree. Heard his name being called, saw the face of some warrior man fill his vision but he could stay with them no longer. Quietude washed over him and he saw no more for a little while.

*

The air was growing heavy and thick. The fight would be a hard one to win, Damek realized. All around him the whispers of incantations of the Ancients could be heard. They seemed to be a part of the walls, not just bouncing off them but coming from them, from deep within the foundations of this magic place. They were standing around Falkhar, circular formation, seven feet from each wall. Their eyes were closed and their aged skin moved around their mouths as they intoned the ritual. Tall and ghostly looking if not for the faint glow of life in their grey flesh. They smelled like dust and rot, all the silk and perfume in Osrillia could not disguise that stench. Old death.

Four of Falkhar's men had hauled up the mirror by two thick chains. The mirror that would keep Arial's soul entranced and drag it from her body after the drey breath had awakened it. Another was washing her body with a sponge soaked with Drow water. All physical magic traces would be cleansed from her skin leaving her helpless, and then they would be able to remove her necklace; her all-powerful protective amulet. If they simply tried to take it from her, they would all die. If she had arrived without it, her soul would have been impossible to entice.

Falkhar snapped his fingers through his trance-like state and another scuttled forward to help him into Damek's cloak, the cloak that would protect him from any unforeseen magic that the young drey maiden might emit. Damek tensed up as he realized his father must have taken it from him whilst he was engrossed in the human. Shame crept up his neck and settled red in his face.

Falkhar's arms were spread wide, he was ready. The hum of the Ancients grew louder and pressure fell upon Damek's ears as Falkhar's malachi magic filled the room. Damek looked at Kaleo; his Shadow Brother and friend. Kaleo nodded his head in a barely visible gesture. He tossed Damek a last, cheeky grin and pushed him off the balcony. Damek fell through the air like a fly through treacle.

Magic always rose, just as hot air did, and near the roof it was at its thickest.

As Damek fell through the congealed power, he watched Kaleo work. Crawling slowly across the walls and down behind the foremost Ancient. Damek saw him free his own amulet from around his neck; Isha's locket. He cupped it in his hands and blew on it. Blue fire erupted in his hands and he hurled it at the Ancient which howled out in pain and surprise, stumbling around the room, knocking the elongated candles to the ground and setting the others alight. Kaleo kept up the display and soon, the entire party was alight, most lay smoldering on the floor, dying again.

The malachi guards set to protect the fragile Ancients were no match for Kaleo's ferocity. He was a well-trained Shadow Brother, albeit not the strongest, and Damek watched as each of them fell to Kaleo's hand and blade, as if he knew how each would die before he made his deadly moves. Shrieks filled the room, curtains were catching alight and dark blood sprayed the floor from gaping wounds in malachi necks, collecting in pools at Falkhar's feet. But he did not flinch. He was deaf to the world.

Damek started to fall faster now and he landed lightly on his feet, marveling at the flaws in malachi magic. It was conditional. Ordinary magic, that of summoning the elements, was attainable with little effort, but any other kind had to be done under special circumstances. The malachi would have to go into a trance in order to channel the strange power; he would be helpless and extremely vulnerable. Of course, this was unacceptable, and a loophole had been found in the system as always. Whilst the malachi was incapacitated, a hidden other would act for him as protection, creating powerful anima. Each had their own and Damek was curious to see what Falkhar had encrypted his spirit with.

Kaleo was nowhere to be seen and Damek went in for the kill.

He had not taken two steps forward before he felt it. The stirring in the plane sent chills down his spine, all the hairs on his body stood on end, every nerve warning him against the shift in dimensions. A rift appeared just to the left and a little behind his impassive father. The plane was being breached. Damek thought he glimpsed scales; perhaps it was a trick of the mind. He unsheathed his claws, felt for the dagger at his side and took another step forward. The snake fell to the floor with an otherworldly thud as reptile skin met stone, borne on heavy flesh. It was massive. Black as night, blue flame reflections dancing off its glittering scales.

It arched its neck, surveying the scene. Damek hesitated. It was a greater force than he had imagined. It towered above him in all its fanged glory, long strands of thick poison oozing from its three-foot fangs. Its bulk blocked the way to Falkhar and its hiss stilled Damek's heart. He gripped the hilt of his blade, feeling the jewel encrusted reassurance. It was a hunter's knife, one he had stolen a few years ago, a Xirunese weapon with which he had slain hundreds of supernatural creatures, and if wielded correctly, it could melt the heart of this magical beast.

One tentative foot before the other and the snake had spotted him. Its eyes met his with calculated fury. Damek drew the blade. It shone in the fire light like an enraged spirit but Falkhar's anima self only grew more incensed by the sight of it. Its scales seemed to enlarge and the skin between them stretch, ready for the strike. Damek was engulfed in a thick mist of poison spray as he rolled right. The snake was not too fast and its moves could be predicted but Damek needed to get close. The snake struck again and Damek let it get closer this time, close enough to try to penetrate scale with claw. The snake came off better for this. Damek was left with a nasty cut in his arm; a nick from one of the smaller and non-poisonous fangs that lined the snake's mouth. Damek's claws had slid clean off the armor of his adversary. He clutched his arm, allowing for a brief inspection before focusing upon the task at hand once again. It was deep, blood flowered under his shirt. The fabric was coated in poison and already it stung at his skin. He tore it off and tossed it aside.

The snake regarded him for a moment before it lunged at him again, fangs bared. The terrible hiss resonated in Damek's ears but he concentrated on standing still until the very last second. He stepped back and jumped lightly onto the snake's head in a single move. His arm threw him a little off balance but he was still strong from his feed and it was healing already. He spread his legs and corrected his weight in anticipation of the snake's next move. It flung its great, caped head back and thrashed its body violently in an effort to dislodge the intruder, but Damek was lithe and quick, ready for each sway and jerk. He gave it half a minute and in the time it took for the snake to find its bearings - Damek leaned over and thrust down hard, leaning all his weight into the strike.

The blade plunged true and hard, driving through the skull and lodging its point in the beast's brain. Magic coursed from the blade tip throughout the body and the heart gave one last beat before it was told to stop. Damek could hear it smoldering within the rib cage. The snake collapsed to the floor and Damek sprang from its head as it did.

The true blood was pumping full course now, the parasite wanted more from him, and he was ready to give it. He turned to face Falkhar, expected to be greeted by his full wrath but the Master malachi stood perfectly still, eyes still closed, having to work harder now that the Ancients were not there to lend their magic. He knew of nothing, his spell had not been broken.

It took Damek a few seconds to work it out, mostly because he found it too hard to believe. He had underestimated his father and his resources. Three more rifts were opening up around him. Fear took hold of him now. Three more similarly massive forms fell to the floor, scaled and terrible. Cold sweat broke out as he realized the challenge he faced. He was after all only one man. He thought of pulling his knife from the skull of the fallen anima but something rooted him to the spot. Was he giving up?

Thoughts trickled through his mind as he stood staring at his death through many eyes. More rifts, more snakes. He stopped counting when he heard them slithering over each other and waiting for him outside the doors to the chamber. They were closing in on him now, blotting out his vision with their massive serpentine bodies. One man...

He turned back to take one last look at his lady. Arial's soul had been awakened by the fire playing across the surface of the raised mirror. It showed no sign of the snakes in its reflection, the battle that had been fought or the chaos all around it. It showed only her and the magenta fire. It was drawing her in. Damek watched in horror as her soul started to emerge from her body, breaking through the natural bonds that held it in place, defying the very rules of the Worlds to get to the mirror and sate her spirit's need. It was all happening so slowly but she was too far away for him to save her, there were too many of them. Her soul was as pure and white as the driven snow; her hair flowed around her perfect face like the river through Eden. She turned her head to him and he gazed into the eyes of her soul, halfway between rapture and doom. In that moment, something inside Damek was forever changed. He could feel the shift in equilibrium as for the first time, understanding of what he now stood to lose dawned upon him. He felt power surge inside him that he could hardly believe.

This must be what Kaleo feels, he thought, what they all hide from each other. So much balance and clarity that there were few limits. Kaleo could have stopped this at any time, he realized, but he had wanted Damek to do this by himself. To reach this pinnacle, this collective thought.

Damek closed his eyes. He dropped to his knees, stone making way for his form like ripples in a pond. Time slowed, matter froze in the face of his power. He lifted his hands like a man holding the Worlds on his shoulders. He could feel the weight of his father's magic, could grasp it as it flowed through the air. He flattened his hands and pushed up. The magic was strong but he was stronger. Slowly and inch by inch, he could feel it give way, feel it crumble and dissipate as it touched the roof above his head. He smiled to himself before he gave one last heave and the weight was lifted. He opened his eyes to blue fire, ashen reptile forms across the floor mingled with the blood of the fallen and - Falkhar.

The Master malachi took in the scene around him with unmasked shock and anger. His eyes met Damek's and Arial's soul fell back into her body. Her back arched and she breathed again, arms struggling against the bonds that held her, blue eyes straining against the pain of having her soul ripped from her body, voice unable to scream her great anguish. Damek could feel that his miracle power had left him, not forever, but for now.

'You,' Falkhar hissed. His eyes narrowed dangerously and Damek knew that this fight might be his last. His father's power was not a well-kept secret. 'I always knew you for a stupid child but even *I* could never envision you as being responsible for the downfall of our entire race!' he spat.

Damek had no words for the evil his father had become, he merely knew that he had to be destroyed before any more had to die for his madness.

'Have - You - NOTHING to say!'

At that, Adonica burst into the hall in a flurry of pink lace and flustered features.

'I could not hold the anima! I came as soon as I could.' Her face froze as she took in the scene. She rushed over to Falkhar's side and clutched his arm like a frightened girl. She hissed at Damek, opening and closing her fanged mouth as a threatened cat does.

'I told you he would ruin everything,' she said into her father's ear, 'what are we to do now?' she wailed pathetically. Falkhar gazed down at her with a mixture of emotions that Damek could not quite place.

'Get rid of the woman, her soul is tainted now and will not bend to my will. I will take care of him,' he said, brushing the line of her cheek with his thumb while cupping her treacherous face with the rest of his hand. She smiled a smile Damek knew from childhood and they kissed one another deeply. She broke away first and smirked at her brother.

'Wicked child,' Damek scorned.

She skipped over to Arial and leant down low over her strained neck, grinning all the while. Adonica's perfect bosom was threatening to burst out of her gown and Falkhar's lecherous gaze fell upon the sight. Damek's face contorted with repulsion.

'Tonight, Damek, you die,' Falkhar sneered, 'you and the barbarian you would betray your people for.'

Damek leapt forward at the same time as Falkhar and they met in the air, claws gleaming and jaws set wide. Falkhar pushed with greater force and they were both sent crashing into the central pillar, dust and rock fragments flying. Falkhar's fingers were around Damek's neck now and try as he might, his muscles could not keep the fearful grip away from his windpipe. Falkhar cocked his head to one side and asked, 'Did you really think you could defeat me?'

Damek could not speak for the pressure. He screwed his eyes up against the darkness that wanted to blot out his vision and was overwhelmed by what he saw then. His eyes now closed, he could see more than when they were open to the clearest night. He could see things that no one could! He could see Falkhar's beating heart, see the blood flow thick through his veins, he could see the energy he radiated; see the weakness in the body plan in a way he had never seen before. The world was made out of light and energy, he had always known this, but now he could see it! It was like an energy aura, tangible and transparent to him.

He started to laugh from pure elation and wonder and Falkhar's facial expression changed. He partially relaxed his grip in confusion for the briefest of seconds but that was all Damek needed. He snaked his arm up toward Falkhar's chest and broke the surface of his father's flesh and bone as easily as he would dip his hands into water. He clenched his fist around the malachi's strong heart and crushed it in his grip.

Falkhar let out a cry of such utter agony that Adonica stopped for one second to look up, her fangs deep in Arial's tender neck. She had wanted to tear her throat out, see what all the fire fuss was about. Not to drink, just to taste. Her wretched brother and her lover were lying on the floor in a death embrace. Damek's hand had disappeared seamlessly into Falkhar's chest and she could feel he was dying.

Damek, still with his eyes closed, watched death with new eyes. The energy fields faltered and changed as he looked on. The life stopped within him on one level and left him on another. It was beautiful and terrible all at the same time. Contrasting colors and vibrating energy levels that he could now witness with all his senses. He let Falkhar slump to the floor, sliding his hand out without a drop of blood spilled.

Adonica froze in terror. Her brother's eyes were still shut and a serene look was etched upon his handsome features. He looked god-like in his state and she let Arial's head fall back onto the stone altar, taking a step back as she did so. She sensed something had changed within him.

'We can talk, brother, the way we used to do.'

Damek opened his eyes and saw his sister. He saw past her outer beauty and saw the person she really was. He did not need any special power to do that. He walked toward her and she backed away slightly. Her one hand was held out before her in a cautionary manner and Arial's precious blood coated her lips.

'You would not harm me?' incredulously, but softly. Her lopsided smile was like noxious gas to him. He moved behind her before she could blink and held her by her pretty throat. A small gasp escaped her full lips and her bosom rose and fell dramatically as she breathed what she surely knew to be her last breaths. Her eyes were wide with fright as her brother leaned in even closer to smell the fresh blood with deep shuddering breaths. Adonica forced her tears back.

'I would have done anything for him,' she said.

'As would I.'

He tore her throat out with little passion or fervor. He let her lifeless form fall to the floor and ran to Arial's side.

Déjà vu. She was so weak. He carried her out of the back doors in his arms. He closed his eyes and looked down at her but he could see only the darkness that greeted every other shut eye in the Worlds. He pricked his ears to the sound of roaring flames engulfing the chamber, running feet coming toward them, many of them. They would need to find a way out and away but his energy was much drained. He ran out into the gardens instead, trying to find a place of quiet and solace.

He laid her down under a giant tree and wondered what was to become of them. He looked up to the stars as if asking for guidance and when he dropped his gaze again, his eyes fell upon Kaleo. He was leaning against the tree as if all was right with the Worlds. He was smiling.

Damek grinned broadly.

'Thank you,' he said sincerely. 'What am I to do now though?'

Kaleo hunkered down and grabbed hold of Damek by the shoulder;

'You must take her to the High Elves, they are waiting for her.'

Damek wanted to ask why but the *how* sprung to his lips first.

'The gate will be open.'

'Are you certain?' Damek asked, 'the gate is never open anymore and going through closed is suicide.'

'It will be open,' Kaleo reassured him, 'go now, they are coming for you. Take these,' he added, holding out Arial's amulet and Damek's cloak. Damek nodded, took the relics and scooped Arial up into his arms once more.

'Thank you,' he said again before taking his leave, 'for everything.'

They embraced warmly and Kaleo gave Damek one last push in the right direction.

'Go well!' he called after them.

Damek hurried through the many winding paths of the parliament gardens. Statues leered at him from every corner, mocking his attempt to escape. He ran half blind into the night. He knew not the exact location of the gate but after twenty minutes of blundering through the mazes, he saw it. Marked by the great sword of the noble High Elf Assay. A nondescript patch of soil and grass would lead him through a permanent porthole to the High Elves. Built decades ago when the political bonds between elf and malachi were strong, in the days before Falkhar.

Damek ran toward the sword as if it were not even there, praying that the gate was open. Just as collision became inevitable, his feet were touching nothing. Light surrounded him, pressed in upon him, and forced him to hide his face.

He awoke to the sounds of night on a foreign planet and darkness broken only by the moons.

Arial breathed uneasy in his ear and he looked around him. Another garden, another sword; a malachi wrought blade this time.

At first, he did not see the forms that surrounded him. That was their way after all. When his eyes adjusted he could barely make out where the armor stopped and the shadow began. He was not alone.

*

Lucio had contacted one of his colleagues and asked if a cab could be sent to fetch them. Ramroth refused to walk for fear of another encounter and Lucio wholeheartedly agreed. He only hoped that the Religion had not intercepted his call.

The cab arrived, a sleek but old model in black finish. Lucio recognized the driver and soon they were on their way to Lucio's cousin's holiday home. They had agreed that this would be a safe place. Ramroth was silent all the way there, collecting his thoughts, formulating the right questions in his mind in order to get the best answers.

Lucio felt dazed. He knew that this ordeal was far from over and that the lives of millions of people hung in the balance. He was still grieving for Mirkisha but knew that if he did not help Ramroth then he would be but the first among many to lose loved ones to this darkness.

The cab pulled into a small driveway and the doors popped open. No words were exchanged and the driver promptly drove away, leaving the two unlikely companions standing alone in front of the post-modern style home.

Ramroth moved toward the door, brushing his fingers across its sleek finish, pressing his ears against the brushed steel. Lucio said nothing.

'Your cousin keeps odd company,' Ramroth said at last. Lucio answered with a frown. 'Malachi vestige,' Ramroth explained as he pushed the door open and flicked on the lights inside. 'One of your cousin's acquaintances is a vampire.' Lucio was not sure what to say. 'No need for alarm,' Ramroth said, humor in his tone now, 'malachi are everywhere and most are good people, or at least they are trying to be.'

'And for a vampire to be deemed a "good person" is to go against their nature,' Lucio ventured. Ramroth looked up in surprise;

'And so we all suffer for our varying sins while the faceless label us as good or evil. That, my friend, is the greatest problem of all.'

The wizard spoke with an age-old weariness that Lucio failed to recognize in its entirety.

Ramroth sat down heavily on a simply carved, wooden chair, closed his eyes and massaged his temples. Lucio took a seat next to him and waited for the questions. When none came he decided to speak first.

'Mirkisha came to me some years ago. She was burdened with a great sadness which she revealed to me in her own time. I do not live an entirely sheltered life but her story struck a chord within me.' He did not want to tell Ramroth of the kiss and all he had seen through it, it was a moment shared between himself and Mirkisha alone. When Ramroth said nothing to this, he continued. 'There came a stranger to her bedchamber one night. These wraiths or kuvuta or whatever name has been given to these demons from another world.'

Lucio placed his head in his hands and Ramroth had to lean closer to hear the pained and muffled words. 'He forced himself on her and she fell pregnant.'

Ramroth struggled to breathe for a few seconds but he did not want to interrupt this all-important testimony. Lucio took a deep breath before emerging from the refuge his cupped hands had provided. The harsh light enhanced his drawn face and Ramroth could see the love he had born Mirkisha etched plainly there. He kept his silent vigil and allowed Lucio to unburden himself.

'She spoke of you fondly, and as often as I think she could allow herself. She spoke only once of her family for it grieved her so, but she told me what she did and why she did it. She said that she could have lived with the pain of giving up all she loved but not with that of being responsible for the loss of everything everyone in the Worlds loved.' He wanted to tell the story as Mirkisha would have told it if she were alive. He knew she would want Ramroth to know the truth of it.

'So what did she suspect of the kuvuta's intentions?' Ramroth asked carefully.

'I think she knew that it was no coincidence. The wraiths had discovered the existence of the army, the winged ones, and wished to sway the odds in their favor by placing a royal of their choosing on the thrown, to ensure they were never summoned.'

'But they knew not how close they were to the leader of the great enemy?' Ramroth guessed. He was starting to understand very well now.

'Yes, that is why she sent him away, to protect him, to protect the Worlds.' Lucio sighed deeply and stood up to pour himself a glass of water. He shouted an offer to Ramroth from the kitchen but he declined. When Lucio was seated again, Ramroth asked,

'What of Arial? I can understand going into hiding to spare her name but why not take her child?' Ramroth knew the answer before it had even been given. Had Ethron not told him so? Lucio leaned back in his chair;

'Two reasons. First, the fact that she wanted Arial to have no knowledge of the interdict and no contact with her half-brother or his father who she was sure would be part of her life in the years that the boy grew. And second, Arial needed to be protected from more than just his influence; she needed to be protected in her entirety in the event of Valador's death.'

There was a silence it seemed that only Ramroth could fully comprehend. He knew that he had known all along, Ethron had confirmed it, but he had failed to admit the whole heavy truth even to himself for it was too great.

'The Blood Angels are no mere weapon,' Lucio professed, as if reading Ramroth's mind, 'Valador was made leader of an *immortal army*. It is his job to call them when the time is right and to lead them into battle.' Lucio raised his eyebrows at his own statement. He could hardly grasp the concept of immortality, let alone an entire army of men who could not die by any other means than by the hands of a wraith.

'I do not understand,' Ramroth began, 'if Valador is the one who holds the key then why is Arial so important? Valador is the one who holds the power.'

'As it stands yes, if he is still alive. But the common law of blood that holds true for all humans provides the missing key.'

Ramroth racked his brains for the meaning in this. In all his studies and experience he had never come across this law of blood.

'Humans have their own magic, Ramroth, as I showed you earlier.'

Ramroth smiled, he knew about Faith and the old stories. Human magic.

'So when Valador dies, Arial shall inherit his power and purpose in accordance with the law of blood because she is half-human?' Ramroth asked.

'Yes. It is all in the blood my friend. At least for us it is. The very symbol of female fertility...the essence of our gods throughout the ages....it embodies so much meaning for my people; pain, sacrifice, life, death, hope. It is why the vampires crave no other but us.'

Ramroth sat back and thought for a little while.

'I must find her,' he said abruptly.

Lucio stood and pushed Ramroth gently back into his chair.

'We do not know where she is. We cannot go picking through the universe looking for one woman, however important she may be. We must have faith that fate will take care of her,' Lucio cautioned.

Ramroth's mouth was open to speak protest but he relented, knowing the priest spoke true. He frowned deeply for a while, seeming to recollect something, and nodded once to himself.

'We will have to aid her in any way we can then,' Ramroth said finally. 'It is time.'

Lucio did not ask for what. He was tired and he trusted the mage. He watched on as Ramroth drew the outline of a circle with his finger on the floorboards, muttering strange things as he did. It sounded like he was asking for something, talking to someone unseen.

He motioned for Lucio to join him inside his invisible circle and Lucio did as he was bid. Ramroth took hold of his hands and in that instant, everything changed. The wooden walls, beams and foundations of the house seemed to come alive. They were breathing and speaking to one another. Lucio could see traces of color on the walls. The hand prints left behind by former visitors in this world of theirs. The circle he stood in was ablaze on the edges with white flames as high as his waist and he could see figures dancing within the fire. They were speaking to Ramroth but he was silent now. He held on tight to Lucio's hands and said,

'Stay with me.' His voice sounded so close but eerily far away. Lucio felt the ground abandon his feet as if it had merely been there as a favor to him his entire life. The white fire engulfed him and he squeezed his eyes shut against the searing light. In one moment it was color, fire and dancing figures, Ramroth's hands enfolding his and bright light. In the next it was darkness, cold and damp. The smell of soil filled his nostrils and goose bumps covered every inch of his skin, bringing back to life all the parts of him that heat forgot. He was alone.

*

Zach was swimming through the space and time of the Worlds once more. Weightless and exhilarated, he took his time to admire the work of whoever had dreamed up this reality. Was this a dream? He was not so sure. He felt the same stirring in his loins that the Oracle, birth giver of time, evoked in her chosen ones.

He saw a blue planet. Time had been allowed to heal this world and the oceans had swollen in gratitude, landmass stood lush and peaceful. As he hurtled toward this place, he could feel the strained muscles in his sleeping body trying to keep up with his mind. The ground came rushing toward him and he was dropped, like a plucked flower, from the hands of the Oracle.

A strange land. It echoed with the memories of its former inhabitants but there was no one to be seen. He cast his face skyward and saw clouds heavy with the promise of a storm. The first drop stung his cheek but he made no effort to close his eyes, it had been too long since he had felt rain on his skin. There were mountains to his right and they rang with the mournful song of a drey.

Zach was pulled from his dreams by the rough hands of Cahan.

'Captain, the human is awake. Corbin. He wishes to speak with you.'

*

Corbin had awoken from his own dreams to a world he too did not recognize. Largely built and strange looking men dressed in boiled leather and scaled armor, armed to the teeth with finely crafted blades and bows.

His wife was sleeping peacefully at his side as if there were nothing amiss. He sat up groggily and felt at the skin on his face. It was healed, perfectly. As if the fire had never touched him. Had he dreamed it all? But then he saw the dragons. Giant mounds of earth sleeping on the dunes. One had raised its head and turned to look at him, scales glittering and nostrils smoldering. It took everything Corbin had to remain calm. Then, as one of the warriors came closer, the memory of his brief encounter with these men came back to him.

'My name is Kai.' A harsh but pleasant accent, not someone who spoke Udaranese every day.

'Corbin,' he said in reply. The man was not armed and his body language was cautionary, not aggressive.

'We are dragon riders. We found you and your people here. We killed the soldiers who were attacking your party. Your hounds are dead but we recovered four from your party including yourself.' He spoke slowly and carefully, pausing in between so Corbin could speak if he wished. 'Your wife speaks of one you lost but it was not by drey fire.'

The image of Raul came back to him and Corbin sought to block it out before it replayed again.

'He was good man,' was all he could manage.

Kai merely nodded.

'You were badly burnt but our herbs and elixirs did what your suits could not.' Kai smiled, as if very proud of his work and Corbin said his thanks. He looked over at the sleeping Eira and stroked her soft hair. Kai was quiet for a while and then he took hold of Corbin's hand;

'They did not touch her,' he said, meeting Corbin's gaze levelly, 'but the damage has been done to her brother. I am sure he is not a danger to anyone here but watch him carefully please.'

Corbin nodded; he could well remember the look in Nyx's eyes as they had killed his best friend and dragged his sister away to strip from her all that he had fought to protect.

'I thank you for all you have done for us. May I speak to your leader?' Corbin asked.

'Cahan fetches him as we speak,' Kai replied. His manner was easier now, as if he had gotten all the uncomfortable business out of the way and now felt sure that Corbin was civil.

The captain stood a head taller than all the others, save one, the one he walked with. They both looked fearsome in their battle attire, shaggy beards, braided hair and wild eyes. Corbin rose to his feet automatically. Four paces away, the taller one stopped and the other continued to walk toward him. A heavily muscled arm was thrown over his shoulders and he was embraced by this stranger as if they were brothers.

'Greetings fellow Captain. My name is Zach. We have much to discuss.'

'I am not sure what has happened here…' Corbin half stuttered.

'We killed the blue-cloaks!' Zach was smiling broadly.

'Yes, thank you, but there are many more and there are others who need our help.'

'No,' came the blunt reply, 'your ship is broken and we cannot leave you here. You must send for help or come with us and your wife tells us there is no help so you will come with us.'

Corbin tried to think clearly. He screwed his eyes up against the mid-morning sun and felt a pair of fine hands encircle his waist. He turned to find Eira looking up at him, smiling a sad smile.

'How badly is she damaged?' he asked.

'Corbin, we won't leave this planet unless we go with them.' Eira said gently. Corbin was about to speak but she cut him off, 'Nyx and I have tried to radio out, there is no one there. It's like everyone is just gone and we are alone.' She looked close to tears and Corbin hugged her tightly to him, looking at the captain of the dragon riders.

'Where do you want to go?' Corbin asked.

Zach nodded and called out over his shoulder,

'Men, let us sit.' They sat on the soft sand and waited for the assembly of dragon lords to join them.

'You all know of our guests, Corbin and Eira.'

Nyx came forward out of the throng and sat down next to Corbin. His look was haggard but he managed a weak smile and did not shake Corbin off when he placed his hand on his shoulder. 'You have all met Nyx and...Cadeyrn?' Zach looked at Corbin in question about his pronunciation. When Corbin nodded he continued, 'He is asleep still for he suffered the worst of the fire, but we shall inform him of our discussions when he awakes.'

Corbin could tell that Zach felt a little guilty about the innocents caught in the cross-fire and Corbin could not blame him, for had he not also found himself wanting in the past in his eagerness for battle?

'I am told that the blue-cloaks we slew are evil men of the cloth who seek to kill all who oppose them and their god so it was a good deed we did.' Zach said firmly. The men greeted his statement with enthusiasm and he smiled. 'A small victory for our long mission. We have traveled far from our homeland to seek retribution for its destruction. We travel to find a man who could put an end to the darkness and help us find our queen,' he said, addressing Corbin and his crew now.

'What darkness?' Corbin asked. He worried at first that this interruption was not part of the protocol but he mistook the fear in their eyes for hostility.

'There is a great shadow that threatens all who live. They destroy entire planets like a dark virus. Killing and smothering all in their path. It is a terrible foe and we have been sent to find a man.'

Corbin was very confused now. A virus that swallowed planets whole and only one man to stop it? He was about to ask for a little of the herbs that they all seemed to be smoking when a phrase caught in his mind and he shut his mouth. Midas had spoken of a "black plague". Eira was looking at him expectantly as if she believed every word said and was afraid he might say something offensive.

'Where is this man?' Corbin asked instead.

Owein stepped forward to draw a map for him in the sand. Corbin twisted his neck to get a better look and frowned at the picture.

'But that is not far from here,' he said, and after a while he added, 'that is Earth.'

Zack nodded to no one in particular and said,

'Yes, it is as we thought and many have confirmed our suspicions. We will fly tomorrow morning.'

Zach wanted it to be sooner but he could not risk first time flyers in a bad condition and the dreya would need rest if they were to carry extra burdens.

Corbin looked over at Nyx and said,

'There are old radio bases there. They may still be in operation and they carry strong signals. From there we can call for help.'

Nyx nodded in agreement.

'We thank you for your cooperation, you all seem like good people and we are glad we could help,' Zach said, as the meeting was disbanded and men started to move away. Corbin was too grateful for words at that time and settled for a smile and a shake of the captain's hand.

'If a war is coming, we will join you,' Corbin said, 'we number but a few but we will help you in any way we can.'

'I doubt that not Corbin,' Zach smiled, 'but first we will hunt and you can show away any doubt my men may have.'

Corbin frowned and asked what they were to hunt for on a deserted planet. The warriors laughed openly at his question.

'We hunt for the desert cat!' Zach roared to tumulus applause, 'Cahan, Delano and Kai will accompany you.'

Three men stepped forward. Kai, the dirty blonde whom he had recognized before, Cahan, the one who had walked with Zack and Delano, almost a carbon copy of Cahan but his build was slighter.

Delano strode toward him and Corbin could see a bruise on his face.

'I'm sorry about...' Corbin gestured to the nasty mark and Delano lifted his hand to touch it as if only just remembering it was there.

'Worry not. Today we hunt and yesterday we forget.' He smiled warmly and Corbin felt more comfortable. When the rest had moved away to tend to fires for the coming meal, Eira included, Delano stayed behind and leaned closer to Corbin;

'You have a pretty woman and a strong arm but do you have the courage to fight a desert cat?' he asked cheekily. Corbin laughed long and loud. Eira looked back over her shoulder to smile at him, the light playing on the fairer strands of red in her hair.

'I am ready if you are,' Corbin replied.

'Good,' Delano said, a little more seriously now. 'We made a burial mound for your hounds and for the one called Raul. When you have been to see them, we shall leave.'

Corbin looked away at these words. Delano took a few paces back and was joined by his drey. Ealunan blocked out the sun with her height and Corbin nearly lost his balance as he gazed upon her full majesty. Till now, they had been far away and not yet completely real to him. His mouth hung half open and Delano took the opportunity to beckon her closer toward the frightened human.

'You may touch her, she will not harm you,' he said.

Corbin could feel her hot breath on his face; see the same shades of gold that bedecked his wife's sun-kissed hair in her scales. She stood tall and proud, a creature his imagination could never lay claim to. Her wings flexed in uncertainty but she was so graceful in her movements that Corbin felt all fear fade away. He held his hand out flat to touch her snout and after a moment's hesitation, she closed the gap, and he felt the heat beneath her leathery skin.

'She likes you,' Delano remarked, 'I think you will ride with us tomorrow. Her name is Ealunan. She has fire inside her that will make your heart melt.'

Words evaded Corbin as the dragon started to make low rumbling noises that he could feel in his body. He took his hand back after a while and Ealunan flexed her wings once more before striding away on her clawed feet. Corbin was instantly saddened once again. A feeling of nostalgia he could not quite place.

Delano frowned and walked back to stand next to Corbin once again.

'Corbin,' he said, the name sounding foreign but well-meant on his tongue, 'we all die. In essence we are all already dead yes?'

Corbin nodded in ascent to this, but was surprised when he was shaken roughly by the shoulders and found Delano looking him fiercely in the eye, mouth dead-set and eyes ablaze;

'No! We are alive! We fight for all that is alive and we shall never die because of that. We all live on through others and as long as even *one* still breathes in the whole of the Worlds, then we all still breathe. Do you understand?' He shook Corbin once again for emphasis.

The warrior spoke true and Corbin felt he had purpose once again.

'Good man,' Delano said, seeming satisfied by Corbin's silence. 'Now we shall hunt. Those who live in your heart join us.'

Chapter 11
Good intentions

Millennia ago, when the human race still inhabited Earth, a group of scientists left their home planet in search of another. It was a secret mission and the records and memory of their departure were lost to the ages. They were to find another planet that could sustain life, for the clock of their destructive ways was ticking. They wanted a fresh start, one where they could learn to work hand in hand with nature and evolve spiritually, free from the oppression and industrialization of modern life.

Many thousands of years later, they returned. They wanted to share with their ancestors what they had learned and give back in return for their enriched lives. They were not received as they had expected and they left as soon as they realized they were unwelcome.

They withdrew from the political capitals and left the people they used to be, not for safety but out of respect. Their weaponry was far advanced and even though they struggled to understand the humans and their behavior, they let them be.

In response to the coming of the alien race, the Fourth World War broke out on Earth and the humans nearly destroyed themselves and their planet again with nuclear and biological warfare.

The Drows sprung from those humanoids who had become embittered and enraged, seeing the primeval soup from whence they came. They refused to acknowledge the humans as their forefathers and shunned all those who did. The High Elves were those who chose to follow the path of their heritage, expanding their knowledge of the Worlds, their never-ending hunger for it and accepting where it came from. And so the elves split. Other factions also broke away but simply in search of new homes. Most lived nomadic lives, small clans favoring forests or water, burnt lands or deserts. Many of them were hunted down and killed by the first wave of anti-tolerance Religion campaigns but a few still roamed free.

Time passed for the tribes until the only defining features that could link them were the same features that had made the humans fear them so. They all stood almost two heads taller than the tallest human, had elongated ears and large eyes for sensory purposes, longer fingers, strange complexions from exposure to different suns and an eerie grace about them. The two prime clans, the High Elves and the Drows, lived on separate planets and conducted all their business independently with only the smallest trace of respect for each other in the name of the past they shared. They had never gone to war but they were no allies, yet here they stood, shoulder to shoulder in the grove that was the portal to the malachi realm.

Damek was not sure what to say or if he should say anything at all. He stood there, drey queen in his arms, bloodied and sweating, staring at a site that had probably not been seen since the homecoming of the elvin race all those years ago.

The High Elves donned armor inlaid with the finest gold leaf and the Drows with that of silver; the old metals. Different gods graced each breast plate and different verses were written upon the suits in a sloping, elegant hand, but they were of the same make. The Drow's perhaps a little bulkier but apart from that, same fabric, same purpose. A skin-armor with regenerative capabilities, able to provide heat and moisture for prolonged periods, could photosynthesize, and camouflage the wearer so that it seemed they merely ceased to exist. The envy of any fine army but sole property of the two Alvars under General Braenden of the Drows and General Carrick of the High Elves. They gleamed under the full moons like assassins of the stars, sleek and agile. The clinging Artificial Intelligence Adaptive Auto Skin Suits outlined and emphasized their bulk and Damek felt heavily out-muscled. Fearsome and silent, all weapons aimed at him. He recognized the Angel-tazer crossbow that the Drows favored and the no less menacing Hasteblade of the High Elves.

'I need help,' he managed to say. The High Elf closest to Damek pulled off his face-piece, shaking out his hair and stepping forward. Damek recognized him, or rather, recognized his father in him. 'Son of Altair,' he said in greeting, shifting Arial's weight in his arms in order to greet the High Elf Prince. They touched foreheads and Alarico said,

'We apologize for the poor reception; we never know just quite who is going to step through this particular gate.' He smiled and Damek appreciated his humor.

A Drow stepped forward to take Arial from Damek, but he pulled her away and snarled slightly, hiding her face with his cloak. Alarico chuckled and waved the soldier back;

'We will escort you to my father's home, now the home of us all, and you may put her in the hands of our physicians.' Damek nodded and the small party turned their backs on him and Alarico, marching back through the palace grounds to their posts.

Alarico looked long and hard at the night stalker. He had seen a few before but this one seemed a little different. Most disturbing was the manner in which he held the woman.

'Are you going to eat her vampire? She looks half dead already.'

Alarico's sense of humor now went wasted.

'Who sent you here for us?' Damek asked, ignoring the jest.

'Our alarm signals went off and we have orders to bring whomever we find at this gate straight to our lord fathers. It seems you are expected.'

Damek thought for a moment before he posed his next question. Elves were strange in the way they answered, never quite what you wanted to hear unless you asked the right questions.

'This woman is important. If there is some quarrel here between you then I will leave.' Damek hardly expected his accusation to hold truth but he needed to know what was transpiring here. Two ancient but silent rivalries where prowling the night together and he needed to know why. The home of them all? Were the Drows perhaps captives here? Never. Elvira would die before her children served a High Elf, and the two princes it seemed, were undertaking the same task.

'No quarrel. You will not leave until our lord fathers say otherwise though.'

So now *he* was a captive, Damek thought grimly.

'Are you working together?' came the impossible question from Damek's lips. Alarico shot him a sideways glance and Damek could make out the glimmering suits of both clans turn the corner in perfect unison over Alarico's shoulder.

'We are working. We are together,' was his reply and then silence as they walked side by side till the dim lights of Altair's home loomed ahead.

Damek remembered reading a human child's fairytale book once. It had been salvaged by Uriool a while back in the Purging Fires and Damek had found the gift highly amusing. The illustrations were a little less frightening than the real thing but the anatomy was quite accurate. They had also assumed that the elves were jovial forest-folk, living in trees and eating berries. Fun-loving and carefree musical folk that helped "fairies" and other creatures of the forest.

The elves had one of the best fighting forces in the Worlds, armed with weapons designed to the utmost efficiency. The Alvar was a name feared by most and challenged by few. However, they were also a race that lived close to the land and had learned to communicate with organic matter and blend their energy with that of the biological world around them. They were not immortal because of some parasite that lived inside of them or some inherent gene but because disease was unheard of. They sustained themselves with Worldly energy for as long as they felt necessary. Death was dealt by another hand or by their own, through neglect or choice. This was a mindset beyond his comprehension.

Damek revered them but kept his distance mostly because he did not know what they were capable of. They were gentle in their mannerisms but always prepared for the worst in all the best ways, courtesy of the nasty streak they inherited from their ancestors.

They arrived on the wooden steps of the great house, torches lit the walls outside, but wind-powered light burned inside. Sleek glass and wood finishes gave the dwelling a pleasant ambiance, the enormous tishgah trees, indigenous to Emara, hugged the walls and Damek was glad to depart from the granite and sandstone that surrounded him most of his life. Altair's home held a simplicity and charm that spoke to a place inside Damek that he did not know was there.

Everything seemed to hum quietly with life and Damek saw many awake at this late hour, Drows and High Elves alike. They really were working together then, setting aside their differences. But why? For war?

'Please, this way,' Alarico said, gesturing to a small door on the right.

'Thank you, Prince,' Damek said, still holding Arial like a rag doll in his arms, unable to give her blood for he was drained himself. He hurried inside, not knowing what to expect but praying that it was not too late for Arial.

Candlelight dimly lit the room. A table was set to one side and three seats set beside it. Two people occupied the room; a young and beautiful Drow witch, from the streaks in her hair, and presumably, her instructor, a sketchy looking individual with solemn but striking eyes.

'Welcome,' said the old man, 'my name is Dunkan and this is Mirian.'

'I am Damek. This woman is badly wounded, she needs help,' Damek replied quickly. He felt very out of place but he had come here for refuge and to seek assistance, not old friends.

'Please...' Dunkan said, gesturing toward the table and Damek did as he was bid, laying his woman down on the hard wooden surface.

Mirian moved closer and touched Arial's brow, then the wound in her neck. She shot him a glance. It was not accusatory but it made Damek feel even more awkward.

'She was bitten by another and...' Damek began.

'And her soul has been exposed,' Mirian finished for him.

She looked up at him again and this time he felt guilty.

'Can you help her?' he asked, trying to keep the note of hysteria out of his tone.

'Hush,' Dunkan reprimanded, 'she is new at this and she must concentrate.'

Damek was not happy at this; they send a novice to help save the woman who was probably the most important being in all the Worlds? He held his tongue however; keen to see how the elves worked their magic. He had heard that it was a spiritually channeled energy that only they had mastered and few had seen in practice.

Mirian kept her eyes open this time, seeing the channels of energy in the woman. They were fascinating, like none she had ever seen before, but perhaps it was because she had never worked on a drey lady before.

Yes, she could see the connection lines to her drey, the fire in her blood and spirit, but there was something else too...her concentration wavered and she could feel Dunkan tense beside her. She brushed her curiosity to one side and focused on the task at hand. The bite wounds were severe and would kill her within the hour. Her soul was weakened from the extraction and her heartbeat was faint. She tapped into the drey-power to try to harness it. Every being had something that drove them and if that force could be awakened, it could be used as a very efficient healing tool.

Damek watched on in hope as the sorceress's hands moved above Arial. Mirian's eyes had rolled back slightly and Damek could see Arial stirring.

The power inside her was phenomenal, Mirian realized as she delved deeper. She had found the essence of her strength but was afraid to touch it. She hesitated a moment longer, knowing that Dunkan would judge her harshly on this deed. It would be her last before she would be allowed to move onto the next level of her training. White wings settled around her shoulders and she knew she could safely continue. She gripped firmly with both hands and felt her skin set on fire, rivers of overwhelming flames swept through her and she struggled not to let go. She was rigid and her hair was flowing around her face as if a hot breeze had caught it. Only the whites of her eyes were showing and, as she started to tremble, Arial's eyes flew open.

Mirian relaxed and stumbled backward, caught by her mentor and made to sit down.

Arial sat bolt upright, air flowing into her lungs in huge gasps. Her wound had somehow disappeared while Damek had been watching Mirian, and the color had returned to her skin. She looked around briefly and upon clapping eyes on Damek, leapt off the table to embrace him fiercely. Damek was taken aback but returned the gesture after a brief hesitation.

'I knew you would not leave me to die. Thank you,' she breathed into his ear.

'She saved you,' he said, releasing her and pointing toward the spent Mirian.

'Thank you,' Arial repeated and Mirian bowed her head in acknowledgment.

'I am so sorry,' Damek said softly. They held each other's gazes for a few moments before Arial looked away and said,

'I need to find Ronan and Ramroth. I need to fulfill my destiny.' Damek was saddened by her words but could find nothing to say in reply.

'You would leave us so soon?' It was a new voice. Damek looked up to find Mirian and Dunkan gone. He recognized the speaker as the great High Elf Lord, Altair. He was taller than he remembered him being, a little older too. His blue eyes shone in the candlelight and his hands were steepled together, his long, blonde hair flowing around a clean-shaven face.

Arial bowed briefly.

'Your Highness,' she said smiling.

'My child, you are all but full grown, I see your beauty grows with you.'

It was clear to Damek that they had met before, but of course, she had been queen not so long ago.

Altair walked toward her and embraced her. A fatherly gesture more than anything else.

'I am so sorry to hear of your loss, many others have suffered with you from many corners of the Worlds,' he said sadly. Arial nodded but said not a word. Damek tried to imagine, for the first time, what it must have been like for her to watch her planet burn, watch her people die.

'Please sit, there is much we must discuss,' Altair said politely.

Arial and Damek sat next to one another and Altair took a seat opposite them both.

Arial had met him only twice before but he had known her mother and her father and her dealings with the High Elves were always pleasant. His children were charming, his wife extended every courtesy and she had a feeling the handsome Alarico harbored a small crush on her.

'As you may have noticed,' Altair began, 'we have merged our forces here on Emara. Our long lost brothers and sisters have joined us in arms against this great foe we all face.'

Damek looked on questioningly and Arial spoke up;

'But you are still too few, they come in numbers too great to tally and for every one of them, twenty soldiers are needed.'

Altair smiled, perfect white teeth gleaming along with his eyes.

'Yes. They creep into the hearts of men and they burn the air from the skies but we will be prepared,' he replied calmly.

'And how is that, Altair? Will you summon every army, and play host while the Worlds are left undefended?' Damek did not mean to sound impertinent but the question begged asking.

'Yes,' came the High Elf's calm reply once again, 'I have sent out pilot vessels as has the Drow king and we have asked every able-bodied army to join us out of free will, for only in that way will we ever hope to tip the scales in our favor.'

'But surely that is a mammoth task,' Arial remarked, 'you would have needed more than half a year's notice to plan such an assault.' But she already knew the answer before he had a chance to give it. 'That is why you left the council, you knew this day would come and you have been spreading word.'

'You are as smart as your mother, my dear, but do you know the whole tale from start to finish I wonder?' Altair asked.

This is what Arial had been waiting for, the answer to all her questions. When she made reply with her eager eyes, Altair leaned back in his chair.

'I know not how much you know, Damek, but your master knew well enough,' Altair said to the malachi.

'I know he wanted to steal Arial's soul.' Damek admitted. He glanced at Arial but her eyes remained fixed on Altair.

'Yes, but do you know why?' Altair pressed.

Damek hesitated and Arial answered for him;

'Because I am the One Prophesy.' She sounded brave but not entirely sure of herself.

'We cannot be sure of that,' Altair said. Arial frowned, as did Damek. 'Falkhar is still a fool, has been all his life, and he got his facts mixed up,' he sighed. Altair knew he had their rapt attentions so he danced around the subject no more. 'When you were still a babe Arial, your father volunteered to become the leader of an army that was created by the council. They believed that an air assault on even grounds was their best chance of defeating the wraiths. The kuvuta had been banished but it was not a question of if they returned but a question of when. The council created an immortal army of drey riders and your father would lead them in battle.'

'Immortal for they knew not when the kuvuta would return?' Damek asked. Altair nodded and said,

'It is never fair to thrust such a task upon anyone's shoulders. Immortality takes its toll on the best of us.' The elf looked weary when he spoke these words and Damek shared his sense of onerousness. Arial was silent.

'The years passed and the soldiers had to leave with their dreya for the people could never know,' he continued, 'they live a lonely existence, scattered amongst the Worlds, waiting for the call.'

'Who is to call them if my father is dead? Will they appoint another or does the duty fall to me?' Arial spoke slowly, her voice quavering a little. How was she to tell them that she could not do such a thing since she did not know how?

'Arial, people often lie to protect those they love,' Altair said carefully, leaning forward in his chair.

'I know that my parents may both still live and I know that my mother banished my father for madness. Ramroth could not tell me why though. He said that there were documents he was asked to destroy and he took me to the council, after the kuvuta attacked my planet, to try and learn what had made my mother flee the land and her family.' She said it all defensively and it came out in a rush, as if she had been waiting to repeat the information, and make it real in doing so.

'The documents Ramroth destroyed made up the bulk of evidence that the army and indeed your family ever existed. Birth certificates, signed papers of consent and so on. Ramroth wanted to go to the council for he believed that he could flush out an enemy or anger someone into letting slip some clue that could explain the reason your mother acted the way she did and trust me, that information is hard to come by, so I do not blame him in his failure.' Altair fixed Arial with a penetrating stare and asked, 'Do you wish me to continue? This tale is a hard one.'

Arial closed her eyes and nodded, licking her lips.

'Very well,' he said, 'your mother was the target of a plan dreamed up by the Lord kuvuta himself. Nagesh knew enough to be suspicious of this army's existence and his wish was to gain a seat on the council, particularly the seat of your people Arial, in order to gain access to information relating to their scattered whereabouts and take them out one by one or, if occasion should arise, have influence to delay the calling of the army for a while longer. Anything at all, as long as he was suitably placed.'

Damek snorted at this preposterous notion but was silenced by Altair's reprimanding glare.

'He knew he needed royal influence so he stole into your mother's bedchambers one dreadful night and planted his seed within her,' Altair said heavily.

Arial made a small noise in her throat and Damek was shocked stock-still. Such things were unheard of. He moved his hand to rest it upon Arial's knee. He could feel she was trembling a little. She made no move to push his hand away, nor did she acknowledge it was there. He could not imagine what thoughts must be going through her mind.

'I am sorry, my dear.' Altair said quietly. He gave her a while to recover before he continued. 'He obviously had no idea how close he was to his enemy since Valador was your mother's husband.'

'Valador.' Arial let the name roll off her tongue, knowing full well the legends but she said nothing more.

'Yes, he is your father. His strong blood flows in your veins and the power to summon the army too.' Altair said solemnly.

'By the law of blood,' Damek breathed, 'Arial, your mother was a human, and that is why the responsibility will fall to you.'

Arial looked at him and they exchanged words without moving their lips at all. Altair watched on with curiosity.

'When the babe began to grow,' Altair continued, 'she sent your father away to protect him and all the people of the Worlds for she knew of Lord Nagesh's intentions. She fled out of fear and shame and she left you in the care of the one she trusted most, for if Lord Nagesh ever realized your importance, he would hunt you down. Ramroth destroyed the documents and the child grew to indeed claim a seat on the council. His mother vouched for him and that was all the proof the council needed.'

'Soren,' Arial hissed, with more venom than Damek had ever heard her speak with.

Altair sighed deeply, as if troubled by all these things he knew, sat back in his chair and said,

'The council has fallen, the kuvuta have taken fourteen planets that we know of and the worst news is yet to come.'

Damek could not imagine what this might be but he waited patiently for the ill news.

'Are you familiar with the Religion?' Altair asked.

Arial scowled and replied,

'Yes, we broke ties and treaties with the humans upon those grounds.'

Damek knew of them too, he had had dealings with them in the past.

'Soren, your half-brother, is a member, being half-human. The humans plan to work with the wraiths in order to bring about the end to their revolution against all those "alien" to them,' Altair said, brows furrowed.

'The humans and the wraiths working together,' Damek sneered, 'this much I have already guessed.'

'Foolhardy and ambitious as it is, they have provided the kuvuta with the means to do their dirty work for them, and given them enough time to grow strong enough to defeat us all.' Altair sounded grim.

'Then anything we do will count for naught?' Damek raged. He was pacing up and down now, hands working through his dirty hair.

Altair remained quiet, staring at Arial.

'Is my father dead?' she asked softly, 'If so then we can continue gathering forces and then I shall call the army, the Blood Angels, and we can defeat them once and for all.' She looked up at Altair and found no answers in his eyes. He reached across the table and took her hand saying,

'That, my child, I do not know.'

'Then what are we to do?' Damek asked, hands planted firmly on the table.

'What we can do. Prepare to fight and try to hope,' Altair shrugged.

Arial sat back and covered her face with her hands. She now knew the truth of it and it was no easy thing to hear but at least she was safe here, for now, and at least she knew where she stood.

'I do not know how to call them.' She spoke so quietly that Damek was unsure of what she had said. 'And that frightens me.'

'You have nothing to be afraid of,' Damek said brusquely, drawing to his full height in a miss-placed protective gesture. Arial dropped her hands and got to her feet in a fury;

'Yes I do! I am supposed to be the One Prophesy but I do not know how and I am afraid!'

Damek's features softened and he sat down again submissively.

'Being afraid is not proof of cowardice Arial; it merely presents us with an opportunity to show courage. Be brave dear child.' Altair's voice was soft and lilting, comforting. 'We have all had a long evening and it is time we ate and rested. Please join me in the grand hall when you are finished here and we can speak more if you wish.' Altair gently kissed Arial on the cheek and left the room.

Damek was staring at the floor and Arial was staring at nothing. He opened his mouth to speak but she beat him to it;

'I do not mind being lied to, I understand why my mother did what she did, I do not blame Ramroth, I do not begrudge this task before me if indeed it is my task to carry out and I bear you no ill for any part you played.'

Damek fidgeted with his hands in his lap and looked up at her.

'But I am afraid,' she finished.

'I am as well,' he said, standing up and slowly drawing her into his arms. 'But we are all here for you and we will find a way.'

Damek's words gave her more comfort than any other she had heard before and she buried her face in his shoulder.

They sat that way for a long while before Damek brushed away her tears, took her hand and led her from the room.

'Let us eat and rest,' he said, mimicking Altair's regal tone. Arial laughed at him and they made their way to the grand hall, following the sounds of more laughter and enchanting music.

The wooden walls around them gave way to clear glass floors that stood three feet from the ground. Wild flowers blossomed beneath them, night daisies and moon roses, pastel pinks and shocking hues of blue. The crickets chirruped and the children, who had snuck out of the hall where their parents and older siblings danced and drank, ran along the halls playing games Arial recognized from her own childhood. Arial knew that the war trumpets would soon sound though, the laughter would die and the flowers would hide. She gripped Damek's hand all the way but released it when they entered the feasting hall.

Here, both the ceiling and the floor were glass and open to the sight of both heaven and earth. The stars covered the night sky, food and drink was plentiful, and harp, drum and violin all played together. The paneled wood was adorned with broad stroked paintings and there were no long, trestled tables and flagstone floors like in Bethriam, but small clusters of benches and rounded tables scattered all around so that if you wanted to dance, all you had to do was stand up.

Carden waved in greeting and Damek grabbed Arial's hand again, making for his table.

Arial vaguely recognized the Drow lord, her dealings with him had been fleeting and few. Damek must have met with him more often though because they greeted each other like old friends.

'Damek, how nice to have you here with us,' Carden smiled.

His wife, Elvira, her brother, Ather and Mirian, his daughter were all introduced to Arial. Arial thanked Mirian again for her help and noted that Dunkan was deep in conversation with Kieran, the elder child and only son of the royal Drow family. They sat at a different table though, close to her own, and Altair's youngest sat with them. Kieran was three years older than his ex-rival, Alarico, making him the same age as Arial and he was handsome in a different way to the High Elf prince. Arial had never seen him before but he interested her. He glanced at her briefly and his eyes were piercing, his full lips curled into a curious smile and Arial looked away.

Alarico came over to greet her, blushing ever so slightly and only for a second. He too, was tall, blonde like his father with soft blue eyes like a clear spring morning set against his dusky High Elf skin. He kissed her hand and bid her sit at his table with his family later on. She thanked him graciously for his invitation.

Damek and Carden were talking business. Arial soon gathered that Damek was a relic hunter and that was how his path had crossed Carden's. Mirian wanted to know as much about dreya as Arial could say between mouthfuls of sweet pie and red wine, while Elvira paid nobody any heed except her son and the pretty young princess he sat with.

Arial found herself staring at Elvira and was startled when she realized Elvira was staring right back. Elvira raised an eyebrow and said,

'Please forgive me my rudeness. My son is betrothed to young Vanora and I am, as any mother is, curious...and a little envious.'

Arial swallowed her mouthful of apples and replied,

'They seem to make a good match. I am sure she will make him happy just as sure as I am that he will not forget you.' She was not sure what else to say.

Elvira leaned closer and filled her glass with more wine, her eyes already a little lazy with drink.

'I hear your planet was destroyed,' she said.

Arial blanched.

'Yes,' she replied stiffly, a clear end to the topic but Elvira was having none of it;

'What was it like? Flying away while the people were being slaughtered?'

'Where are you going with this?' Arial asked, she was done being polite.

'Nowhere. All I mean to say is that sometimes things happen that we did not foresee and did not welcome but have to deal with for the good of the whole. Us women have the hard way of it more oft than not. I am uncomfortable with my present lot but I see you are worse off and I just want you to realize that.'

'But why?' Arial asked, much hurt by the ice queen's words.

'Because pain makes us stronger. Acceptance makes us hard and that is what we have to be. Use the anger. It will be your best defense when the time comes.'

She was a woman hard done by, Arial assumed. She had become bitter and hard and she did not want to be the only one.

'I disagree,' Arial said firmly. Elvira arched her eyebrow again and gripped her glass tighter.

'Understanding and forgiveness are the things that should drive you and will provide you with the best defenses,' Arial finished.

Elvira downed her glass of wine and looked questioningly at the drey queen.

'Perhaps you are right and I am an old crone,' Elvira said, smiling suddenly. Arial relaxed. 'You young people think you have the way of it and perhaps you do!' she was gesturing with her re-filled glass and sloshing it over the white cotton tablecloth. In an instant, Kieran was by her side, gently laying hands on her shoulders.

'Mother, perhaps you and I can retire early tonight. Would you like that?' Elvira gazed lovingly up at her son and placed her already half-empty glass down.

'Yes, alright then, take an old, drunken woman to bed. I shall be glad for the company for I fear I shall fall asleep on the way there.'

All harsh tones had melted away and Arial pitied her. Her known world was falling into another and she was set in her ways, being left behind. Kieran helped his mother up and winked at Arial, leaving her a slight crimson color. They left through the less-crowded back door and Arial did not see them again.

'My wife is a fish swimming upstream,' Carden confided in her once they had left.

'Perhaps you should help her swim then instead of watching her drown. Please excuse me,' Arial said flatly. She stood up without waiting for a reply and walked toward Altair's table, leaving Damek and the Drows behind.

She was lost amongst the throng of dancers and Damek could not see where she was seated amidst all the moving bodies.

'Well, well,' Carden said, 'planning on taming the fire maiden are we?' Damek grinned in return to Carden's jest.

'She has been through much the last couple of days; please do not take anything she says too much to heart,' Damek said, standing up to go and find her.

Carden took a generous swig from his goblet of mead and muttered to himself,

'Sounds like my wife.'

Damek made his way through the crowd to the High Elves' table. Vanora now sat on her father's lap, Alarico sat talking to Braenden, the High Elf warrior and Delwyn was stroking her husband's hair.

'Did Arial come this way?' he asked, trying to sound casual.

'She came to bid us goodnight and then she left for bed,' Alarico piped up.

'I see,' Damek said, a little perturbed that she had not bothered to wish him a goodnight.

Carden and Mirian walked over to the table too and Damek turned to walk away. Mirian grabbed his sleeve as he passed and whispered,

'She sleeps in the east wing tonight vampire. A private, open-roofed chamber I told her take, for the night air will do her good.' Damek thanked her and strode off toward the east wing, jostling against sensually intertwined bodies moving to the beat of the Drow drums.

Carden took a seat next to Altair and they watched Damek depart from the hall.

'Ah, my friend, I fear we are getting too old for this sort of gathering,' Carden said wistfully as he watched the young slide past one another provocatively and dance in circles grasping the next, spinning faster and faster to the beat of the drums. Delwyn threw back her head and laughed heartily. Altair looked up at her in surprise.

'Why, I remember dancing this very same dance with you, Carden, not so many years ago,' she said.

Carden and Delwyn's betrothal had been the first attempt to reconcile the clans but another dispute had broken it.

'You were young then, my dear, and less full of strange ways,' Carden jested.

Altair smiled broadly and added,

'Would that you had put up with her instead!'

Delwyn pinched him on the arm and Vanora followed her mother's suit.

'When will I be old enough to join the dancing father?' Vanora pleaded as she watched Kieran dance with another.

'When Kieran asks you, sweet child,' Altair said kindly. She pouted at her father's words but her mother gave her a stern look and she stopped.

'My son wants to dance with you Vanora, but I have told him to wait. Only eight seasons will pass and then he will come to you.' Carden was as impatient as the princess to seal the deal but she was only fourteen and still too young.

'Love waits for no one,' Delwyn sighed. 'I have seen the way our two new guests look at one another. Love waits for no war either it seems.'

Altair looked meaningfully at Carden. The Drow lord furrowed his brow.

'Nations have been lost to love,' Carden said, still staring at the dancers.

'They have also been saved. Let us not forget Limneth,' Altair countered.

'You both have many cases in your defense, but perhaps it is not even so. He is an immortal vampire; she is a drey maiden who will not live past a hundred years. Their match is an unlikely one and I am sure they know that themselves,' Delwyn threw in.

They were all quiet for a little while and Delwyn noticed the look in her son's eyes.

'What say you, Alarico?' she asked, eager to hear what was on his mind and on his heart. He looked up unabashed and said,

'Let us test him,' without hesitation. Yes, she had raised her son well.

'Who shall we send?' Delwyn asked.

'I have just the man,' Carden said, a cunning look creeping across his features.

'If you say Hronn I will have to forbid you anymore of my fine wine!' Altair declared mockingly.

Hronn was summoned over just as soon as they could tear him away from a pretty, young elf and was sent to Arial's chambers.

'This seems a little cruel,' Vanora said, not old enough to understand exactly what was going on but wise enough to grasp the concept.

'Sweetling,' her father said, 'love can be dangerous and in times like these, it is always best to be safe.'

Vanora nodded.

The drums stopped beating and a softer tune filled the air. Kieran came sidling up to the table and asked Vanora to dance.

'Just a small one,' he promised as his father fixed him with a reprimanding glare. With no other objections, he picked Vanora up, swept her off her feet, and whirled her around the dance floor whilst she screamed in delight.

Altair, Carden and Delwyn all clapped in time to the rhythm and Mirian looked sideways at Alarico.

'I suppose we should dance too,' he said to her, 'just to keep them happy.' He gestured to their parents and she agreed, if a little reluctantly, but not as reluctantly as he.

*

Arial's room was open to the night sky. The stars were different here and she realized just how far away she was from her broken home. Her parents could still be alive, she had a brother out there somewhere ready to exterminate the Worlds and she still pined for her drey with an ache she could barely stand. She could still feel him though and if she was not mistaken, he was drawing closer. She needed him now more than ever. She knew now that her place was here, where the war would be fought, but she needed to have him by her side. She was grieving for her mother too, the woman who had suffered so much and suffered it alone. She wondered where her father was, if he was still alive, and if she would ever see him.

She ran her hands across the satin sheets of her bed and enjoyed the cool, night breeze as it played across her bare shoulders. Delwyn had been kind enough to provide her with an array of garments so that she could finally discard of her old chiffon raiment, bloodstained and travel-worn. She was now adorned in a loosely fitted gown that was a little too long for her, but allowed her skin to breath. It was ruby-colored and sat low off her shoulders, flaring at the sleeves and trailing across the wooden floors.

She was combing out her hair when there came a soft knock at the papyrus sheet that served as a door.

'Who is it?' she called out. No reply came; the panel was merely slid aside. She craned her neck to make out by firelight who stood at the entrance. It was someone she did not recognize. She stood up and asked, 'Who might you be sir?' The man was well built and wore black pants with no shirt. A chain hung around his neck and an animal's claw hung from it, curved and menacing in the gleam of the stars. He had waves of chestnut colored hair and dark, brown eyes, liquid and swimming.

'My name is Hronn,' he replied. A deep, baritone voice, melodious and inviting. He was no elf but Arial could not place him.

'What are you doing in my chambers?' she asked, quite affronted that he should be there in the first place, no matter what the excuse.

'I have been sent by the royal families as a gift.' He bowed low and straightened with a flourish, his hair bouncing around his comely face. Arial considered this statement for a while. What sort of gift, she wondered. She knew it was many a tribe's custom to send a gift to the bedchambers of the guest but surely Altair would know better. *She* was no lustful man. She was a *queen*.

'What sort of gift?' she asked suspiciously.

'The kind you will enjoy,' he replied, smiling at her graciously.

'If this is leading where I think it is then please take your leave, I have no need for carnal amusement and tell your lord that we shall have words come morning.' Her tone was haughty and harsh. She was insulted and baffled at the same time and was not sure what to make of the situation. Hronn looked just as affronted as she and he frowned ever so slightly at her;

'My lady has it all wrong; I have been sent to keep your dark thoughts away by providing light conversation and entertainment. I was not sent here to share your bed with you if that is what you mean.'

Arial blushed deeply at her own assumptions;

'Sorry, I just thought that...'

'Never you mind,' he interrupted, 'many a fine young maiden such as yourself has assumed many things about my intentions.' He smiled wickedly and Arial suppressed a giggle. He was very attractive and she could only imagine how true his words were.

'Still, I need no counsel but appreciate the gesture of good will,' she said with finality.

'I am also not here to provide counsel. That is why wards and council-men exist. I am here to provide light conversation and entertainment,' he repeated.

'Well then,' Arial said, sitting down heavily on the bed, 'this is very awkward, what shall we talk about since you refuse to leave?'

Hronn smiled.

'I can see you are in no mood to talk. I shall show you something instead!' he said brightly.

His manner was jesterly and she found it laughable but curious all the same.

He walked over to her and knelt before her, taking her hands in his. Arial was clearly uncomfortable by the close contact and pulled her head away a little.

'Close your eyes,' he said. Arial gave him a look close to mistrust and he said, 'I am not going to kiss you, they do not pay me enough.'

She placed her hand over her mouth to stop from laughing. This man was very easy to be with and she felt all her frigidity melt away.

'Very well,' she assented and closed her eyes. He was still holding onto her hands when he said,

'Now think of an animal, any animal that walks the Worlds and is smaller than this room.'

Arial tried to remember the dimensions of the room and think of an animal that would fit inside it and was not a fish.

'Do you have one?' he asked.

'Yes,' she answered, with eyes squeezed tightly shut like a child at a magic show. She felt Hronn's hands release hers and after twenty beats she wondered where he had gone.

Something jumped up next to her on the bed and she opened her eyes in surprise. Hronn was no longer in the room; a dark and sleek panther had taken his place and was lying lazily on her bed. Her mouth hung open in shock as she gazed upon this creature who had not roamed the Worlds in many years and the likes of which she had only witnessed in history books but had always wanted to see.

'I was thinking of a chicken,' she said almost breathlessly.

'I eat chickens for breakfast,' came the lazy reply. The panther was talking to her! Its pink tongue moved in its fanged mouth as it spoke with Hronn's voice.

Hronn watched the many expressions that crossed the young queen's face.

'You may touch me...if you wish to,' he said.

Arial looked long and deep into his green cat eyes, wondering if she should resist temptation and if this was not some sort of trick. Need took precedence over caution and she reached out with a trembling hand to touch the black pelt. It was as smooth as honeyed milk under her caress and once she became braver, she ran her fingers through it with more vigor; all the while her mouth was a small O of wonder and enjoyment.

Hronn the panther started to purr softly causing Arial to abruptly withdraw her hand and the panther leaped off the bed landing on the floor as a peacock. The brightly colored birds were native to these climates but Arial was impressed again nonetheless. He spread his regal tail for her and curtseyed. 'Your Majesty,' the peacock said.

Arial laughed out loud and called for more.

For a small while, all her thoughts and fears disappeared as Hronn took her through a show of almost every animal and bird she had ever seen or wanted to see. He spoke to her all the while, making her laugh and doing silly things. He became a snake and coiled his cold, muscled body around her arm, he became a butterfly that tickled the end of her nose when he sat there and then he roared the mighty roar of the desert cat that made Arial's ribcage reverberate, before she told him to shush or he'd wake the others.

He became her panther once more and leapt upon the bed beside her again. She was tired and she lay her head down on the soft midnight fur of his flank.

'What are you Hronn? An Adare'?' she asked, gazing into the expanse of the Emara sky.

'No. I am a shape-shifter my lady,' he replied. All jest was gone from his voice. Shape shifting was frowned upon by many and illegal to perform in most nations. The wielders of this strange art were usually outcasts and employed to do terrible things with their powers. Terrible or humiliating. Some roamed free but were called demons wherever their true identity was made known. They were also very rare and Arial had begun to wonder at the truth of any of it. Now she knew.

'*Who* are you then? Answer me that instead and redeem me of my rude question.'

The cat sat up and nuzzled the side of her face.

'I am Hronn the shape-shifter sweet lady; I am whoever you want me to be.'

His voice was no more than a whisper in Arial's ear and she was so lulled by it. It drew her in and made her want to hear more of it. She looked up at his words and found not a panther but a man. Ramroth was sitting on the side of her bed, his creased smile shedding light on her heart. She leant forward and hugged her ward, tears threatening to spill for the second time that night.

'I am so happy,' she managed.

'Do not cry my lady,' Hronn said, brushing her tears aside with Ramroth's fingers.

'Do not tease me so then,' she said through a smile, inches away from Hronn's masked face.

'How then shall I tease you?' he asked, his wizened old face turning into the face of a young squire with whom she had been infatuated when she was very young. She laughed again, slapping him softly on the arm;

'That was ages ago, that is not fair!'

'A more recent affair then?' he grinned, the smile of the squire turning to the smile of young Alarico.

'Your hair is too neat,' she joked and Hronn vigorously mussed up his hair. Arial giggled again. Alarico grabbed her by the waistline and declared his undying love to her, lifting her up and laying her down on the bed.

'Do not be so cruel, he is a boy with a crush and that is all,' she reprimanded.

'What then of this boy, a boy no longer though?' Hronn shifted into Kieran and Arial was startled. Up close he was far better looking than he had been further away. Perhaps it was a trick of the light but her heart beat faster still. Kieran's face was older and less childish than Alarico's and his gaze was impenetrable and sincere.

'I cannot say that I love you but what of one night queen of dragons?' he offered, smiling the same self-assured smile that Kieran did when he thought he was not being watched, sliding his hand tantalizingly up her leg on the outside of her gown.

'This is absurd!' Arial said, sitting up and pushing him away, half laughing, half angry.

'What of this then?'

Arial turned back to Hronn only to find herself staring into the green and gold pools of Damek's eyes. They seared her with intensity and seemed to undress her where she sat. She was frozen to the spot. She had been willing to let herself get lost in this little game of Hronn's, but feeling the stirring inside of her that she had let herself feel with Hronn for pure amusement, suddenly became palpable and real. It was a game no longer and Arial could say nothing to get Hronn to stop. It was not even Hronn anymore in her mind.

Damek moved himself closer to her and raised his hand to brush her soft cheek. He surrounded her with his strong arms and she let herself fall into him.

'Do you love me?' he breathed, the hot air from his lips brushing the small of her neck. He placed a tender kiss just below her ear.

She had wanted this so much but had not known it. His protection enveloped her, his voice stirred her and she was irresistibly drawn to all that he was. She leaned her head to one side subconsciously so that he may have better access to her, his hands climbing up her middle, his sweet smell upon her…her eyes flew wide open and she yelled,

'No!'

When she looked again, it was Hronn's arms she was in and not Damek's and she was ever grateful that she did not do something she would regret.

A noise at the door made them both look up. The real Damek stood framed in the doorway wearing a grim expression. Arial leapt up off the bed, pure shock upon her features.

'So this is what you left for,' he asked, gesturing at Hronn.

The shape-shifter got to his feet and walked out of the room once Damek had given him a dirty enough look and let him pass.

'I...cannot explain,' she finished. How was she to tell him that it was *his* arms she had succumbed to?

'You need not explain a thing to me. I merely came to bid you a goodnight and see if there was anything else you needed. It is clearly unnecessary.' Damek folded his arms across his chest and stood uneasily in the doorway. 'Goodnight,' he added, turning to walk away.

Arial narrowed her eyes and stomped over to where he stood, grabbing his sleeve.

'You came all this way to bid me goodnight and are angered when you find me in the arms of another? I do not believe you.'

'Believe what you will but I am not angry!' His voice rose and his tone gave him away.

Arial smirked with one side of her mouth.

'Yes you are. You feel for me as I do for you and you are angry.'

A strange blank expression settled over his face at her words and she backed off, trying to fend off the embarrassment and rejection but when she looked into his eyes, she did not see the refusal that she feared would be there. She sat down heavily on the bed, now fearing what her words had done.

Damek was before her in the blink of an eye, kneeling as Hronn had done but this time she did not draw back.

'The love I bear you frightens me.' His eyes were imploring and his voice was sincere. 'For me to feel this way is rarely spoken of amongst our kind. You have given me light and hope and strength. Things I thought I knew about but have never truly grasped.' He hung his head in shame. 'But I am what I am and I would have fed you to the fire for my weakness if it were not for the help of an old friend.'

He knelt there at her feet like a lost disciple. She placed a hand beneath his chin and raised his head so his eyes would meet hers. They sat like that for a long time until Arial broke the spell and leant down toward him.

'*I* am the fire,' she whispered.

He met her lips with tender surrender and they shared the sweetest kiss that the night had to offer.

Arial felt as if she had waited her whole life to share that moment with him. He gently nudged her back until he was on top of her and she moved her hands down and under his cloak, pulling it from his frame, unable to stand the wait for his rare touch. Their kiss intensified as he felt her need match his own and he was tugging at her robe, burying his face in her naked chest and breathing in her scent like a man who has found oxygen after long years of slowly suffocating. Their movements were fevered and passionate, their kisses long and fiery. They held on to each other as if the break of day would tear them apart. She ran her fingers across his bare back and along his long jaw-line.

He closed his eyes, giving in to all the pleasures he had for so long denied himself. He hauled her up to sit on top of him, admiring her naked form down to the waist, thighs exposed to the kisses of the stars. She pulled at his shoulders with urgency and he savored the way her eyes devoured his every move. He traced his lips along her shoulder, hot breath against her flesh and she moaned low and long in his ear. He held her tightly and felt as if he needed to be closer still, lose himself within her compelling embrace. He threw back his head and cried out in anguish;

'I cannot do this!'

He leapt off the bed and thrust his cloak back on.

Arial bundled her robe up around herself, pain and confusion in her eyes.

'I cannot do this,' he repeated, softly this time. He stood framed by the moonlight, hands on his hips, breathing hard. He refused to look at her. She stood up and walked to him. She put her arms around him tenderly so as not to frighten him away a second time. She searched his eyes for an answer but could find none.

'Damek,' she whispered, 'stay with me tonight.'

'I cannot,' he whispered back, barely able to talk from the pure proximity of this woman. He kissed her fiercely before taking his leave and closing the door behind him only to stand in the hallway a tortured man. Arial held her fingers up to the door, knowing he stood just beyond it. Damek put his hand against hers so that he could feel her warmth through the papyrus.

'I *will* protect you, even from myself,' he murmured to the night.

*

Sirena was dreaming, she was almost sure of it. She was standing upon a raised platform, an ocean of darkness spread out before her like some giant, black quilt. All were ready to do their duty, all were ready to purge the Worlds of the unclean. They were watching her; she could feel their empty eyes on her. She felt proud, like a mother. She spread out her arms wide and called to them. They came, eager as children. They were all around her, swarming up the platform one by one just to touch her. Soon they were upon her and the shadows felt cool against her skin. The shadow wraiths swirled around her body and groped eagerly at her exposed flesh. The feelings they stirred within her were intensifying. Her heart quickened and her eyes flew open. Soren's eyes were staring back at her.

He was half-way done with what he had come to do but she had only just awoken to the reality of it. At first she was scared but that feeling soon melted to be replaced by another; pure exhilaration.

She writhed beneath her new kuvuta lord in ecstasy, enthralled by his power and the feel of his long claws pulling at her skin. She was wreathed in his shadow and time seemed to stand still. Made his for the first time, not the other way round. He possessed her in a way she could never have imagined and she cried out in elation, savoring every second of his rough touch, every heartbeat that he was inside her, every brutal thrust and every ounce of pain that he wrung from her willing body. She was overcome with his power and presence.

Afterward, he left her bed and went to stand by the open arched window. He still kept his silence and Sirena was not sure if she should speak at all, but the words gushed out before she could hold her tongue.

'What happened to you? I did not know it was possible to cross over completely! Has your father seen you?'

Soren turned, slowly but irritably. He gave her a look that could chill bones and she shrank back, covering her nakedness with the discarded blanket. He turned back and spoke to the night instead;

'I am still me, I choose this form now.'

Sirena leaned forward again, a smile spreading across her features. He even sounded different. More aware, poised, controlled. No longer the man she married, but the man she hoped he would become. This time, she kept quiet, waiting for him to speak again...

'Tomorrow I will go before the brothers. I will speak openly to them,' he said at length.

'As a representative?' Sirena asked.

'No, as their leader!' he thundered. '*I* am their leader, not Velasco and not my father. I hatched this plot even if my father sewed the seed and I will be the one to bring it to fulfillment.'

Sirena shivered. It was one thing for *her* to have borne witness to the kuvuta but the brothers might not be so open-minded. Yes, they knew who their allies were but the sheer sight of these beasts might breed doubt in the minds of a few. She had met his father before, his hatred burned in his eyes and his dark nature was so palpable it left a taste at the back of your throat.

'Do you think it wise?' she enquired timidly.

'I think you are all fools,' he said, 'we have put this off for far too long and it is time.'

'But what of this Blood Angel theory?'

Soren was upon her in an instant. He loomed over her like the demon plague he was and grasped her cruelly by the chin, forcing her face upwards. She was no longer his master and he would deal with her the way he dealt with everybody else.

'I have had enough of your words woman. The human in me made me weak but now I know. I know that nothing can defeat us and I will devour these Worlds.'

Sirena's heart beat faster as his words fed her lust for war.

'Then we begin tomorrow?' she asked, 'you will lead us into battle and we shall have our war?' She was on her feet now, the blanket left discarded once again.

'Yes, we shall have our war. We shall tear out the hearts of all the unclean and feed their souls to the fire of eternity.'

He could see now what he had always seen in her. Her unyielding need for bloodshed that matched his own. She was a strong woman but he did not need her any longer.

Sirena walked over to him and gently draped her slender arms around his shoulders. The cold was acute but she relished it.

'And if I carry your child? We shall raise him well, to be like his father. A new breed.'

Soren felt nothing. Not as a human feels.

'There is very little difference between our two races,' he said flatly, 'only choice separates us. And weakness perhaps. But once you have made the choice to be strong...'

He stared blankly at her for some time, and eventually she let go of him. He had changed so much.

'I will prepare the brothers,' she said, knowing that she would receive nothing from him anymore unless he chose to give it freely. He stood thinking upon that while she dressed. He did not look at her hungrily anymore, she noticed, like he wanted all that she could give and knew she was holding back. He held the power now.

'Will you stay here tonight?' she asked, already knowing the answer.

'No, I will see my kind tonight and when the sun rises, we will take another planet.'

Sirena thought to correct him, it was Velasco that decided when and where the attacks took place, but his tone brooked no argument and she knew that from here on out, blood would be shed on the kuvuta's terms, on Soren's terms, and that no one was safe.

*

Cold Barrow. Not so cold in the height of summer, Adisa reflected happily.

It was the festival of new moons that night and dusk was settling on the landscape. The moons were rising red against the azure-blue sky and Adisa could make out the looming figures of the jagged mountains in the distance, slightly darker than the sky they pierced.

'Have you come to help or stand around like a half-wit all night?' It was her mother, calling her from down the way. She turned her head and could make out the twinkling fairy lights that had been strung up in the valley for the party. So much preparation had gone into the event. The guest list included every able-bodied person in Lord Tanvir's land and even the feeble were urged to come, horses being sent to carry them. It was to be a night like no other. Free wine and ale, the first sweet harvests and no expense had been spared.

Adisa's brother was part of the band that was playing and she and all the other lord's servants would be serving at the tables. Adisa was very excited. All her friends would be there and Niyol would be there too. She skipped and ran down the footpath to join her mother.

'Young lady, get your head out the clouds, there's much work to be done!' her mother scolded.

Niyol was feverishly impatient for the toasts and speeches to be done with. His father, Lord Tanvir, had asked him to say a few words too, since he would be lord over the holdings in a few short years. Niyol had no love for politics and all the formalities and duties that came with being a ruler. He became bored easily in all his classes except for history and the art of war. He was seventeen and a strong man. He could wield a sword along with the best of them and his squires cheered him on whenever he took on one of his lord father's guards and won. But wielding words of diplomacy did not come so easily to him. He was still young and he yearned to be free to be so.

The first time he had seen Adisa was in the kitchens. He could not sleep that night and had ordered the bakers to stoke the stoves early and bake him some fresh bread.

She had come stumbling in, hair bedraggled with hay, eyes still bleary and movements marred by unfinished sleep but he watched her, transfixed, as she collected bundles of wood and lit the stoves. Her hair was like autumn, her eyes like a clear day and her voice as she sang to herself was like a bell ringing in his heart.

'More like a gong going off in your pants!' his older sister scoffed but he paid her no heed.

From then on, he had tried to sneak glimpses of her as often as he could. She worked in the kitchens though, so how many excuses could he possibly think of, to be there day in and day out, to see her delicate hands as they kneaded the dough, her beautiful, round face streaked with flour?

One night, he waited outside the doors until the others had tired of playing card games, and the head bakers had drank all of the wine he had given them as a gift. He had tiptoed past the snoring mounds of bodies and stood behind her as she packed the deck of cards neatly together. She bent over to blow out the candle but he had sheltered it with his hand and she had been so startled to find him standing there with her in the kitchen. Eyes wide and breath stopped short.

'My lord,' she had said, curtseying in an awkward manner.

'My name is Niyol and you are Adisa.' That was all he could think of to say, standing there in the rapture of her simple beauty, the smell of bread and yesterday's pie filling the room.

She had giggled at his strangeness and soon they were talking like old friends. She showed him how to make the bread, how you could do almost anything to old man Sanders and he would not wake until the cock crowed. He, in turn, showed her the gardens, taught her all the names of the flowers and had shown her how to loose an arrow from a long bow.

He arrived every night to fetch her once the others had gone to bed and the castle was theirs. The secret was theirs too and over the weeks, they got to know each other very well. He was a gentleman though and never touched her. Adisa was not used to such behavior, she was no maid but it felt good none the less, to be treated like a lady. She cherished the stolen moments and her heart thumped so loud when she bid her friends and family goodnight that she thought it might give her away but it never did.

Niyol had bedded a serving girl or two but Adisa was different, she was smart and funny and he wanted her to feel special.

The night before the new moons festival, no one had slept because there was simply too much to do. Adisa did her work dutifully but was angry at the thought that she would not see Niyol that night.

'Here, what's this then?' One of the bakers had found a letter but he could not read and Adisa had snatched it from him and ran away quick as lightning before any of the others had a chance to see. It was from Niyol, he had written to her telling her to meet him under the weeping willows further down the valley on the night of the festival. She was instructed to sneak away, once the dancing had started and the drink was flowing freely, so that she would not be missed.

Butterflies danced wildly in her stomach and she could hardly wait. Her prince, her Niyol.

Niyol did his duty, made the toasts and blessed the land and the people loved him, he could hear it in their cheers and his father gave him an approving nod. He watched Adisa serve the table two down from his, the gentle arch of her neck as she poured the wine, the way she laughed and joked with the guests.

When the flutes began to play and the jesters started to dance on the tables singing their songs, he politely excused himself and left his father's side. He did not care that he would be missed the entire night and risk his father's wrath. He needed to be with her.

Adisa watched Niyol get up and their eyes met across the brightly lit lawn and all the people sitting at the tables talking loudly. She put down her platter of syrup fruits and hurriedly made her excuses. As soon as they left the circle of light and the voices were drowned out by the sound of the rushing river and the frogs bellowing at one another, they joined hands and ran alongside the embankment, laughing at their own trick. They passed a few couples in the darkness with the same idea as them and waved merrily at them. No one could be identified in the darkness that cloaked the valley and so they had nothing to fear.

When they had walked for a long enough while, and were sure they were alone, they sat down by the brook, bare feet dangling in the water. They spoke half the night away. They laughed and kissed and threw things into the water, scaring the frogs and silencing the crickets for a few moments. The stars were fading and dawn was going to break in a few hours but they were far away from anybody else, lost in the moment of their youth and each other's company. They were lying down on the dewy grass, watching the constellations fade. He rolled over and kissed her deeply.

'You are very special to me Adisa,' he said, face composed and serious. Her own face was framed by the wild daisies and wet grass. She had never looked more beautiful.

'How special?' she asked teasingly, grabbing at him playfully.

'No, you don't understand,' he said, getting to his feet angrily.

'I was only playing,' she said, sitting up and looking hurt. Perhaps she had spoiled the moment. Did he not want to lie with her? He was busy fiddling with something in his pocket and Adisa was starting to get frustrated. 'Why do you court me so and then leave me unsatisfied? What is it you want from me?' She was angry and Niyol had not meant for it to happen like this. He turned to face her and his expression was so soft and worried that Adisa was confused again.

'Please stand up,' he asked.

She did as she was bid, brushing the stray grass and soil that clung to her skirt. He grabbed hold of her hands;

'Stop, you are perfect just the way you are.'

Their eyes met and for a fleeting instant Adisa thought she knew what was coming but it could not possibly be. She was a serving girl and he was to be lord of the lands, a highborn. He dropped to one knee nonetheless and she clasped her hands over her mouth in utter shock. She tried to wrench him to his feet again simply because she did not know what else to do.

'Damn it woman,' he said, breaking free from her feeble attempts, looking up at her in frustration. 'Do you always have to be so damnably stubborn?' he asked, a smile breaking out on his handsome face at last. 'Now,' he continued, settling nicely into his original position, 'I want to make an honest woman of you and I cannot imagine going through a single day without your warmth. I want to bend a knee to the conqueror of my heart. '

'But...' she started, hands over her mouth again.

'But nothing, can you not see that I love you? Will you marry me?' He held in his fingers a silver ring studded with purple stones. Adisa's eyes started to fill with tears of such joy that she did not know what to do with it all. She fell to her knees before him and kissed him fiercely.

'I'll take that as a yes?' he asked, through mouthfuls of her overflowing show of happiness.

That early morning, just before the star had kissed the land, they made love on the grass beside the river. Slow and gentle like summer's first rains. Afterward, they lay next to each other, naked and in silence, listening to the sound of the valley coming to life. She propped her head up on one elbow, strands of hair threatening to fall into her flushed face.

'What will your father say?' she asked, her brows furrowed with concern.

Niyol sighed.

'He will say what he always says; "find a woman with child bearing hips and have sons!"' he roared, lifting her up by the waist and laughing.

'It's not funny,' she said, 'put me down!'

He did and she crossed her arms huffily across her chest.

'Perhaps I should marry a man with more sense.'

Niyol frowned and pulled her closer to him.

'Don't say such things. We will find a way. You have the power to darken my skies with the harsh things you say,' he said softly. She relented and put her arms around him, breathing in his musky scent. The rising star seemed to go behind a cloud and they both looked up. A black cloud. The sky darkened.

Chapter 12

Progress

Soren had never felt more alive. He rode a beast born of black flames and together they wreaked havoc upon this tiny planet. Human heathens with no gods but the moon and sun and stars. They gave thanks to water and ground and praised no being, believed in no afterlife. Sinners.

He watched his brethren drive hordes of screaming people before them, cornering them, filling the air with poison. Blood ran in rivers. The beasts tore flesh from bone, arguing over the spoils. Women twisted baby's necks to save them the pain, men made feeble attempts with blade against darkness. The grasses and trees withered and died and the castle walls crumbled with the sheer weight and force of his army. He could smell the blood and the fear and the burnt corpses and it only made him want more. He hacked at the heathens with his claws, blood-drunk and frenzied. This was what it felt like to be alive, to have power, to wield fear into the hearts of those he hated most. And god would cast his enemies down…

They stood beneath the smoldering weeping willows; ash falling upon Soren's shoulders like snow, the smell of the tar that the everglades had become permeated the air.

'Today the nations will begin to fall one by one.' He was speaking to Esyago.

'We moved too slowly before, your humans feeding us planets they thought were far enough away and safe enough to take,' Esyago hissed. Soren's lieutenants, Malik and Izyan growled their assent.

'All that has changed now. We will take them when we please and we will swallow these Worlds whole,' Soren said firmly. Esyago smiled beneath his cloak of shadow. 'They will no longer hold sway over us, I will see to it,' he continued, 'they are weak, and they need to be guided but, they are an asset. They will provide us with the means to move on and grow stronger. Many more galaxies await and there will be no warning.'

Soren could see that he had been wrong in waiting. This place was theirs for the taking and take it they would. Retribution waited for no man.

'Should we initiate the black star Lord Soren?' Esyago asked his new leader.

Something stirred in the grass by their feet. A young woman, naked and bleeding. Her legs had been crushed but still she made feeble attempts to move. She was clawing her way to the man that lay near her. He was dead already.

'Heathen,' Soren spat. He spurred his beast forward and he slashed her pretty little face off. Her teeth and gums bared, her skull shattered, she died with a shudder. His beast began to eat what was left of her body but Soren pulled at the reigns.

'I will meet with the humans now. Initiate the dark star; drink the light. Tonight we make another.'

*

Uriool walked into the hall where the battle had taken place. Adonica lay where she had died. The cremators would come and fetch her soon. The great columns were broken in places, the ancients lay like shriveled corpses against the walls where they had been flung and the anima ashes littered the stone like snow.

His malachi Shadow Brothers had become very strong.

Scorch marks marred the walls like shadows and Uriool tried not to flinch at the sight of them. He could feel something stirring in the devastated room but wrote it off as magical vestige.

Falkhar had been taken to his room where physicians were working on restoring his broken heart. How ironic, Uriool thought as he fingered Adonica's soft hair. Her throat had been ripped out and she would not ever recover from the wound. Falkhar was stronger, older; his body had taken more true blood. He closed her eyes and went to see his master. He had been summoned. He placed the silken black gloves over his scarred hands and climbed to the tower.

The room smelt strange, like death had been and gone, had left empty-handed. He stood framed in the doorway, silent as ever, the angel of mercy.

'Leave us,' Falkhar commanded and his physicians scurried from the chamber clutching their strange array of medicines and herbs. Borrowed magic from those who knew how to heal better than they.

'Come closer, Uriool.' Falkhar motioned with his hand from behind the netted drapes of his bed. The half-breed did as he was told, taking a few steps closer to his master. 'You chose your alliances well, you have been shunned by all others while I welcomed you with open arms, plucked you from the fire in the name of love for my sister and I raised you as my own.'

Uriool tightened his fingers into a fist and relaxed them again, the memory of the Purging Fires still fresh in his memory. Nothing of that night had faded, not the pain, not the scars and not the screams of his parents. 'I have trusted you and called upon you in my times of need and now I have one last thing to ask of you.' Falkhar was weak now, perhaps too weak and Uriool could see it pained him to speak where his throat had been half crushed.

Uriool was listening to all that Falkhar said and it was true. The humans had come to his village many, many years ago and burnt it, burnt his friends and family at the stake, burnt it all to the ground. His father was a Drow and his mother was a malachi, Falkhar's sister, and the Shadow Brothers had come for her and the child, only to find it was too late for her and almost too late for the boy. The Deep Forest Drows had all but been wiped out and Uriool was one of few that had remained. He had kept his silence ever since, a boy of twelve with the weight of the world on his shoulders measured in grief. He had been a good pupil though and always listened. He traveled to his people's planets sometimes, always watching and listening. He had no real place in the Worlds but he had a place to rest his head at night; with the malachi, but his heart constantly yearned for the forests. The sunlight streaming in through the canopies, the life that surged beneath them, the wind and the water; the simpler way of life. He had had enough stone now, enough scheming and struggling.

In an instant he was beside Falkhar and the old vampire had to turn his injured neck slowly to look at him. Masked face, gloved hands, silent as the grave from whence he was plucked.

Uriool removed his gloves and touched Falkhar's forehead, no fever to show for the agony his body was suffering, growing a new heart for him.

Falkhar tried not to shudder beneath Uriool's hands. They were smooth and shiny in most places but puckered and twisted in others. His skin had the same green tinge to it that his father had donned but it was mottled and grotesque looking, flawed by the hunger of the flames.

Uriool watched Falkhar inwardly flinch with a detachment that had become second nature to him. Uriool was not angry with Damek, was more than a little fond of him in fact. He knew of love and he knew of hate and he knew what the combination of those two could yield. The only thing he did not know was fear. The night his parents had been thrown into the flames by the groping hands and accusing voices, it was not fear that he had seen in their eyes; only love for one another and hatred for those that would tear them apart. Uriool also knew about justice and freedom and he fought for them all the time. Justice for the malachi, freedom for what was left of his father's people. He had never allowed himself to love another for he knew they would just fade away like all his other great loves. He had lost everything to the fire and now... now the fire held hope.

He had brought the human for Damek, he had watched the two Shadow Brothers talk, and he had watched them defeat Falkhar and the Ancients, but had left when the fire had spread, taking refuge in the gardens. He had then watched Damek and the fire maiden disappear through the gate.

Falkhar was clutching at his scarred hand now, all previous whims forgotten in his desperation.

'You must find Damek. You must kill him and bring the drey maiden back to me. There may still be a chance. Do you understand?' Falkhar said, looking imploringly up at Uriool.

His eyes told of anxiety and loss. He had loved Adonica dearly but had never been able to show her. Only when the Worlds were gone and the humans were at his feet could he be free to do as he wished. His people would no longer care for formalities and other eccentricities, only for blood, only for the hunt, the way their ancestors were. She was dead now and his dream was dying with her. He needed the girl, she could still be used, forced to bend to his will, but he needed Uriool to bring her to him. As always though, he was unable to read what lay hidden under Uriool's mask. It was porcelain, white like spilled milk; no holes for his eyes or mouth, only for his nose. Black markings ran like lightning across its smooth surface. Damek had found it and given it to him as a gift. It had been a Verashkai Prince's mask and Uriool treasured it.

A strange child, Falkhar thought. He never said a word but he did as he was told and Falkhar had tried to explain his vision to him, not knowing whether or not he understood.

Uriool was looking out at the moon, lost in thought apparently.

'Do you understand?' Falkhar repeated.

Oh he understood, Uriool thought, he understood very well. Religions. Millions of them all across the Worlds. Many gods and goddesses, so many rituals, so many different names but a few things made them similar; do unto others, respect, humility. Sometimes the message got a little lost or misinterpreted along the way and was then used as a weapon. People tended to read too far into things, dissecting the words and their meanings, trying to find significance until none of it made sense any more. The perpetual need to *understand* when all you had to do was *be*. He was done carrying out revenge, done with the hatred in his heart and in the hearts of others.

Uriool slid his fingers, which were resting on Falkhar's head, down to his neck, without looking down. He did not need to say anything, words were beyond what he needed to convey, what he needed to do. He snapped Falkhar's head clean off his shoulders in one move, and walked away without a backward glance.

He was going home. He was going to find the fire.

*

Not many people could speak to their dreya, not any that Valador knew of. For all he knew, he could be the only one. It had happened when he had been faced with the choice of immortality. He had been torn, not sure which path he should choose for his life. He had stepped outside of the council chambers and into the daylight. He needed to think, he needed advice. Valcan had strode up to him but stopped short of nuzzling his neck the way he always used to. Valador had looked up into his large eyes and a connection was made.

If you do this then remember always that it was your choice

Valador had been taken aback by this. Valcan was speaking to him, inside his head. He could hear the rumble of strangely accented words, heavy-tongued and broken, but there none the less.

'I must do this for the people.' Valador spoke out loud, not knowing how else to speak. Valcan had inclined his head in acknowledgment of the two-legged reasoning, a gesture Valador would soon come to grow accustomed to.

It will not be easy

'Nothing ever is.'

It was a revelation; he felt a bond stronger than the one he had known before if it were possible. On the battle fields they were flawless because of this new-found method of communication. Valador never questioned it and Valcan never explained how or why.

We have been speaking all the time,

He had said once.

Now, Valador was falling into the dark abyss of madness, and no bond, however strong, could bring him back. Valcan nudged at him with his snout. He could see that although his wound had healed, the sore in his heart grew worse with every unwilling breath.

'I used to see their faces at night. Now I see them all the time,' Valador breathed, lying on the gravel, not even bothering to find shade against the fierce star anymore.

You need to eat

'I need answers,' Valador retorted, 'and a strong drink.'

Valcan wrapped himself around his keeper in a hallowed way, knowing how this would end.

'I cannot help but feel guilty. Why did she send me away? I chose immortality over her, I chose a life that did not include her and she banished me from her sight.'

What is immortality?

'You tell me, you seem to know a lot more than I do.'

Valador was greeted by silence. Valcan had explained to him the complexities of the rider-drey relationship. Dreya did not need keepers to survive and the riders could live their own lives too, but some unexplained force drew them together. A bond that made them merge so strongly that when one died, the other nearly perished in their wake.

I do not understand you sometimes

'I know. I have become weak and selfish. The one thing I set out to do and I cannot find the strength to do it. Can the Worlds suppress you into non-existence? Can they forget me and snuff out my life force?'

You seem to be quite capable of doing that all by yourself Valador

Valador laughed. Valcan was right.

'Are they here?' It was the first time he had dared to ask the question for he could already feel the answer in the air like some shadow passing over, dark and suffocating.

Yes. Do you want me to call the others?

Valador stood up and looked Valcan in the eye.

'I am not fit to wash the feet of my soldiers let alone lead them into battle! Look at me! What do you think has become of them if I look like this! What hope could there possibly be?'

Valcan paused before he answered. Dreya chose not to interfere with the lives of men. Let them travel they roads they must. Guide them, answer their questions but let them be. It is in their nature to make mistakes, walk blindly, hurt one another and fall into traps. They were there to protect them as far as they would allow...

Many died long ago but there are enough who still live on

Valador looked at his drey as if he had lost his mind.

'They died? In battle? What battle?' He gestured wildly at the empty skies like the madman he had become. Valcan was patient. He had had many years of practice.

Do you remember what I told you on that day beneath the white tower?

Valador stared blankly at Valcan for a while, blinking stupidly in the noon light before abruptly walking off. Valcan let him go. He would follow him at a distance to make sure he did not do anything too absurd.

Valador felt betrayed often but not so much as now. The sand covered his boots as he dragged his feet along, wishing this earth would swallow him whole and be done with it. All this time and he could have simply made a choice.

No choice is ever simple. You did it for your people

Valador spun around and started throwing anything he could lay his hands on at his beloved drey.

'I HAD A CHOICE AND YOU NEVER TOLD ME!'

Valcan spread his wings, kicking up dust in whirlwinds and pinned Valador to the ground. His keeper struggled to wipe the sand from his eyes and spit it out of his mouth but Valcan paid him no heed.

You made your choice and you never asked

'I could have chosen to go back, I could have chosen not to be immortal! I could have gone back.'

He was crying now, great sobs of gut wrenching grief and loss. Valcan let him go and sat back on his haunches.

She did it for you. She sent you away but she loved you. You would not have chosen any other path until a few days ago and what will that help you now? You have come so far to let it all slip away. You make me sad

'She loved me?' He was speaking more to himself than to Valcan.

There are people coming for you. People who need your help

'I cannot give it to them.' Valador had resigned himself to that fact. He was not the man he once was, no one had taught him to live with this burden, but he had chosen it, and now he only wanted peace. 'I am sorry,' he said; tear stained face looking up at Valcan.

I may not understand why you are doing this but you do not need my forgiveness any more than you need anybody else's. Our kind will live on and your kind will too. Evil will never triumph in a place... where there is so much light!

He spread his mighty wings once more and raised his head to the star; it glistened off his scales like the promise of all things good.

You are a good man Valador and you are loved, never forget that

'Thank you... for everything.'

Valador could have gotten to his feet but he did not.

Valcan got up and started to walk away. Valador could hear his strong steps upon the ground and soon the cry of mourning went up. It echoed off the mountains and in Valador's heart as he made his final choice.

*

They were looking through the record books. Great volumes, pages stained yellow with age and coated with dust, each one more fragile than the one before. They threatened to crumble at the lightest touch.

Carrick stroked the stubble around his mouth and pushed his golden hair from one side of his head to the next, staring intently at the records. Altair had a difficult hand to read at best, looping and whirling like his fingers were the ice skaters and the pen the skates.

'There!' Altair said, peering over his Alvar commander's shoulders and jabbing a finger at the paragraph he had found.

"*They attack, as dawn breaks, in great numbers. The sky darkens and then the blood rivers flow.*" He was reading from an eyewitness account from long ago; the first wraith attacks. Carrick made a sound in his throat but said nothing. Altair read on, "*They ride great beasts of doom that spew poison from their mouths and tear the flesh off the people, never satisfied in their hunger for blood. Some of us escaped on our ships but many more died. Carnage. Fear. I have never seen any foe as fierce as they.*"

Altair did not look up once he had finished. Ather leaned closer to his sister and said,

'The star pirates would not know a fierce foe from a dead one. They are merely cowards and thieves.'

'Is there something you would like to share, Ather?' Delwyn asked. Her tone was polite and enquiring but Ather sneered at her and said nothing. Elvira spoke for him since he refused to speak directly to a High Elf.

'We simply find it hard to take the word of any star pirate as truth. They lie and they plunder, that is all they know how to do.'

Admiral Runako held his hand up in a subtle gesture to his Chief Captain, Dafina. He did not wish to start a fight and further discredit his race in the eyes of the ice queen, Elvira, and her poisonous brother.

Altair raised his eyebrows as if in amusement and read on;

"The dawn came and brought with it the wings of demons. These creatures of shadow are strong. We must have slain some of them in battle but those of us who fled did not see how and those that did lie dead. Their corpses not left for the cremators, but to the deadly rays of darkness that was once our refuge. They tracked us through space, seeking us. They would come twenty for one of us until we numbered but a few." 'This testimony was taken from a commanding Shadow Brother. Would you believe the word of a malachi?'

Ather remained silent but his eyes showed fear. The Shadow Brothers were the best of the best. They drained dry entire villages in their glory days to feed their strength. Assassins and hunters that were never seen or heard. He cast a glance at Damek but the vampire remained motionless as if the words of the fallen and fearful meant nothing to him.

The assembly was seated in a small coliseum that held thirty. The two royal families were there with their chief scribes, the Alvar commanders and few representatives from the races that had already arrived. Sivan was there from the Wazimu. His hair was water flowing down his shoulders and his face was hard as stone, his features sculpted by the water. He wore no clothes like the others and his eyes were hollow and empty. Thorr had come too, with his warsaur nailed feet and scarred body; Ailfryd had sent an elvin ship for him and his people. Thorr had not enjoyed the flight but his people were impressed by the elvin technology and weaponry and their questions were endless.

A few others were there too. Arial represented the drey keepers as well as Lord Elaeth, an older drey lord from the southern kingdoms. He said little. His hair was already flecked with grey and his drey had seen many seasons pass. Damek had said he would call the Shadow Brothers, those who remained unmoved by his actions and still wanted to fight. The Adare' were yet to appear, always late and always with excuses. The wizard, Toireann, had sent a message ahead to say that he would bring them and rally his own people. The cleya of Lar would be much needed and appreciated. The hairless monkey people, the doirya, had already arrived. Caleb spoke on their behalf as Grand Chieftain. He was larger than the two guards that sat at his side. Their kind was not used to this sort of gathering or setting. Delwyn had given them the forests in the east and promised them no trouble from the others. The humans were also noticeably absent. No one had been able to make contact with the group that called themselves the Rogues, the ones who openly opposed the Religion, and the Faith priests had all but been hunted down and obliterated. By now, news of their deceased King Felias would have reached them. Perhaps they were affronted by this and would refuse further truck with those who had had a hand in his falling, but Altair seriously doubted that. Felias was a drunken fool with fewer ties to his homeland than was appropriate. Altair had whispered a few words into well-chosen human ears but the choice, in the end, was theirs. The kikubwa were coming in on the next flight. Dunkan had been sent to seduce them with magic and hope to lure them over. Altair's gaze roved over the rest of the assembly, marveling at all the races that had gathered.

'Father, father! When can I see the fayres?' Vanora had pleadingly enquired before the meeting. Delwyn had answered for him,
'Child, there are people you will see today that are very different from anything you have ever seen before. Try to hold your tongue and do not stare.'

Vanora was now sitting opposite a portable bubble of liquid that held the largest fish she had ever seen. No, not a fish, a man, no, a fish. She could not decide but it scared her. It had scales all over its arms and a long tail like an eel. Fins covered its flanks and the side of its head. It was three times the size of General Carrick and he was five times the size of her. Fangs protruded from the sides of its mouth and gills that looked like knife wounds ran purple and jagged along its neck. Its eyes were large and bulbous and cruel looking. Aysel, her father had called it. These maji would guard the rivers and oceans and Vanora believed that she would never go swimming again.

General Braenden decided to say what was on his mind regardless of whom it may offend;

'We need to post one strong battalion with every two weak and so spread our force. The suns rise east and north-east for the next week and so we need our strongest divisions there.' His broad shoulders moved to the rhythm of his words as he gestured beyond the room and his pale green eyes swallowed the light, illuminating them further.

'And if they break through our "strongest division" Braenden, what then? Should we not hold some of our force back?' Alarico had his mother's mind but his father's manner and Delwyn smiled at her son. He was learning fast.

Braenden frowned and Carden said,

'Yes, you are right. We should have three strong-holds along their path so that they are weakened and our greatest division should be at the center.' He had leaned forward and was tracing lines on the carved wooden table with his pale, ringed fingers.

'Where will we put the people, the women and children?' Vanora asked. Such a soft spirit, thought Altair. Too soft, thought Elvira.

'We have decided to place them underground, for now, in the caves at Agrum and Utorea.' Carrick replied. He was taller than Braenden, his fair hair was a thick mane and his eyes a lazy blue, his dusky skin in sharp contrast to the pale cast of his companion.

'Escape will be impossible,' Thorr remarked.

'Defeat is not an option,' Braenden countered.

'Defeat is likely.' Sivan's voice was like boulders plummeting down a steep ravine. It echoed off the dull wood like something from another world. 'Our plan was to assemble here on this single planet rather than allow so many to be destroyed,' he continued, 'the battle will be fought at the place of our choosing and the host will soon be great, but we will not make it without the dreya army, we may be defeated if they are not called.'

Everyone in the hall looked to Arial now. She was well-rested and her hair shone in light waves of spun gold. She wore a simple green dress but no simplicity could hide her perfection. She glanced at Damek but could not hold his gaze.

Last night they had sat together writing messages to their people asking for help. No reply had yet been received but she did not want to make any excuses. The survival of the Worlds rested on her shoulders. Sivan had brought news of her father's death and now she held the power, the responsibility, but she did not know how to use it.

'It will be done,' she replied coolly.

'Yes, but when will they come?' Elvira was prompted by her brother to ask.

Arial did not know what to say.

'Such are the secrets of the drey keepers,' Damek spoke up, 'we all have our secrets.' He looked meaningfully at Elvira and spared a nasty look for Ather whom he had never liked.

'We need to know!' Dafina interjected, 'we cannot hold off the aerial attack alone. When will the magic slingers come? We cannot fight without their magic either!'

'Everyone stop for a moment,' Delwyn said, loud enough for all to hear, 'hopefully, our host will be so great that where we are going to put the women and children who are not fighting will not be an issue. There will simply be no space and no resources. In the same breath, our host will be so great that how many more come will be irrelevant.'

'Will not be an issue?' one of the perions thundered, 'they will need our protection!'

'Irrelevant?' someone flustered.

'As I hear it,' Delwyn said dryly, 'you did not all bring your full forces here, you left enough behind to protect your home planets, as much as that will help, so we will send the women and children that you brought with you - home.'

The perion looked uncomfortable and confused and asked,

'You just said that what we left behind will not be enough, what if they attack our homes? Our people will be left defenseless!'

'They will do no such thing.' Delwyn was on her feet now. 'We will play on human pride and that alone is enough to lead their full forces here.'

'How can you be so sure?' Renata asked shrewdly. Delwyn smiled and said,

'Can you not see? We have what they want. We give them a holy war.'

Altair and Delwyn exchanged looks and the assembly pondered her words.

'All our women and children fight,' Thorr said, changing the topic and breaking the awkward silence unawares, 'they strap the babes to their backs and the little ones fight with vigor enough.' His voice was grave, he knew what they faced. Altair had shown him the images of the black holes that their satellites had picked up. 'The demons will not go unpunished.'

'I can fight too,' Mirian said. Her hair was silver now, streaked with black, and Elvira took a deep breath. 'We can wield our magic. It will be of great value. Whether or not the Adare' come,' Mirian finished.

Altair frowned but said nothing.

'We do not know how these creatures operate. Your magic may be used against you.' Sivan said cautiously.

'So then why do we wait for the Adare'?' the maji translator asked. The maji was signing to him through the transparent bubble, for if he were to speak out loud; hearts would explode in chests.

'We fight fire with fire!' Ismet shouted, his cloven hooves clattering against the wood as he stood. Alarico wondered how they could even stand up with the weight of their massive curled horns on their heads. The perion smelled musky and the prince was loath to sit beside him but duty called. The goat-men came from the mountainous and barren planets further north and were a primitive race but good fighters. They fought with long spears with strange bells attached to the handles. They had fierce and beady black eyes and they could move two tons with one mighty heave of their horned heads. He could never tell the women apart from the men. He knew the maji were hermaphroditic so there could be no confusion, and no one had ever seen a male fayre even though they definitely existed, but perions and giants always confused him.

'So we fight death with more death then,' Carden sighed.

Ismet sat down again and rolled his eyes, nudging Alarico. Sivan continued;

'We sacrifice much but we have everything to gain. The presence of you all will far outweigh the carrying capacity of this planet, however large and well-kept it may be, but this is not our greatest threat, neither are the kuvuta themselves, but the dark stars they leave in their wake must be stopped. It did not happen last time, this new devilry, but something must be done. Several have merged already and more are formed each day that passes.'

'How are they being formed?' Dafina asked. As a star pirate she had battled many but *too* many was another thing entirely. She knew how to spot the event horizon, knew how to spot them from afar before it was too late, but she did not know how they could be stopped any better that any other member in the assembly.

'The kuvuta suck the very light from the space they occupy when they attack a planet, they thus cause it to collapse upon itself and a black hole is created,' Sivan replied.

General Braenden shuffled some papers to break the silence.

'Can they not be transformed into white holes?' Damek asked, 'or perhaps we could use strong opposing magnetism?'

'Good suggestions,' Sivan replied, 'and ones we have already thought of, but they are all merely plausible and have never been attempted before since we have never had a problem with them on such a scale. They are a natural force of nature but they threaten to consume the Worlds if they are not held in check. There is one option we have not yet looked at,' he finished, looking at Altair. The High Elf knew of what he spoke but was not sure that the lady in question would agree.

'I will speak to the Adare' when they arrive,' was all that he said.

Everyone seemed to accept this without question; some wizard who had the ability to stop dark stars. It was not unheard of.

Caleb tensed next to Altair.

'What is it?' the High Elf asked. Caleb grunted;

'Wyrms.'

Altair smiled, he had hoped they would come. The ground beneath them shuddered and heaved forth a creature that made Vanora gasp in horror and set the doirya off in a display of bared teeth and howling, leaping from the light fittings and howling some more.

'This is a fucking circus,' Ather hissed. Elvira said nothing; she too was having her doubts about Altair's plans though. Many people were on their feet now, crying out to be heard among their peers. Fingers were pointed and accusations made.

Meanwhile, the wyrm pushed through the floorboards and slithered heavily across the floor to find an empty seat, dragging its translator behind it.

They lived underground, they were five foot long and every bit of them was repulsive and chilling. They had no eyes; long slits in its face were used for sniffing out prey and mates. They fed on decaying flesh and had the teeth to show for it plus a worm-like body with short, stubby arms and hands. Long and soiled claws that could navigate through dense rock sat on the end of each finger. Their bodies were smooth and undulating.

The wyrm hissed and bared its fangs at the doirya. They were natural enemies since the wyrms destroyed the doirya's tree top habitat with their burrowing and the doirya retailiated by throwing rocks at them whenever they surfaced.

Altair had simply hoped everyone would be mature enough to put their differences aside since this was clearly a time to band together.

Ather decided to speak. It was now or never.

'What exactly constitutes as a sentinel being these days!?' he fairly cried, 'are we to be classed with this vermin?' He gestured at the worm-man and spat in disgust in his blind face. Roars of agreement sounded around the hall.

Vanora got up, her nerves almost frayed, amidst the shouting, and sat beside the wyrm. She took a napkin from her pocket and wiped the spittle from his face. Everyone grew silent and watched the young princess. The wyrm sniffed at her for a while and took the napkin from her. She gave it to him, trying not recoil from his horrendously long and sharp claws, blackened by the soil it lived in. He sniffed the napkin and hissed at his translator.

'He says thank you.'

Vanora smiled shyly and returned to her seat. Ather watched her with growing hatred and Delwyn watched her with growing pride.

Altair knew it was time to speak, while the throng was still silenced by their shock.

'I know it must be hard for many of you to be here. Know this though; any living thing that has the will to live and fight for that right is a sentinel being! We are here to pool our ideas and discover how best to do that. Put your petty differences aside, save them for times of peace and boredom.' He stared sternly at each member of the assembly and a deeper quiet fell over them all like his words were magic. 'If you do not wish to be here then leave. I will not stop you. No one will.'

After that, there were no more outbursts. Ather still whispered occasionally in Elvira's ear but no one paid him any heed.

It was decided that the people would indeed be placed in the caves until further notice and that the doirya would protect them overhead from the trees. Each race would assume the position in the best terrain they knew how to fight in. Each great Alvar would protect the front and the rear. Magic would be doled out to those fighting with weapons, as much as could be spared until the Adare' arrived.

Renata was hovering near to Delwyn as she preferred to address her questions to the female in charge rather than the male. Fayres were a fiercely feminine group who kept their males locked away purely for procreation purposes. They were said to outnumber them ten to one. This, they said, was to ensure the continuation of peace. It worked relatively well but the queens took on a masculine role in any case, nature working out the balance. They were half the size of any human most of the time and lived in hives, feeding off strong magic collected and stolen from others. They had feathered wings, when they chose to show them, that shone in the sunlight. Each one was an image of outstanding beauty but this was also rumored to be a façade. In true form, it was said, they were ugly creatures, but they used the harvested magic to make themselves more appealing to their magical prey. They too, would be using their magic for they could wield it and store more of it better than any of the sentinels. Altair had never been keen on magic but he knew that it would play an integral part of the battle and he needed to play every card in the deck if he hoped to pull this off.

Vanora had been looking forward so much to see and speak to the fayre but Renata was cold and preoccupied. The crown on her head glittered but her eyes were dead and she hardly spoke, in obvious disdain at having to attend a meeting where predominantly males featured. Her gaze slid disapprovingly over the assembly and she did not even care to return Vanora's greeting.

The butterfly people, however, were far more interesting. They too had wings; fragile and dusty-thin like moths. They were the size of Vanora's finger but they were more than able to fend for themselves. As they drifted around the hall, talking to each person in turn, Vanora noticed the evil-looking stinger that each possessed. It was curved and black, dripping with poison, and her mother told her never to upset the enganya for a single sting would leave the victim paralyzed for life, unable to move or shout for help or ever do anything again. Their innocent smiles and playful behavior gave no sign of this though. Delwyn had said they live in great colonies in trees and if an enemy threatened them, one would sacrifice their sting and their lives so that the rest could live.

Naira was clearly the one in charge; the other enganya followed her wherever she went. She came to sit on Vanora's nose and tickled her cheeks with her wings whilst Carrick and Braenden argued about which Alvar should stand in the front line and the doirya argued with Altair about which forests they wanted.

'Are you ready for the battle little one?' Naira asked. Her voice was like the tinkling of a tiny bell. Vanora had not thought about this before.

'I am not sure what plans father has for us. I shall do as he commands,' was her reply.

Naira stroked the bridge of the elf maiden's nose and leaned in closer until Vanora was almost cross-eyed with the effort of trying to keep her in sight.

'The fayre will ask you to join them; she will try make you one of them. She wants your beauty for herself and *no one* else.'

'That is nonsense,' Vanora giggled, 'she does not even want to talk to me!'

'She is watching you though. Be careful of these new people Vanora, not all are good.'

Vanora crinkled her nose up and Naira hovered in front of her. Vanora could now see that the enganya was right, Renata was looking at her and did not avert her gaze when she saw Vanora had noticed.

'Father would never let evil people sit in his assembly and *you* are new, should I then not speak to you either?'

'There are degrees of darkness; some have been deemed acceptable but you are right, no evil men or women sit here today but some are... opportunistic,' she looked over her shoulder to the malachi Damek. 'Some are bitter,' she pointed to the Drows. 'Some are careless and reckless with other's lives as well as their own,' the star pirates were pointed out here. 'A few are dim-witted,' she giggled, glancing at the monkey-like doirya. 'And some are just tricksters with pretty faces.'

Vanora looked at Renata again who was voicing her opinion about sharing living space with the warsaur.

Runako was asking where his ships would be needed the most; Elaeth was asking how much of a good idea it would be to allow the cleya loose to fight since he deemed them barbarians with no regard for life, and Vanora knew it would be a long time before this meeting would be over.

Naira left her to go speak secrets into someone else's ear and Vanora got up to sit next to Arial. The drey queen was far more beautiful, in her opinion than the fayre, even when she looked sad and far away like she did now.

'What is the matter?' Vanora asked her.

Arial looked down at the doll face of the High Elf Princess. She looked like her mother but had the compassion of her father and his kind eyes. Arial smiled and said,

'I will tell you if you promise not to tell anyone else.'

Vanora nodded her head solemnly.

'I am afraid,' Arial confessed.

'I am too, but we are here together and all will be well.'

Arial was warmed by Vanora's words but not comforted.

'The wyrm says all will not be well if the wraiths get hold of you. He says they will tear your face off and feed it to their beasts,' the wyrm's interpreter whispered. Arial's face fell and her brow creased in anger.

'Tell him to keep his thoughts to himself,' she hissed.

The wyrm inclined his head in Arial's direction but said nothing else.

'It will be alright,' Arial said to Vanora, taking her small hand in hers. She looked up at Damek and he stared back at her.

'Do you love him?' Vanora asked, catching on to the intensity of their looks. Arial sighed.

'Yes but we are very different from one another.'

'Mother and father are very different too,' Vanora said matter-of-factly, 'Kieran is very different from me.' Arial had nothing to say in reply but she looked up from their conversation when she heard her name being mentioned. She was listening in to a half-finished conversation.

'...only if Arial can use her sway and call all the drey riders. We need a strong aerial attack or we will be done for.' General

Braenden was pointing at her accusingly and speaking loudly enough for everyone to hear. She could feel the anger and fear coiling around her stomach and all the way up to her heart. All eyes were on her again.

'We have been through this, General, have we not?' Altair asked in a low voice.

'We want to hear it from her. We want to know that we stand a chance!' Braenden countered. Altair knew it had been wise to keep the secret of the Blood Angels but it seemed they would give her no rest since it was truly only the dreya that would be able to put up any kind of real fight, just as it had been decided all those years ago.

Arial got to her feet, looked like she wanted to say something, but then merely walked out of the room. Elaeth also got to his feet, helped by the rod he carried.

'Have you no faith in our people?' he asked, 'they will answer to her call, have no fear of that.' Altair had told him nothing of the Blood Angels either and the drey lord was under the impression that it was merely the reserve armies that the queen would be calling, not the greatest force to ever live.

'I saw the letters she wrote myself and the troops will be coming as soon as they receive the summons. Why do you pester her so?' he finished. He then too, took his leave.

'Then it is settled,' General Braenden said, feeling a little embarrassed, 'we are ready.'

Altair shook his head slowly and stroked his jaw;

'Not yet. I know you are all eager but we need to wait for the others.' Altair also knew that he needed to wait for Arial to discover how to summon the secret army before he could make plans to start the war.

'You do not truly believe that the humans and the cleya will join us do you?' Elvira snorted.

'It is not just them that we wait for,' Sivan interjected, 'the drey riders and Adare' as well as the Shadow Brothers must come too. Then there are the tribes we wait for as well as the naizhan.'

Damek stiffened slightly in his chair. Only two of his Shadow Brothers had said they were coming so far. They numbered seven in all, his faction that is. He knew he could count on Kaleo and Tariq but the rest had been loyal to Falkhar, as far as he could guess. Now Kaleo was telling him that Damek stood next in line to rule and that the people were clamoring for him to come home. Damek could not think of anything worse. Kaleo had not yet been able to make contact with the remaining Shadow Brothers on Damek's behalf and he would have to hope that his letters struck home. He could not risk traveling back in case his father was still alive and in hiding somewhere, hungry for revenge.

'They are right, Braenden, we need to gather our force to its full before we can orchestrate the war's beginning,' Carden said.

'Till then,' Carrick said, 'we train and we drill and we perfect our battle plans and formations until all can work as a single unit.'

'We are ready,' said Thorr.

'We will call in the rest of the fleet,' Runako said.

Everyone seemed eager to begin the preparations and welcomed the time that had now been promised them.

As the assembly started to file out of the hall, Altair made his way over to the vampire who had spoken little and did not move to leave now either. He sat hunched over with his head resting on his balled fists. Altair sat down beside him and moved his feet as they rolled the maji out of the hall in its giant liquid bubble. He was silent for a time before he said,

'You must go to her.'

'She does not want me to.' Damek sounded defeated and Altair understood his heart's turmoil.

'When we send Riko, there will be precious little time left for life's problems and even less time to resolve them,' Altair warned. Damek looked up, shock in his eyes.

'Riko works for *you*?' Damek asked, 'that is how you know so much!' He paused for a moment, his brow creasing, 'but how did you know that Arial would escape from Falkhar?'

Altair smiled and answered,

'We have more than one double agent among your ranks, young malachi.'

Damek nodded and stared down again. He sighed deeply, his thoughts returning to Arial.

'There is no resolution for us,' he murmured.

'You will have need of each other before the end; I can promise you that much,' Altair said solemnly.

'The end,' Damek muttered, 'there is no hope then, we shall all perish.'

'I know you do not have that little faith in her,' Altair said.

'I have no faith in myself,' Damek replied quietly.

'Have faith, for it is all we have left,' Altair said gently.

He stood and left the hall. He wanted to spend as much time with his family as possible and he hoped the others were doing the same. It was going to be difficult. So many different people flung together in the mêlée, with no prior warning or practice, no real or intimate knowledge of one another. Only prejudice, past battles fought face-to-face and a stringent indifference was all that ever bonded races together. That was the way the Worlds worked.

*

He could hear voices now, as he struggled for breath. One was harsh, the other that answered sounded like Ramroth. The voices were whispered through the earth like water trickles through sand. Lucio wondered if it was time to start praying.

'I told him to stay with me, he must be lost.' Ramroth was quite flustered. He had lost contact with Lucio somewhere over the mountain, or was it through it? He started to panic.

'You had better find him before he drowns or suffocates!' Maya said sternly.

'Well,' Ramroth snorted as he tried to locate Lucio telepathically, 'perhaps your meetings should be held somewhere a little less underground and then things like this would not have to happen!'

Maya shook her head.

'Found him,' Ramroth said, eyes staring and unblinking, fixed on some invisible sight ahead. He clasped his hands together and pulled up with all his might. Lucio was a heavy man. The ground yawned open and bore forth a mud-soaked figure who lay curled up on the floor in a fetal position. This feat had drawn the attention of a few of the wizards but most were far more interested in their own acts. They waited for the man to stir. Lucio coughed once, then again, and a large clump of soil came up and out. Some of the small audience clapped and then turned around to continue their conversations.

Lucio pushed himself up with his hands and looked around. A collection of strange faces were staring at him but apparently, none wanted to touch him or help him.

'What happened?' he asked, spitting out more dirt and wiping his hands down the front of his trousers.

'Ramroth never was any good at traveling,' Maya said, as if that could explain anything. Ramroth shot a dirty look at the sorceress but she ignored him.

'Sorry,' Ramroth muttered, extending a hand and helping the priest to his feet. Lucio shook his head and managed a small smile. He then looked around him more closely, ignoring the awkward silence.

He was still underground, that much he could tell. The cave they were in had clay for walls, ceiling and floor. It smelt like it had been here for thousands of years. Light came from tiny flames like those a candle would bear, millions of them, placed all around the walls. When he looked closer he saw that where natural ledges permitted, and within holes in the walls, many jewels had been set. They glinted and twinkled like a thousand stars and gave the cavern its strange reflective light. Lucio felt as if they were in the belly of some great earth-and-treasure-eating beast. The weight of the mountain around them groaned and shuddered slightly as it adjusted its mass. Lucio started, but when no one else paid any heed, he relaxed a little.

There were about two hundred people in the cave. Most were seated cross-legged on the floor or leaning against the walls, deep in conversation with those sitting closest to them, and some were performing magical displays to the amusement of their companions. Only a few stood on a slightly raised platform. It was more that the ground sloped upward a little than anything else. The witch who had spoken first stood there and a very dark-skinned man was standing next to her. The dark-skinned man was terrifying. He had strange eyes that leered at Lucio and tattoos that swirled around his face. An odd looking Adare' stood to his right and Ramroth was giving them all dark looks.

'Why are we still here? Are you still busy formulating a plan?' Ramroth enquired.

Lucio was not quite sure who the question was directed at but everyone in the clearing grew quiet and looked up at the old mage.

'We have not quite gotten round to that yet, Ramroth. We are still deciding what to do with Ethron's ambitious apprentice,' Taigo replied sternly. He was a wise Adare' but a foolish man. He came from a little-heard of race that lived in a far corner of the Worlds. His beard had never been trimmed and he wore white silk to denote his rank among his own people. He was hard but not cruel, difficult but not unfair. 'He interrogated and left for dead a human. He used his magic illegally and must pay the price,' he finished. His voice was grave and serious but Ramroth had to try to stop laughing at the pure ridiculousness of it all.

'That human had interrogated Ethron, driven him to insanity, and killed many others! Besides, that is certainly not our most pressing issue here Taigo,' Ramroth replied, voice a little raised.

Lucio moved back and sat to one side on the cool ground. He was not sure how this was going to go but it was not what he had expected. He had expected perhaps a few old men sitting around an ornate table, not a rabble of youths and bickering men that no one seemed to be listening to.

A few of the young wizards close enough to hear the conversation had conjured up an image of Toireann being hanged, Taigo a towering figure of white flame above him. Toireann was sniggering and asking them to stop. Taigo narrowed his eyes and said,

'I will not let justice fail to serve the weak just because the Worlds are in danger. For what will it all come to then?'

'Danger!' Toireann cried, 'it is on the brink of destruction!'

'And what would you have us do young apprentice? It has always been our policy to let the battles alone. That is not what our powers were made for,' Maya said. She seemed to be just as stubborn in this instance as Taigo.

Toireann was, by now, extremely frustrated. He had been trying to talk with these people for the past four hours, but no one wanted to listen and the rest of them were doing what Adare' did best; not much of anything at all. He felt like a child again. Being made an example of and being forced to accept their ludicrous views. He had let Ramroth down; he had let Ethron down too.

'He would have you fight as I would,' Ramroth said, taking a step closer to the Adare', 'where is Ailfryd?'

'He did not come,' someone said. It was a young wizard that Ramroth recognized by face, one of Ailfryd's apprentices. 'He sent a letter to tell us he waits with the elves. They all do. They have many great names on their guest list already. Runako, Renata, Arial…'

Someone had sent a flock of birds careening through the air above them. Lucio ducked. Ramroth was lost for words. He looked confused and disbelieving for a moment before he managed to ask,

'The elves have been calling arms? Arial is with them?' He grabbed the young Adare' by his shoulders and shook him. His eyes told of the punishment for a lie.

The Adare' nodded vigorously.

'She is with them. Many are. Ailfryd has told me,' the young mage stuttered.

'The High Elves and the Drows,' Toireann added, 'they have drawn many from far and wide. They wait for us and for the humans. A few others too I believe.'

'We have not given them reason to believe we were coming,' Maya interjected.

Ramroth looked exasperated by this stage and Lucio looked quizzically at him. He walked over to Ramroth while the others continued their debate.

'I thought they would not need persuasion on the matter of survival,' Lucio remarked, 'is there anything I can do or say? Nobody seems to be paying much attention.' He gestured to the crowd of wizards, blue plumes of smoke rising from a far corner and the sounds of many hundreds of insects making it hard to hear anything else. 'At least we know Arial is indeed safe,' he added, with a reassuring smile.

'Yes, that is a very good thing,' Ramroth readily agreed, 'but as for the persuasion, just try stay out of it, we have our own way of doing things, albeit a bit strange,' he added, looking around at the haphazard way that his colleagues presented themselves, 'they will come around eventually.'

Lucio looked over at the tall, dark man gesturing wildly at the woman, and highly doubted that they would be out of here any time soon. Lucio chose to ignore Ramroth and turned around with his arms raised to address the throng of Adare' from all over the Worlds.

'I know you are all scared,' he began, amidst murmurs and conversations trailing off, 'perhaps you are not scared at all and believe that this war will not come to you or that if it does, that you can fight it alone.' He had everyone's attention. Toireann caught on to Lucio's idea to appeal to the masses and added his booming cleya voice to the priest's;

'You cannot fight this battle alone but fight you MUST.'

'This is ludicrous!' Taigo roared but the two men spoke on;

'The darkness is coming,' Lucio warned, 'will you challenge it or will you let it run unchecked?'

'Stop this ridiculous propaganda!' Taigo commanded.

All heads were turned in their direction and there was a strange silence.

'It is NOT propaganda!' Toireann thundered in return. He raised himself into the air, closed his eyes and parted his hands. A giant volume fell into his outstretched palms, plucked from thin air it seemed. He stayed hovering there whilst the pages ran amok by themselves, flipped furiously by invisible hands. They stopped, just as suddenly as they had started and Toireann opened his eyes.

'We all said these words...' he began, obviously wanting to read from a piece in the book.

Maya shook her head and said,

'Do not think you can use guilt to force us into following you blindly into a task not set for us.' Toireann ignored her and continued speaking above her head at the rapt audience of young and old, strong and frail.

'We promised to uphold our individual laws and the Worldly laws that govern us all. We promised never to intervene in choice nor use our powers to harm an innocent,' he paused dramatically, 'It is a Worldly RIGHT to live and be free, we sway NO man's choices but our own and we WILL do harm to those who are guilty!' His oration was beginning to work and the wizards were buzzing amongst themselves, many nodding their heads in agreement, fireworks exploding in approval. 'For too long have we sat on the side lines, too long have we laid our natural talents to WASTE!' he cried to the sound of tumulus applause.

'That is quite enough, Toireann,' Taigo said quietly.

Taigo had been chosen to fill the position of High Adare' and the book had appeared to Ramroth when Ethron's spirit had left his body to be signed. It had irked him to add his ink to the page.

'You have broken the law,' he continued, 'it is not for you to decide who is guilty and who deserves your punishment, which is why we steer clear of such things.' He spoke calmly now, he had decided that it would fare him no better to scream and shout and he did not want to waste the energy.

'But you put us through TESTS!' Toireann objected loudly.

Lucio wondered what these tests involved but decided he would rather not know.

'We passed,' Toireann implored, 'ALL of us sitting here, we passed. We are worthy to wield our magic, we have been chosen and so we must *choose*!' Toireann was back on his feet now, clutching the red leather bound book like it was the only piece of driftwood in a vast and endless sea.

'That may be so, but it does not give you the right to run around doing as you wish. Have you forgotten everything that Ethron taught you, or just the better half?' Taigo asked. This was a clear insult. Ethron was known to be a little evangelistic and passed it on to most of his pupils, much to the displeasure of certain rigid individuals, but the High Adare's words were law and until he passed, there were no questions asked. Ramroth was worried that the young cleya might retaliate but it seemed he was calmer within than he seemed on the outside.

'If it were not for me and my actions, Ramroth may not be alive. I did what I had to and so should we all, we must FIGHT!'

'No,' Taigo objected, 'Ethron did the right thing by keeping his mouth shut. His burden was the knowledge of the Blood Angels and he did what he had to. That is all.'

'That was HIS contribution!' Toireann roared back.

Ramroth wondered how Taigo had found out about the Blood Angels. He probably now had access to all the records. Toireann must have known through Ethron. The rest, however, were still to be filled in…

'Who are the Blood Angels?' the same young wizard from earlier asked, and the cry was taken up by the others. Phantasmagorias of flying figures were sent up, blood dripping from their wings and crude jaws. Ramroth thought they were good anima and wondered who had created them.

Taigo raised his hands up in a bid for silence. Ramroth saw the smile spread across his face and suddenly he understood. This would be his trump card, to continue living the lie.

'The Blood Angels are an army of great magnitude and strength specifically designed to obliterate the wraiths and have been trained for many years. They are immortal, they have waited for this dawn and now, they will fulfill their destiny,' he declared.

Cheers came from most of the assembled Adare'. The war would be taken care of. The darkness they had all heard being whispered across the Worlds would be obliterated, and all they had to do was nothing. Only the older wizards among the congregation were yet to be persuaded. One such man stepped forward, his stubble silvery blue and his eyes crinkled beetles set deeply in his aged face.

'I am a healer of sorts and my work never ended in the Era of Chaos. Not only the battle wounded,' he shuddered a little at the memories and continued, 'but the after effects too. Yes, I helped many a limb regrow and helped settle many a troubled mind, these are the effects of war, but I had to help the women too. The babies were born deformed, acid deposition poisoned lakes as the shadows scattered throughout space. Many died, and countless lives were ruined. The Black Ash is not so named for naught. Many planets were lost, no habitation being able to take place for many years after. So many displaced...' He shook his head slowly, 'I refuse to believe any single army, no matter how great, can quell such an atrocious force.'

Taigo did not look too happy at these words but he could not argue. He had been but a baby himself in those dark times.

'Not only that, Taigo,' Ramroth said quietly, 'but they will need our magic to fight them I believe. Metaphysically speaking, only our magic will reach them. Mere blades in hands of men will do nothing.'

Taigo's face was trouble-creased now. He knew in his heart that Ramroth spoke true. Toireann used the moment of weakness to launch his attack again;

'Ethron may have done the right thing in your eyes but look where that got him – tortured for months and eventually killed!'

'We all have to make sacrifices for the greater good,' came Maya's cool reply, referring to Ethron's silence. Ramroth could not believe that she was still not convinced. Toireann looked defiant, standing there in his swirling black leather cape, bare-chested and tattooed. He looked just the part.

'Then we shall all follow his lead and die doing what is right. There is no greater good!' Toireann said.

By now the people were starting to get riled up even more. Perhaps he had been wrong, Lucio thought. There was always room for revolution in the hearts of the brave and young. He looked upon the sea of faces, all from different walks of life, the youngest perhaps seventeen and the oldest – he could not guess – centuries? They were all bound by magic though. The ability to wield it and to use it for good.

'War is for the young and the foolish!' Taigo was battling to get himself heard above the hubbub but that was how it always was. There was never much control among those who practiced their art. He wondered how Ethron had ever made any progress but then he realized that Ethron had not tried to control them at all. He would have just let them do as they please and through that freedom, they respected and obeyed him. 'Perhaps,' Taigo said quietly, 'this one is for neither.'

Toireann and Ramroth both fixed him with intense looks. Maya grabbed his arm and said,

'Do not relent now, this war is not ours. Let the others who can wield fight!'

Toireann's face hardened and he faced the crowd once more;

'The Blood Angels will not win this war for you! I go to fight; I take my people with me. Do as you wish!' And with that he stalked off. Ramroth hurried after him but Lucio stayed rooted to the ground. The crowd looked torn and he could only imagine what was going through their minds. Some probably didn't want to fight, some believed the Blood Angels would save them, perhaps a few were as afraid as he was and perhaps more wanted the opportunity to wield their magic to the full?

Many had already started to leave and Maya looked startled and panicked, like a deer caught in the headlights. Lucio walked over to her. She was beautiful. Her hair was cropped short and framed her delicate heart shaped face. Her hazel eyes were heavily lidded with kohl and she looked enchanting by the light of the many jewels.

'Why do you oppose this cause so?' he asked her. She looked at him as if she was about to ask who he thought he was but suddenly, her harsh attitude faltered.

'These young Adare' need guidance. Some are too powerful for them to ever know and that is why we do not fight. It is too dangerous.' She made a good point, Lucio had to admit.

'But you put them through tests right? Tests that, I assume, screen them for too powerful an ability or volatile personality?' He enquired. Taigo had joined them now.

'It is impossible to tell a powerful magician that he may not practice,' Taigo said, 'if we find his intentions to be ill, we can strip him of the right, but magic knows no bounds and the individual with whom we find no fault is free to practice, no matter how strong he or she may be. All we try to do here is give these people a home, a fellowship and a safe environment.'

Lucio nodded.

'I do not think they will *all* fight,' he said, a last ditch effort to console these two misunderstood people. He glanced back over his shoulder and saw that most of the magicians had gone. The light cast eerie shadows against the walls and the jewels glowed brighter than before in the absence of so many people. The bloody angels were fading with no one to keep them solid and wildly colored scorches were left in the wake of the random magic that had been used. The smell of sulpher hung in the air.

Ramroth caught up with Toireann.

'This was not how I wanted it to turn out Toireann, we are not rebel leaders.' Ramroth was out of breath and a little angry.

'Firstly,' Toireann countered, 'you started it and secondly,' he gestured wildly about him, 'no one is following me, they are following their hearts.' He placed his hands on Ramroth's shoulders and said, 'It is time my old friend, it is time we too were free.'

Ramroth watched him go with the same mixed feelings that had assailed him the last time they parted.

He found Lucio staring around himself accompanied by Maya and Taigo, too few Adare' still left loitering in the chamber for either of the Adare' to feel much comfort.

'Will you come?' Ramroth asked them. Maya shook her head and Ramroth knew why. Taigo said that he needed time to think. 'I will see you there, friend, Ramroth said.

He led Lucio away, down the winding gravel passage that would take them outside. He did not wish to have another mishap any more than Lucio did.

'I feel sorry for you all but not in a patronizing way,' Lucio remarked, as they walked the road that lead out of the mountain. Ramroth frowned before answering,

'We are given this tool, this amazing ability, and we are taught how to refine it but not how to use it to our full potential. For many people, that is frustrating. That is problem number one.'

'What is problem number two?' Lucio asked, already half knowing what the answer was going to be.

'We are the same but we are different. We travel the Worlds but we have no real place to belong to,' the wizard replied. He was quiet for a while before he added, 'We belong to our magic but we do it no justice.'

'I have seen you do very impressive magic Ramroth!' Lucio remarked.

Ramroth raised his eyebrows;

'You have not seen anything yet.'

Chapter 13

The resistance

Cadeyrn had never been to Earth before. His great-grandfather had been taken there on a tertiary institution field-trip for his historical studies class and he had later done his thesis on it. His illustrations did not do justice to the true beauty of this blue planet though...

It sang of strength and serenity. The ruins of the Super Empire could still be seen, the massive buildings that once stood proud and mighty, several thousand feet into the air, like fingers pointing accusingly to the unknown above. Now only the tips of those steel titans could be seen, poking up from the ground that had swallowed them whole. All the old relics had long since been plundered and now, only vast wilderness remained. The place was cursed, many had said. No man could find peace there. But Cadeyrn could not believe it to be so. He could not remember when last he had seen a more beautiful planet. Even Bethriam, he had to admit, all but paled in comparison to this diverse and spectacular realm. Most planets were too close to their stars, had too much wind, not enough water. Bethriam, for all its beauty, was mostly mountainous, and it spewed forth more hot rock every day. Earth had it all. Earth was a woman of rarest quality, a balanced maiden with just enough fire, just enough ice. His great-grandfather had told him that it contained so much ecological diversity that the humans were forced to relocate, and it had been declared a protected area. Anybody living there would be doing so illegally. All the splendor, all the marvels, the utter perfection and the humans had nearly destroyed it all.

The ground rose to meet them as the blue of the endless oceans faded into the horizon. They landed near a lake with a polished glass surface, flanked by tall naked trees. In the distance were steep hills, small and swift rivers running through them. The winters were dark and brutal here but they had caught the early spring and the aroma of it hung sharp in the still air of noon

Cadeyrn was riding with Kai and his dragon, Valeo. The ride had been both exhilarating and nerve-racking; Cadeyrn was glad to dismount but lingered to stroke the snout of the creature that had let him ride.

'This is the birth-place of my drey's ancestors,' Kai said as he stared around him in wonder, 'they say the Earth spewed them from the molten lava of its belly. They were hunted to near extinction and the few that were left flew away in the great meteor storm of 2040.' Kai bent down to scoop up a handful of sandy soil. 'Earth,' he muttered to himself. Straightening up he added, 'The humans never could bond to the dreya. Too much fear.'

The others started to land one by one, the ground shuddering beneath each mighty paw. The creatures shook their heads, snorting and billowing smoke from their nostrils. Some took off right after their riders had touched ground, spreading their leathery wings and gliding low over the lake, plucking massive, glittering fish from it as they went.

Everyone stood in a group, waiting for their captain to address them. Corbin and Eira came to stand with Cadeyrn, and Nyx soon joined them too. He had enjoyed his flight as much as the others.

Eira still had her backpack with her and some sparse equipment. The riders all watched them intently as they set to work packing it out and laying it all down on the ground.

'Trinkets for the local ladies?' Ionhar asked, gesturing at the paraphernalia that littered the floor. Eira picked up a rectangular object with handles on both sides, tapped a few buttons and a bleeping noise started up.

'No, actually, we are the only sentinels in this vicinity. No ladies for you then I'm afraid.' She winked. Owein stepped behind her and inspected the device from over her shoulder.

'It is a diagnostic probe,' he said to no one in particular.

'It doesn't have a very wide range but we are definitely alone for a good hour's walk in any direction,' Eira confirmed.

'That does not help us much,' Zach remarked. He had joined the group at last after having climbed the nearest small hill with Delano.

'We know that already,' Delano smirked.

'It also says there is a small military base roughly one mile that way,' she said, pointing east, 'perhaps they have radio equipment.'

Corbin nodded.

'We'll go check it out,' he confirmed.

Cadeyrn went to fill the canteens at the water's edge whilst Eira and Nyx sorted the rest of the equipment out.

'We are heading west,' Zach announced, 'our dreya sense something there, perhaps it is the pair we seek out.'

'Shall we rendezvous back here at night-fall?' Corbin asked.

'Yes. If we have not found them by then, we shall have to wait till dawn to continue our search,' Zach said. He clapped a hand on Corbin's shoulder and added, 'Good luck.'

'You too,' Corbin replied. And with that, the two companies headed in opposite directions.

The riders were following the dreya. Some walked ahead of them, their massive rumps swaying in time to their rolling gaits and some flew overhead. The riders had donned their lighter armor and walked with swords in hand. Earth was not a hostile planet but the few, sparse occupants were rumored to be. Thieves and plunderers with no place in the Worlds outside the wild and forgotten. They had made the abandoned underground mines their homes. Fetid pariahs armed with crude and cruel weaponry.

The men walked on through the heat of the day, and the landscape of near impenetrable pine trees on their left gradually gave way to softer country. Wooded and rolling hills were cleaved through by a broad valley and after four hours of hard walking, they took to the wing, agreeing that their quarry must lie further ahead than had previously been suspected. They flew slowly the rest of the day, scanning the ground for signs of life and at dusk, landed in a savanna. The hours had become slow and hot, punctuated by the shrill cry of the beetles.

The riders dismounted and drank deeply from their water flasks. Zach had his hand to his eyes, scanning the horizon for any signs of life other than the teeming mass of flies that amassed in their wake. Every rider had squatted down in the dust to rest. The horizon shimmered and seemed to be on fire. The sweat ran down their necks and backs. All was still.

Delano thought he could hear something in the distance though, like a song carried gently on the wind. The dreya had heard it too, their ears pricked and heads turned to better catch it. He stood up and inclined his head in the direction of the eerie melody.

'What do you hear?' Zach asked, his arms folded across his chest. And then it came to his ears too – dreya song. A cry that could be mistaken for no other, the song he had heard in his dream.

'A drey in mourning,' Kai said softly.

'It is being sung by a closer descendant of Kylan than any of our rock dreya,' Owein added, gesturing to Abiro and Ealunan, 'evolution shrunk the vocal chords to make space for less but more accurate fire.'

Everyone was on their feet in an instant, a chance to see one of the ancient war dreya of old was an opportunity not be missed.

'Relax fellows,' Delano laughed, 'he sings far away, his voice will be heard for many hundreds of miles when he reaches the end.'

Zack looked troubled; he knew that it was very probably Valcan and that if the great drey was singing this song, it meant that they were too late.

'We need to find the tracks,' he said to Kai, a note of desperation in his voice as the images that the Oracle had shown him went racing through his mind's eye. The rider nodded and grabbed Cahan, Delano and a few others who ran in different directions in order to find the spoor sooner. After twenty minutes, the song had grown louder still and Delano came running back with good news. He had found the prints but he did not know how far back they led.

'Mount up, riders!' Zach said, 'Delano, you will lead the party. You can read the tracks from up high.'

Delano nodded. The riders took to the sky and flew arrow formation behind Delano.

Valcan's tracks came from the plains west of them. His path led mostly straight but soon Delano was having trouble reading the tracks. The dry and yellowed grass led to low scrub which led to bigger trees, thorny and green with spring. He touched down and the others followed suit.

'How much further?' Zach asked Delano. The rider shrugged and answered,

'Perhaps twenty meters. His gait here is starting to settle.' He drew a ring around the massive paw print in the sand, pointing out weight distribution and angles.

'Kai, wait here with the others, I will go on ahead, alone,' Zach instructed. The riders did as they were bid, standing stock still and alert. They waited and watched as Zach crept further into the dense foliage until they lost sight of his leathers.

Zach followed the tracks as well as he could. They led to a clump of trees that stood in a small clearing not two meters wide. A figure lay in the sand and sun, forsaking the cool shade. The Oracle flashed painfully through Zach's mind, the image of her face fiery and fierce. He was afraid. The man lying on his back looked no more than a bundle of bones and rags. Zach took a few steps closer, whispered words echoing in his mind, the Oracle not giving him a moment to concentrate or decide what to do, so he stepped closer still.

His men were out of sight, he found, as he looked back, and he was alone with the man in the sand. Zach cautiously leaned over him. A rider; he wore the inlaid boiled leather and dragon hide and carried the steel. The tracks led right back to him. His drey had been the last thing he had seen.

His face was aging even as Zach stared on; it looked as if the man had lived hundreds of years. Deep set wrinkles were busy crisscrossing his face and neck like some elaborate map of the Worlds being woven by invisible hands. It must be magic, Zach thought. There was always a catch. Valador could not be more than 150 years old. His eyes were squeezed shut and his mouth was taught. His hair hung long and bleached bone-white around his face. His sword lay discarded. Zach could see this was no ordinary rider. His build was big for such an old man and his features were harder that any Zach had ever seen. This *must* be him. The tapestry of age stopped spinning and Valador's features relaxed. Zach felt silly for thinking he would find anything more. Valador was a warrior from long ago, a myth from older days. What had he expected? He asked himself, a fine strapping soldier who would wield his sword and leap upon his legendary drey to rescue the Worlds from the darkness? Zach felt like a child and sighed deeply. Why would the Oracle want him to find and old, dead rider? Zach straightened up, angry that he had come so far, confused at what he had been told and had seen, that he had dragged his men and their dreya across space for days on end, for the memory of a legend, for nothing. He leaned over again, peering into the old man's face curiously.

'Valador,' he breathed, his eyes roving over the great sword at his side, the words inscribed in old Bethrimian upon its blade, the hilt a grand drey crying ruby tears, and the fine armor that had molded itself perfectly to the man's body. He leaned in closer still, trying to visualize what he had looked like years ago.

Valador's eyes flew wide open and he grabbed Zach by the arm so suddenly that the captain fell over backwards and was left without a breath. Valador tugged desperately at Zach's arm and the captain composed himself. Staring into those wild eyes, he allowed himself to be pulled closer and listen to what he had traveled so very far to hear.

'You are from my dreams!' Valador said. His voice was parched and strung out, like a thick strand of cobweb that refused to break after being stretched to its limits. Zach frowned but said nothing. 'You come to me always and now, here you are.' Valador closed his eyes again and placed his head back down in the sand. Now only his lips moved but he did not stir. 'You never speak; you just stare at me and I see myself in your eyes. The reflection of myself as I age, not as I have always been.'

Zach had no idea what Valador was saying but he listened intently all the same. 'I am leaving now, I am so very tired.' He closed his lips and his head lolled to one side.

'No!' Zach yelled, unsatisfied, 'you have to help us!'

Valador smiled a toothy grin;

'Yes, they are coming. The Blood Angels will answer the blood call...' he trailed off and Zach had to shake him again to hear the rest of the puzzle.

'You need to tell me what to do!' Zach fairly cried.

Valador opened his eyes for the last time and looked at the dream that had haunted him of late, finally understanding.

'You are here to do what I cannot, what I never could. You are here to lead,' He said as he dragged his sword closer to him and thrust it into Zach's hand, clasping the two together as if to make sure Zach would never let it go. His death rattle was peaceful, his eyes shed a last twinkle and Zach set the old man's head down.

To lead

To lead what, he thought, gazing at the blade in his hand.

He did not move for some time, just sat there staring at the ancient warrior, toying with random thoughts, playing with the weight of his new weapon, finding it to be more than perfectly balanced. He did not even hear Llstar and Kai come to sit down next to him.

'That is a fine sword you have there Captain,' Llstar remarked, brushing his fingers along the edge to test the sharpness and swearing quietly as it drew a bud of red blood. Zach looked up and saw Kai staring intently at him.

'What did he tell you?' Kai asked.

'He told me to lead,' Zach said after a while, staring at the ground between his feet again.

'The humans are back, they found us,' Brenin said, bursting through the undergrowth to deliver the news and then darting back in again. The trio got up and walked toward where the rest of the guard was standing. They were in deep conversation with the Rogue humans and Zach strode into the middle of the discussion.

Corbin looked up and started explaining at once, still short of breath from the long run. They had found the base quickly and had stayed hard on the riders' heels ever since. It had been a long and difficult journey.

'We radioed out and there were reports flooding in from every corner of the Worlds,' Corbin said, gulping air down as he spoke. Eira looked close to tears.

'It was terrible,' she gasped, 'people were being attacked as we listened...' she trailed off. Cadeyrn's face was set and his look was hard.

'This is the same force that took Bethriam. They will not stop until we kill them all.' Kai's voice was strong and certain, he looked at Zach expectantly and Zach could feel the pressure of his men's eyes on him.

'There are others who are running, many are going to Emara,' Corbin explained.

'The High Elvin planet,' Owein added.

Corbin nodded;

'It seems they are forming an army there. A signal came from a small planet not far from here confirming it. They are calling all able-bodied sentinels to arms. Now.'

Zach was silent for a moment. He was still unsure as to why the Oracle had led him here. Should he stay and try decipher the riddle or should he do what he knew he should; lead these people to the common cause. The elves, it seemed, had a plan as usual.

'We will fly to Altair,' Zach decided, 'perform the rituals for Valador and prepare to take off.'

He strode away and Eira turned to Corbin and he drew her closer to him, looking at Cadeyrn and Nyx, all that was left of his team. They had heard some chilling reports across the radio link and now, were preparing to join the thick of it. Uncertainty was sketched on Corbin's face as he held his wife.

'It has to be done,' Nyx reassured him.

'Besides,' Cadeyrn added, 'this reeks of Religion.'

'Definitely,' Eira agreed. She had been horrified by the voices streaming in from far away planets, the shrieks of the wraiths and the snarling of their beasts, but she knew there was no hiding when it came to the Religion; you had to stand your ground and fight and it would be the same with these wraiths under their employ.

After an hour had passed and the prayers had been said, Valador's body offered to the fire, they all prepared to leave. Zach clambered uneasily onto Karo. She craned her neck and turned her head to get a better look at him.

'Do not worry about me,' he said. Karo flicked her head back in a characteristically arrogant gesture and they took flight. Zach had to smile at the big human, Cadeyrn, holding on to Kai's waist for dear life leaving the rider battling to concentrate without bursting into laughter himself. Zach tried to shake the uneasy feeling that had settled on him and the guilt at the empty answers that had been all he could offer his loyal men. They had traveled far with him and all he had to show for it was a sword.

To lead

They broke atmosphere quickly for Earth's protective cocoon was only a few hundred miles thick. The clouds broke above them, the inky black of space embraced them, and then Zach saw something that he could not even hope to see in even the wildest of dreams. Every member of the guard and every Rogue looked up to see hundreds of thousands of dreya and their riders streaming past in the space above and around them. They traveled in groups mostly, they were all fully geared for war, including the dreya, and the ones that flew close to the party all looked at Zach as they rode by, glancing at the sword he held in his hand and dipping their heads in acknowledgment when they saw it.

Llstar looked at Zach and Zach looked at the wonder of such an army. Their flight patterns were perfect. The formation and skill was immaculate. Every soldier looked as if he had spent his entire lifetime training day and night, every muscle was honed and every weapon was sharpened so that it sang as it soared through the still air. He felt elation and pride surge through him at such a sight. He felt tears sting his eyes. All thoughts left him as he drank it all in. All purposes save the one he now faced. The Oracle sang to him, she sang to him of the Blood Angels, she sang to his very heart of battles to be won and everything else faded to grey.

Zack looked back at his men, shiny eyed. He sheathed the ruby sword that had been given to him and him alone. They all knew what the Oracle had led them here for now. Every doubt was dispelled by the majesty of this great army that filled space and heart alike.

'Fall in!' Zach cried, his voice as full and commanding as ever, and the riders formed up behind the closest hold without question and watched their captain race to the front where he would lead the flight straight to Emara. To the last battleground for freedom.

*

Arial was standing on one of the many rooftop terraces that adorned the palace buildings. She could see for miles from up there. She could look directly down and see the star-warmed courtyards, once tranquil but now teeming with life. Beyond the ornate gardens, where still more people lay by the river and ambled across the lawns, there lay the orchards and meadows, the snug villages and open fields, lakes dotting the landscape like puddles on a giant lawn. The largest contained little green islands off the shore and Arial could see the temples built upon these for the Great Energy. Hazy, green mountains lay in the distance, cupping the land like the hands of a moss mother. Between it all though, scattered amongst the landmarks and majestic scenery, the babble of a thousand tongues could be heard, leather wedge tents pitched everywhere with their heavy, wooden frames packed closely next to each other, temporarily erected until the newcomers could be assigned a piece of land.

Arial had been watching them arrive all morning and most of the afternoon. There were many today. The lesser tribes of smaller planets had finally succumbed to Altair's call and were turning out in droves such as she had never seen. The cooking fires wound smoke amongst the trees, the horses whinnied and the men practiced their archery and various other combat skills whilst their chiefs spoke and negotiated with the High Elves and Drows.

Arial recognized a few of the tribes from various markings or previous dealings. The Abenaki of the east, the Savari of the north, the Gau of the south and the Benat of the west, were all present and accounted for. The Four Stars. Smaller tribes fell under their rule but the Four Stars were the strongest of the Free Nations.

They were all practicing spear-throwing with the warsaur and while injuries were rife behind the tribal lines, the warsaur warriors stood stock still while steel and wood streaked past without so much as a scratch. The Four Star tribes were ganging up now, pooling their resources in order to save their individual pride in the face of the laughing men with nails in their feet.

She also recognized the Brule, purely from the burn marks scarring the thighs of the few women warriors. They were an eastern tribe. The Yallup were from the south. Their accents told her as much. She could hear them because they were closest to the courtyard walls and she had once received a gift from their southern Gau prince when she was ordained. One tribe had faces painted red with what looked suspiciously like blood and wore bones around their necks and in their long, matted hair. They stood near the Abenaki camp. Another had rocks, with holes drilled through them, tied around their ankles and wrists. They stood with the Gau too. Arial wondered how they were able to move so swiftly with all that extra ungainly weight as one of them jumped into the air, twisting around as he did and catching the arrow meant for the tree behind him neatly between his two flat palms. She recognized the Takya from their dark orange skins and somber faces. They did not join in the activities nor speak to any of the others. "Hostile brutes," Ramroth had always said, "Greedy for land and game". They stood with the Benat.

There were at least threescore more but Arial had given up trying to search her memory. The flags and banners of the north-men waved idly in the wind. They alone favored the steel over the bronze, wood and rock. They rode upon fine horses whilst the others rode outlandish wolverines and large cave dwelling marmots or simply traveled by foot. Arial's gaze roved over so many different faces. Some were painted, some masked and if it were not for these then Arial could hardly distinguish one dusky complexion from the other. They dressed in many different garments, woven all over the Worlds by different hands and for different purposes. Loincloths, leather, chain-mail, skins, beads, tattoos, silks, colored fleece and heavy cottons. It was a feast for the eyes and imagination. It was all that Arial could do but stare. She never thought she would ever see such a grand sight, nor would she ever again she realized.

A handsome young warrior from the Gau camp looked up and waved at her, smiling broadly, small white teeth made for grass and root-eating blinking in the light of the star. Arial smiled back. It was good to be part of something so vast. Her heart grew heavy though as she watched the same young man look down and carry on with the cooking. A friend next to him said something whilst sharpening his axe and they both laughed. So many people from all across the Worlds. So many individual lives were at stake. None of these men or women would be going home unless Arial could discover how to call the Blood Angels.

She had scrutinized her drey-necklace for hours, even tried talking to it, clasping it tightly, anything and everything, but to no avail. Altair had told her again to be patient. Damek had stopped her in the hallways asking if she was alright, if she needed anything, saying that he believed in her, but the more he said it, the more frustrated and hopeless she became.

'Are you going to watch them all day or would you perhaps like to have some lunch?'

Arial turned around; it was Damek.

'With you?' she asked. It came out sarcastically but she had only meant to hide the hope in her voice, the emotion.

Damek stared long and hard at her before saying,

'If you would prefer that I leave you alone I will.'

Arial was struggling to breathe.

'I did not say I wanted that.'

She was not sure how to handle the situation ever since that night in her room.

'Have you been crying?' he asked, taking a step closer. 'I want to be there for you, help you if I can,' he said. Arial turned away.

'No one can help me. I have to do this myself.'

Damek frowned.

'There are so many people who are willing to offer you help and advice. Will pride not let you take it?' he asked.

Arial spun around; red rising in her cheeks;

'How dare you!' was all that she could say.

Damek had known that the discussion was going to turn out like this. She was pushing him away, trying to keep him at bay, which was what he should be doing as well, but he just could not bear to do it. Time spent apart from her was like falling from grace. He felt anger rise in him like bile. The anger of being denied this woman, the anger at having his heart torn in two, the anger at her for wanting to push him away so much he hardly still believed she had ever loved him at all.

'I am responsible for all those people down there!' she said, 'I do not know how I am going to save them because I am so hopeless and useless but I *must*, and you want to talk to me about *pride*!' She was nearly in tears again but Damek had had enough;

'I have told you a thousand times that you have to get over this fear, you *will* find the way!'

Arial was shaking her head wildly, golden curls flailing, refusing to hear the truth until she suddenly stopped. She could feel something deep inside her soul, something she had been afraid she would never feel again. It felt as if a heart-string were being pulled taught, the unnatural slack that was there before disappearing. She looked up hardly daring to believe.

Damek was so frustrated he could scream. He wanted nothing more than to help her but she would not let him.

'Are you even listening to me!' he yelled, lunging for her in an attempt to shake her out of her trance and make her understand.

A shrill shriek cut across the air. His arms were outstretched and he hardly had time to register or understand the look terror on Arial's face. Strong talons grabbed at his shoulders and he was flung clean off his feet and into the wall behind him, bricks crumbling and dust flying. Blood sprung from his wounds, warm and thick. He looked up and saw the cause of his numbing pain. He stood taller than Damek had envisioned, his scales glowed in the light like his maiden's hair and his eyes were fierce and opaque, their depth unfathomable and fearless. Smoke curled from his leathery nostrils and he stood hostile with his chest puffed out, scales standing on end and tail ready to strike. Damek was truly afraid.

Arial could not have been more petrified. Her Ronan had come to her at last but now he stood before her and the man she loved. Every muscle in his body and the posture he held indicating that he meant to kill. This man that had tried to harm her would die and Arial could see he meant it. Arial was pleading silently, hoping he would somehow be able to ignore instinct and listen to her, feel what she felt through his haze of misplaced anger. She could not touch him, his scales simmered red-hot with his fury. Ronan lifted his tail higher, ready to strike. He hissed and spat forth bursts of flame and sparks.

'Please!' she called out. Her heart appealed to him, crying out silent desperation and he stopped. Ronan lowered his tail reluctantly, recoiled the barbs and turned to face her.

He was going to hurt you

Arial stood blinking at him like a fool for a few seconds before she replied,

'No, we were just having an argument.'

Ronan turned back to give Damek an ugly stare before relaxing his body and turning to greet his keeper.

I found you

Arial was in tears, the joy of being near Ronan again was immeasurable. She reached out to him and he nuzzled her affectionately. She caressed the folds of skin behind his ears like a lover, burying her face in his warm neck.

'How did you find me,' she breathed. Ronan inclined his head and blinked his eyes.

My bretheren told me you would be here

Arial stared at him for a moment in disbelief. She looked over at Damek who was busy assessing the damage done to his shirt since his body had already healed.

'Should wear my damned cloak more often,' he was muttering, casting nervous but angry glances at Ronan. Arial ran over to him in a fleeting moment of reckless abandon. She embraced him tightly around the neck and kissed him deeply on the lips.

'Thank you for believing in me,' she whispered before running down the stairs and out of sight leaving him alone with the drey. 'I will be back soon!' she cried over her shoulder and then she was gone.

Damek was stunned for a few seconds and then he remembered where he was and with whom. The two sized each other up warily before Ronan took off, leaving Damek in the wake of his great gusts of stirred air.

Below, the tribesmen's cries of wonder went up as Ronan glided effortlessly over their heads. Many of them had never before seen a drey and Ronan was a sight to behold indeed. Damek watched as he perched himself atop of Arial's bedchamber. A giant bird of prey, he looked, from where Damek stood. Horned and terrifying. He would not lightly cross a dragon in the future, he decided.

*

Arial rushed down the stairs, two at a time. People made way for her as she ran light-footed down the corridors, across the courtyards, finally arriving at the grand hall. The Drow guard let her in without question and she burst in, face flushed, clutching her dress.

A westerner was sitting with Altair, his brow furrowed as he looked over maps spread out on the table. His fair hair hung in dreadlocks around his face and his arms were covered with leather bands, signifying high rank. He did not look up.

Altair walked toward her and pulled her to one side.

'What is it?' he asked.

'I am ready. Send Riko,' she breathed.

*

The walls were brick and flint and the statues were carved wood. This was an older church. Smaller and further away from the main compound. Dust motes hung in the air as the last of the sunlight filtered lazily through the high windows before being snuffed out by the night. Altar boys hurried about, lighting the candles and incense for the evening ceremony. The lamb lay tied down on the altar; hours of relentless bleating had left it silent.

Most of the priests were already assembled. Sirena sat near the front, alone. Her hands were folded demurely in her lap and her hair was pulled back behind her ears. Velasco stepped up to the altar and the chanting that had filled the air stopped. A wind blew in from one of the many cracks in the heavy wooden door and the candles sputtered. Silence.

Velasco's somber eyes roved over the audience. He clutched the small knife he held to his breast and he took a deep breath.

'We are here tonight to pay homage to god; we are here to sacrifice unto him so that we may be blessed,' he intoned.

'Amen,' came the solemn reply from the many lips.

Sirena was having trouble breathing. The incense was stifling; it choked her like the foggy fingers of a demon. Her eyes were watering and she was so cold. She had declined to speak at the gathering; she did not want to have any part of the ceremony tonight. Everything was different now. Velasco was droning on about how the loyal would be rewarded and so on and so forth. Nothing mattered anymore, she realized. She could not take her eyes off the lamb. The leather straps had cut into its soft flesh, mucous was streaming from its nose. She closed her eyes only to open them and find the lamb was still there. It struggled feebly for a few seconds before it lay still again, brown eyes staring straight at her.

Distant thunder rolled through the sky. A storm was coming. Sirena could smell the rain and she wondered if any amount would ever be enough to wash away her sins. As the first flash of lightning illuminated the church, the bloodied and mangled face of a milkmaid played before her eyes. The cow she had been tending had been ripped open from nape to navel, its guts spewed across the charred barn floor. A lamb had been there too. White fleece stained deep red, eyes staring lifelessly at her.

Soren had taken her to the planet he and his kin had destroyed. All the so-called guilty heathens dead and eaten, all the unclean blood painting the roads, piles of flesh and bones almost all that remained. Fleeting screams for mercy or death abruptly cut short or left to linger a few moments longer. Streams of entrails dripping from the black fangs of the creatures they rode. The dawn air making steam from the still warm corpses. No, she decided. It would take more than rain to cleanse her.

Velasco was busy lifting his blade, ready to sacrifice an innocent. For *what* she wondered. Redemption? For they would all need plenty of that before the end.

The chanting had started again, low and ominous, drilling through her ears. She could not bear to watch but she saw the blade rise as if in slow motion, saw it arc in the air. The lamb's eyes were wide with fear except, she realized, it was not watching the knife, it was looking up. Up into the cavernous recesses of the church's domed roof. Sirena followed its gaze and out of the darkness swooped a figure wreathed in shadows blacker than those it came from. Startled cries were sent up from the priests as the creature swooped low and grasped the lamb, clutching it in its claws and carrying the bleating creature back up to the beams.

The assembled men stumbled over one another and pointed upwards, whispering furiously amongst themselves. No one could see where it had gone. The dark and dusty vaulted ceiling swallowed everything in its recesses.

Velasco opened his mouth as if he wanted to speak but as he did so, the lamb fell back to the altar with a dull, wet thud. It was a bloody mess. Throat ripped out and life force gushing. Only Sirena was properly afraid. She alone knew who sat up there in his lofty perch, watching and laughing at the mortals below him. They had all fallen silent now, waiting for some explanation. Velasco was drenched with the splattered blood, it was running down the few stairs that led to the altar and Sirena lifted her feet as it crept closer toward her. The assembly did not have to wait long to discover the true form of the perpetrator. Thunder rolled louder, lightning flashed brighter and those who sat closest to the back felt the chill of something colder than stormy wind creep up their necks.

Nathaniel saw it first. The others were still busy staring skyward but he had sought the source of the frozen fingers that wound their way through his bones. It was not as big as it had looked up there on the altar but it frightened him more now than it had then. It walked upright like a man but Nathaniel had never seen any man like this before. Cold eyes grazed his face painfully and shadow choked the breath from his throat. He walked past him, clawed hands fingering the pew railing leaving massive scars in the wood that peeled and recoiled from his touch. It was all Nathaniel could do not to faint where he stood and so he sat down. Heavily on the bench. The others followed suit as soon as the clawed creature stalked past them and they felt, rather than saw, his presence like some collective subconscious.

He walked past Sirena without so much as a backward glance and she felt the cold in her heart spread throughout her body. It was almost too much to bear. He reached the stairs and the blood clotted and blackened beneath his feet, a river of tar bubbling and hissing. Velasco fell to his knees before the creature. The shadow-man made a gesture like pulling a hood from his head and his face was revealed beneath the dark mirage. Skin black as ebony, swirling and moving like the passing of all the shadows in the Worlds. Its eyes focused on the kneeling archbishop, fixing him with a gaze so powerful that Velasco started sobbing quietly.

This was no man, thought Velasco, this was a dark angel sent to him by god to help him with his task. Soren had been right; these creatures were truly ethereal. Velasco could feel the power emanating from this being, strong and pulsating like a divine heartbeat. The other priests had also gathered around this strange force that drew them toward him inexplicably. They were all kneeling before him and pleading with their eyes.

Sirena had walked to the back of the church unnoticed. She would not submit to this evil. She had borne witness to the carnage she had so craved and it had opened her eyes. She looked back before leaving the building. Velasco had spread his arms out wide and was basking in the blackened mist that wrapped itself around him like a man devoid of all sense.

'Dark angel, we will do whatever you ask of us.' His voice shook with reverence and all the others were whimpering like the dogs they were. Sirena closed the door.

*

There was a turmoil of grey clouds rolling in. They became heavier and darker with each gust of wind that drew them nearer and soon the rain was falling in sheets, the fat droplets pitting the dust in the courtyards and a cold wind pulling at the makeshift hovels and tents.

Altair was gazing out at the army, wondering where he was going to put them all since he had received news that the naizhan had arrived and Toireann had sent word that the Adare' and the cleya were on the way too. Damek had confirmed that three of his seven Shadow Brothers were arriving within the hour. Contact had been made with the humans, more breakaway factions and civilians willing to rendezvous at specific secret flight areas to fly in and help the war effort. The human kings, they had not been able to sway. They had neither the courage nor the power to summon armies anymore. It would be left up to the individual to risk his life.

As each army arrived, their generals were debriefed and temporary land for their men was allocated. The army would then be flown to their battle stations with captains left in charge while the commanders would stay at the palace to engage in war councils that lasted hours on end and held daily. It was vital that every group knew their place and coordination was the key.

Altair was weary. He hardly slept now that the time was drawing near. Delwyn was also constantly busy ensuring medical, housing and resource needs were met. She was tirelessly working with the diplomats and emissaries to check that everybody was happy and that no one with prior struggles stayed too close to one another. It was a monumental task and Altair thanked her every day for her hard work.

Alarico sat on the war council with Carrick, as did Kieran with Braenden. Vanora traveled with her mother and Mirian, he was told rather angrily by Elvira, was honing her skills under Dunkan's tutelage. Elvira herself was assisting Altair as the captains and commanders came rolling in. She took register and notes on specific needs, passing them on to Delwyn on the front line. So far, they were ninety million strong and counting. Altair was worried about resource availability but Toireann stepped in just in time...

'You would not BELIEVE the opposition I received,' were his first words.

Altair smiled and Ailfryd gave a knowing nod. 'I bring but three hundred Adare' and four thousand cleya warriors but I have Water Adare' and many who can manipulate crop. I hope that will be enough.'

Altair stoked his jaw line thoughtfully.

'How many Adare' are warriors though?' he asked.

Toireann seemed to be considering the question before he answered,

'Perhaps one hundred but the others can be trained.'

'And who will do the training, Toireann? You? Your cleya?' Ailfryd asked dryly, 'we have twenty days at best to make ready.'

Toireann smiled;

'You underestimate us.'

Altair nodded and thanked Toireann for his contribution. The mage moved over to Elvira's table to give a head count and added,

'We need only soil and water, where you place us makes no difference,' He said, referring to the cleya. He looked up in thought for a little while and then added, 'Perhaps an area where fire hazard will not be too much of a problem?'

Altair looked out his window again and watched as the cleya headed out of the gates toward the waiting aircraft. They looked formidable with their tattooed skin and dark semblance. Naked but for tiny loincloths that covered their fronts. Only weapons; their bare hands. The crowd parted for them and a hushed silence fell upon the encampments as news of the cleyas' arrival spread.

Elvira joined him at the window.

'I for one will be glad that they are out there somewhere. Neither man nor beast, no matter how ominous, stands a chance against them. Perhaps I myself should make bed in the Urki mountains amidst all the roaring fires and war cries,' she laughed. Altair was quiet for a while.

'Where will we house the wizards?' he asked at length, knowing it was an issue close to her heart and one they almost saw eye to eye on. To his surprise she replied,

'Why, here of course.'

Now Altair looked up questioningly. 'All the better to keep an eye on them,' she shrugged.

Altair grinned broadly.

Chapter 14

Waiting

Ramroth was next in line for an audience. He had been standing in single-file for two hours. He was baffled by the amount of races who had answered the call and by the sheer variety of people. Some of them, he realized, he had never even seen or heard of before.

When he first arrived, he had come marching around a corner at a brisk pace and it had felt as if he had run into a solid iron wall, but when he had looked up, he had seen that it was a naizhan warrior. The naizhan were a biologically mechanical race. Muscle and sinew wound around steel and pistons. Blood and oil flowing through pipes and veins. The monster had lowered its head and gazed blankly at the tiny fleshling that had blundered into its path.

'Please. Move.' It had said in monotone.

Ramroth had stepped aside and watched as four of them moved forward in line. Their metallic footsteps making dull clunking sounds on the wood. Ramroth could only stare in horror and wonder at these creatures. Surely they could not be considered sentinel? A man had grabbed him by the sleeve of his cloak. It was a western tribesman. The Benat had said in hushed tones,

''Tis a good thing they come. Their armor will make good against the shadow.'

Ramroth knew that this would be the only opportunity for him to study the races he knew little of in great detail. To ask them face to face of their customs and anatomy. More than anything though, he wished to speak to his lady. He needed to apologize, to explain and to give her any counsel he could, as he knew what was expected of her.

As soon as he finally entered the hall, Altair rose to his feet and pulled him to one side.

'You must tell no one of the Blood Angels, do you understand?' Altair whispered.

Ramroth nodded in understanding.

'Thank you for looking after her Altair,' Ramroth said, clutching the High Elf's hand tightly, 'I thought I had lost her forever.'

'It was the malachi who brought her; it is *he* you should be thanking. Now come, old friend, we have much to discuss.'

They decided at length that Ramroth and Taigo would draw up a list of names and abilities, assigning each individual Adare' to a group that would perform a specific task. Ramroth thanked them again and asked,

'Where is Queen Arial, I really must speak with her.'

'If she is not with her dragon then she is with her vampire,' Altair said without looking up from the paper he was scrutinizing. He could almost hear the unspoken protest on Ramroth's lips.

*

Arial sat beside a clear stream, spanned by a series of small footbridges. The sky was bruised even after the rain and the light was fading. She watched as the colored lanterns, which were strung from the trees, lit up one by one and the tiny insects of the land gathered around them. A swarm of enganya flew around one of the many trees in the palace gardens that had been assigned to them, wings whirring in the dusk air, chattering away around their hive. She felt a presence behind her and turned around. Of all the people she had been expecting to call on her, it was not this man...

'I do not have long; my people wait for me en route to speak with Altair.'

Arial got to her feet with a frown on her face. Tariq did not seem hostile but she found it hard to trust him.

He read the doubt on her face and stepped back.

'I came to apologize,' he quickly explained, 'I was following orders that I should not have, but I did not know the truth, for I would never have led you to him if I did.'

Arial opened her mouth to speak but he cut her off. 'I did not come here to make excuses, I do not expect you to forgive me either.' He moved forward again now. Arial was silent, regarding him suspiciously. 'I came to give you this.' He held out his hand and gave her a small vial of liquid. 'For the life I would have taken from you, I give you another.'

He did not pause to hear her reply nor accept any words of thanks for his gift. He turned on his heel and walked away. The shadows of falling night barred him from view after a few minutes and Arial looked down to inspect her gift.

She held the vial up to the last of the light. It held no more than a few precious droplets but that was enough to give away its identity. Arial had heard of this but had never seen it. She doubted many had. This must have been worth a fortune and the secret of its existence fiercely guarded. The blue, viscous liquid swirled within its glass restraints unaided. It was the elixir of life. Nobody knew exactly where it came from and so its rarity was unrivaled but it was rumored to be maji tears, and they never cried.

Arial took a deep breath, realizing the full measure of this sacrifice and hastily hid the tiny vial between her breasts.

Now, another approached her. She wondered if it was Tariq coming to claim back his excessive token but it was not. She would have recognized that gait anywhere. All composure left her as she gathered her skirts and ran toward her ward. She half jumped into his arms and nearly wept with joy at the mere sight of him. He hugged her back with that same alarming strength that she had come to love.

'I thought I had lost you forever,' he sighed.

Arial laughed out loud.

'If it were not for you, I would have been,' she said, pulling back and holding him by the shoulders, staring straight into his eyes. 'You taught me well Ramroth.'

The old Adare' had never been more flattered in his life and he held back the tears that threatened to spill over onto his wrinkled features.

They sat down next to the stream while the sky threatened to break out in rain once again and spoke of all the things they had done and witnessed while they were apart.

'I knew the malachi would be up to something,' he grumbled, 'I hope their alliance proves better in the future.' He looked meaningfully at Arial but she did not catch his message.

'We wait for a few more and then we wait only for the hammer stroke to fall,' Arial said, biting her lip, and Ramroth knew that she was still afraid.

'All that Altair has gathered here will deflect the blow and your army will slay them all.'

He sounded so sure that Arial could not bring herself to argue. She had indeed seen with her own eyes the multitudes, looked upon the maps that marked their positions and she had to admit that it surpassed impressive.

The sounds of carousing mobs of drunken north-men reached their ears in that moment of silence. Let them enjoy the night, she thought, for it may be among their last. Fireworks burst into the sky above them; green and blue sparks flaying the darkness and distracting the young drey queen.

'I have never seen fireworks before!' she exclaimed.

'No doubt the work of some reckless Adare',' Ramroth said, shaking his head as he remembered the crowd of young wizards in the mountain. He looked at Arial's upturned face, the wonder in her smile and the gleam of the display reflecting in her eyes. It was then that he realized that although she was childlike in nature, she was a woman grown now. She had no need of him anymore; he had taught her all he could.

'You must go and partake in the festivities,' he said, getting up and brushing off his robes. 'You are young and have more energy than I.'

Arial knew why he wanted her to enjoy the night. He too, was afraid, for all his bravado.

'Thank you for coming to see me, I will seek you out later and we will speak more,' she promised, giving in to his request without hesitation.

They embraced again and Arial called out to Ronan. He flew from his perch on her bedchambers, hearing her quiet call from all that way. He swooped down and landed lightly on the grass beside her.

Ramroth watched the special pair with pride and reverence. Arial shone so brightly with her new-found bond that Ramroth felt his heart could break.

She hitched her skirt up and around her perfect legs to mount her drey. Ramroth could understand why the malachi felt the way he did. Arial was a rose in a bed of thorns even when compared to the most beautiful of women. Ramroth was an old man but he had not lost his eyesight and although he felt for Arial like a father for his only child, Arial's loveliness could not be denied.

She leant down from the neck of Ronan to plant a tender kiss on his cheek, her warm skin brushing against his, her sweet scent filling his nostrils and in that moment, Ramroth forgave the vampire everything.

*

The festivities were taking place in the temporary tribal camps outside the palace grounds. The night air was alive with the smells of ale and wine and all manner of meats and fresh bread, cooked beneath the ground on coals.

Arial had not meant to make a grand entrance but it was difficult *not* to astride a fire drey. Ronan glided down low over the camps, his wings skimming the tent tops causing coupling pairs, red-faced and flustered, clutching deerskins, to come tumbling out and see what the fuss was about.

Kemen was busy tending his horse while Erromon and Mikel stoked the fire and stirred the sweet, spiced wine. The north-men were mostly all drunk by now. Their flutes mingled with the drums of the westerners, and drink was being exchanged. The west-men drank a strange milky concoction that was five times as strong as that of the traditional northern drinks.

'And it makes you more potent!' Danel cried, making ludicrous gestures with his strong arms.

'Easy now,' Luken said, prizing the cup from his lieutenant's grasp and replacing it with a flask of water, 'the night is still young,' he warned.

Luken had seen Altair earlier that day and his men were to be moved out to the white lakes alongside the Savari north-men, and he wanted them ready for the journey, not puking out the night's frivolities outside their tents. He adjusted a bead in his fair, dreadlocked hair and pushed the tent flap aside to speak with Kemen.

'Have you spoken to the elf yet?' Luken asked.

Kemen turned around and chucked a brightly colored bridal to one of his grooms and continued stroking his mare's face.

'Which one?' came the reply. Kemen's dark eyes smiled, his black plaited hair hanging before them. Luken smiled back.

'We leave at dawn. We ride our beasts since the journey will take a full day. Do we ride together?'

'Ha!' Kemen laughed, 'your xanti could never keep up with my horses.' Kemen referred to the big dogs that the westerners rode. Fangs the size of a man's hand, big bulky shoulders. Luken stepped closer to the Savari prince and inspected the creature he was caring for.

'Your horses are like women. You tend their every need and whim. I heard that on long quests, your men like to make use of them in much the same way...shall I get you a stool Kemen?'

The dark-haired prince made a swipe at his cheeky friend but he missed. Luken ducked at the last minute and came up behind Kemen, planting a foot on his arse and pushing him right over. Kemen roared with laughter and Luken helped him get up.

'Your Majesties?' A young serving girl was at the door of the tent. Kemen had his hands on his knees and was panting for breath. He gestured for her to continue. 'There is something happening in the Gau camp, your men want to know if they have leave to go see?'

Luken tightened the straps on his arms and brushed the hay off his leather pants. He looked Kemen up and down with his heavy chain-mail and ornate helm.

'We ride together?' he asked again.

Kemen nodded and led the way down to the southerners camp.

The entertainment down there was far more extravagant. The guests, too, were of a greater variety and Kemen was glad for an excuse to spend the night here instead. The fires roared red and green around the magic slingers who had come. Fireworks brightened the night sky. The dancing girls whirled around in satin shifts and clinking bronze trinkets that dangled from their ears and ankles.

The Gau loved their piercings almost as much as the Savari loved their horses, thought Luken.

Kemen was already transfixed, ogling a particularly beautiful southern specimen in an orange and purple wrap, using her belly to hypnotize him with wave-like motions. The prince was busy trying to fish gold out of his pocket for the camp-follower when Luken grabbed him by the scruff and led him away to the sound of much protest.

'Will you not keep an eye on what your commander spends his "hard-earned" coins on?' Luken hissed at Mikel. Kemen's lieutenant shrugged and said nothing. Luken shook his head.

'There! Over there!' Erromon cried.

Luken followed the direction Kemen's lieutenant's fingers pointed in and a great ball of fire erupted from something on the ground.

'This is more wizardry,' he said dismissively, waving his hand idly in the air, 'why do you drag us all this way for magic tricks?'

'Those are no magic tricks, Prince.'

The voice had come from the shadows and Luken turned around, trying to find the source.

'That is *real* fire.'

The same voice, a little closer this time and from the opposite direction. All the men were looking around now.

'Show yourself,' Kemen demanded.

Out of the shadows and from their left and right, stepped two beautiful women. They were identical in every way. Same deep brown eyes, same raven hair, long bronzed legs, tattooed bellies, scantily clad in the softest cat-skins, with pierced ears, navels and noses.

'Well well, if it isn't Yera and Yuli,' Kemen said, taking his hand off his sword. It was the infamous twin bodyguards of Prince Jakome. Stealthy and deadly, their reputation was known throughout the Four Stars. It was said that their mother bedded a Shadow Brother and that they were the result of the love affair, tearing the hearts out of their victims to satisfy their occasional thirst.

Luken highly doubted that. Only true vampires carried the parasite, it could not be passed along in any other way. He did not disbelieve the ferociousness of the sisters but some rumors simply went too far. He was sure Kemen felt the same, they knew these two rather intimately, but he could not speak for the others who regarded them so warily, you could swear their legendary fangs were out already.

'Careful, Prince Kemen,' Yuli said, referring to his easy manner, 'we could have your tongue for merely uttering our names.' She giggled at her own joke.

'You are on Gau ground now,' Yera added.

'What do you mean by "real fire"?' Kemen asked.

Yera walked toward him, encircling him as she spoke and caressing his hair with her long, hennaed fingers.

'Have you not heard? The beasts of fire are here,' she whispered. Luken frowned.

'To be fair, only one for now,' Yera added.

'But more will follow,' Yuli finished, 'thousands they say, to help the poor boys with even poorer sword skills.' They both laughed and ran ahead to where the fire was last seen.

Kemen and Luken looked at one another and shrugged, following the sisters into the crowds.

True enough, there in the middle of the throng bustling one another for a better look, was a fire-beast. *Dreya, dragon, umuriro.* One of the largest Luken had ever seen. The last time he had seen one was when the queen, Mirkisha, had come to visit his homeland. He did not know the maiden who stood beside this great beast but he wanted to very dearly from the moment he could tear his eyes away from the umuriro to see its keeper. It seemed Kemen did too for he shouted very loudly,

'Make way for Princes Kemen and Luken!'

They strode forward, the crowds parting for them as they went.

Luken could see elves, perion, tribes' men, star pirates and even a few fayres among the many faces. He wondered what the fayres were doing there but when he glimpsed past the masses and into a nearby tent, he could see why. Their males, it was said, did a poor job of satisfying them. The men of the other sentinel races would do anything they asked in reverence of their great beauty.

'I am Prince Kemen of the north and this is my good friend, Prince Luken of the west,' Kemen said, introducing them, 'and who might you be?' he asked, bowing low and kissing the fair maiden on her hand.

'Why, she is Arial, the queen of *umuriro!*' Jakome said loudly in mixed Udaranese and Gauan, his hands raised in the air, and the cry was taken up by the people.

Luken could see Arial was blushing by the light of the bonfires that whisked sparks and smoke into the clearing sky.

'You are a long way from home, Your Majesty,' he said, as he took his turn to kiss her royal hand.

'I have no home left,' she replied sadly and Luken could see the sorrow in her eyes.

Ronan could see that the attention was being drawn away from him, so he threw another ball of flame into the air, and the crowds went wild again. He posed and flexed his tail to the shrill cries for more.

'Typical male,' Arial muttered, stroking his gleaming scales.

'Why not leave him for the people and come talk with us?' Kemen suggested.

Just call if you have need of me

'Very well,' Arial said, to the obvious displeasure of Prince Jakome who had greeted her first and wished to show her his impressive royal guard. As the southern prince scowled, the other two princes led her away, finding Yera and Yuli who led them to an unused tent further away from the throngs of celebrating folk.

Once they were comfortably seated and served spiced wine and fresh bread, Luken asked,

'Is it true that a thousand more will join you?'

Arial looked at the strange people with whom she now sat. The twins, whom she did not know, and had only heard of this very night, and the other two were newly ordained princes of the north and west. Could she trust these tribes' people?

'I am sorry to disappoint you Princes, but perhaps only a few hundred more,' she answered, 'our numbers were greatly reduced in the attack on my planet and I must rely on aid from other kings and queens.'

'Was it the shadow that came for you?' Yuli asked, moving closer to Arial, draping her slender arm over the queen's shoulders in sympathy. She spoke the common tongue well enough but it rolled oddly from her lips and the words were drawn out.

Arial stiffened a little at the close proximity but realized that she was on foreign ground and that she must try to be accommodating.

'Yes, they come with the rising star and they slaughter all who stand in their path,' Arial replied solemnly.

Kemen frowned and said,

'Surely they cannot be so formidable that no one stands a fighting chance?'

'Look around you good man,' Luken answered for her, 'do you think all this is for naught? Altair would not have called every warrior from across the Worlds if he did not believe otherwise.'

Yuli was on her feet in a heartbeat, her thin blade drawn and laid across Kemen's neck.

'That is how fast they will kill you,' she hissed playfully, 'except it is not my sweet breath and the touch of my bare breast which will be the last things you feel, it will be the stench of the wraiths and their shadows will swallow you whole.'

Yera laid her head down on Arial's lap, hand resting on her thigh.

'Forgive my sister; she likes to play with little boys,' she purred.

Kemen's face was contorted with outrage but Luken was chuckling quietly. He looked over at Arial and explained,

'They know he bites the bait so easily that they leave me alone now!'

Yuli snapped her head around and jumped up to straddle the younger prince.

'You will be next,' she warned, licking her lips.

Yera got up and brushed her thick, dark hair out of her eyes.

'Are you well prepared for the battle ahead?' Arial asked, sipping her hot wine, the sweetness of it burning the back of her throat and soothing her tired body.

'Do not worry, Queen Arial, we are always well-prepared!' Kemen said, lifting his glass in toast to his self-proclaimed ever-ready super army.

'Wraiths like horse flesh best of all,' Arial remarked, copying the twins' mischievous air now that the wine had loosened her tongue.

'We have many horses,' he retorted, 'rather my steed's backside than my own!' and everybody burst out laughing. Luken swore loudly in Aban. It was gruffer than the clicky Aben, far less complicated than Savan and Arial begged to be taught some lilting Gauan. This language, however, of the two sisters, she could not wrap her tongue around no matter how hard she tried and more laughter greeted her efforts.

'*U-wak-tu-oh-ay*,' she tried. By this time, Kemen was holding his sides and tears ran down Luken's face. That was no word for a lady and when she found out its meaning, she blushed deeply, slapping Yuli lightly on the arm but joining in the laughter none the less.

Arial relaxed much more and they spent the night talking of battles and *umuriro*, drinking and fornicating. Arial had little to tell on the latter but for the stories she lacked, the others more than made up for. Yuli and Yera were more than happy to re-enact and the tears of mirth were rolling freely by the time she had to bid them goodnight. It was such a pleasure to be away from tedious war councils and all the familiar faces, and spend an evening with strangers who welcomed her as warmly as one of their own.

Eventually they left the tent to walk outside and get some fresh air. They walked among the many tribes' people, greeting them and stopping to talk with them as they went. Yuli and Yera pointed out who was who with the help of the by now, very drunken princes.

'That is Princess Maitea of the Abenaki easterners; see how she loves to wear the snake?' Yera said. Arial craned her neck to see better and sure enough, the princess sat on a pile of silken cushions, snakes draped around her neck, arms and thighs. Her fifteen husbands sat around her, drinking and laughing loudly.

'She believes their venom will make her strong if she drinks it,' Yuli added.

'And does it?' Arial asked in alarm.

Yuli shrugged;

'She will not say but I will bet Luken's pretty head that no poison will hold sway over her no more.'

'Fiend of a woman!' Luken mock-cried. Yuli fended off his attempts to kiss her and continued to point out more people;

'That one there is Kalil, chief of the Atakape`, tribe beneath Abenaki. They will eat the wraiths so that they can hang their boiled bones around their necks.' She brushed her fingers around Arial's neck and a shiver went up Arial's spine as she watched the Atakape` warrior. It was blood on his face, she was sure of it now. He sneered, as she walked past, at one of his serving men and she could see the filed and stained teeth in his ugly mouth.

'Queen of fire beasts!' a man cried out to her as she passed with her new entourage, 'will you save us with your creatures of flame and wing?'

This was exactly what Altair had warned her of, but she felt that these people had come this far and deserved a little hope to brighten the dark days that lay ahead, even if it may be false.

'Yes,' she whispered as she walked by, clutching his free hand and squeezing it tightly, 'tell the people that I will not let them down. You will see home before the end. The Blood Angels will come.'

The man smiled broadly and nodded eagerly.

'Ronan?' she called finally, after hours of walking and talking. The princes looked around, searching for the person she was speaking to.

'No Ronan here Highness,' Kemen said, gesturing about him with a sweeping hand.

Arial smiled as her drey came striding through the crowd toward her, heavy shoulders swaying, paws making no noise in the thick dust.

Kemen looked over at Luken.

'Wish my beasts would come when I called,' Kemen slurred.

'Aye,' Luken replied, 'that would be a thing.'

Arial mounted Ronan and thanked the people from her lofty post for their hospitality and promised to return.

'The drink is always free for one as fair as you!' one of them cried.

'Come see us soon! Bring the beast!' another yelled.

Arial smiled and looked down at her friends.

'And thank you for a wonderful evening,' she said sincerely.

Yuli and Yera both boosted themselves up and kissed her lightly on either cheek. Identical, Arial thought.

'What makes you different?' she asked. Yuli grabbed Arial's hand and thrust it on her bare breast.

'What do you feel?' she asked. Arial could feel nothing but the soft skin of Yuli's breast and the hardness of her nipple against her thumb.

'Now feel mine,' Yera said, taking Arial's other hand. Arial's expression dawned in understanding and she said to Yuli,

'Your heart beats faster.'

The twins nodded and leapt down onto the soft ground.

Kemen stepped forward to kiss her hand again and thank her for gracing them with her presence before making way for his friend. Luken also found his way up but he kissed Arial full on the lips. She could taste the sweet wine on his searching tongue and had no time, and little need, to pull away. Without a word and leaving Arial quite breathless, Luken swung down, took his friend by the arm and they turned to leave. Kemen swept Yuli right off her feet and hoisted her over his shoulder as she shrieked with glee while Yera hung on Luken's free arm, turning to wave as they walked away.

Interesting

Ronan remarked as he took off in a cloud of dust, amidst the roars of the people, their clapping and dancing. Arial looked down at the camps they were leaving behind. The fires burning high, the whirling dancers and the beating of the drums that still throbbed through her ears. She was almost level with the glittering lights of the star pirate's ships that hung in the air like floating ghosts. The ladders that hung over their rails were full of people clambering down to join the festival. Drink was spilled and singing filled the night air.

'Do not lie,' she teased, 'you loved every minute of it.'

*

Ramroth decided to try and get an early night. There was much to do in the morning. His quarters were on the far side of the palace and enough distance was between him and the festivities for him to be able to rest. Except for the drums. They resonated through the wooden structure like the heartbeat of a monster.

His dreams were troubled. He dreamt that Arial was falling into a dark abyss and that he could do nothing to save her. All the while she was crying out his name, reaching out to him, eyes wide with fear and the drums kept beating. He awoke with a start.

The day's light was streaming in through the paneled glass wall of his bedroom. He was drenched with sweat. He took a shower, standing beneath the cool stream of water until he felt refreshed. He donned his cloak, drank herbal tea and strode down into the maze of courtyards with purpose.

'Ramroth!' It was Taigo. He stood beneath a poplar tree that had grown over the heat-baked walls. Ramroth walked over to join him. There was a small, make-shift table that had been set up for their use, pen and paper, two rickety chairs and nothing else.

'The Adare' have been told to meet us here so that we can take register and start sorting this rabble out,' Taigo said.

Ramroth looked around him. The noisy vendors cluttered the sidewalk and there was hopelessly too much hustle and bustle for them to get anything done here. Elvira's idea of a joke then. Well, he would fix this soon enough. He called out loudly that by order of the High Elf Altair, this courtyard was being requisitioned, and that everybody would have to ply their trades elsewhere. There was much muttering and grumbled obscenities. This was prime space since most of the traffic came through here.

'Barricade those doors, will you,' Ramroth said to Taigo, once the last of the crowds had left, 'make sure nothing can disturb us.'

Taigo nodded and Ramroth set to work on the opposite entrance, ensuring that only those with magical ability could step through. He drew the Line of Difference, a pale yellow streak across the cobblestones, barely recognizable but impenetrable to non-wielders all the same. They simply would not come this way; find another menial task to do that would lead them elsewhere. The art of illusion. Ethron had been mildly good at it, passing on what little he knew, but Toireann had been hooked from his first spell and had mastered it. That was his trade. Ramroth hoped his feeble attempt would hold.

Ramroth was an Adare' of many trades. He could do a little bit of everything but had not *perfected* anything. He had sacrificed the knowledge of one for the knowledge of many. He had studied all the arts tirelessly and though he could not perform them as well as his fellow Adare', he had an intimate understanding of magic as a whole and this, he had discovered, was an art in itself. He was the only one who had chosen this path. All the others became obsessed with a specific sphere of magic that they had discovered their powers bonded with best, and would bend all their will upon it.

Ramroth touched the table, closed his eyes and grabbed the edges. It was weak wood, it would do his bidding. He pulled hard and the table began to stretch.

Taigo cocked his head to one side and said,

'It is not very straight.'

'You do it then,' Ramroth retorted, knowing full well that Taigo was a Barricade Master and little else. Taigo nodded his head in accent and they both sat down to wait.

Soon enough, the Adare' started filtering in through Ramroth's special entrance and sidled over to the table when they felt like it. Ramroth sighed deeply as he started to take note of the undisciplined wizards. There were only three columns to fill in; first name, ability and level of mastery. Nothing else mattered. Race, age, family - they were all irrelevant and shared only by the mage if he or she wished it. You became part of a new clan when you joined the guild. All else was left behind. Your loyalties lay with your new brothers and sisters.

'Blair. I am a level Three Pathfinder.'

Ramroth was impressed. The highest level that could be achieved without crossing over to other planes, and being left there forever, was a Five. Very few ever reached this level and even fewer arts were of substantial power to even be classified that highly. Pathfinders could reach a Four.

'How much distance can you span and what type of materials have you learnt to bend?' Taigo asked the obvious questions.

'I can span -' but Ramroth cut him short;

'Show us.'

The young Adare' was taken aback but did as he was told.

Blair stood with his feet planted firmly and slightly apart. As Ramroth watched closely, Blair took a deep breath, closed his eyes and began to bend the cobblestones he stood on. His hands cupped and his muscles straining, he lifted the few he needed and pulled them clean from the ground they had been embedded in for hundreds of years. He threw them up into the sky above them and they exploded into a million pieces, each suspended and slowly rotating. He thrust his hands forward and created a bridge that stretched all the way from where he stood to the far corner of the palace walls.

Ramroth stood and craned his neck to see. It was a long way away, the end of his path, and it looked solid enough.

Blair was taking strain but the bridge never shifted. Ramroth grabbed hold of the wall with the same magical hands he had used to pin Lucio with not two days ago, ripping part of it from its foundations and placing it on the bridge, five feet above their heads. He spun the stone into a crude ball and made it roll across the path to test its stability. Perfect.

'Thank you,' Ramroth said, as he smoothed out the stone and replaced the wall.

Blair opened his eyes and lowered his hands, the bridge dissolved and the cobblestones fell back into place within seconds. The whole exercise had taken him five minutes. Ramroth sat down and took up the pen, scribbling out what Taigo had written.

'You are a level Four,' he said matter-of-factly, 'you were graded wrong. Please move over to the side.'

Blair had a massive smile on his face and the other mages cheered for him and clapped him on the back.

'We've all been graded wrong!' they cried, laughter raining in the courtyard.

Ramroth sighed again. Taigo looked over at him.

'Perhaps you should do the testing and I will record the findings?' the High Adare' suggested.

Taigo was giving Ramroth the authority that belonged to him and Ramroth wondered why.

'Very well,' he conceded, trying to discern what warred behind Taigo's eyes. 'Next!'

The Adare' came rolling in and never one at a time, never in an orderly queue and Ramroth was starting to get frustrated. Blair had not stood where he was told to but had moved on to stand with friends, re-enacting his test with excessive hand gestures. He shook his head and tried to concentrate on the task at hand.

'My name is Seme and I am a Water Adare', level One,' a pretty young thing next in line stated. Taigo duly recorded the information and looked to the next candidate, obviously not wanting to waste their time on such an insignificant mage who would be of little use. She looked over her shoulder at a friend calling out her name and started to move away but Ramroth grabbed her hand to stop her. He could feel it there. The power. That was his *true* art, he could see the gifts of others, see the potential they held from his extensive studies of the subject matter and this Adare' could do better, he knew it.

'What can you do with this glass of water?' he asked her, placing his mug in front of her on the table.

Seme frowned;

'Not much. I can make it swirl around and maybe tip the cup but that's about it. I've never worked on anything with much more mass though,' she admitted.

'Humph,' Ramroth muttered, 'I do not believe you.'

She looked up at him, startled. Her name was called out behind her again and after a brief glance at the culprit, Ramroth encased himself, Taigo and Seme in a Relative Silence bubble.

'Perhaps not under tutelage,' he hinted.

Seme was not sure what to say but she decided that the truth would have to do. After looking round and satisfying herself with the knowledge that no one would hear their exchange she said,

'Umm…I went to a lake with my sister and some friends…'

'Go on,' he said gently.

'Well…my sister was in trouble. We had all had a little too much to drink and she was going under.'

'You could not go in after her because you cannot swim,' Ramroth guessed.

'Yes,' she admitted shyly.

'Then what?' he prompted.

'I…I moved the water so she could breath.'

'You moved an area of water around her because you knew where she was?' he pressed.

Seme looked down, fiddling with her fingers.

'Speak up girl,' Taigo said.

Ramroth cast a dark glance at the High Adare' and he fell silent.

'It is alright, you are not going to be in any trouble,' Ramroth promised.

'I moved the whole lake. I didn't know exactly where she was and I panicked.' She said it so quietly, her voice ringing with such desperation, that Ramroth had to struggle to make it out but he had his confession. Magic laws stated that unauthorized use of excessive power would result in the perpetrator being stripped of his or her power, unless extreme exception could be proven.

'It is alright, my dear,' he said gently.

'I have not been able to do it again,' she said in a rush.

'That is something we will have to remedy,' he said, a slight twinkle in his eye. 'You had confidence because you were intoxicated and you had the need to perform for someone you loved, not some old wizard with a marking sheet. We will practice.'

Seme looked overwhelmed with gratitude and excitement.

While Ramroth had been absorbed with her, his bubble had slowly stretched and burst. Other Adare' had been listening in on this conversation and now some of them stepped forward, made bold by Ramroth's promise of leniency.

'I too have wielded better under illegal circumstances but I do not know how to do it again,' one said.

'Me too!' chorused another. The cries were taken up and Ramroth could see that about thirty of these mages had untapped potential and were desperate to learn how to use it. They were encouraged to step forward one by one so that their stories could be heard.

Many of them, it seemed apparent after a while, had invaluable skills like Iker, a presumably level Two Shield Adare' and Esti, a Fire Adare' that it was soon discovered, could create fire, as well as bend it to her will; not a skill your average Fire Adare' possesses. Demond could morph biological matter on an impressive level. The last time Ramroth had seen anyone do anything like that; he had been watching his own master at work. Lore was a Pulse Adare' using shock waves and not electromagnetic waves like the others. Elezar was a very strong Storm Adare' but storms needed space that he had never had access to and his air and water abilities needed work.

'All of us need help,' Demond said, 'we have just been tinkering about with our powers, no real pressure. We all thought we had time, we all thought it was fun. Yeah, sure,' he said, looking around, 'some of us took it seriously and some of us were curious about how far we could push ourselves but most, like me, had no one to push us and now we face a *war*. We have *lives* to protect, we have a duty.'

Ramroth was glad that they were all thinking in straight lines now. The others were all rallying around Demond, clearly the most talented, and they wore somber expressions. 'We need to learn,' Demond finished, 'who will teach us?' His fair features were darkened with worry but his broad shoulders stood proud as he asked for a leader, speaking for all who stood behind him.

Taigo looked at Ramroth and Ramroth met his gaze. The High Adare' nodded ever so slightly and Ramroth knew it was time.

'I will,' Ramroth said.

There was movement in the crowd and smiles were breaking out. 'But then it will be done my way or no way at all,' he warned, finger pointed at the eager faces of the crowd. 'Form a line!' he barked and everybody did as they were told, scrambling for a better place.

Ramroth drew scorched lines into the cobblestones; blocks on the ground that would be assigned to groups that would work and train together, soon to be fighting side by side on the battleground.

'High Adare' Ramroth,' the first in line said, 'I was graded as level Three but I think I can do better. I have learnt many new illusionary spells. May I show you?'

Ramroth looked over at Taigo who was seated beside him. He seemed to be taking this all very well and Ramroth was surprised. It was a coveted title, one that was *earned,* and now it had been thrust upon Ramroth without much ado.

Taigo put his hand on Ramroth's shoulder;

'What will you have me do?' he asked, 'my barricades will protect an army in its entirety, but lead these people, I cannot.' He was smiling, if a little sadly, and Ramroth relaxed.

They went through the mages together, assigning task teams and marking those who needed extra attention with a red cross next to their names.

'We will use the fields north of the palace to practice. Iker, you will set up the perimeter to avoid casualties and I expect you all to be there at dawn,' Ramroth said sternly.

The Adare' all nodded eagerly and took note of whom their task-team members were. Hands were shook and boasts were exchanged.

'They will always remain wizards,' Taigo laughed, 'not even you will ever be able to change that.'

When all was said and done, and the elvin suns were sitting low in the sky, the mages all formed a semi-circle around Ramroth. The book was pulled from thin air as Toireann had done previously and Taigo scratched his name out, replacing it with Ramroth's.

'High Adare' Ramroth,' the crowd chanted, 'we accept your authority and you accept your responsibility. You will uphold the Adare' laws,' they all said together, Taigo's husky voice added to the chorus.

'And you will lead us into battle!' a voice from the back added.

'Into battle!' they all agreed enthusiastically.

Ramroth signed and the book snapped shut, vanishing from sight and leaving only the dust from its pages lingering in the air.

'Thank you,' Ramroth said. He was not sure just how thankful he was but he would take care of them, it was now his duty as well as his wish.

The Adare' started to leave in groups, chattering excitedly. Ramroth was shuffling papers, deep in thought. His thoughts were not on all he had accomplished that day, or all the work still needed to be done, they were of Mary. The brief student he had lost, the girl who had given her life to save his. He wondered if it could have happened any other way and as he cast his thoughts back, a vivid flash of her umanok came to him. The rush of wings against skin, the sear of coal-red eyes and the heart-gripping fear as blackened fangs and tawny talons took what they wanted. He jerked his head up and looked at the entrance to the courtyard, his special line crossed by another girl, not part of the guild, not tested, and therefore, not able to cross the line. But there she stood. Ramroth could hardly believe his eyes but he composed himself.

'You,' he barked, pointing at the girl who was staring about her at all the wizards, wonder slackening her sharp features, 'come here...'

*

Otorea was a small planet that orbited near Terrius, its larger sister. It was plagued by heavy storms and the landscape was constantly bathed in an eerie green light. The frequent tornadoes made permanent inhabitance difficult, but that was not what the planet was utilized for. Otorean gems were plentiful on the planet but found nowhere else. They were sold across the Worlds at exuberant prices. It was how the Religion garnered the means to drive their war. It was also where they gathered to discuss their plans for extermination.

Some of the people believed the propaganda and the lies that they had been fed and were signing up to join the military wing, most simply turned a blind-eye and there had been word of those who had decided to go against their god, and the dark angel he had sent, in order to fight alongside the enemy. A few of these rebel groups had been intercepted and wiped out along with the rest of the Rogues but it was inevitable that a few would escape and make it to…

'Emara? But that is many light years away. How would they have had the means to get there? We have confiscated all space vessels in keeping with our grounding laws. They would never have been able to get their hands on church property!'

Soren was seated at the head of the table; Lord Nagesh and Esyago flanked him, standing on either side of him like the bodyguards of the devil himself. Umar, Malik and Izyan were also present, preferring to stand at the door instead of sit around the table. They had nothing to say to these fragile beings.

Soren was listening to the priests argue amongst themselves and was growing impatient. Riko sat to his left. She was curling a strand of hair around her finger until he glared at her. She abruptly stopped, folded her hands demurely on her lap and lowered her eyes. He would like to deal with her later in ways that only he knew how but that might not come to pass. He was still a man after all but business came first.

'Private enterprises, dear Diego. They have money hidden from us and the means to power their own operations,' Velasco explained as if to a child. He sat to Soren's right and spoke for him most of the time. 'Either that or the elves provided transport for them.'

'But…'

'It does not matter,' Soren breathed and the issue was immediately dropped. Diego's mouth snapped shut and everyone turned their attention to their leader. His shadows and swirling darkness fell across the table, fingering those he sat closest to. His blank eyes bore into his human allies and he waited for the next menial topic of discussion to be brought up. No one said a word and Soren smiled inwardly. At least they knew their place.

'Riko?' he asked and Riko looked up.

'Yes. I have seen this Emara. I snuck aboard as a human ally as you asked and when we landed I boarded the next ship flying out. It took a week, for the human traitors number but a few and so I had a chance to see much,' Riko said.

'Tell us,' Velasco ordered.

Soren saw the brief flair of defiance in the shape-shifter's eyes.

'Their army is colossal,' Riko said, 'they wield strong weapons and wear even stronger armor. They train relentlessly by day and night perfecting an art they have already perfected. That is just the elves.'

Velasco sat back in his chair. 'There are more,' Riko continued, 'many more who have joined! All the people called from all across the Worlds. They have magic! Their numbers are too great to count and their banners cover the blue sky till a shadow seems to fall across the land and travel with the wind.'

Velasco looked to his fellow priests and then to Soren.

'Do we have a force great enough to overcome these odds?' Velasco asked for no one else was brave enough to. Soren remained silent for a while and Velasco became worried that he had over-reached himself but after a while, the angel's face broke into a grin and he said, as if with the words of god himself;

'No army can defeat us. Our cause is noble, their hearts are wicked. We will smite them down and they shall never rise again.'

The assembled priests all crossed their hearts and sent up their silent thanks.

'We must strike now,' Riko interjected, 'they wait for no one else,' taking advantage of the quiet.

Soren turned his head to stare at Riko. He watched her squirm under his gaze with immense satisfaction.

'I think we should send a probe attack to see if she speaks true,' Velasco said, arms folded across his chest.

'Why would she lie?' Diego asked curiously. Velasco gave him a pleading look and answered,

'To lure out and destroy our black army of course! It is our only weapon! We know our Religion soldiers number but a few thousand. They are assassins, not foot-soldiers, and they will not last one day against an elvin Alvar. They will remain on the Home Planets and keep order in the streets. That is why we need the black plague and that is why we need to discover how great the enemy force truly is!'

Soren sat forward in his chair and leaned toward the Supreme Archbishop until he was but mere inches away from his face.

'Do you doubt us, Velasco?' He drew out his question agonizingly and Velasco fought for breath as tears stung his eyes from the noxious gases that came with every syllable.

The priests fell silent again, a collective breath was taken. Yesterday, one among them had dared challenge the dark angel and no one wanted to see a replay of those events. They hung on his every word but they feared him very much.

Riko sat quietly, also watching, but with satisfaction not apprehension.

'I…it is her that I doubt,' Velasco grated, groping for words and pointing at Riko accusingly. There was a pause and Riko's heart beat fiercely in his chest. This would be the moment…

'And well you should,' Soren said, a smile spreading across his wicked features.

The color drained from Riko's face. Soren turned his attention to him now, and Riko knew it was now or never.

He leapt up from his chair, taking his tiger form as he did. His front paws touched the ledge of the window and he was half-way into his eagle metamorphosis when lord Nagesh grabbed him by the tail and pulled him down to the stone ground with a thud. He turned and hissed at the wraith, white fangs bared and claws out.

'You will get nothing out of me!' Riko spat.

Soren nodded at Esyago and the kuvuta helped Nagesh hold the shape-shifter down. Riko became a small mouse, slipping from their grasp, and tried to scurry beneath their clawed feet and away to freedom, but Soren lifted him up by the tail half-way to the door and held him up close to his face. Riko turned again, back into the orange cat and made a swipe for Soren's face.

By this time, all the priests sat cowering in the far corner, not wanting to be caught in the cross-fire.

Soren flung Riko to the other side of the room, Riko's claws missing his face narrowly. Stone cracked the outline of Riko's body, so strong was the force with which he struck the solid wall. Powdered dust settled over the onlookers and Riko cried out in pain. He fell to the ground in female form and held up his hand to Soren. He had not wanted to beg for the life he had been willing to sacrifice, but in the end, the will to live on had won.

'Will you not give me another chance?' he asked, 'I have done all and more that you have asked of me.'

'You were never mine to ask anything of, Riko.'

The wraith was advancing and Riko knew that he would not escape. Six kuvuta and a handful of deranged priests that would rather die than help him; the odds were not in his favor.

Soren was upon him and as everybody watched, he pushed his toxic essence out and into the helpless figure that lay at his feet.

The black flames and gases consumed Riko in mere seconds. They poured out of the kuvuta's palms and open mouth like black water from a stone statue. His cries echoed across the stone floor and off the walls with such clarity, that every human in the room felt his pain as if it were their own. Riko's body struggled against death and he morphed into all the forms he had ever taken; High Adare' Ethron, the imp that had been spying for Falkhar, creatures that no one had ever seen before, men, women, elves, cleya and all manner of strange races, all wearing the same pained expression, and then it slowed down till Soren bent down low over the body of a man with an animal claw strung around his neck.

'There you are,' he said, as Riko's true face emerged, the last that would ever look out upon the Worlds. Soren tore it off in one foul gesture and flung the wet skin down to lie alongside the smoldering corpse of the shape-shifter who had betrayed him.

He straightened up and looked at the priests, all huddled in the corner and desperately trying to regain their composure. The blood from Riko's face dripped from his hand, falling blackened on the floor and hissing like the stones themselves were on fire. He flexed his claws and grabbed the priest closest to him; piercing his shoulder and watching the blood run down his robe. The priest's face was set in a silent scream, his body twisting in pain.

'We attack at once with full force. You,' he said, gesturing to the wraiths that surrounded him, 'you will find the woman of my blood and you *will* kill her!'

Nagesh inclined his head toward Soren but said nothing. This vengeance, this was a human trait and it would serve his people well. Two faces of hatred glared out from his son's soul.

'Take this,' Soren said, pulling a torn piece of white cloth from within his robes, 'give it to your beasts so that they may find her sooner.' Esyago took the rag without a word. 'Any questions?' Soren sneered.

Velasco and the others looked upon the six kuvuta that stood towering above them. They looked into their cold, dead eyes. They looked at the seared body that lay at their feet, the crumpled face that Soren had torn off, empty holes where eyes should have been. They looked at their comrade writhing on his knees in the merciless grip of their dark angel. No one stirred and no one said a single word in protest. A piece of stone fell to the ground from where Riko had been thrown. Diego jumped.

'Boo,' Soren said softly, a cruel grin on his twisted face.

*

It was nearly dawn; they had ridden the whole of the previous day and half the night to get to their position. The last of the long line of soldiers had finally fallen in, three hours ago.

It was a charmed landscape that they had walked through. The hills rolled away to join their bigger brothers in the distance, the fishermen's masts rocked lazily on the placid lakes, the streams ran clear and warm and teemed with life. They marched through dewy meadows, trampled pastures and the smell of freshly cut hay. The men had been merry and the fresh air had bolstered their morale but Luken knew that the land would soon be scorched and bloodied. The spring winds did nothing for his spirit.

He was sharpening his blade next to where Kemen lay sleeping soundly. Kemen was always just teetering on the edge of snoring, something that had always bothered Luken, except now. Now he sat there listening to it. Luken's locks hung in his face, the anxious sweat was instantly dried from his brow by the morning air and all the while the 'shring-shring' sound of the whetstone on the knife could be heard.

Kemen groggily opened his eyes. The image of Luken swam into focus, sitting beside him, not saying a word and sharpening the knife that his father had given him. Luken looked up at the awakening Kemen.

'You had better get rid of these wenches,' he said, gesturing to the two naked, slumbering females that lay across the tent floor with the point of his blade, 'we have armies to train. Plus, they are flying all camp-followers out at noon. The water and food is rationed enough already.' His tone was gruff and Kemen did not feel like Luken's moods so early in the day already.

'Have your senses taken leave of you? Why do you pester me so at this hour?' he demanded. He pushed the heavy blankets from himself nonetheless, stretched and pulled on his riding breaches, trying to keep his balance in the tiny tent. His princely things had been left behind much to his dismay and by Luken's command in order to save time and space.

'I am not pestering you,' Luken scolded, 'just get these bloody women to the rear of the camp! We have a war coming!' He stood up angrily and flicked the tent flap open violently.

He stood outside for a while, breathing deeply and waiting for his friend. Kemen came out a few moments later, still buttoning up his vest and pulling his boots on.

'Talk to me,' he said. He meant it earnestly and Luken relented. It was no use being angry with the fool for long.

'I am a little anxious is all,' Luken replied.

They stood on the hill and looked out at the camp. Dead fire-pits dotted the landscape and a few stragglers were still busy readying for combat practice on the far fields. 'I have heard stories of these beasts we are to fight,' he elaborated after a while, 'a merchant from Mayne was making his way toward the palace and he passed my army last night. He said his cousin had just come from an attacked planet and that he had seen them. He said they were like dark demons that ate flesh and lived in darkness.'

'Well then we fight by day!' Kemen joked, but when he saw Luken's face, he knew now was not the time.

When they had received the call from the elves, Kemen and Luken had been more than willing to join the adventure. The two were always eager for a good fight and something to do other than sit through tedious council sessions. They had fought countless wars together and wanted to prove themselves against a presumably immortal foe. They had persuaded the other Two Stars and all the tribes on all their lands to join them, an intricate task at best. Kemen could see Luken was beginning to wonder what they had let themselves in for. The thought had crossed Kemen's mind too but he did not like to give voice to his fears for it made them all the more real. Luken spoke his mind though. He was afraid.

'How many times have we heard about "demons" that cannot die, that suck out your soul, that will eat your cattle, steal your first born and bed your wife, hmm?' Kemen asked. He put a hand on Luken's shoulder, 'and we have fought and killed them all. Masked men. If they can bleed, then we shall bleed them out. Nothing lives forever.'

Luken seemed to be a little buoyed by Kemen's words but he countered;

'And what of the dreya? They are our great hope and Arial said she can bring but a few hundred.'

'Pah!' Kemen exclaimed, tying his last bootlace and gesturing wildly about him, 'women always lie!'

Luken broke into a grin and helped Kemen load his arrows and sword onto his horse.

Kemen rode his massive stallion, black as nightshade with green, blue and red-woven bridal and saddle-blanket, the colors of his flag. Bells were strung around its tail and hooves and though Kemen thought this piece of traditional battle attire was brilliant, Luken could barely stop laughing.

'It tinkles like a kept cat!' he roared.

'Well that creature smells like a common dog!' Kemen retorted.

Luken's xanti hound looked up and snarled. Kemen's stallion whinnied and paced to the side. The xanti were an ancient breed of wild fighting dog that had been trained to carry soldiers into battle. They stood half as high as Kemen's tallest horses. Their shoulders were bigger than the rest of their body, carrying strong neck muscles and a large head. Their tails were docked at birth and teeth had to be filed or they would grow too heavy to run with. Kemen looked down disdainfully at Luken's drooling steed and shook his head as Luken smacked it hard on the flank to spur it on, raising musky hair and dust.

Soon, they neared the top of the hill. Just beyond the crest, their two armies practiced with sword, axe and bow, side by side. The two princes had led their armies into battle together a few times and by now, the two tribes had learnt well enough how to amalgamate their individual skills. The Benat were excellent close-range bowmen whereas the Savari had stronger bows better suited for far range.

However, some degree of accuracy had to be sacrificed for this longer range so they provided cover for the Benat "sharp shooters" who would sneak in close. The enemy would be taken out silently and efficiently. They had even earned quite a reputation and so it was with almost every faction of the armies. Where one lacked, the other made up for the weakness. It was not all smooth sailing though and fights regularly broke out.

Luken and Kemen made their way down to the training grounds, greeting soldiers and being saluted in return as they wove a path through the sweating men. Giant water buckets had been placed at various points to slake the men's thirst and camp-followers brought fruit piled high in woven baskets every hour.

Luken stopped at three swordsmen parrying with one of his own spearmen. He dismounted and walked toward them. They stopped at once, breathing hard and saluted their prince and commander.

'Right,' he began, 'I like the idea of three swordsmen to a foe because that is probably what it is going to take to slay these monsters but,' he warned, 'they will not be fighting with spears.' He grabbed the shaft of the spear the Benat was holding and waved it about. 'They will use claws and teeth and noxious fumes as well as black-magic and shadows.'

A small group had gathered around the display and was listening intently. 'We will need longer swords,' he said, pointing to the short blades the three Savari were holding and then to the long swords of a few of the on-lookers, 'it may impair your accuracy with its weight but it will keep the wraith at bay. One clean sweep is all you will need. I recommend the head,' he said, running his finger across his throat. The men laughed and heartily agreed. He considered the blade he held in his hand. After the magic had been doled out, it seemed the steel was always wet. 'You,' he continued, pointing at his spearman now, 'you will ensure our foes reach the ground on their feet. They ride fearsome beasts. This will work like any other mounted attack. Bring down the beast, slay the footed enemy.'

Everybody nodded and Luken picked up a discarded spear to demonstrate. He acted out flinging the spear at an imaginary beast then rushing in with long sword in hand to slay the wraith.

'Very good, but what if the beast still lives?' Kemen asked from atop his giant black horse.

'Axes my friend,' Luken smiled, 'BIG axes.'

Luken clapped a few of the soldiers on the back and told them to spread the word. He then hauled himself back on top of his xanti beside Kemen.

'You trust them to take your orders across the entire army?' he asked incredulously.

'Yes. They will come up with wilder and better means than I by the time it has traveled ten men,' Luken smiled and they continued riding through the grounds, watching the men at work.

After a while, they came upon a group of people who had built a crude rig to imitate the creatures they would be battling. It was comprised of a wooden beam that when released, would swing from a tree and a sack of potatoes that sat upon it. Two axe-men stood holding a foot each of a spearman who would be launched into the air for extra height, he would throw his spear and land softly on the grass. Axe-men in place, would rush forward to bludgeon the beast and rush away again. Arrows were launched into the potato sack and splintered beam after which, two swordsmen came forward to finish the job, using the Benat close combat technique of "fling-fighting" where two men would join hands and take turns at hacking and parrying, the other gaining momentum as they swung round again.

'See?' Luken boasted proudly.

Kemen just smiled and shook his head.

By noon, it was time to practice battle formations as a whole. Who would be where when the horns sounded and so forth. The two princes decided to go with their newer and less outdated tactics that they had thought out together.

'Do not tell our fathers!' Kemen jested as he drew the sketches in the sand for their lieutenants. Erromon liked the plan as well as Danel and so instead of rows of each individual faction being laid out like a chessboard, groups would stand together as units. Ambush groups would line the riverbanks and strong attack bands would work together on the field. There would be no "army" to attack or focus undivided effort on.

The west and north Stars were acting as a shield to the river beyond, which wound its way down to the palace grounds thirty miles back. They were the last defense on this side of the river, but no one knew for certain how or where the enemy would strike so for all they knew, they could be the first line of defense against a southbound strike.

Once horns had been blown, drums beaten and the men drilled until they could barely hold a sword with one hand, Luken and Kemen called a halt to the training, instructed the men to feed and water their steeds like they were their own children and only then get a good night's rest.

They all waited for war. Altair had been very clear on the fact that it could come at any time and that they should be prepared always. Watchmen were posted all around the camp and the star pirate ships were closely watched for any signs of warning signal fire. The previous night, a drunken pirate had been stumbling around holding his torch and panic had flared up in the Gau camp. A message had been sent down by the captain of the ship, expressing sincere apologies. All rum was emptied out over the rails of the ships and the offender strung up by his ankles, over the stern, for the rest of the night. By morning he had drowned in his own vomit and the lesson served everyone well.

Kemen and Luken were bruised, sweaty and dirty from the day's hard work. Kemen had received a nasty cut above his brow and Luken had broken a finger but they felt good. Their men had done well and they enjoyed being out there on the training grounds with them, face to face and sword to spear.

They reached a twisted tree that burst unexpectedly from the surrounding scrubland on the outskirts of the camp, watching the elvin suns go down, and the shadows grow longer, while resting against their beasts. Luken stroked his xanti's matted fur while Kemen fed his horse the last oats he had left in his pockets. They were quiet for a long while…

'I shall want to be a father soon,' Kemen remarked, as the last ray of light threatened to fall from the sky.

'More than like, you already are,' Luken remarked matter-of-factly.

'Well then, I shall want to make an honest woman out of the mother of my next child.'

Luken smiled but said nothing. The crickets started chirping, an endless night-time symphony on this planet. 'Do you think we are ready?' Kemen asked.

Luken wasn't sure exactly what Kemen meant but he did not care to answer him anyway.

'You had better hope to *my* god that we are because *your* god clearly does not hold you in high regard,' Luken snorted, gesturing at Kemen's swollen forehead and at the blood and dirt sitting in his stubble, 'just look at your face!'

Kemen frowned slightly then stroked his jaw line with a mischievous grin on his face;

'You are just jealous.'

Chapter 15

The last day

The star had risen bright and early and Ramroth had eaten a hearty breakfast. The great hall had groaned under the weight of the food, since all the guests being housed, not only within the palace itself, but also around the complex, had to be fed. This included two hundred High Elves, fifty Drows, a few odd captains and permanent guests as well as four hundred Adare', bringing the total to roughly six hundred hungry mouths. The cooks did not complain though, a few of the mages were secretly helping them. If Altair knew the fires his stew was cooked on were magical, who knew what he might do. Ramroth chuckled to himself.

He had also seen Arial and spoken to her briefly, enquiring after her health and apologizing for his prolonged absences. Juggling the training of a few hundred Adare' was no mere task, it was a commitment. She had laughed him off and told him that all was well and congratulated him on his new high rank. He deserved it more than anyone else, she had said sincerely. They chatted about his new students and how their training was going, all the mishaps that had been narrowly avoided thus far and Altair's watchful and hilarious gaze upon them at all times, as if he were the teacher and they the pupils.

'Are you sure all is well?' he asked her once more before he bid her goodbye for the day. She looked so sad beneath her smile that he could almost not bare to leave her. He caught the glance she shot across the room, followed it, and found Damek, pushing food around his plate and toying with a glass of standard-issue blood.

'He came to see me again last night,' she confided, 'we did not talk much, he just held me until I fell asleep.' She sighed and Ramroth was unsure of what to say. It was so unheard of for these two very different races to fall in love that he had almost no authority on the matter.

'Love gives us room to hope,' he suggested.

'If I love then there can be no hope. We must be granted one night only and know that death waits for us at dawn. There can be no other way.'

Ramroth was deeply saddened by her words but he knew she spoke true.

'Do not deny yourselves then,' he said sorrowfully.

'But Ramroth, there *is* hope. I have to believe that I can save these people and that is worth more than one night,' she said with urgency. Ramroth nodded, hugged her tightly and left the great hall. He could not help her in this. In this she was alone.

He stepped outside and set his mind upon his many tasks for the day. After breakfast, which he asked not to be dragged out too long, the Adare' would convene in their courtyard and would be debriefed.

'Please, everyone, settle down,' he called. Taigo stood at his side and the mages slowly finished their conversations and looked up at the speaker. 'Today we are going to be practicing some very interesting spells where you will be expected to work together in order for us to execute the battle moves I have in mind. Murmurs of curiosity and excitement rose from the crowd and Ramroth signaled for silence again. 'In light of that,' he warned, 'I expect everybody to be on their best behavior. Altair is worried enough as it is; I do not wish to give him even greater cause for concern by setting loose a rabid band of magicians. Are we clear?'

The mages were laughing amongst themselves but he could see that his message had sunk in. They started to leave without being asked and Ramroth turned to Taigo whilst there was still enough commotion for them not to be overheard.

'I spoke to Altair again today; he wants to know if Maya is coming.' Ramroth's tone was bordering on pleading and Taigo knew that a lot of pressure was probably being placed upon Ramroth which, in turn, meant that a lot of pressure was going to be put on him. 'I am loathe to ask you, it is just that…I know you are…involved…and she will not listen to me…I discovered her.'

Taigo knew Ramroth spoke true. It was not that Maya disliked or resented Ramroth but deep down inside, she had to blame someone.

Maya had been very young when Ramroth had first realized her power. Her adolescent years still lay ahead, but with this new responsibility laid upon her, it was difficult for her to stay young and enjoy herself for very long. No one had known how to teach her though, and the one time that she had used her magic, people had died. People she loved and cared about. It was not a story often told but she used it as an example to her students, the ones who had extraordinary and dangerous gifts, the ones who needed guidance the most. She claimed she was not trying to scare them into submission but she and Ethron had never seen eye to eye on the matter. She was a brilliant teacher nonetheless. She was also the most powerful of the Adare' and they needed her. Maya could create anti-matter. She was the only Adare' in known history that could. Without her cooperation, they could not hope to win the war. Not against the enemy itself but against that which they left in their wake.

'No one ever gets *involved* with Maya,' Taigo muttered, 'it is complicated,' he explained when he saw Ramroth looking at him strangely.

'I just thought you could speak to her,' Ramroth pressed.

'Yes, well, she will speak with no one,' Taigo countered hotly.

'Perhaps she is making a decision then?' Ramroth suggested lightly, 'these things take time.'

They started to follow the other Adare' toward the training grounds.

'What of Mirian?' Taigo asked, changing the subject.

'I see her tonight,' Ramroth replied, 'I must try to help her. It will be hard. I do not have nearly the same amount of experience that Maya does.'

Taigo could see Ramroth was deep in thought and left it at that.

Ramroth created a podium out of reeds for himself to stand on and be heard. Taigo went to stand with the rest.

'She will not come,' he said, before walking off.

Ramroth called for quiet for what felt like the hundredth time. He had stayed up late putting final plans together from his first inklings and now it was time to see how well they would work. When the rabble had settled down, he outlined his plans. Each Adare' had been given special one-on-one training so far, but they had yet to learn how to work together. A mage always operated alone and so this concept was new to most of them. Ramroth wanted roughly five types of assault teams. The first type would consist of Elemental Adare'. Fire would be the weapon of choice against the kuvuta but rock and wind would help herd them into position.

The Water Adare' would assist in damage-control if any of the fire got out of hand and threatened the other side.

The second type would be an aerial assault team. The Levitators would carry the Pulse Adare' into the air so that the devastation would not touch the ground troops. The Electromagnetic Pulse Adare' had been taught how to channel energy to assist the Pulse Adare' in order to create a bigger blast radius. The wraiths used no electronic weaponry but the EMP could cut out star pirate ship controls and that would be devastating. These Adare' were therefore strictly forbidden to wield their own power directly.

The third and fourth teams would have a single element in common – strong teleporters working alongside them. The Shield Adare' would guard the remaining women and children as well as travel to the Elemental Adare' if anything got out of hand. The Pathfinders and Barricade Adare' would go to areas where they were needed most when retreats and regroupings were required. They only had five Telepathists among them. These individuals would have to cover the entire planet, deciding whose call was most dire. They were training the hardest.

The fifth and final group was Ramroth's most daring and exciting idea. He had done some research and wanted to try something that no one had ever tried before. True enough, most of his ideas would be difficult to achieve at best. For a single Teleporter to carry a minimum of ten Adare' would be a challenge none of them had faced before. For one Telepathist to tune in to the cries of one-fifth of a planet's people would tax their very spirits. It was not unheard of but it could be done. This plan, however, was new.

Ramroth had always suspected that the imagination carried some form of physical mass, however small it may be. He had delved deep into Dunkan's archives and discovered the paragraph of proof he needed buried in the depth of magical records that he had waded through. In short, an Illusionist could only create an *image* and project it into the mind's eye of another. It took a great deal of imagination and creativity to do this and all that energy temporarily siphoned off some mass from the being's essence. Ramroth's idea was to get the Biological Morphists to tap into that energy mass and make it solid, a palpable illusion that could be used with force of body instead of just mind and also, therefore, to a far greater audience. The wraiths would probably be impervious to any terrifying image thrust upon them but if it were made into something real that could harm them; then they were on to something.

'You are a crazy man,' Taigo grinned when Ramroth had finished outlining his ideas. They had been met with great enthusiasm, however, and it seemed everyone was eager to start practicing. The Adare' had remembered the teammates they had been assigned before and started working straight away. Ramroth moved among the groups, giving advice and correcting them when they were wrong, congratulating them when they got something right.

Toireann had joined them for the day, the cleya would do well enough without him, and his place was with his family. Also, he was the strongest Illusionist they had and Ramroth believed the others could learn much from him. He stopped beside Toireann now; he was with two other Illusionists and a Bio-morpher. Ramroth saw that the illusions projected by the weaker wizards were difficult to morph but Toireann's illusions were so powerful, that even a level Two Bio-morpher could grasp them and make them real.

Toireann was laughing manically at his two-story high scorpion that had been given life in the eyes of not only one but all. The women shrieked and the men applauded. Ramroth called Demond to help with the weaker Illusionists and soon, they had mimicked Toireann's armor-plated beast. They were smaller and far less detailed but it was a step in the right direction. Toireann snapped his fingers arrogantly and his armored giant gobbled up its lesser duplicates with ease. Bets were being made on whether anyone could create anything to rival the mighty level Five's illusions but it soon became clear that Toireann would be their key player on the battlefield.

Ramroth was becoming more and more hopeful as the day wore on. The Elemental Adare' were working well together and the Teleporters could carry at least five mages with them over many, many miles, bringing back snow to prove their distance. Fire swept the land like a plague and massive walls of water put the flames out with a hiss that rang in the ears like the whisper of a god.

The Levitationists were carrying Adare' to heights they had not even been able to achieve by themselves. Pulses coursed across the bleak sky as if some great, magical storm was playing out above them. Ramroth could feel his heart under pressure each time a blast emanated from the sky. His ears rang and his skin was a tingling mass of flesh. Magic sat hunched in the air like an unseen beast and the fayres wasted no time flocking to the gathering to consume all that was left discharged and unused. The ground started to split underfoot with the effort of so many minds and the weight of so much magic. Birds steered clear of them, great, yellowed clouds circled overhead and it was getting harder to walk or even stand up straight. Ramroth was pleased. Still, they had much practice to go through before they would be ready to face such a fearsome enemy but many of them felt they were up to the task; an ingrained Adare' mentality that Ramroth would have to bend ever so slightly if only to keep them wary.

About one hundred mages had clambered onto a Pathfinder's bridge and were jumping up and down on it, desperately trying to break it and test its strength while the rest cheered from below as the Pathfinder sweated it out. Ramroth was watching with great interest, at this massive display of teamwork, when he felt a tap on his shoulder. He turned around only to stare into the face of the one Adare' who had said she would not come.

'Maya,' he said in surprise, 'you came.'

She nodded briefly, sadness in her eyes but determination as well.

'Taigo had nothing to do with it,' she said, eyebrows raised as if indignant to their efforts to sway her own decisions. 'I came because...I suppose it is the right thing to do. A chance for us all to do the right thing,' she finished.

Ramroth smiled;

'We are glad you decided to join us.'

'They want me to try one tomorrow, one of the smaller ones that was formed only yesterday. It used to be a planet I visited often, but all that light is gone now and they want me to fill the void. I do not know if I can do it.' Her tone was somber.

'I believe in you,' he said, 'we all do. You know you can do it.'

Maya looked around her at all the mages clapping atop the bridge, three hundred now and still, the bridge held.

'My my, Ramroth, you really pulled this rabble together,' she said, sounding impressed and changing the subject as Taigo had done earlier.

'It was not all that easy,' Ramroth conceded, 'they are like children without parents or rules.'

'I am still afraid for them,' she said.

'Do not be,' Ramroth replied, 'for *they* are not.'

Maya laughed and Ramroth laughed with her.

'I hear you have found a Tarayelo' she said after a while.

'Secrets travel fast in this place,' he muttered. Maya raised her eyebrows again;

'You have told so few?' she asked.

'It is her gift, her decision,' Ramroth countered, quietly but firmly.

'You play a dangerous game,' she warned, 'she is someone's child.'

'As are we all,' Ramroth defended, 'do you think it any less fair that all these people risk their lives?' he asked, gesturing at the wall of suspended wizards above them, Taigo standing with them, cheering along.

'That is different, Ramroth,' she hissed. 'Do not play that card with me. She knows not her power and she will not die by the hand of the enemy but by her own…'

'Only if she does not learn,' Ramroth interjected.

Maya frowned at him and her full lips became a thin white line. Ramroth moved closer to her.

'I am told she has been training for a few years already, has mastered elements and healing, those are not powers to be judged lightly. She has learnt how to control, only not how to wield this specific gift. She wants to help,' he finished, looking Maya square in the eyes and taking her hands in his own. Maya sighed;

'And I suppose *you* want to try and show her how,' she asked, looking down at the ground, an expression on her face that Ramroth could only guess at. He let her hands go and called down to the Adare'. The day's practice session was over; the elvin suns were setting once more. Dawn, next day, and they would resume. Strength and endurance would become part of their every day.

Everybody complained out loud and sauntered away to the palace gardens to enjoy the last the daylight had to offer. He was surprised that they seemed not nearly as drained as he did, but time would tell of their true stamina.

'Actually,' he said, once everyone was out of earshot, 'I thought you might want the honor.'

*

Delwyn had been busy with final round checks as asked for by Altair when he had called in to tell her that Riko had been sent. His hologramatic image had looked wretched and Delwyn had had no words of comfort for him. She did not like lying.

She was now standing with her hand blocking the setting suns from her eyes, staring out at the rocky mountain landscape that seemed to leer out at her from every direction. It glared red and angry, like the promise of the war to come growing ever closer.

'Hallo!' she called, like a child looking for its lost hound. Vanora stood by her side. Instructed not to speak unless spoken to, she had been silent for almost the whole day, which was a definite first.

It was impossible, Delwyn thought. Many battalions of perion resided here, they could not all have simply disappeared. Hooves clicked on the hard rock, horns jutted out over an outcrop. One of the goat-men poked his head out from behind his hiding place and stared quizzically at her.

'Can we help you?' he asked uncertainly. Delwyn frowned;

'We?' She walked around the other side to where he was crouching and saw only him and two others, dozing in the double shade. She looked back over her shoulder and wondered how many others lay sleeping in the shade of the giant boulders. She turned back to look at the perion and he answered her question before she could even ask it;

'We will fight in the darkness, so we sleep in the day.'

'Very well,' she shrugged, not able to deny such simple logic. 'Is everything all right here? Do you have enough water and food supplies?'

'Yes,' he replied flatly, and then, 'thank you,' after a brief pause.

The silence here was oppressive. Delwyn could hear the sun-beetles screeching and almost nothing else. She looked around her again at the desolate landscape and found it hard to believe that anyone could live here comfortably.

'We are quite comfortable,' he said.

His manner unsettled her a little. Delwyn nodded her head stiffly and bid the perion goodbye. Vanora did the same, bowing slightly, leaving the perion looking as confused as her mother. Delwyn lifted her skirts and picked her way back down to the waiting ship, her daughter in tow.

'Highness,' the pilot said, as she walked up the stairs, 'there is a message for you from the fayres.'

Delwyn struggled not to roll her eyes. That particular race of vivacious females had given her enough grief to make up for all the others who had provided almost none.

'Very well, let us go see what the problem is now,' she said, trying to keep the edge out of her voice. The pilot smiled at Vanora as if they shared some private joke and eased the vessel into the air, skimming just above the surface of the ground. They negotiated rough terrain that eventually smoothed out, for two hours, the shadows of the clouds running across the surface of the land as if the suns raced one another, until they finally arrived at the fayre strong-hold.

The forest they had asked for, no *demanded*, Delwyn remembered, was one of the deep, old forests near the upper belt of Emara. They had left it relatively untouched but Delwyn could sense that they had claimed it as their own in another way. All the creatures seemed to hold their breath where before they had made the trees seem alive with their sound.

It was eerily quiet. In fact, Delwyn thought, it had been like this almost everywhere she had been of late. It seemed as if word had traveled quickly and now the waiting game had really begun. All the armies had ceased training and seemed to be resting up instead. Even the war councils at the palace had nearly stopped altogether. The commanders had been given leave to stay with their men permanently and would receive word if any changes were being made. Wherever she went, men sat quietly sharpening blades and stirring cooking pots with almost religious care. Words were exchanged in hushed voices and glances were thrown around as if the enemy were to leap out, without any warning from the powers that be. "The quiet before the storm" Vanora had said. When Delwyn had looked at her strangely her answer had been,

'I read it in one of father's old human books.'

Here, however, in this dark and wet forest, the quiet was not one of pre-war; it was one that held a more dire threat. Delwyn was loath to spend more time with these creatures and she could sense that Vanora was too.

They stood quietly, holding hands and waiting. No one ever found a fayre, they found you. Vanora whipped her head around at the first rustling leaf and snatch of whisp-ish laughter.

Delwyn knew of their games and refused to be pulled into them.

Giggling and whispered words beckoned Vanora and she ran to find the fayres despite herself. She spun around in circles, trying to locate the ever-evasive creatures of the forest. Faster and faster she spun as the sounds surrounded her. It seemed to come from within and all around. She was starting to get dizzy; the world was becoming a blur, a continuous haze of greenery and whispered words until her mother grabbed hold of her arm and pulled her closer. Vanora closed her eyes to stop the giddiness and when she opened them, Renata stood before them, as tall as her mother. Vanora had been unaware that fayres could change their size at will. Renata stood on higher ground, beneath a tall tree. A mossy slope ran from the tree and seemed to cling to the air, making the small space damp and strange-smelling.

'Would you spoil our fun so soon, Delwyn?' Renata asked.

Delwyn smiled politely and replied,

'You called me to play games?'

Renata scowled and gestured to another to come forward. A fayre with pink-tinged skin flew out from behind her. Her hair was plaited flowers and she wore no clothing that Vanora could see.

'Please take the...Elf Queen...to see what I have seen,' Renata said slowly. The fayre nodded and flew away, beckoning for Delwyn to follow and singing an eerie tune as she went.

'Vanora?' Delwyn asked, pulling her by the hand.

'I think I will stay here a while,' Vanora replied distantly. Renata smiled. Delwyn fixed the fayre queen with a threatening glare, not wanting to say outright that no harm should befall her child but boring the message in nonetheless.

'I shall watch the girl until you return,' Renata said, sickly-sweet as the honeysuckle that adorned her hair. Delwyn squeezed Vanora's hand and walked away slowly, turning around every now and then until she disappeared into the undergrowth following the pink fayre.

They were alone for a full minute before Renata spoke, just staring at one another.

'Vanora...' she said, letting the name roll off her tongue, 'white wave.'

When Vanora frowned Renata explained, 'It is what your name means, in an ancient human tongue.'

Vanora was not really concerned with what her name meant. She was fixated on the fayre that stood before her. No, she did not stand; she hovered just above the ground, her dainty toes being kissed by the wet moss beneath her. Her eyes were the most brilliant of aquamarines, even more beautiful than the dragon queen's and her hair folded itself around her face and shoulders like the dark hands of a lover. Her skin was pure white, tinged with the faintest of greens, and her limbs were long and graceful like the weeping willows that her father had had planted in the gardens. Today, she too wore no clothes. Ivy was wrapped around her waist and shoulders carelessly, and trailed onto the floor. Vanora was mesmerized by her preternatural beauty. Her papery-thin and feather-like wings were there one second and then gone the next. Flitting in and out of existence like far-away stars.

Suddenly, Renata was right in front of her, Vanora could feel her breath cold against her cheek. It smelt like morning dew and jasmine.

'You are such a pretty child,' Renata whispered, tracing lines across Vanora's face like a blind woman. Her lips sliding over the elvin words like a charm. Vanora wanted to brush her fingers away but she could not. Renata danced around her, whispering flatteries into her ears and touching her. Vanora closed her eyes and gave into the strange sensation despite herself, not wanting it to end, even though her skin almost crawled beneath the fayre's touch. Renata was lifting Vanora's hair to her nose and smelling it as if she had never smelt anything as sweet, running her fingers through it and trailing it across her face. Her lullaby was hauntingly beautiful. She kissed Vanora's cheeks and lips; she glided in and out of her vision and breathed strange scents into her face and across her body. Vanora was hypnotized.

*

Delwyn had been led to the stream that flowed through the forest.

'Quietly now,' the fayre warned, finger pressed against her full lips, 'you might scare them away.'

Delwyn said nothing but slowed her pace and peered around the last tree to glimpse this scene that Renata had been so adamant she see. At first, she saw nothing and looked up questioningly at the creature that hovered above her shoulder. 'Look closer,' the fayre crooned, pointing at the water. Delwyn sighed inwardly, focused her gaze and then, she saw. Figures moving in the water, dancing. The water was dancing. There were four of them; they appeared to her as well-built men with flowing hair and long, sinewy limbs. They stared straight through her, and the splashed water from the river that they threw playfully at one another, sprinkled her feet and ankles.

'Nymphs?' she asked disbelievingly, the old human name escaping her lips first. They were rarely ever seen by anyone. Delwyn had never seen them before. Altair claimed he had, but he had seen women of course, beautiful women.

'*Zimun,*' the fayre corrected, 'the children of the wazimu,' the fayre intoned, nodding her head solemnly. 'They come to aid us since their parents are too precious to be risked.'

Delwyn knew this to be true. The elementals were forbidden by whatever force of nature had created them to never soil their hands with the affairs of Worldly creatures, especially in war.

'They will fight?' Delwyn asked, not able to tear her gaze away from them.

'Oh yes,' the fayre answered, 'like the warriors they are.'

Delwyn frowned.

'They are not warriors; they are the guardians of the elements,' she corrected.

'What do you think guardians do best?' the fayre asked rhetorically.

'I must talk to them,' Delwyn said, straightening up.

'No!' And suddenly the fayre was as tall as she, grabbing hold of her arm and pulling her back; 'no words you or I possess are sweet enough for their ears to hear. Do not scare them away.'

Delwyn relented but only because of the anguish in the fayre's voice. She lingered a few moments longer before she turned on her heel, her own child more precious to her than the sight of another's, however rare and special they were.

*

Renata stopped abruptly in front of the young elf maiden and Vanora opened her eyes.

'Why are you saying all these things to me?' Vanora asked, 'is it because you want me to stay with you?' she pressed, remembering the enganya's words.

Renata smiled gently and took Vanora's hand in hers.

'Will you?' the fayre queen asked.

Vanora considered the statement and was unsure of what to say. What did Renata want with her? Her pause was the wrong answer and Renata's face dropped. All flattery and pretense was discarded as her features hardened and her face became a cruel mask.

'You are so soft, so indecisive!' She screeched and Vanora jumped at the sudden change. 'If you will not stay with us and you would rather yield your beauty and purity to that scheming prince...'

'He does not scheme,' Vanora interjected indignantly.

Renata moved closer still and pierced Vanora with her ugly glare.

'You are too soft,' Renata repeated, 'if you stay with him, he will break you. How do you suppose you will defend yourself against him?' Renata shook her head and took a step back to regard the elvin princess with a mixture of disdain and disgust plain as day upon her face.

'How will *you* defend yourself now when all you have is your beauty?' Vanora asked simply.

There was a moment's pause, deliberation perhaps, and then Renata grabbed Vanora by the shoulders and the world went dark. It smelt like old forest, rotting debris and damp.

'Open your eyes,' Renata commanded and Vanora did as she was told. Where once the beautiful Renata stood, was now a decaying mass of fleshy skin, mottled with dead leaves and wet soil. It clung to her corpse-like figure, the skin green and black, the eyes empty in their sockets. Long claws hung from her wrinkled hands and fangs protruded from her ugly mouth. It looked like Renata had been buried for two whole moons and had then clawed her way out of her grave. She looked like the swamp monsters Alarico always teased her about, the creature that watched you play by the river side from some dark hole crawling with unimaginable things, watching and waiting to grab you and feast on your soft flesh...but somehow...somehow she was not afraid. It was not the icy grip of fear she felt around her heart...it was love.

When Renata calmed down, the world was once more a bright place, her form had life again and the rays of the sun filtered through the canopy and rested on her ethereal face. She tilted her chin defiantly as if daring Vanora to say anything unkind. Vanora was going to say no such thing. She now, finally, knew what the fayres were.

'You are beautiful inside too,' she said instead, 'it is only you that cannot see it.'

Renata frowned and her ever-set jaw slackened a little. This child was not afraid. Renata knew in that moment that perhaps she would not be able to steal this one away. She smirked stiffly and tears fell down her cheeks.

'Why are you crying?' Vanora asked quietly.

Renata looked long and hard at the young princess.

'This is a war unlike any ever seen before. Do you understand that?' Ranata asked harshly. When Vanora's face remained placid Renata grabbed her by the shoulders again, trying to shake some fear into her for it was all that would keep her alive. 'A war on an entire planet!' she hissed, 'not just a single battlefield, an entire planet encompassed in war! Every nation Altair could summon with the time given to him, every man with sword in hand against a single enemy, every prayer to every god being said in one collective breath in one place....' Renata trailed off and Vanora placed her hands on top of the fayre queen's.

'Greatness is within us all. You need not fear,' she whispered.

Renata stared at her wide-eyed and whispered,

'But what else do we have?'

'Vanora!' Delwyn had emerged from the dense forest cover and called out to her daughter.

'I must go now,' Vanora said to the fayre. Renata nodded her head slowly and reluctantly let the child prodigy go. Underestimation was something she did not favor but it seemed she had done it again.

Delwyn tried not to rush to Vanora's side but seeing the fayre so close and with such a pained expression on her face, it was hard.

'Do you want to see the nymphs?' Delwyn asked as soon as she was within arm's reach of her child.

'I want to go home please,' Vanora answered.

'Very well,' Delwyn said without hesitation, for she too felt no need to linger any longer. 'I bid you good day,' she added stiffly to the fayre. Delwyn took Vanora's hand and they started toward the clearing where their ship waited for them.

Renata ran forward in one final attempt;

'Stay with us,' she pleaded, 'we can keep your beauty forever as it is, protect you from fate's cruel grasp!'

Vanora smiled, pulled her hand away, carried on walking and left the fayre queen behind.

Renata's true form flickered with her grief and she cried out loud, clawing at her face and body like a woman possessed. Delwyn looked back, astonished at this display, and could not decide if she should falter in her steps or press on with greater haste.

'Leave her be,' Vanora warned, over the desperate mewling of the rejected queen. Delwyn nodded her head and they quickened their pace, putting ground between themselves and the maddened creature.

'Why does she want you to stay?' Delwyn asked and Vanora could see the shock in her eyes.

'She is afraid,' Vanora replied, closing the door behind them and smiling again at the pilot. Delwyn sat down carefully in her chair and asked,

'Afraid of what?' Vanora looked out of the window as they climbed, trying to see the fayres one last time.

'Of letting go.'

*

Delwyn asked the pilot to stop in the gardens and drop Vanora off. Vanora had been looking out of the window, as she always did, forever dreaming as her father seemed so oft to do, and she had spotted the mages throwing snowballs at one another in the height of a summer's night. When she had seen one of the balls sprout wings and go hurtling back to its sender, she had begged her mother to let her stay and watch.

Delwyn had been reluctant at first, purely because of her husband's subtle misgivings, but she had relented fast. Vanora, she had decided, was growing up hopelessly too fast and whatever had happened between her and the fayre queen had made her age that much more. She would indulge her childish whims for as long as they still existed.

'Not a word to your father though!' Delwyn had warned with a mock stern look on her face and a twinkle in her eye. She hugged her daughter tightly to her before she leapt lightly from the hovercraft.

Delwyn nodded at the pilot and he took her to the palace entrance. She walked the stairs heavily, like a woman tired of clinging to the remnants of hope. She needed to see her husband, to be comforted by his gaze.

'He is in the royal quarters my lady.' She was told by one of the guards.

Good, she thought, he is finally resting like everyone else seemed to be doing. She pushed the door open gently and found Altair reclining on the white linen sheets that covered their bed. He looked up when she entered and she smiled, closing the door quietly behind her.

'You look as weary as I feel,' he commented, reaching out for her as she came closer.

'Yes, weary,' she replied as she was enfolded by his arms and brought down to rest next to him, 'the full scale of this war has only just begun to sink in.'

'How so?' he asked in a bemused manner.

Delwyn sighed.

'There are so many of them, Altair. So, so many.'

'This is a good thing,' he said, rubbing the top of her hand with his. She rolled over to face him and said,

'Thank you. Without you we would all have perished.'

Altair laughed;

'I only give them all the means to do what they do best.'

'War?' Delwyn asked.

'No, live.'

Delwyn smiled a full and bright smile.

'Perhaps *we* should live once more then?' she asked playfully.

Altair returned her smile though his was far more mischievous.

'We shall live a thousand times before this day is through,' he said, grabbing her by the waist and pulling her down on top of him.

Delwyn sat bestride the man she loved most in the world, as he pulled up her shift around her slender waist, his strong hands caressing the soft folds where her thighs met even softer skin. His face grew grave and she asked him what was wrong.

'Our beautiful planet, our home, must be forfeit,' he said sadly.

'I need a new bathroom anyway' Delwyn said lightly, waving her hand disdainfully. Altair broke into a smile that mirrored hers and kissed her deeply, cupping her face with both hands.

'I would now finish what your hands and lips have started,' she whispered, making her way down his chest, her hair trailing across his chest.

Moments later, there came a knock at the door.

'We are busy,' Altair said roughly.

'My lord,' came the fervent reply, 'it is a matter of great urgency.'

Delwyn sat up and stared disbelievingly at the door. The hour was so late as to be early. Was there no rest for the weary?

'By whose account?' Altair wanted to know.

'Everybody's I think, my lord.'

*

It had taken three bribes, one slit throat and two days to get Sirena to Emara. The planet looked like a paradise, the way pictures of Earth had once looked hanging up in Soren's office except here, the land mass was joined, and the waters glistened even from way up there with the two stars that it orbited.

Sirena remembered that they called these stars their suns and that the ground was called earth and not soil, as her people had once done. It held a magic that she never thought she would experience. It was like going home.

Her ship landed at the main docking-yard and she asked one of the off-duty hovercraft pilots to take her to the palace. The Drow had looked at her with great contempt, eyeing her forehead and robes with suspicion.

'You are Religion,' he had said flatly, 'I think you are on the wrong side of the line.'

Others, standing nearby, had laughed at his statement and Sirena had felt her pulse quicken and her face flush. She grabbed him by the collar of his sleek skin-uniform and hissed,

'I am on the right side of the line for once in my life. You know not what I have borne witness to!' And her eyes spoke all the truth he needed to hear. 'Now please,' her voice shaking with distress, 'take me to Altair.'

The guard had been so shocked that he had uttered not a word and had simply climbed into his craft.

Sirena sat in the back, staring out of the windows. Soldiers littered the landscape. Their weapons glinted in the sunset. Millions and millions stretched as far as the eye could see and she knew more lay beyond the horizon. An army that could drink a planet dry, and would. Men of all colors and nations, brandishing a multitude of colored flags and singing hymns from faraway places in tongues she could not even hope to ever understand. They all stood there, ready to avenge the lives that would be so wantonly taken from them. And as Sirena gazed upon their masses, their war banners and shining helms, she knew that they would wrest that precious prize from the wicked, from her own people. They would fight till none had breath left to draw.

The craft glided down to the palace of the High Elves and Sirena's thoughts took her away from the valor of man and to the fear of the unknown.

She had joined the Religion at a very young age, seventeen to be precise. She had left home to study their doctrine and had fallen in love with all that made sense, that gave her a place in the Worlds, a righteous one, and had then gone on to join the church. She rose in rank after a few short years. She had had a vision and that was when they lifted her to prophetess rank.

One true vision, she thought ruefully, and it had been of god reaching out for her. She did not have one again but fabricated them to appease the masses and hold her powerful station. Velasco had been her mentor and lover for a time, before she met Soren. She immediately succumbed to Soren's weaknesses and his potential power and they had been married soon after. The Religion's rise had been slow but eventually, a secular state was born and the wars began. She had reveled in the knowledge that the heathens were being put to death, safe in her home at night. But Soren had taken her to bear witness...

She had watched babes ripped from their mother's arms and cast upon rocks until they cried no more. She had seen cities overrun, put to flame, women ravaged and men squirm in their own entrails. She had seen smoke mark their demise, their blood darken rivers. She had seen a thousand crying faces, pleading eyes, outstretched arms, and prayers uttered by bloodied lips with no tongues left for prayer, only the mouthed remnants of silent pleas for mercy.

No excuses could be made, no justification for what she had helped to do. Blind belief drove all her actions and gave them meaning, no matter how obscene. Now she believed she had the power to do one last thing and this belief was the only thing that kept her from gnawing at her own wrists until the nightmares seeped away with her spilled blood.

She had dreamed of ending it the very night Soren had come to her, no longer a mere man driven mad by belief, but a creature born of hatred and fear of himself. She was afraid that it would happen to her too. Then she had realized when she saw the others succumb to his power that it was far from the end. She still had time and she still believed.

The craft came to a halt and the doors opened and it was too late. A massive crowd of human avengers, now calling themselves the "piashish", had gathered outside the palace gates to ask for more firewood. They had seen her and it was too late.

She walked the first few paces with as much dignity as she could muster as faces dawned in recognition and then scowled in hatred as her blue robes betrayed her and her marked forehead burned with shame where before she had worn them both with pride. In seconds, she was swallowed by the crowds of accusing glares and pointing fingers. Hushed voices became howls of anger and anguish and still they did not fall upon her. Were they fearful of her presence or was it that they would not sully their hands? She found out as soon as the first rotten cabbage was thrown. When they had finished raining what little they could spare they began throwing things out of willful abandon. Shoes, bracelets, whole clumps of hair torn out by maddened grievers but she would not run for refuge.

By the time she reached the doors, she was covered in vile spittle, bloodied clothes, hair and rotten fruit to match her already flourishing bruises. The guards did not even question her; they merely dropped their crossbows and watched her silent ascent of the stairs. Her head held high, she entered the sandalwood-scented refuge of the palace, the mob screaming for her blood behind her.

'I must speak to Altair,' she said, with all the grace of a queen.

*

Altair quickly pulled on his shift and sandals, not quite believing what he had heard. A Religion emissary, come to him. But of course, of all the hundreds their church comprised of, he should have known that at least one would break away.

'I will return,' he said to Delwyn as he hastily kissed her on the forehead, 'this I must deal with now.'

She was crying but he had no time to decipher her tears. The door to his bedchamber was flung open and he marched down the hallway to where Sirena waited for him. He walked past one of the guards on his way and said,

'Bring him please.'

*

Sirena had been given new clothes to wear as she waited for the High Elf Lord. Her others were beyond restoration and she did not want them against her skin anymore anyway. The elvin robe she had been given was simple but elegant; it rippled across her skin with feathery fingers until she wondered if she should be allowed to wear anything at all. She adjusted her low slung belt and looked up as the door to the room opened. It was Altair, the Summoner of Armies. He walked toward her but stopped a few paces from her.

'This, I must say, is a surprise,' he said.

Sirena could hardly say a word. She had always wondered what he would look like, this man that she had heard so much about, how he would sound. She could clearly see his resemblance to her own race and wondered how she could have denied it so long.

'I come to ask you for help,' she said in a clear voice.

Altair smiled kindly and gestured for her to be seated opposite him. It was a small room with a fireplace and two armchairs. Scrolls lined one of the walls and the windows that opened out onto the gardens had been closed. She could feel the close air in the room but felt its suffocation appropriate.

'Are you running away, Sirena? Where do you wish to run to?' Altair's tone was not unkind but Sirena knew that his question needed to be considered and answered seriously before he would continue talking to her. She sat quietly for a few moments, wondering if this was some kind of trick.

'I run back to something,' she said at length.

'Well then,' Altair said, 'what can we do to help?'

Sirena told him first about the wraiths and about Soren. He nodded politely but Sirena had the feeling that he probably knew all this already; she was surely not the only one who had decided to redeem her soul. She paused, trying to read his face but he leaned forward, grabbed her hand and said,

'Go on.'

'But you have heard all this!' she cried, feeling guilt and shame at his sudden close proximity. She was afraid, she realized.

'Yes,' he said softly, 'but you have not.'

And that was when Sirena told him everything. Things she had never told another living being. The tears fell hot and angry down her cheeks and he clutched on to her hand ever tighter, listening raptly with the gaze of an elder child listening to the woes of the younger.

'I did not come here for any kind of forgiveness,' she blurted out at the end. Altair had asked for hot, spiced tea to be brought in and she sipped it gingerly at first until she realized how much it calmed her nerves, then she called for another.

'This, I also know.' Altair conceded, 'you know forgiveness is something that starts with you. How can you ask another to do something that you cannot?'

Sirena nodded.

'Then the question remains, my dear, what can we do for you?'

Sirena knew the ways of the elves, had studied it at length since they were the main focus of the Religion's debates. She knew they had cast aside some of the characteristics that defined mankind in order to move away from the chaos. Vengeance, she was sure, would be among that list.

'I need to go back and destroy him,' she said carefully.

'Revenge?' Altair asked.

'That would be half of it,' she replied, deciding not to lie, 'the other half would be the rational woman in me who knows that this must end. He cannot be allowed to live on.'

Altair nodded slowly.

'You want us to send someone with you,' he said, not asked, and then added, 'why?'

Sirena lowered her eyes and said,

'He is too strong. In many a manner and in ways...I fear... over me.'

Altair considered the woman who sat before him. He stood up and walked to where she sat. He placed one hand on the back of her chair and the other; he carefully lowered onto her stomach. She looked up at him, tears brimming in her eyes.

'We will send the best,' he whispered.

Sirena nodded and gasped a small, 'Thank you.' Tears falling unhindered down her pretty face. 'I don't really deserve it.'

'None of us truly do,' he said, straightening up and gesturing for someone unseen to come closer from the far end of the room, 'that is why we are all so lucky to be surrounded by "sinners" like ourselves. For in them you will find yourself and you will find mercy. You will find god.'

*

He had been listening to the unfolding drama with half an ear. His thoughts dwelt not with the now but what was to come. The *now* he understood. The future, however, needed to be assessed. The Religion woman would lead him to Soren, the man he must kill. Altair had come to him with the proposition as soon as he had arrived on Emara, made his presence known and services available. He had come for the chance to avenge his family and all the other families who had been destroyed by the fire. A new fire had been struck now and he went to see it as soon as he had agreed to put down the monster.

She had been sitting alone by a small stream when he had first glimpsed her. Talking to another, one of old magic. The stars had set and the drey queen was illuminated by tiny lanterns and the fire from her soul. Uriool had stayed where he was, savoring the aura of a savior. Her heart beat pure and her blood sang true. Her skin was the parchment the future would be written on, her hair, the fabric of time. The One Prophesy. And his eyes had met hers for the briefest of seconds. He could see nothing of course, as others naturally saw, but he saw her as no other did. He saw her whole life flash before him in that instant; like a long line of snapshots on a thin piece of string and his heart was saddened. He could scarce take his eyes off her afterward. He watched as she mounted her drey and flew away, and his heart, as it had been for so many years, was torn.

'Sirena.' The voice of the High Elf Lord waded through the mists of his thoughts and found him. He looked up. 'This is Uriool.'

The half-breed made no move to shake her hand but merely inclined his head slightly in acknowledgment.

'He does not speak,' she said slowly.

Altair smiled as only a man of great knowledge could.

'He sees,' he replied.

'And you will accompany me?' she asked, trying to peer past the porcelain mask upon the strange man's face.

Uriool said nothing and moved not a muscle.

'He has agreed,' Altair said, 'some time ago now but *you* can lead him directly to Soren and we will not need to waste precious time searching.'

Uriool moved closer to Sirena and she had to concentrate on staying still so that she would not run away. This creature was unlike any she had ever encountered and she had seen her fair share of races far and wide. Altair caught the look on her face and explained, with a hint of irony in his voice,

'A half-breed.'

Sirena looked away and tried to hold the man's gaze for she knew it was upon her, could feel it with an astonishing certainty.

Altair took a deep breath and clasped his hands behind his back.

'Uriool is special. He is of both vampire and elf.'

Sirena looked meaningfully at Altair as she digested his words. The man that stood inches away from her could snap her spine in two with the same movements she used to crush a twig.

Uriool lowered his unseeing gaze and reached out as if to touch her stomach. His gloved fingers hovered inches from her belly. His hand snapped back and balled into a fist. He looked at Altair and the High Elf met the painted eyes of the mask. He inclined his head ever so slightly and Uriool looked away. Sirena locked her fingers around her stomach and took a deep breath of resolve.

'It will take two days to get there in the ship I came on but that should be enough time?'

'No,' Altair said, shaking his head, 'you will take one of our vessels; it will get you there faster.' Sirena nodded. 'Are you ready?' Altair asked, taking one of her hands, and she could tell that the half-breed was silently asking the same question. She thought about seeing his face again, she thought about all the millions that had died already and she thought about the creature growing in her womb. She looked at the demi-god that stood before her, felt the power he emanated, the capability.

'Yes,' she said, 'and we will save time now that the skies are empty.'

Uriool tensed suddenly and Altair felt the air grow cold even as dawn approached.

'Time we have just run out of,' he said darkly.

'No!' Sirena breathed, holding on to Altair for support.

'You must go now! Go quickly!' Altair all but shoved the two of them toward the door. 'You cannot fail!' he cried after them as Uriool hoisted Sirena up over his shoulder and vaulted out of the window instead.

Altair looked out at the skies, inky black with wings and shadow, growing with every breath he took to steady his heart. 'And so it begins.'

Chapter 16

War

Lucio had been taking in the last minutes of night. The coldest hours just before the sun rose. It had always been his favorite time of day. It was as if the world held its breath, waiting for the sun to break the horizon, like a disciple waiting for his savior. Calm and still, expectant. Suddenly, from down below, the crowds grew still and he peered over his balcony railings, wanting to see what they saw. The people started to part for someone, a woman. A cry was taken up and something was thrown. Soon, there was chaos, and as the woman drew closer through the masses of human volunteers and refuge seekers, he saw why.

She donned the midnight blue Religion robes. She had the mark upon her forehead and she wore a scowl that marked her shame. By the time she had reached the steps, she was bloodied and bruised. The people were screaming obscenities, hurling anything within reach at the lost Religion prophetess, Sirena. He watched her sadly as she climbed the steps with all the dignity she could muster and inwardly praised her for her courage. He only hoped she had come for the right reasons.

He looked back at the crowds, looked upon their faces twisted into masks of hatred and vengeance. They looked like barbarians hollering needlessly for blood. He knew they were a young race but they were older than a few and they should know better…by now at least, and he could feel something inside of him well up and brim over.

'PLEASE!' he cried, his hands raised to the air in surrender, 'please stop!'

The tears rolled down his cheeks and the people looked up at the madman.

'Why should we!' someone yelled out, pointing an accusing finger at the closed doors. 'Give us one good reason why we should not go in there and tear her apart!'

Lucio lowered his arms and placed them lightly on the railing. Pain like he had never felt before tore at his heart.

'But there are so many,' he replied sadly, 'which one will you have me give.' More angry yells greeted his question but a few had grown quiet, waiting to hear what the Faith priest had to say. His reputation was great but his influence was small compared to so many others. What reasons could he possibly give that would justify pure evil going unpunished? So many had died as a direct result of her words and prophesies. Good men and women, innocent children. What reason could there possibly be?

'For thousands of years now, we have been trying to determine where our place is in the Worlds,' he began. Some shook their heads and merely walked away but others stepped forward to replace them. 'We pour over ancient texts, riddled with the errors of our ancestors and their inability to grasp the *now*. We dissect the meanings of these scripts and come up with a story that suits us best. That story, more often than not, becomes a platform for anger and fear instead of one of love and respect.'

'God wants her to BURN!' a young mother called up and the crowd cheered for her.

Lucio sighed.

'Don't you see? God wants no one to burn. He gives you this amazing, natural ability to choose for love and all you can do is build cages for yourselves.'

The people craned their necks to hear better and a few tribes' people from the nearby camp had left their cooking pots and weapons to listen to the commotion. 'We each build our own you see and hers is grand indeed. It is she who is plagued by the choices she has made, she who has to carry the burden.'

'And what of *our* burdens?'

Lucio looked at the lone man who had asked the question. He had the look of one who has lost much in his eyes.

'Yes,' Lucio admitted, 'we all carry burdens. That is the way of the Worlds as the old saying goes, but when you learn to love yourself, as you would have others love you, you are able to carry these burdens with more ease. She has chosen to live in hatred, is incapable of forgiving herself and *that* is why she suffers.'

No one had an answer for this and so Lucio continued; 'The Religion are a mislead people. They cannot *see* what they are doing. Their fear makes them blind and it is our duty to help them, not scorn them.'

A riot almost broke out at this statement. He held up his hands for silence and after a long while, the outrage subsided.

Lucio stared long and hard at them, like children who had erred.

'People will ask us, when this is over, they will ask us "Why? Why did you let this happen?" and you will answer them with the truth!' he said, angrily shaking his fist at them. 'You will tell them that there existed two worlds. You will say that they pretended to be civilized in ours whilst we pretended not to see the savagery of theirs. Until it was almost too late.' His hands swept across the space in front of him and he added, 'That will be our burden.'

The people were deadly quiet once again. Some of the star pirates had joined to listen too, hanging from ropes and leaning over the rails of their ships.

'It does not matter what you call your faith, how you choose to pay homage or what those before you wrote. What matters is that you try to be good people, that you honor your life and learn to love. For without love, there can be no forgiveness and no hope.'

He left the balcony and the staring faces down below and went inside to be by himself and to pray for a miracle. It could not be so hard, he thought, for life to be allowed to live on.

*

Arial, Vanora and Ronan were lying on top of the retractable roof of Arial's chambers. They had become tired of staring out of windows, tired of waiting. Arial lay on her back now instead, head resting against Ronan's belly, watching the stars wheel past with the night.

'Bethriam would have been out there somewhere,' she suddenly said, 'one of those stars out there would have been ours.' She pointed a finger to the heavens above, listening with half an ear to the speech that the Faith priest was giving and Ronan tracked her gaze.

'The fayres tried to steal me away today,' Vanora said, keeping in tone with the somber statements of the dragon queen. She had joined them about an hour ago after spending half the night with the mages in the gardens. Her dress had been singed and her nose was red with cold from snowballs. She had not wanted to go to her parents and try to explain so she came to see Arial instead. They had become close friends of a sort over a short period of time and they enjoyed talking together.

Arial frowned;

'Troublesome pixies,' she muttered.

Arial had never had time for the fayres. Tricksters and riddlers. They had almost fooled her out of her mother's locket once. Arial believed they must have succeeded because she never could find it again and had harbored a grudge ever since.

'I am glad they did not steal you away from us,' Arial said, smiling at Vanora. The elf maiden smiled back and Arial felt happy for the first time in days. She had her drey by her side and tonight... tonight she would go to Damek. She had argued with herself back and forth one hundred times over, but she had decided that life was fleeting, only love was eternal.

She curled a strand of hair around Ronan's scales absentmindedly and continued her silent reverie of the stars. A select few shot past in their last glorious blaze and somehow she saw her life reflected in them. Ronan shifted beneath her, disrupting her thoughts, and her hair got pulled along with him.

'Ouch,' she said, disentangling her hair from him.

Sorry

He said distractedly. He rose to his feet and stared up, with renewed interest it seemed. They had grown clever, these beasts of darkness. They had cloaked their coming and he had felt them too late this time.

Arial's heart grew cold with fear. She got to her knees and somehow, Vanora's hand found her own. It gripped hers tightly and Arial could tell she was not the only one made afraid by Ronan's restless movements.

'Are they coming?' Arial asked quietly, looking to the east only to see the slight glow of a coming star. The only time such a sight had instilled horror within her instead of awe.

They are already here...and they come for you first

*

Kaleo watched on as Tariq sucked hungrily on a blood pack.

'Careful friend, we have only brought so many,' he warned playfully.

Everybody knew of Tariq's insane thirst. He was stronger that anyone on their donated blood allowance and Kaleo had been with him in the days when he had drunk human blood straight from the vessel. It was a sight to behold.

Blain was sitting in the far corner. He wore a strange expression that Damek could not fathom as usual. Damek looked at his three comrades. He hoped they would be enough. Quinn had not answered his letter and Shona was in hiding with her brother, Daray. He had fed off another and the Apostles were out for him.

Kaleo caught the look upon Damek's face and walked over to him.

'Where are your thoughts?' he asked, leaning against the wall next to where Damek sat. They had been housed in a windowless cellar by request. They had forsaken their UV-drugs for the time being. It weakened them somewhat and they would wait until the last minute to take them.

'He thinks upon his woman?' Blain asked, absentmindedly picking at his teeth and glaring at Damek from under his shaggy, dark mane. Damek felt the anger in him rise but decided against a fight. It would do no one any good. Only Kaleo understood.

'She is not my woman,' he said instead.

Blain shook his head, got up and stretched. When he had walked to the other side of the room and was out of earshot, Kaleo put his hand upon Damek's shoulder and asked,

'Will you not go to her?'

Damek sighed. He knew what would happen if he did.

'It is too difficult,' he said at last.

Blain strode over to the two love-sick malachi. He had had enough of this foolishness.

'What you two need,' he said self-assuredly, 'is a good fight.'

Damek looked up at him disdainfully.

'Actually,' Tariq interjected, dropping his empty bag on the floor, 'I agree. That should shake the madness out of you.'

Damek smiled despite himself. Perhaps he did need to tear out a throat or two.

'These wraiths, they seem to be worthy adversaries?' Blain asked. Tariq laughed quietly and Kaleo raised his eyebrows.

'We will need a plan,' Damek conceded.

Tariq sat on the cold floor and asked,

'Will we use any magic?'

Damek shook his head;

'We cannot afford to have anyone out of action.'

'Yes, but for the one out of the fight, the one in it will more than make up for.'

Damek considered Blain's statement for a moment before answering,

'Altair said he does not advise it. He has asked that anyone who can afford not to wield, should indeed withhold, for we are not sure what effects such a great amount of free magic will have.'

Blain snorted and cried,

'The effects? The kuvuta will die of course!'

More laughter greeted his blatant reply.

'Perhaps…' Damek trailed off.

He realized that they all hung on his every word even though Tariq was leaderless by his very nature, Blain thought him a fool for falling in love with a drey maiden and Kaleo was wise enough to think for himself. He stared at them all for a moment before realizing that they were waiting for him to lead them.

'We have several options,' he began, sitting up straight and focusing his thoughts. 'We can equip someone with a few different spells, direct anima attacks and so forth,' he said gesturing with his hands, 'but how much is that truly going to help?'

Blain was nodding his head, Tariq was sucking on his fourth blood ration and Kaleo was deep in thought. After a moments silence, Kaleo asked,

'So what do you propose?'

Damek looked meaningfully at Tariq.

'He is the only one strong enough,' Damek said, nodding his head at the thirsty malachi.

'Strong enough for what?' Tariq asked darkly, blood trickling from the corners of his mouth.

'Strong enough to call a Daemon,' Kaleo answered for Damek.

'You want to summon someone?' Blain asked, his face disbelieving, then excited.

'It is the only way,' Damek shrugged.

'Who will protect the caller?' Kaleo asked. Damek looked to Blain and then to Kaleo.

'I will,' Blain sighed, sensing that Damek was sizing them up.

'He needs only a pulse-shield, if we feel anything, we will come straight back,' Damek said hastily.

'And I suppose Kaleo will try to keep up with you?' Blain chuckled. Kaleo grinned halfheartedly, knowing full well Damek was the one who was going to shoulder the greatest burden.

'Walking with a Daemon is no mere thing Damek,' Tariq warned, 'it will possess you at times. It will leave you at others and who knows what it may take with it when it is done.'

'The risk is worth it,' Damek said with finality, 'it is the only way that we can make a real difference. Otherwise we will be like the rest; pitting strength against strength and I have a feeling that we may come off second best.'

'Damek is right,' Tariq relented.

It seemed they had a plan and Damek was glad he had voiced his opinion. He had been thinking about it for a while but it was a monumental task and he had not been sure how the others would react. Whenever this had been done in the past; it had been done to ask advice, not to do battle, and fourteen Ancients performed the summoning, not four naïve assassins and relic hunters. They reacted like the friends they were though and he was sorry he had ever doubted them.

When they had first arrived, they had all wanted to hear Damek's account of Falkhar's defeat and Adonica's death. Damek had told them everything, from their master's plot to the fight that had ensued. He left out the part that he had still not been able to fathom though. Altair had asked him about it, said he had sensed it within him. Damek had said that he did not know how it had happened and the High Elf Lord had launched into an explanation about how Damek had seen the World as it truly was and that energy could be harnessed as easily as it could be expended. Damek wondered if he would ever feel that power again. Perhaps it was with him all the time, on some subconscious level. He could not be sure. They had all taken the news well though and supported him fully.

'Give me some of that!' Damek said, reaching out for a blood bag while Blain dangled it enticingly in front of him. Tariq watched on hungrily and Damek was glad they were all together again. Soon, they were all feeding happily and sharing stories of all that had come to pass since their last mission when suddenly, Kaleo sat bolt upright. His breakfast clutched in his hands so tightly, Damek thought it would burst.

'What is it?' Blain asked.

Damek could feel something too, though obviously not on the same level of intensity as Kaleo.

'I feel it,' Tariq said, getting up off his haunches and staring at the ceiling as though it were cursed. Blain convulsed ever so slightly at the same time Damek did.

'They are here,' Kaelo said in hushed tones.

'Then we must prepare! Tariq yelled. He began stripping off his clothes with the help of Blain. The Daemon needed to pass through the naked skin of the caller or his form would be tainted.

'We need water!' Blain bellowed. Kaleo dropped his food and started running water from the tap. Damek swallowed the rest of his blood ration and started taking his UV-drugs, shoving the rest into Kaleo's hands.

There came a furious knocking at the door and half a second later, two women came bursting through. They were identical in every way and their attire left so little to the imagination that Kaleo was not sure where to look.

'A bit late!' Blain cursed.

'There was no warning!' one hissed while the other grabbed Damek by the arm. Her grip was fierce and her tone brooked no argument;

'You must come now!'

Damek looked at his Shadow Brothers, confusion on his face.

'We will get ready, you go with them,' Tariq said, not wanting to waste time arguing.

'I will meet you on the other side,' Kaleo said reassuringly.

'No!' the woman closest to Blain yelled, 'you must all come now!'

'Give us a break!' Blain yelled back, 'we need time!'

The women sized up the situation. The two who were engaged in undressing and throwing water everywhere could stay but the other two would come. Only one had been asked for but there were too many wraiths for him to come alone.

Damek looked at the hand that held him and saw the blood smeared across it. He needed only one moment to know whose it was.

'Kaleo,' he said, his eyes wide with fear and his face drained of all the blood he had consumed moments before, 'you must help me.'

*

As soon as the first finger of light touched the land, it was snatched away by the dark cloud that gathered above them. Arial got to her feet and Vanora followed suit. Ronan was pacing restlessly, his wings flaring and bouts of blackened smoke billowing out of his nostrils.

I cannot fly you away, they are everywhere.

'I told you we would stay and fight. We stand a better chance in there,' she said, pointing to her chamber down below, 'the entrances will filter them.'

Ronan nodded his great head and got ready to defend the lady of his soul. Arial and Vanora dropped down and backed up to the far corner, away from the door and window. She pushed Vanora gently behind her and gave her what was supposed to be an encouraging look, but she doubted her face had shown exactly that. Vanora did not seem too afraid and asked no questions. Arial was grateful for that. She could not deal with telling a child she may be facing the last seconds of life, without breaking down.

A few minutes passed, they passed like treacle from a spoon and soon, Arial could hear the wings. It sounded like a swarm in her head, growing ever louder and filling her heart with dread. For a moment she felt as if she stood at the edge of an abyss, the darkness alive with moving shadow and wings. She took a deep breath and then, they were upon them. She tried to temper her heart as she heard the war cries being sent up outside. Voices crying out together, an effort to drown out the sound of death. If they could be brave, so could she.

Vanora clutched Arial's skirts and she looked down again. The princess looked up at her and Arial's heartbeat slowed. This child needed her right now and she could think clearly again. The moment was stolen by the heavy thud of a kuvuta against the glass window to her right. Arial stared at it for the briefest of moments and all the fear came rushing back to her as if a dam wall had broken inside her heart. It leered at her, the face of death. It pulled its fist back to break through the pane but before it could, the glass was broken for it. A spear came careening from somewhere down below and impaled the monster where he sat upon his beast. The shaft shot through the window, shattering it and scattering pieces of glass and tar-like blood at Arial's feet. The wraith hung on the sill for a few moments before slumping over the side and falling into her room.

Arial stood in shocked silence for a moment. The spear must have been thrown over forty feet and with perfect accuracy. That was how far the nearest camp was. It would not be enough though. Arial could feel it in her blood just as sure as she could hear the wraiths running up the stairs, that not even tenfold-hundred warriors with spears that could fly true every time, could save her from the fate that awaited her.

Ronan stood before the door and as the first wraith slammed its body against it, mistaking it for normal papyrus; he set lose a burning ball of fire that erupted in the hallway beyond. Arial tried to shield Vanora from the intense heat with her body. The heat-waves ruffled her golden locks and singed the tiny hairs on her arms. When she looked up again, black corpses lay smoldering in the corridor beyond like a carpet. But more were coming. They charged up the stairs, some still on their beasts, while others clamored at the window. Many were taken down by arrows and spears. The fierce Gau tribe below defending the fire maiden's fortress with every breath they could muster and every spear they could spare and arrow they could loose.

Ronan was bombarding the hallway with fire and soon, the building started to burn, along with the foul creatures that swarmed all over it. It would not last long though, Ronan could only breath so much flame. Soon, the sulpher in his stomach would be used up and he would have to rely on brute strength alone.

He looked over at her and Arial gained courage from the look in his eyes. She took two steps to where the first wraith lay dead and pulled at the spear that had slain him. She wrenched it free and stood in front of Vanora again. She would not die so easily. Let them take if they must but she would not give.

Ronan threw his last flame, stood back and curled his tail to the front. He bared his fangs and roared so loud at his would-be challengers that they stopped for a moment before they continued their advance.

Something moved at the window again and Arial spun around, spear pointed forward, sweat running down her brow. Dark figures on the sill, two of them, but they were not wraiths.

Yera and Yuli jumped down and drew their twin double-bladed war-swords. Their bodies were painted the fiercest of reds in bands across their legs and faces, their teeth flashed white as they met their foe and Arial watched them dance like a child mesmerized. The way they wove around each wraith that came through the windows; it looked as if they were merely performing an intricate step with a partner. A neat slice across the neck was the kiss of death for every kuvuta they danced with. Figures lithe and strong, feet never missing a step, hair flicking around their faces like the wings of a crow. Arial could feel Vanora watching too.

Ronan felled four of the creatures neatly in half, for every mighty sweep of his tail, and every now and again he would beat his massive wings to push the enemy back and give them a moment's respite to catch their breath.

Another swooped through the window, leaping off his steed, arms outstretched and mouth agape. Arial spun just in time and drove the point of the spear through his terrible eye. Cold, black blood ran down her fingers and wrist and she rubbed it off on her robes. It had started to burn already.

Yuli stopped for a moment to look over at Arial and the kuvuta that lay dead at her feet. She smiled and Arial grinned back wildly. It felt good to kill them, even one, for you could almost hear the souls they had taken whispering out of their mouths as they took their last rattling breath.

Arial pushed her hair back and looked over at Ronan again. He blocked most of the door and had not been injured yet. Yera and Yuli took down any who got passed him and any who managed to get through the window. How long could it last though? As these thoughts raced through Arial's mind, the ground began to shake with the great footsteps of another beast, one of those they rode only bigger, much bigger.

Arial could see it through the narrow crack of doorway she was exposed to. It looked like a creature from her nightmares. Steam came off its ugly body and black liquid spilled from the corners of its twisted mouth. Horns curled out from its head and a kuvuta sat holding on to them. He was taller than the rest and held a silver long sword in his hand. Vanora let out a small cry and Arial tried not to shake where she stood. The wraith looked at her and pointed his sword straight at her. Ronan rushed forward and the two massive beasts wrestled one another. Biting and snapping, tails flashing, blood being drawn. Ronan roared out in pain as one of the sword blows swung true and stabbed him just below the shoulder. Arial wanted to drop her spear and run toward him but Vanora desperately held her back. Ronan struck out in return, grabbing the kuvuta by the waist with his strong jaws and flinging him to the far side of the room.

Yera and Yuli were being swamped now. Ronan's battle with the beast had left many more free to enter the room and they had their hands full. Sweat was beginning to pour off their bodies but their movements were as swift and tireless as ever. Arial envied their skill.

A roar that made the very floor shake signified the demise of the black creature that had taken Ronan on. Ronan lowered his tail and the beast slid from it, hissing and spitting, still trying to fight when the battle had already been won.

Arial cheered out loud and she did not see the wraith that crawled toward her until it was too late. Vanora screamed as the wraith reached her first. Her cry stilled Arial's heart and she turned around only to see the kuvuta that Ronan had flung, with its arm down Vanora's throat. It pulled out her tiny beating heart and the High Elf Princess fell to the floor in a heap of dead limbs.

Arial did not hesitate. She ran forward, spear held out in front of her and jaw set. Tears were streaming down her face in the few seconds it took her to reach him. He deflected her thrust as easily as if she was a child with a toy and he grabbed her by the throat. He was weakened but he was still strong enough, and Arial struggled for breath, her feet dangling inches above the floor. He stared into her eyes and said,

'Soren has saved a great fate for you.'

He lowered her, increasing his grip in case she decided to struggle.

Arial's eyes widened in fear as his mouth clamped down on hers. She closed her eyes and gave in to the feeling that swept through her. She had fallen into that winged abyss...it was so cold...It was over in seconds. He let her fall to the floor and no sooner had her body met the hard wood than the wraith was decapitated by her drey's jaws. His body fell to the floor beside her but she hardly noticed. She crawled over to where Vanora lay, her little body lying at a cruel angle. She reached inside her robes and brought out the tiny vial. The one Tariq had given her. She poured the few precious drops down the girl's throat and laid her back down. She could feel her own strength leaving her just as she could see something stirring inside the elf maiden.

What happened! You should have called for me!

Arial could only stare up at her drey. The cold had started to crawl through her like a plague and he lay down beside her, his wing enfolding her like a cradle.

*

The steady stream of wraiths had slowed and Yera left the rest to Yuli while she rushed to the dreya queen's side. She fell to her knees and held Arial's hand.

'What can I do?' the warrior maiden asked in her tongue. Arial loved the sound of it and she closed her eyes for a moment.

You cannot go

Ronan's voice brought her back and she looked up at Yera.

'Bring me Damek,' was all she could manage as a massive tear ran from Ronan's eye and fell warm on her breasts. Yera nodded and scrambled to her feet, dragging her twin sister with her as she killed the last wraith.

Arial would see her last love. She would fight to make it that far.

'Thank you, for being here with me,' she said to the drey beside her and something close to peace stole over her troubled heart. His wing tightened around her and she waited.

Chapter 17
Death

Damek took the stairs four at a time in his effort to reach his lady. He did not know how dire the situation was. The twins' Udaranese was so poor that he could hardly understand their crazed ramblings. They kept switching to their mother tongue and gesturing wildly, and this had a more profound effect than any message he could linguistically understand.

Kaleo said not one word. He was too afraid for his friend. He could hear Damek's frantic heart beating deep in chest, alive with hope and dread in equal measure. The heart of a malachi beat like a stone turning in a loamy grave, slow and wont to cease all together. Only true blood could quicken it, or true love. He could scarcely keep up with the man before him.

Damek was running almost flat out. He could not believe the pace that the light-footed Gau were setting. All he had to guide him was fleeting flashes of bare flesh or raven hair as they rounded the next corner. He had walked these passageways a thousand times before just to listen to her breathe as she slept, but the chaos around him blurred his senses, and he was glad for the guides. He could smell them now, all around the palace. He could hear the clicking of their foul tongues as they screeched orders to one another, could hear the baying for blood outside as if it came from within.

Blood was spilled and the smell of it filled his nostrils and made his head swim. He could hear the sound of shadow brushing against shadow, the battle cries of the still brave and standing. He smelt war and he knew then that it would be all he smelt for many days yet to come. The decay, the hot life-force of thousands seeping into the hungry ground, the sweat, the fear and the death.

As they came close to the last corner, however, he smelt something different. It assaulted his senses not in waves, but like a wall of stench so vile, that it would block the passage for any weaker creature than he. Kaleo hesitated. Damek tore on.

Char-grilled darkness. He had only smelt it once before and then, the wind had mercifully swept it away. Now he confronted it full on and struggled not to gag. Layer upon layer of burnt kuvuta like a black sea spread out before him. The walls still smoked, obscuring his vision and filling his nostrils and small fires still fed off the dead and dying.

'Who could have done this?' Kaleo asked in disbelief.

'Ronan,' Damek said, more to himself than to his companion. How many had come for her? Hundreds. He should have been with her, should have known this was going to happen. He should have been with her. His heart recoiled in dread and he had to force himself to move forward.

The Gau maidens were edging along the walls, finding footholds in peeled wood and shattered windowpanes. They were barefoot and the wraith blood boiled and hissed beneath them, deadly even in death. Damek tried to find hardened islands within the ocean of liquid shadow and Kaleo followed soon after. Damek rushed ahead as the heat still emanating from the walls and ceilings impeded the sisters.

He could smell something else now and that smell was as sweet to him now as it had been when he had first cast his face to the white tower that day. It cut through all the others and he could almost taste it so near was she. He steeled himself and faced the doorway to her bedchamber after negotiating the black tide. He clambered easily over the dead beast that lay in his path, blocking the entrance with its massive bulk, holding onto the ugly, curled horns for support and vaulting up and over.

Ronan had put up a courageous fight and many more lay dead in the room. Some were severed clean in half and others, it seemed, had had their throats slit as if by some enraged lover. The cuts were so clean that only a dribble of blood escaped them and they lay crumpled on the floor in neat little heaps as if a dance had been danced and they had died from pure exhaustion. Damek glanced at the two strange women who had come to collect him with new eyes. So these were the twin killers that he had heard so much about. A good thing then that they had been there in his absence. His eyes quickly scanned the room for Arial as Kaleo landed lightly beside him.

All Damek could see was the great drey curled up in the far corner. He was wounded, but not grievously so. Brightly colored blood stained his scales. The little elf princess was kneeling before him, weeping silently. She had dark blood all over her lips and throat, splattered all the way down her front. She looked like a malachi child after her first true kill. He could tell it was her blood though and he pitied whatever pain such a child was made to suffer. His eyes met hers as she looked up, and Ronan stirred his wing. There...a cascade of gold...and shadow...

Damek took measured steps toward the trio, trying to breathe easy and still the mad beating of his heart. It thudded in his ears and he thought he might make deaf every creature in the room. His shoulders were hunched in painful anticipation and the sweat poured off his face like hot rain. He calmed his heart with great effort but it grew heavier with every step he took that brought him closer to her and when Ronan lifted his head, snorting softly and flexing his scales in angst, his gaze fell upon her and his heart broke at last.

Her eyes were closed, one hand rested lightly in Vanora's and the other stroked Ronan absentmindedly. Her lips were as black as night, the soft skin around her eyes and nostrils too. Even as he watched, the shadow growing within her crept out of her ears and into the roots of her lovely hair. It seemed to seep out of her skin like some dark star was pulling black water from her.

Her eyes slowly fluttered open and Damek was afraid but he needn't have been. The same brilliant shade of blue shone through that always did, the blue of a sky drenched in light. He fell to his knees and Vanora made room for him. She shuffled a little to the right and Damek felt like he should ask her if she were all right but he had eyes only for his lady now.

Shadows poured out and curled around her. He could feel only the tearing of his heart and the tears that rolled freely. Everything else was numb, as if it belonged to another body and was not his own. He reached out and stroked her soft face. She smiled, her eyes blinking weakly.

'You came for me.'

Damek pulled her over to him and she lay in his arms as light as a feather. He just nodded his head and pulled his lips together to try to stop the torrent of tears.

'Of course I came,' he managed at last.

She reached up and stroked the hard line of his jaw.

'Oh to have loved someone as beautiful as you,' she murmured and Damek tried not to squeeze her so tight that she would die. He was not beautiful...

He looked up at the others, searched the different faces for any trace of hope but he found none. He could barely look into Kaleo's eyes for what he saw there chilled every bone in his body.

*

Kaleo watched on in statuesque horror. The death he had witnessed flashed before his eyes and he could do nothing to save Damek from this fate. Perhaps the Ancients had been right. Perhaps there was no place in a malachi heart for love; the feed was the only intimacy they knew. Would the parasite not let them alone?

Kaleo slunk deeper into the shadows and tried to tear his eyes away from his broken friend but he was transfixed and he clamped his hand to his mouth to stop the mournful cry that threatened to escape his lips. A cry for his lost woman and for his Shadow Brother.

Damek was looking at him now and no amount of will could mask his terror. He shook his head slowly and closed his eyes to save Damek from the sight of them. He could do no more.

There was movement at the window and Damek's head snapped up. His eyes were slits of menace and his fangs were fully bared. His energy senses were starting to return and he would obliterate any wraith that came within reach of him. It was no kuvuta though, it was a human.

*

Lucio felt the room grow darker. It was like the night had become a deeper shade of black and he could not understand; it was dawn! He walked outside and there he could see, just on the horizon, not a sun that rose, but a shadow. They were here. They were moving fast. They were coming this way. Lucio's forehead broke out in sweat and he cried out to the people down below;

'They are coming! Sound the alarms!' The voice did not sound like his own. It came from a foreign tongue that stuck in his throat like a fat toad. His face drained of color as he watched the descending darkness. His hands squeezed the railing until they were as white as a virgin's veil. He needed to get out of there and fast. He was no match for even *one* of those kuvuta and he had to either hide or find some sort of protection. He did not fancy his chances running through the passages like a trapped rat and decided instead to vault over the balcony and onto the nearest wall. It was covered in vines and he could climb to the roof with relatively little difficulty and from there, he would be able to better see what was going on, and what the best course of action would be.

He leapt from the ledge, planting his hands firmly on the rails and throwing his legs up and over. He landed hard against the wall and his palms burnt red-raw as he struggled for a decent grip on the rough plants. By the time he had struggled to the top, he was drenched in sweat and very afraid. The wraiths were nearly upon the palace compound now and he had still found no place to hide or anyone to protect him until he could. He chanced a backward glance and his eyes grew wide with fear. No time.

He ran as fast as his legs could carry him across the rooftop, pumping his tired arms and ignoring his ragged breath. He was by no means an athletic man. He worked out in the simulator once a week but that was about it. Now, his limbs found an energy he never knew he had, and he was glad for it.

A massive beast came shrieking from above, swooping down with its glinting claws and rolling tongue. Lucio skidded to a halt just before the end of the roof, ducking his head low to avoid it. It reeled upward again but Lucio had lost his footing and was sliding away.

He caught on to the edge of the one-way looking-glass roof and could feel his legs kicking at nothing. He took a deep breath, measured up his chances and decided to drop down. He landed safely on a window frame; shattered glass, dead wraiths and people within the room beyond. He held up both of his hands in the Worldly sign for peace and tried to catch his breath.

'I am alone,' he managed to pant. When the postures in the room relaxed and it seemed no one had the slightest interest in him anymore, he slowly dropped himself down and into the chamber. He scanned the room; dead kuvuta, a dragon, two vampires, a High Elf child, two tribes-women and someone dying.

He rushed over to the woman. The vampire who held her hissed slightly at his approach but he held his hands up again and moved slowly this time.

He knelt down carefully next to the night stalker. He could feel the eyes of the dragon on him at all times, could hear the quiet sobs of the elf. He concentrated on the woman however. He had never seen anything like it before and he had been practicing medicine for many years now, in deep dark jungles, on far-away planets, in hard-fought wars and amidst Chaos magic unleashed. This though, was beyond his expertise. He could tell from the very moment he laid eyes upon the affliction. It looked like the essence that made up the kuvuta had already bonded with her blood, was fighting to replace it somehow. It enveloped her and poisoned her like a disease. It seeped out of her every pore in its attempt to surround her and there was nothing that Lucio could do. He took her hand. It was warm, too warm, but her heart was cold. The life was leaving her and another trying to destroy whatever it would leave in its wake. Lucio could feel all eyes on him now, but the vampire closest to him bore holes into the top of his head, so fierce was his stare. Lucio looked up and shook his head slowly just as Kaleo had done moments before.

'There is...there is nothing I can do.'

Damek cursed under his breath and squeezed Arial's hand tighter. She had opened her eyes again and looked around.

'I heard a voice,' she said, a little deliriously.

Lucio frowned.

'Mine?' he asked.

Arial found the face that the voice belonged to and smiled.

'Yes. I heard you speaking earlier...'

Lucio thought for a moment but then he remembered. This place was not so far away from his own chamber and she would have heard him talking to the people twenty minutes ago. He smiled nervously.

She was very beautiful, this dying woman, and she had an impressive audience to watch over her. From the leer of the dragon, he could tell she was his, and he could almost say the same for the vampire.

'Do you want me to say something for you now?' the priest in him asked. Most likely she did not practice any faith that he knew of but he could think of nothing else to say or do.

'You speak with such passion,' she said slowly, her brow furrowing ever so slightly. 'Where is your god though when you are far from home and shadows swallow Worlds?' She spoke so softly and when Lucio knelt down to better hear her; he saw the blue of Mirkisha's eyes staring up at him. It could be mistaken for nothing else. Tears sprung to his eyes and he held her head gently.

'God is in us all,' he whispered. Arial nodded and closed her eyes. Lucio looked to the vampire but he had eyes only for the woman.

'Who is she?' Lucio asked.

'She is the queen of the dreya,' the vampire replied solemnly, 'she has saved us all.'

That was all that Lucio needed to know. He looked up at the others again. She was dying and they could do nothing but watch. He could see the breath in her ebbing as the shadows pushed the air out to make space for themselves. The sweet smell of natural magic still clung to her and it was like watching his love, Mirkisha, die.

'No,' he breathed. He laid his hands upon her, focusing all the energy he could muster. He could feel the vibrations now, as the smoke hissed dangerously out of her lungs, recoiling at his touch. It promised to come back though and Lucio was bewildered at what else he was supposed to do. There was nothing more, truly.

But Arial's eyes flew open. She had been given a few more minutes. Some miracle had come and chased the fog away, if only for a short while, to give her the time she needed. She reached out for Ronan again and when he brought his snout under her hand, she clung onto him for support. She could feel his love and power but she was in too dark a place for him to save her now. The priest had said that god was in them all. She was no longer afraid, everything made sense to her now.

She was trying to say something, Damek could tell. Her black lips were struggling to sound it out but the priest had given her some time.

'What is it Arial?' he asked, lifting her up by the shoulders.

'You...' she struggled, 'you must drink...'

Damek looked down at her, horrified by what she was suggesting. She held him by the side of his face and she was pulling him down.

He saw her weak heartbeat struggling against the skin of her neck; like a small bird caught in a net, and suddenly he was overcome with desire.

'I cannot,' he stammered.

She only smiled at him and pulled him ever closer. This was a fight he would not be able to win, he could feel it. He would sink his fangs into her forbidden neck and drink the sweet blood. It would set fire to his soul and he would die with her. Tears shook in his eyes as he held her tight.

Kaleo stood over him now, a keen look in his eye. Damek looked up in bewilderment at Kaleo, eyes pleading for guidance. He was so afraid that he could hardly move.

'Tell me what you see, Damek,' she whispered.

'I see you,' he breathed without hesitation.

'No,' she said, with a firmness that surprised him, 'tell me what you really see.'

Her eyes were wide open and she was staring at him intently, the blue searing him like flames. He tried to concentrate, tried to focus on something other than the sound of her beating heart, the smell that came from her hair, her hands, her tender skin and the desire of a different kind inside him. He squeezed his eyes tightly shut and roared out loud in frustration and torment. His chest reverberated with the sound of it and Vanora's hands were clamped over her ears.

When he opened his eyes, he was calmer, the room was warmer and he could think clearly. His full energy had returned to him and the wood breathed around him, each splinter alive. The elf princess glowed white and energy flowed outward from her at an alarming rate yet she retained her form perfectly. The drey was a wreathing ball of pure fire. It was beautiful to watch, like fireflies weaving a form into being. The malachi beside him, his Shadow Brother, was a shifting mass of water-like substances composed of strange blue and purple hues, all shifting and mixing like the current deep beneath the sea. The kuvuta lying sprawled on the floor looked exactly the same except perhaps duller in color than usual. He paid them almost no heed. Damek took a deep breath before looking down.

She was a sight to behold! It was like a million rainbows had decided to live in her eyes and in her smile. She shone so brightly that his limbs deflected her rays and cast slight shadows over her. He could see the inky darkness trying to surge through her and it diminished her colors somewhat but she still took his breath away. A star in its brightest days of youth and light. The tears were rolling again.

'I see you,' he said again and this time she seemed satisfied.

'It will be alright,' she promised softly, 'you must drink now. It will be alright.'

'She is right,' Kaleo assured him. His hand rested gently on Damek's shoulder. 'You will not burn. You need her strength to channel the Daemon and you need to take the shadow from her. You are perhaps able to suppress it, or at least the Daemon will be, but she *cannot* be left with it. Take it instead and use it.' Kaleo's hand squeezed his shoulder with his final message before he let go and took a step back.

Vanora got to her feet and without being told, followed suit. Ronan did not move an inch but Damek could tell from his posture that he wanted Damek to take the shadow from her as much as anybody else did. She deserved it.

Damek looked back down at her and saw that she was fading fast. He drew her closer to him, hesitated, and then closed the gap when her small hands clutched desperately at his collar. She was so impossibly warm, so sweet and when he finally sank his teeth into her he rolled back with her in pure ecstasy. Her blood burnt wild and free, it sang like a chorus of angels through his body, it filled his heart and flooded his spirit. He had never felt more complete, more whole, and she clung to him like a lover in the thralls of passion. She did not flinch, she did not pull back or struggle, but pushed deeper into him and his tears flowed into his mouth as freely as her blood.

She gasped out loud as he withdrew, and he held on to her tightly, licking the last precious drops from his swollen lips. He was sobbing now, rocking back and forth with her in his arms. He thought he may have felt something close to god in that moment. Something that held them closer to each other than mere flesh and bones could ever hope to.

'Stop,' she whispered, for her voice was no more than the flutter of a paper wing against the symphony that roared in his ears. He still held her but he ceased rocking, tried to stop sobbing if only to hear her better and he gazed down at her beautiful face. The rainbow lingered, the darkness was gone.

'For a while,' he choked out, 'I thought I would die sharing my love with you, but now I see…' he broke off and she stroked his face so softly Damek thought he might never stop crying just remembering that touch and the look in her eyes. '…but now I see, you are the one who must die to share it with me.'

She was quiet for what seemed like a very long time and Damek was so afraid that it was over. She opened her lips one last time though to speak to her love;

'Every moment with you contains a life-time's worth of love,' she whispered, 'we have shared one hundred times over.' She smiled at him and the light in her shone very brightly again, like a fading star's last moment and Damek could feel why. They were coming, the army. The cheers went up outside as the angel warriors fell down from the skies and upon the enemy. Arial did not open her eyes to hear them; her smile only grew broader still.

'Say a prayer for my Blood Angels,' she said and the last of her light left her.

Damek pulled her closer to him still and felt the last of her heat seep into his skin.

'I love you,' he whispered into the ear of the lover he thought he had never known.

Yera and Yuli watched on helplessly as the beautiful *umuriro* woman died in the *njade's* arms. They held on to each other and cried quietly. Lucio was at a loss for words. But the crowds were cheering outside as the slaughter was forgotten for the briefest of seconds. Salvation had arrived and she may have saved them all. Lucio said his silent prayer as she had asked and knew that he had done enough. He moved toward the crying elf maiden and drew her closer to him. She was in a terrible state and he knew they would have to move soon if they were to remain alive.

'Come.' It was one of the tribe women. She held out her hand and her eyes were pleading and insistent, 'we know a place.'

He followed them out of the room, the two warriors with the little girl in tow.

He could only pray now. That was all he had ever been able to do anyway.

*

Ronan rose and gently nudged Arial with his massive snout. He was beginning his mournful song but it sounded beautiful to Damek's ears. It drowned out the sound of animated shrieking that was beginning to fill his head. The Daemon had been summoned. It was climbing into his skin and Ronan's song was all that kept the pain at bay.

The dragon looked down at his maiden once more, before taking off into the sky beyond with such force, that Damek was nearly blown back where he sat. Ronan soared high into the air, singing his song of lament while tearing down the wraiths as he went. It was a sight Damek would remember forever.

He laid Arial gently down and Kaleo stepped forward with a sheet from the bed. Damek could only watch as her pretty face was covered. He had no tears now. The Daemon was stealing them all, drinking them up with a long-harbored thirst. He could feel her power buoy him though; shield him from the awful force within him. He could feel the creature clawing its way into his mind and body and he wondered how he ever would have coped without her sacrifice.

He looked at Kaleo but Kaleo could only stare back.

'I have no words for you,' Kaleo said sadly. He could see the Daemon in Damek's eyes now. It glittered with malevolence and thirst. It spoke of pain and destruction. 'Can you control it?' Kaleo asked uncertainly.

Damek said nothing. He bent down to scoop Arial up into his arms. He lay her down gently on the bed, placed one last kiss on her silken-covered forehead and faced the window. His grief was starting to drown in something else, something stirring deep, deep within him.

'Today, I feast on shadows.'

Chapter 18

Pestilence

Izyan had never seen a force like this before. They could be defeated, these little swarming ants with their sticks and stones, but it was the greatest host he had ever seen at one single time and he was thrilled beyond reason.

He could see the others were too and he had to try to keep them at least a little calm. All these stinking bags of tender flesh and bone so eagerly amassed to be torn apart. All the innocent faces, all the unfulfilled dreams.

Most of the surface of the planet was dotted with armies. Some small, some giant in comparison; these each filled with would-be warriors who would try to defeat them. Izyan smiled a cold, hard smile. He would have them fighting each other before the day was out. He would fill their hearts with such terror and doubt that they would turn on each other like the weaklings they were. They would feast upon one another's flesh and stab their brothers in the night while they slept.

Esyago had been sent for the girl. Soren believed her important in some way. That was the human in him but Izyan had kept his thoughts to himself. Let him have his petty feuds if it meant that he would lead them across the span of the universe, bloodshed and destruction left in their wake.

Malik was coming from another angle with the greater part of the army and from there they would spread like the plague. They would fill this land with darkness; sow the seeds of fear and dissent. Blood would flow, green land and blue ocean would be black, sky would be smoke, the stars would cease to shine and Izyan would make an army of limbless soldiers to bear witness to the horror.

He swept down low over the treetops. He had sent some of his own to inspect the northern forests but they had not yet returned. Suddenly, screams filled the canopy, the cries of wraiths.

He could hear mighty branches snap as beasts were brought down, their roars of pain giving testament. No matter, losses would be had. He signaled for the others to follow him and not go down to inspect, as the shrieks grew higher in pitch before they were abruptly cut off altogether. He could see the glittering host of the High Elvin army on the horizon across the sea. Like so much gold-plate spread across it. He urged his beast on faster, pulling at its glistening skin and digging his heels in while it snorted and spat in protest. Today he would taste elvin flesh and victory would be his.

*

The naizhan were an ancient people. Their history went back to the dawn of time when their planet was the first to see creatures crawl from the swamps to breathe air. They grew wings, grew stronger bones, grew longer fangs. They started to swing from the trees and jump across the land. Soon, they started to walk upright and make tools. Much later they learnt to meld these tools to their bodies. They became their own gods, they recreated themselves. There were no rules, only progress. There was no limit to what an individual could achieve using what he had already been given at base-level. Procreation was forgotten, DNA could be far better encoded by pre-programmed systems.

They would fight the kuvuta not for freedom or love of land and home; they would fight them because they did not belong in the system and needed to be destroyed before further contamination occurred. The old fleshling king had not even needed to call them. The naizhan had gone to him, knowing him to be statistically the most likely leader to gather an army.

Now here they stood. Their ancient cousins, the kikubwa, stood behind them. They would be the second wave, to pick up anything the naizhan had missed.

They had agreed to fight for five hours and rest for three. This was calculated as the most efficient use of energy resources yielding the best result.

Rows upon rows of glittering giants stood steadfast in the face of the oncoming swarm. Illegal weapons were loaded, extra ammunition was shared, red eyes gleamed in the darkness, and not a single sound was made. The kuvuta came charging at them and it was too late before the wraiths realized that this was unlike any race they had ever encountered before. Had they fallen upon a normal naizhan citizen, they would have perhaps found a weak spot; an eye made of gelatin and nerves, a limb perhaps that the individual wished to keep, but these naizhan were built for the battleground. Computer-equipped brain-ware working alongside their natural brains gave them the ability to calculate faster, move more swiftly, but still have the initiative and reflex of a sentinel. No flesh was exposed; all was encased inside the solid metal that could be found on their planet alone. Simulated and controlled micro-stars had to be used to melt the special metal and the planes were chaotic enough to give total flexibility yet total protection. Weaponry was designed to take out maximum numbers with minimum effort and energy usage. These beings, it seemed, were bred to do this. Ironic then that this was their first war. It would also be their last.

The kuvuta reigned down upon them, spewing forth shadows and black fog. Naizhan heat sensors cut through their veils so flesh could be found and bone could be broken. Armor kept the shadows from the lungs and skin of the naizhan and it seemed they were an impenetrable force. Soon, the wraiths were surrounded. The naizhan mowed them down like grass underfoot. They sucked up the shadows, pumping them deep into the ground that would be wasted soon enough anyway and then the kikubwa had their turn...these beasts who had stolen from them, stolen life. They would pay now. Backs were broken by bare hands, shrieking beasts trampled and flung and black blood was stamped into the ground by the angry mobs.

When the waves eventually stopped coming and the shadows seemed to steer clear, the naizhan began to hunt.

*

The Abenaki were a fierce tribe. The most barbaric of the Four Stars, the most feared for their darker rituals and brutal ways. Cannibalism ran in a few, sacrifices were made of sentinel flesh and they worshipped the crueler, harsher gods than their sister tribes did. Their faces were painted with the angry red and orange clays of their lands and their spears were sharp and deadly. Some had carved for themselves fangs out of their teeth and wore the hair, bones and skins of their foes, fashioning themselves fearless, but when the darkness came at last; it was more frightening than even the bravest of them had imagined.

The shadows swooped down without penitence. Cowardly fighters. They stayed high and flew low randomly and in packs. The jaws of their beasts snapped and ripped at flesh like demons on wing, dripping toxic liquid onto those who survived, and carrying the rest up high, while those below watched in horror as they were tossed about like toys and eaten alive. Blood literally rained down and soon it seemed as if every warrior cried red tears and leaked red sweat.

The plan had been to lure the kuvuta near and low, and run toward the mountains as if in retreat. The mountains they ran to were the domain of the perions. And it seemed their plan was working. Once the kuvuta were within range and their retreat blocked by the narrow, jagged pass, the perions rolled massive boulders down the mountainside. They flew with such speed and velocity that anything caught in their path was instantly crushed.

The Abenaki clung to the face of the cliffs and prayed out loud that all the rocks flew true and did not roll slow enough to catch them at the base. Soon, it was realized, that this trick would only work so many times and the kuvuta learnt quickly. Then the fighting engulfed them. Abenaki and kuvuta alike being crushed by the rolling boulders that the perions had started hurling with their bare hands, and shoving with their great horns, to save time. After a while, lifeless and mangled perion bodies joined the rocks that fell from above and the scales were severely tipped in the shadow's favor.

Queen Maitea looked around her in dismay. Her warriors were falling in whichever direction she looked, the ground becoming thick with their lithe bodies. She was protected by the snake, of that she was sure. No beast would eat her and live and that thought alone gave her comfort.

She thrust her spear deep into the belly of a snapping, winged giant and stepped quickly aside as its entrails spewed forth, noxious smoke seeping out of the wound. The kuvuta landed lightly on his feet beside his dying beast and snarled. It was a sound from her darkest nightmares. She gripped her spear tighter and began circling the foul creature. She dodged a torn leg that fell heavily at her feet and used the slain beast as a wall between them. He had no weapons, no blades, no illegal arms, nothing save his claws and fangs, the darkness he breathed. He was calm, enjoying the chase while she struggled to concentrate.

She faked to her left and planted a foot firmly on the body of his creature, pushing up with all her might and bringing her spear into a double-handed grip. She coiled in the air and came down directly in front of him, mouth open in a battle cry she learnt as a young princess from her war-mongering uncle.

The kuvuta merely cocked his head to the side, watching her slow progress through the air, sidestepping her as she landed.

Her spear was stuck in the ground now, firmly, where moments before there had been a wraith. Before she could spin around and face her foe, a terrible force collided with her back and pushed through her stomach. Her knees buckled below her as her spine snapped and only this loathsome thing poking out through the middle of her was holding her up; a clawed fist. The nails were twisted and the parts of her where flesh met his skin burnt like all the seventeen hells her people believed in. She cried out silently, her mouth a giant O. He snarled again, pulling her backward so he could make that hateful sound right in her ear.

A voice broke through her pain, cut through the darkness swirling around her.

'They are here! THEY ARE COMING!'

Maitea did not think she could take any more ill news. What was here? *Acanacra* himself? Come to claim her as his own and drag her limp form to the underworld? But no, this cry was one of hope. And she dared to hope in that moment, to believe in more than just the pain that consumed her, the hatred that burned like an unquenchable thirst inside her. She raised her head to the sound; a young Brule' warrior. Her thighs were burnt black from initiation. The woman was pointing upward, a mad smile upon her blood-stained face. Maitea followed her finger, lifting her face to the heavens in a last act of faith. And there they were, glorious beasts with leathery wings and fiery breath. There were *so many* of them!

Maitea sighed. It was her last breath. She did not waste it in terror for the ears of her enemy nor did she waste it on the battle for another. She let loose what air in her remained so that another may breathe it in and feel the same peace that she felt now.

The Blood Angels were here, the dreya queen had spoken true.

*

Shield Adare' can hold off an attack for twenty minutes, perhaps longer. They cannot hold full power for any longer than thirty, they cannot protect entire armies, you cannot inflict harm upon the enemy any better than he can inflict it upon you while you are in that protective shield; it is simply there to cover a retreat or protect innocents from magic wielded by our Adare'…there are many more that are in greater need than you, we are sorry.'

Ramroth's head was swimming. The amount of pleas coming in from all over the planet were phenomenal. His Telepathic Adare' were supposed to be filtering the information. Instead, they were bringing it all to him, making *him* decide who received aid and who did not. Ramroth did not scold them too harshly though; it was no easy task that he had given them. He restricted each to a narrower area for a shorter period of time so that they would be less bombarded. He had already sent his best Pathfinder to the perion mountains. They were out in the open, trapped from above and below. They needed a way out and fast. He had three groups of Fire Starters in the field, positively wreaking havoc. He was yet to unleash Toireann and Demond. He was going to wait until the kuvuta had decided to land in substantial numbers in some place. For now, it was mostly an air assault and escape routes and shields were working the best.

Lore was working down at the palace district some three hundred miles away. A level Three Teleporter had taken him there and returned in two-point-three seconds. Ramroth was thrilled and set her to work on the rest right away. Some were coming back now.

Blair was drenched in sweat. He guzzled an entire liter of water before he was cautioned to drink no more.

'Are you able to go out again?' Ramroth asked, 'the Doirya need you to create an *inviting* path…' Ramroth asked.

Blair smiled mischievously before replying indignantly,

'I am fine; perion goat-men are heavy is all!'

Ramroth let them all laugh, have their moments of fame, beg to be sent out into the field and prove themselves. The time was a-plenty. What most did not understand, was that this was going to be a battle of wits, of endurance. It would not be over for days yet. They would be tired, hungry and thirsty but unable to slake any of these desires since they suppressed their magical ability. Lack of sustenance only enhanced it in fact, and they would be baying for Ramroth's blood before the end, before they had seen what he could drive them to accomplish.

He had been told from roaming scout parties that his Telepaths were doing well. He had them drilling the Seers minds. The plan was to tap into their thought-streams, follow them back to the source and then hammer the beasts until they collapsed. With fewer eyes, the enemy would be weakened.

Shouts of panic went up somewhere nearby, disturbing all thoughts of progress and Ramroth rushed over. It was Elezar. One of the Transporters had brought him back from half-way across the world and he was badly burnt.

'What happened here?' Ramroth asked the Teleporter in hushed tones. He did not want to cause a stir within the encampment if he could help it.

'An accident High Adare',' came the reply, 'he got caught in the fire of a *Blood Angel*.'

The boy's eyes were so wide you would never have guessed that his comrade was close to bleeding to death. Ramroth wondered darkly who had leaked the secret information, but she had managed it, Arial had called them as she said she would, as she was destined to do, and Ramroth was so overjoyed that he grabbed a random Healer by the sleeve and thrust her in the general direction of Elezar without a word.

'Tell me exactly what happened,' Ramroth demanded.

'They came swooping out of the sky like…like angels!' the Teleporter gushed, 'they are twice as big as the black beasts and I swear it, ten times as strong. Elezar was in the eye of the storm and his black robes swirled around him just like smoke because of the gravity loss and they must have mistaken him - '

'Never,' Ramroth interrupted, 'they would never have mistaken him and even if they did, he would not be here to tell the tale.'

The Teleporter was silent for a moment and Ramroth cut him off before he could speak again, 'Warn the others to stay out of the Blood Angels' way. I shall ask the Telepaths to spread the word immediately. Wherever *they* are, we need not be.'

Next set of youngsters in, after the Teleporter had scuttled away with his precious news, was Seme and Esti. They were flushed with effort but both were smiling in triumph.

'She set fire to more than a hundred wraiths and I flooded the Marshal Plains,' Seme gushed, 'I can *drown* them!'

Ramroth smiled gently and guided the two to the refreshment tent.

'Be careful,' he warned when he left them, 'over-confidence is as much your enemy as the kuvuta.' And how true his counsel would prove in the moments to come.

Another cry sounded from not too far away and again, Ramroth rushed toward the sound. He pushed the throng of Adare' aside and elbowed his way to the middle.

Toireann. He held in his arms a broken and bloodied Demond. Blood tracked across his cleya face like a tiger's prints and his eyes were wide. His mouth kept opening and closing and every now and then, someone around him would scream as Demond's body convulsed so violently that you could hear bones crack and sinew snap.

Ramroth stood before the kneeling cleya, something more than rage possessing the wizard's features. His worst suspicions come true it seemed.

'You go too far Toireann,' he said, low enough for no one else to hear. Toireann could utter no words. Just the same blank expression and no words to join it.

Ramroth snatched the Adare' from the Illusionists arms before the whole crowd had to witness the horrid spectacle and hissed at an onlooker,

'Do not let him speak until I return!'

He stalked away from the circle and made for the solid wall of darkness that surrounded their camp now, that the stars had set again, and there was no light to breach the gaps in the dark clouds. He did not need to see where he was going; he did not need anyone else to see where he was going either.

Toireann; foolhardy idiot. He had cost someone their life with his stubborn streak. He had wanted to go out and attempt an air-illusion. Ramroth had forbid it, telling him to stay with his people until he was called. No, it always had to be done his way.

The body he held convulsed again, the neck breaking in the process this time, bloody froth from Demond's mouth running down Ramroth's sleeves. Ramroth lay the Adare' down on the cool grass and said a quiet prayer for him. Something had come to claim his body and Ramroth would have to end it for him. He struck up a flame and it burned brightly over Demond in that brief second of violent light. His body had become a nesting ground for evil. Beneath his skin, things the size of Ramroth's arm twisted and wriggled, feasting on the lovely, soft entrails and organs within, fighting for the most tender parts.

Ramroth lowered his flame and brought it closer to Demond's face. He was conscious again; face so bleak he could have been dead for hours already. His gentle eyes pleaded silently, filled with a pain Ramroth could only imagine and he needed not one more second to decide. He brought down his fire with such force, driven from grief and hatred, that he surprised even himself.

Ramroth inspected the smoldering corpse and poked at the hatchlings still encased within the body. They did not stir. Ramroth rolled the body over and saw, through the torn clothing, the blackened veins spreading from the orifice where the live-young had been planted. He held his composure for one maybe two seconds before he threw up all over the grass beside the host.

He had suspected that the kuvuta grew in numbers this way. They had no females that he had ever seen or heard of, so what womb could they use save the body of another? Ramroth's thoughts traveled to Soren, the monster at the heart of it all, and how he had allowed his dark race to grow. How many had been given to the cause he wondered, how many had had to endure this horrific death? Ramroth fought the urge to vomit again.

When he traveled back to the light of the camp, he went to go see Toireann, not because he was angry or because he needed to exact a reason for the madness, but because Toireann would need to beg forgiveness from someone who would only forgive him if they saw he *truly* meant it and not just on a whim to silence him. Someone who knew the extent of his error.

*

It was dawn again, the second day of darkness. The only way Dafina could tell was by the smell of it. She hung over the railing of her mighty ship, weary but not willing to close her eyes just yet. The fight had been raging for the whole of yesterday and most of the night. Her armada hovered over the palace district, the warsaur and Gau tribe battling the last of the legions that had been sent to the palace beneath her and her crews. She had seen the swarms approaching like something out of a nightmare. They were upon them before she could get her people properly prepared and in their battle-positions but it made no difference.

Cannons were fired, smashing small holes through the nigh impenetrable cloak of black around them. They flew by on their ugly creatures and snatched fistfuls of pirates right off the decks. Ropes were strung down; suicide missions took place, brave men hanging on with one hand, slashing wildly at the beasts with the other. More gun shots were fired every second than she thought she had heard in her entire life at space. Projectile nets were launched to snare the beasts, but they just shifted through them, and an empty space was left where they had been moments before. The tazers did not seem to have an effect on them either. It was as if they were made of something other than flesh, yet when one was injured, blackened blood poured out. It was madness. It had been like fighting against a solid wall. Where one fell, more kept coming.

The numbers started to thin out eventually but that was for both sides and before they knew it, they were back to square one, with even less resources and strength than moments before. Fire, they soon learnt, did better than most weapons simply because the wraiths were too quick for them. Clothing was torn and stuffed down bottlenecks, lit and sent flaming into the night sky. Two of her ships had burnt down, pieces of flaming wood sailing away, screaming star pirates going down with them.

How utterly helpless they had been for the better part of the battle. Just when she believed they would be overrun by sheer numbers, her prayers were answered. The dreya had come. They shone like beacons in the shadow, flame cutting giant holes into the fleeing foe. They lit the sky like a chorus of angels. Dafina knew she would never see anything like it ever again. The riders looked like they had trained their entire lives to do just this one thing. The way they dived and swooped and banked right back out, their flawless formations and their fearless faces. The fire the dreya bellowed forth seemed to cling to the air, spreading through it, feeding on it and only dying out minutes after. A sea of writhing fire in a sea of retreating shadow. Blows simply glanced off the dreya scales, their roars mercifully drowned out the terrible shrieks of the wraiths, and their talons could cleave a kuvuta clean in half. They glided through the air as if finding a path already marked out, especially for them. Tails flicked, fire rolled, great wings pumped and all was chaos and death.

That had been hours ago. The wraiths had been driven off and the people had been left in the wake of those magnificent beasts and their riders who had come in their time of need, blazing a trail in pursuit and leaving without a word.

Strange, how Dafina had expected silence then, after the deafening sounds of battle had traveled on. But she had been foolish. Men and women wailed in agony, others shouting orders, masts hammered into quick repair, great fires roaring in the distance, and the cruel hiss of protest it gave as it was smothered by water. Dafina took a deep breath and gathered her wits. She needed to report to Admiral Runako and she needed to have a full account of the losses when she did. She walked her deck, clipboard in hand, marking off the dead and dying. She knew the cries would haunt her till the day she died. They were a strong people, a harsh people. They knew no home save the wood they stood on and held little pity in their hearts for those among themselves stupid enough to get killed, but this was different…in this they had no choice.

"Just fucking KILL ME!" and *"Don't TOUCH me! It's INSIDE MY HEAD!"* rang out across the decks. Medics poured buckets of blood over the railings, mops merely painting the wood red and nothing more. Her hands were shaking by the time she was done on just her own ship and she dispatched others to tally the remaining ships.

As she stood staring at a man she knew well, clutching his mangled face and moaning softly, rocking back and forth, two Adare' appeared behind her. She spun around, not being used to this kind of magic. It was a young girl and a man who had brought her.

'My name is Seme,' the girl said. Dafina estimated she could not have been older than her own daughter and wondered what she was doing in a place like this. 'The water is already being poisoned by the kuvuta; you must not drink from the rivers anymore,' the young mage said.

Dafina raised her eyebrows.

'Well then I hope you have some alternative, magic slinger, for my men must drink somehow, we must clean the wounds…' she gestured at the bodies propped up at funny angles all around her with an exasperated look on her face. Seme, also looked on at the horrors, and her delicate face drew together as if she wanted to cry but managed not to.

'I will make you water,' she said quietly. She drew a flask out of her robes and held it out for the star pirate to inspect. 'This will be adequate for your ships and all their men.'

Dafina nearly started laughing but stopped herself when she saw that the Adare' was serious.

'What, this? You must think me a fool,' Dafina said, shaking the flask up and down in front of Seme's face.

'Bring me a larger container,' was the only reply she got.

Dafina narrowed her eyes and snapped her fingers. A sailor stopped in his tracks and came running over. Dafina said something to him in such accented Udaranese that Seme had no idea what she had asked. A tub was brought out a few seconds later, Dafina's bathtub.

'Show me,' she challenged, her eyes still slits. Seme did as she was bid, uncorking the flask and tipping it upside down.

'We bottled clean water before they came. We knew this would happen,' Seme was explaining, 'there should be enough for everybody...'

Dafina was no longer listening. The flask should have been empty by now but water kept tumbling out of it as if some great dam was contained within it.

Seme saw the look on her face and hurriedly tried to explain further,

'I take a little pure water and I expand it. It will not quench your thirst as well as it should because it is thinner, but it will do. It is all we have.'

Dafina nodded and tried to look composed as she stared at the full tub of water before her and the still full flask.

'How much can you...stretch it by?' she asked slowly.

Seme shrugged her shoulders;

'As much as I want until it simply becomes a gas.'

'How long will this...moderately-stretched water last us, Seme?' Dafina asked, frowning.

Seme looked a little afraid before she answered,

'Four days. That is calculating at its current form. Four days.'

'Four days...' Dafina said under her breath. From what she had seen last night, she wondered if anybody would survive that long or, alternatively, if they could hope to defeat the great darkness in such a short time.

'It will be enough,' Seme said, placing her small, cold hand over Dafina's.

The man behind them lurched violently.

Dafina ran over to him and placed the back of her hand over his forehead.

'He has a fever,' she said, looking up at Seme as though the water-bringer must now heal the sick too. Seme moved forward and sank down to her knees, a troubled look on her face.

'He looks -' she began.

'He looks what?' Dafina yelled, afraid of the tone in the young woman's voice. Seme looked up at Dafina and her eyes were wide.

'I think they have used him as a host,' she whispered.

'What do you MEAN they've used him as a host!?' Dafina bellowed. She made to reach for the sailor but he convulsed again, his mouth open in a silent scream. His back looked like it was being pulled at the spine from above and below. It arched at such a terrifying angle that Dafina could scarcely look. Her hands flew to her mouth and shock stilled her string of curses.

Seme gingerly pushed him over to inspect his rear, but when the things started to move beneath the skin, she yelled for fire and snatched her hands away.

Several others rushed over. A few said out loud the cusses that Dafina had wanted to say, some crossed themselves and made the Sign. Only two were brave enough to pour rum over the body and then only one could bring himself to throw a match on his writhing comrade.

They all stood back and watched the man writhe and scream, watched as his skin melted away while he still twisted like a man possessed. There was silence on the ship now and neighboring vessels were edging closer so that the other crewmembers could see what was happening, what all the fuss was about, and why a man was on fire. Someone wanted to throw water on the now smoldering embers but Dafina caught his hand and shook her head.

'We cannot spare it,' she said. She looked at Seme and Seme stared back. 'Fire then?' she asked.

Seme nodded her head;

'Yes, you need to tell the others.'

*

Umar had a plan. There was a group of humans that had been causing trouble for two days now. They were equipped with heavy artillery; massive cannons, automatic-rifles, tazers strong enough to bring down a beast and long-range explosives. Umar had received a message about their whereabouts at long last. They were resting up for the day in the weak noonday light on the plains to the west of the mountain range. How to sneak up on them was the question now. If the humans saw them, they would launch a full counter-offensive and the mission would be useless. Umar decided that they would instead, sneak through the forest to their rear.

One of his captains had voiced his disapproval almost immediately. His argument was that the humans would not have taken refuge so close to the forest if they were not sure that it was safe. Murmurs of approval greeted this statement. There had been rumors of things in the forest, above and below ground. No one could give a proper account or sufficient evidence. It was starting to become an annoyance. Whatever the case was, the forests were being given a wide birth at this point and many now argued against an attack straight through one of them.

Umar had scowled deeply and clenched his fists so tightly that blood had oozed from his palms.

'We cannot go high for these drey-beasts and we cannot go low for you are all too afraid,' he gestured widely. *'Are* you afraid?' he asked after a pause. No one spoke, no kuvuta was ever afraid and so, it was decided.

They were on foot, leading their beasts by crude metal rings through their nostrils. Not a sound was made and everyone, including Umar, was a little jumpy. The forest, too, was unnaturally quiet. No annoying birds sang, the stream seemed to have run dry and all the little animals were holding their breaths, or so it seemed to Danja. He thought that he would rather be airborne and take his chances with a living, breathing enemy that he could see and try kill, than walk through a forest that scared him with its mere simplicity. Something was happening, of that he was almost sure. He chanced a sideways glance at the lieutenant. Stern faced, tight-lipped. Umar had always been too quick to make rash decisions and one day, Danja thought bitterly, he would pay the price for it.

They walked slowly at first but with every few yards covered without incidence, the lieutenant's courage grew. His impatience grew too as his need to achieve his goal burned inside him. And the pace quickened. Soon, the forest had smothered them in darkness, their companions' far overhead, and the natural canopy yielding almost no light. This was when their eyesight was at its best and Danja started to relax a little. At least he would see the fool brave enough to come for him. That was all that really mattered.

His beast snorted and veered off to the right a little. Danja yanked him so hard that blood dripped down onto his hand from the creature's nose. He did not care.

He was looking around more closely now that the stars weren't obscuring his vision. There were claw-marks on the bark of the trees that clustered around the crude path they walked.

'Perhaps we should stay off the path?' Danja suggested to no one in particular and no one listened anyway. He stopped for a moment and placed his hand over one of the markings. His claws fit perfectly and a small shiver went up his spine. This was ridiculous, he thought angrily. He was kuvuta, he was not afraid of anything, only everlasting light. He drew back from the tree and noticed that the scratch marks ran all the way down and across the ground. He followed them for a little while until they abruptly stopped, a small mound of disturbed ground marking the end. Danja frowned.

'We keep moving!' Umar shouted out to his kuvuta battalion. Most were lagging behind by now. Umar was becoming uneasy and that made him angry. He pulled hard at his beast but it did not want to continue. Umar's temper had reached its limit when the beast started to snort and paw at the ground. He drew his sword and felled its head in one clean stroke. Umar looked wildly about him at any others who were acting out similarly and cut off four more heads before the creatures decided they would rather suffer in silence.

Danja had silenced his own beast with his hand. As much contempt as he had for it, he did not want to be without it. Something had happened in these forests and he was becoming less and less inclined to find out what. The atmosphere was becoming very tense. Danja was looking about for others who might be feeling the same as he; run, face the consequences later. Being afraid and not wanting to die, Danja convinced himself quietly, were two completely different things. Then he saw the movement beneath the ground and in an instant, he was not so sure anymore. He stopped where he was, just staring at the ground where moments before, he could have sworn, something moved beneath it. He could now feel Lieutenant Umar's eyes boring into the back of his head but he did not care. Nothing would make him take one more step, nothing.

Umar slowly took out his whip. Enough was enough. He would show them that they would do as he said, no matter the cost, and they would not be afraid of anything other than him. The metallic spikes at the end of his cruel whip clicked together like tiny, bloodthirsty animals as he moved closer to the fool who had halted the march. He cracked the whip backwards and still, the offender did not move. Umar brought the instrument down hard and Danja's knees buckled beneath him. He made not a sound and Umar whipped him five times before he got the first syllable out of him and it was not a stammered apology laced with pain, nor a cry for help. Danja was laughing. Laughing and pointing at the ground in front of him.

Umar lowered his whip and tried to make out what was funny. Upturned soil; that was all it was. Like something had perhaps tried to dig a hole and failed. The other kuvuta who had all stopped to watch the punishment were also trying to see the source of the incessant laughter. They thought all they could see was soil too, until it moved...

Something was emerging from the very ground where the punished wraith's face lay inches from. His laughter had become even more frenzied and as they watched, a great creature emerged from the ground in one foul movement, grabbing Danja with its impossibly long claws, soil clods flying and then, it was gone, so fast that if you blinked for more than a second, you would have missed it, back into the soil from whence it came, Danja gone with it.

Now the wraith's beasts were going wild; some had flown away, the rings being torn from their noses in an effort to keep them grounded. Some were rearing up, snorting so madly that great globules of black spit leaked form their noses and mouths. Panic was not far away for their riders either. There was a stunned silence while everyone looked around wildly.

Umar waited, sword in hand, for the next one to leap from the ground. He would cleave it in two and show this creature from below what he was dealing with. Silence...

...And then the attack began.

Wyrm after wyrm sprang from the ground, claws slashing wildly at the air. They could smell where the wraiths stood from down below but if they had moved by the time they broke surface, they had to find them by touch alone. They screeched wildly, a pitch that not even the kuvuta could boast. Blind eyes seeming to lock onto a victim as easily as if they could see. They grabbed each one and pulled them down into the ground like twigs in a sand pit.

Umar was horrified at the speed and grotesquery of this new enemy. They were large too, twice as large as any of them, and they had the strength of twenty. Kuvuta clawed uselessly at the soft ground around them, crying out wildly like pigs to the slaughter.

Umar's face was grim, his fist tightened around his blade and he readied himself for death. It came swiftly; it even looked as if it had a smile on its face as it grabbed him. He dropped his blade and concentrated all his effort on trying to stay above ground for who knew what would happen once they had you beneath. He grabbed at roots and they snapped, he grabbed at staunch grassy tufts and they gave way effortlessly, burning his hands like fire. Umar grabbed a fallen blade, lying on the forest floor that rushed past him. He saw his comrades going down, arms flailing wildly, fear in their eyes. It was all becoming a blur and Lieutenant Umar thrust the knife deep inside his own neck. The blood poured cold and black as his vision swam in and out of focus. His last sensation was of his feet giving way to soft ground, his legs becoming cold with the damp soil, the sharp sting of teeth biting into his flesh and then...mercifully, nothing.

Chapter 19

Famine

The High Elves had fought in wars before, not so many as the Drows perhaps, but enough to know that discipline and superiority in force, and not necessarily numbers, was what counted most in the end. This, the High Elves had. The energy they harnessed was used for more than just feeding themselves and keeping creature comforts. They mined the best metals, they harnessed the best technology and they were supreme in their fighting force. No armor could stand up to the weaponry they wielded and they trained hard to be the swiftest and most steadfast.

General Carrick had eased his grip on his halo-blade that first morning as he watched the enemy amassing. There were so many of them that they darkened the skies with their foul smoke and wings. The High Elves to his right and left had done the same, relaxing their minds and sharpening their senses. Battle-dances came from deep within and the less one thought, the more grace with which the moves came.

The cloud had grown, the hum of war growing with it. Carrick had adjusted his battle armor, the skin-suits that were coveted by so many. It clung to his massive form like an expertly spun web and he derived great comfort from it.

When the two armies met, it was a perfectly pitched battle. Both sides were quick and agile, both were formidable to almost any other, but pitted against one another, it was a hard battle to win. The black beasts seemed to have more substance to them and were hooked and snared by the invisible energy nets far easier than the kuvuta who rode them. Once the kuvuta were down though, the real battle began. The combat skills of every High Elf was tested like never before and they realized that they had under-estimated their enemy despite all of Altair's warnings.

That had been the first day. It was now dusk of the third and still the kuvuta came in relentless waves. It was near exhausting but none of Carrick's men showed any signs. They all kept themselves clean, recharged and ready. Discipline. The only way to stay sane in a world of darkness and blood. They burned their dead every morning, prayers were said and nothing was forgotten. In a few minutes, the battle lines would be fairly gleaming with rows upon rows of High Elves ready to lay down their lives, as they had been the day before and the day before that.

Carrick was a proud man then, watching the still faces ready for combat, their brilliant form on the field, and the militaristic attitude even in such a peace-loving nation. The cloud had formed as it did every morning and Carrick knew it was Izyan that led them; oldest perhaps of all the kuvuta, save Lord Nagesh himself. It seemed that his sole task was to hammer the High Elf Alvar into near extinction but Carrick was having none of it.

'CHARGE!' he bellowed. And his legions had fallen upon the kuvuta armies without mercy. Hundreds were slain on the third day with a savagery unrivaled. Their halo-blades cut through wraith-shadow like butter. Pulse-bows were used to clear space when too many fell upon any single elf. They were able to vault and dodge more often than not, but if surrounded by too many wraiths, pure force would be the elf's undoing.

Carrick nearly died such a death, but he parried every thrust beautifully, beating back attacks from every side. His skin-armor gave him a lot of flexibility save in the small of his back and he was half a second too late for a kuvuta from behind. The wraith had launched himself off his beast and fell upon Carrick, cleaving a neat scratch in his upper arm with his demon-blade. Carrick had pulled his sword up and out of the last wraith he had slain and severed the head off the attacking kuvuta in one, clean, practiced movement.

By the time the darkness had been pushed back again, many had died. General Carrick had regrouped and counted all lost. A few hundred at most when hundreds more of the enemy lay shattered beneath their feet. Carrick sighed. He knew that this was but a tenth of the full force the kuvuta wielded. He knew all too well of the sufferings of others...

Prince Alarico traveled among the others and brought news daily. He was with his family mostly in their hidden location in case the rabble armies decided upon revenge against the wrong people.

The High Elf Alvar was resting after the savage battle when Alarico's voice sought Carrick out in the throngs;

'Carrick! There you are. I find you always in the heart of your army.'

Carrick laughed grimly and responded,

'Would that I were the heart.' Alarico saw the cut on his arm and his expression darkened. Carrick waved his concern away. 'Tell me,' Carrick continued, changing the subject, pulling Alarico to one side and dismissing his guard with a polite gesture of the hand, 'how is your father? Is your mother well?'

'They worry,' Alarico replied wearily, 'there is so much suffering...'

General Carrick frowned.

'Yes. I have seen as much. We try to move often, we do not like to linger with our dead but it seems others do not share our feelings,' he said.

Alarico nodded and said,

'I have also seen this. They do neither burn nor bury their dead. It is as if they will themselves to be the same; dead and forgotten.'

'Perhaps they do not want to forget,' Carrick suggested. 'In any case, it is not healthy and we try to help them but they become aggressive when we do.'

'Who are the main culprits?' Alarico asked carefully.

Carrick shrugged;

'Mostly the weaker tribes of the Four Stars. The ones they do not have direct command over and are not used to such things.'

Alarico looked around him at the wounded and the piles of dead, their dark bodies glistening with fuel for the burning.

'I doubt if any of us are,' he muttered. The prince was quiet for a moment before he leaned in closer to his general and added, 'The people become restless. I have seen men mutiny, and fine soldiers turned renegade, be put to the sword as example. They say they feel "trapped" by the shadow, as if in a dream and long to be free from it. Their despair grows with every day beneath these dark skies and I fear that madness will be our undoing. These people who sit and watch as their dead rot. They do not drink, they do not speak. The ground grows black, the rivers churn into sludge and all the while, their hope dies with everything else. Fights breaking out over water and food, restless sleep snatched before the next horn is blown and they must stand; ready to fight like warriors fallen from the sky instead of ordinary men with families.' Alarico shook his head as Carrick listened intently to him.

'But there *are* warriors from the sky, Alarico. The dreya queen has done us a great service. We shall win this war with their help. It is true what you say, about the falling of the ranks. Our people fare well enough but there is only so much, as you say, that an ordinary man can take. These dragon warriors fight unlike any other I have seen.'

Alarico nodded in agreement.

'They say there is a band of these drey-warriors that travel from camp to camp, telling inspiring tales to the most down trodden of us. Perhaps I should seek them out?' the prince suggested.

'I think it wise,' Carrick agreed, 'I need some good news too.' He smiled jovially and Alarico laughed, though he did not miss the hidden grimace of pain upon the general's face.

'Another thing,' Alarico said, as he made to leave once more, 'never go without your armor. There is talk of…implants occurring.'

Carrick's expression darkened but he inclined his head and bade his prince farewell.

That night, they were on the move again. They were trying to steer clear of the fires dotting the landscape that marked the camps of others, but sometimes it could not be helped. They spread before his Alvar like a blanket of flickering stars and they had no choice but to venture through them. They headed for a camp that looked like it housed humans and Adare'. Perhaps they would be more welcome here, perhaps not.

As soon as the army came into sight, Carrick realized the full extent of Alarico's words although the soldiers in charge there assured them it was better there than elsewhere.

'Over the way the tribes' men are holding a mass ceremony, burning some of their warriors as sacrifice and trying to consume the kuvuta flesh to gain their power,' one of the humans told him. Carrick was not impressed by this news. He ordered his soldiers to rest for a while and to share what food and water they could. 'We are glad to see you,' the young corporal said, 'it has been hard. Our weapons give little reprieve and mostly it is diminished to hand-to-hand. My people are simply not strong enough. If it were not for the Adare', we would have been done for a long time ago.' His voice was weary and sad. Carrick pitied them, these people from whom they had come. It seemed impossible. There was no use trying to teach them otherwise either, they had chosen their path.

He looked over the man's shoulder and saw two men strung together from a crude post. They looked half-starved to death, beaten and bloodied. He gestured toward them and asked,

'What happened to them?'

'I had their tongues cut out,' the man replied without even looking their way. He looked up at Carrick instead and said, 'They were ranting about the end of the Worlds and how we would never defeat them, saying that they would make a womb out of us all or feed us to their beasts while we still lived.'

'These things do happen,' Carrick said carefully. The human threw his bones into the fire and licking his fingers replied,

'Yes, and we shall not speak of them.'

Carrick stared at the bones blackening in the flames and thought of his fallen comrades. Carrick was soaked with their blood every day, had to piece together the parts of their bodies left uneaten as best he could. The human leaned closer and grabbed Carrick by the collar, his face illuminated by the flames beneath it like an image from hell.

'Fear will kill us before they do...if we let it.' And those were the words that stayed with the general. He thanked the humans and Adare' for their hospitality and ordered his army on the march. Dawn was coming.

'Why do they come with the dawn?' one had asked, 'when they see so poorly by the light?'

'They come with dawn to their backs so their enemies can be blind and then they race into the night to meet them,' was Carrick's reply.

'I do not want to stop at anymore camps,' Carrick had confided to his second in charge. 'We shall gather for news at dusk and avoid all other contact. I will have none of this madness infect my soldiers,' he said gesturing about him wildly. Men had been stuck on posts, blood still leaking out of their mouths. Charred remains were left of those that had been eaten out of pure hunger. They looked like the walking dead, waiting for their time with a savagery that Carrick had never seen before. The light had left the eyes of too many. The atrocities they had seen, and been forced to take part in, had left their mark.

Carrick was surprised at how quickly it had all happened. Then he remembered what his grandmother had always told him as a young boy. She had lived with the Nomad Elves of the Flooded Worlds for a long time. It was always raining there, she had said. The clouds hung low over your head so that you felt you had to constantly stoop to evade their clammy touch. It rained so much that it felt you were being rained into the very ground. Many of the people that were not used to it became subdued and would not talk or eat much. She had said that the rain had gotten to them, made them feel trapped.

"Never let it rain inside your head, Carrick," she had warned, *"for if you let it, all is lost."*

*

General Braenden was in his element. Slaying these dark brutes was like a welcome release. Finally, after months of planning and training and endless talks, he and his men were pitted against a force worthy of their blades. At least that was how the Drows saw it. The High Elves possessed stony-faced calm when the darkness greeted them. Disciplined and flawless. The Drows, however, willed the wraiths closer with their grinning faces and ready swords. Every single Drow was eager for the kill, they thrived on it. Wave after wave broke upon their shields and they laughed all the harder. Butchery. Black blood painted their masked faces as they eagerly climbed over the dead bodies of their own fallen to reach the next shadow-wreathed opponent. Tirelessly they fought until the enemy tucked tail and flew, trying to regroup as the Drows ran after them, hacking at their flanks ruthlessly.

Braenden encouraged the bloodshed. It took their minds off the great losses they themselves had already suffered. By mid-day they rested till dawn, until the war horns raised them. They brought the priests in to burn the dead; they themselves said no prayers and did not mourn the fallen. They were soldiers who had done what any soldier must; kill and be killed.

In their minds, this war would never be won and that was why they did not succumb to the madness. They expected no one to help them or save them. They never expected the sun to rise peacefully again. This was their world now and they reveled in it, living from one battle to the next, one crushed foe to the one who would follow, until they either perished in the fray or marched back to camp. Resolute, without hope and strong because of it.

'Akker,' General Braenden called his captain, 'I grow tired of waiting.'

'Waiting for what General?' the battle-hardened Drow asked.

'For dawn,' Braenden smiled. Three claw marks marred his handsome face now. It gave him a leering, dangerous look.

'What do you propose General?' Akker asked, returning the grin.

'Day raids,' came the cool reply, 'we send squadrons out to follow the wraith retreats. We take them when they are at their weakest.'

'But a few men against an army in retreat?' Akker asked, confusion knitting his brows.

'No, they will form groups, as we do, and we will pick off the ones who hold the lines. We will kill the kuvuta on their own ground. Our ground,' he corrected himself.

Akker seemed to consider this for a moment, fingers working at his lips and jaw.

'I have assassins for just this sort of task. We will have to borrow High Elf armor; it will blend better with the light.'

'You will strip them down and paint them with this clay,' Braenden countered, a fist full of it held tightly in his fist. Akker nodded although he did not much like the sound of it. 'Tell Carrick he can tag along if he wishes, his men will not need much paint.'

They both laughed and Braenden poured a strong herbal tea, that had been brewing for some time, into two cups.

'When do we begin?' Akker asked.

'Today.'

'Very well, I will assemble the men.'

'Good.' Braenden seemed to think for a moment before saying, 'We need to distribute food.'

'To who, General? Our soldiers are all rationed well enough.'

Braenden put his steaming cup down on the floor before him. He did not look up when next he spoke;

'I am not a soft man, Akker, never have been.'

Akker wondered if he was expected to say something but chose instead to stay still for the moment. 'But a hard man can feel pity too,'

Braenden continued, 'and perhaps this is what angers me. Do others need my pity? For if I were they, I would not.' He picked up his cup again and blew softly at the steam, sending it wafting away slowly. 'We know this land well enough now, we know how to live off it, but I fear others less resilient and resourceful than us will perish before long. Whether by pure hunger or the madness that makes a man slay his own because of it.'

There was a silence and Akker decided he was needed to speak now;

'I shall find what food we can spare and send distribution parties out. I shall tell the men that you do not want armies dying on our doorsteps for the beast will grow stronger eating the flesh.'

Braenden nodded carefully, his eyes still not meeting his captain's. The shadows of the great scavenging buzzards that plagued the sky could be seen painted on the sand and Braenden sighed. Yesterday they had marched past a camp in frightful conditions. He wondered how men could fall so quickly into disarray but chose not to linger on all he had seen. He believed there was something else too, that made the people irrational. The magic in the air that was being discharged around the clock was starting to take its toll. It cloaked the stench of the wraiths with its sulphric fumes and sat beneath everyone's skin like an uncomfortable afterthought, and it was clouding the judgments of many a good man. However, it was a necessary trade-off and without it, they would have all perished within the very first day.

'Another thing,' he added, before the captain was out of earshot, 'bring Mirian to me. Our numbers grow weak. Tomorrow she shall have the chance to prove herself.'

*

Camp life. War life. Living from one kill to the next, one fitful slumber to the meager meal that was thrust beneath your weary face. Sweat, blood and dirt worn like a second skin. Holes were dug so that the men could sleep hidden, until the restless sentries sounded the war-sirens. Some had gone mad. Out of frustration, lack of sleep or water, who knew? Blood-drunk savages, who had forgotten their own names in the mindless terror of it all, had been made from once respectable men.

Danel had been grievously wounded in yesterday's battle and Edur had been appointed to take his place. Luken had watched Danel die, battling for each shallow breath as the medics in the fetid tent tried to stem the flow of blood. It was better this way, Danel had told his prince as Luken clutched onto him with clammy hands, what was a man to do with no feet and no hands?

Luken had walked outside when it was over and found Laila waiting for him. She did not make to move like the woman she was. She did not loop her arms around his neck and whisper things into his ear that might chase the shadows away. She just stood there, looking at him as if she alone in all the Worlds could see him, her hair swept by the wind, the sword that hung by her side cleaned meticulously of all black blood. And then she was gone.

'Can you believe this?' Kemen asked. His eye had been lost on the first day and a dirty bandage covered half his face. He stood at one of the many medic-tents dotted around the large camp. He was gesturing towards a long line of grim-faced soldiers who were being led into the darkness within like sheep to the slaughter. Luken wanted to laugh but did not. After all, it was not funny. 'Never in my life have I fought such a foe whereupon return from the field I must bend over, hike up my small clothes and have someone inspect my arse.'

Luken could not help sniggering. Kemen raised his eyebrows in disapproval before he too began to chuckle.

They walked together towards the battle-tent. A new plan was being hatched by the sneaky Drows; day raids. Kemen pushed back the flap and Luken walked into the stuffy enclosure. It seemed that everything smelt like death and disease. Herbs had been handed out to stop the tide of general war-illnesses but many still suffered.

It smelt like shit and fear, like blood and vomit and sweat. Luken wanted to gag.

Five captains sat cross-legged on the swept floor and the two princes sat down to join them.

'Day raids?' a burly Benat warrior fairly cried, 'have they lost their minds!? We shall be sent to the butcher at all hours now!'

Luken ignored him and Kemen frowned deeply.

'The men will not like it,' Edur murmured his agreement.

'We will lead them,' Mikel said solemnly. He spoke for himself and Erromon.

'Foolhardy Savari!' the Benat Captain spat.

'Luken, please control your dog,' Kemen whispered.

Luken smiled and said calmly,

'Madras, please leave the room.'

Madras' face swelled with indignity and he stormed out of the tent.

'Thank you for volunteering,' Luken said to the Savari lieutenants, 'but I will be glad if some of my men accompany you.'

They then spoke of food-rationing and strengthening the watches, but they all knew that the raids would be that which would make all the difference.

After an hour or so, the six remaining men emerged from the tent. Madras was standing on the lip of the poisoned well like a self-proclaimed prophet, yelling about madmen and the plots they hatched. About how the princes would feed them all to the kuvuta and they would never see home again. He was doing a fine job of working the men up and Kemen moved to put a stop to it but Luken held him back. The last thing they needed now was a death on their hands of someone who had decided to speak out. It would confuse the men even more. Fights had already been breaking out, tempers flaring over the smallest of things and Luken had had enough.

He walked over to the well, the man making room for him as he went, and he stood right in front of the heretic, waiting for him to stop and recognize him. He droned on for another minute before he realized the very prince he was insulting stood right before him.

His face contorted into an ugly sneer and he pointed his finger at Luken.

'And here stands the war-mongering dog who will see you all killed so he and his lover, of house Savari, can live alone upon your rich lands.'

There was an intake of breath and a ringing silence as everyone realized that Madras had gone too far. They watched as Luken folded his arms across his chest and met the captain's gaze calmly.

'You say I take my friend, my family, for a lover?' He asked quietly but his voice carried well and everyone heard. Madras' finger started to shake, he pursed his lips and said,

'You are together all the time...you touch each other often and talk much...' It was as feeble an answer as any that could have been given and Luken laughed long and loud, the men joining in with him. Luken vaulted up to stand next to the enraged captain and slung his arm around his shoulder, a broad smile on his face.

'Then I suggest we all wrestle you from your warm xanti, dear Madras, for I fear you spend far too much time with that beast,' he said in a mock-serious tone. Now everyone was roaring with laughter and Madras had gone an even deeper shade of red.

'What of you and your plans to lead us all to death!' Madras screeched. If he was made a fool of in public after making such serious claims, then his argument would count for naught. It was customary among the Four Stars. Luken stopped laughing, a stern expression covering his face. He turned away from the idiot captain and addressed the crowds instead. Quite a few had gathered by now, news of a man's folly traveled fast.

'Yes,' he said solemnly, 'I will lead you to your death.'

Madras looked like he wanted to say something, a triumphant look in his eyes but Luken turned calmly toward him with a finger pressed to his lip and a strange look in his eye. This small gesture miraculously stilled the captain and everyone listened to what the Benat Prince wanted to say.

'Death comes to us all you see; would you not have it for a cause? Would you not have someone lead you there under the banner that proclaims all you stand for, song on your lips and courage in your heart?'

There was silence for a while.

'Madras, perhaps you chose the wrong the words,' he said, turning to the captain again, 'perhaps you want to know why I *send* you to slaughter?'

Madras did not answer.

'Alas, many princes do,' Kemen said sadly, 'but not I, not Kemen. We do battle by your side. The gods sent you to your death by giving you your first breath. I ask only to lead the way there. Be your instrument to greatness.'

Someone shouted something from the sea of faces and Luken nodded, replying,

'Aye, 'tis greater to live than to die, but if you must die…then how be it? Like you lived! Free, strong and with a good leader to guide you!'

A few claps and whoops of approval greeted his statement but he silenced them with upraised hands.

'I lead you into the darkness, I lead you to a terrible death by the hand of an enemy so horrifying that we almost dare not utter the name. I lead you willingly, I watch you spill blood and die for our lands, I watch you as day after day you follow me and you do not question. I plot and I scheme to save your mortal souls, even when I doubt we will ever see home again. I know you bleed, I know you suffer, I know your nightmares are much the same as your waking hours. I watch my people die and I weep night after night as I eat the same food that you do, squat over the same holes you do and take up arms with you. We all die. We all suffer. We all bleed. Except one follows and one leads.'

Luken climbed down from the lip of the well to silence. He walked back through the crowds, to where Kemen stood with a stunned look on his face. Madras was silenced and no blood was spilled in doing so. The men were quiet, all watching Luken with strange looks on their faces.

Kemen hated the god-like silence and broke it by clapping Luken on the arse and saying,

'I think I will check this one myself!'

The spell was broken, all the soldiers rolled on the ground laughing, tears of mirth streaming down their dirty faces. Order or at least some form of normality had been restored.

The two princes walked in silence over to the edge of the mountain where they had made camp for day-light hours.

'Well done prince of pretty words,' Kemen joked.

Luken gave a half-smile.

'Will it last?' Luken asked, 'my words will pale in comparison to what awaits us tomorrow again.'

'But that is exactly the point you made!' Kemen said, 'now they *know* they are going to die, perhaps they will stop worrying so much about it.'

Luken snorted and remarked,

'You would think there was another way.'

Kemen shook his head and said sadly,

'It is like this everywhere; dissension and anarchy. The kuvuta will have us all mad before the end. Besides,' he said darkly, 'it is the time between battles that neither I nor the men can stand. That limbo between here and there. The battle brings us together again, clears our heads.'

'This is what the day raids will bring,' Luken agreed, 'something to hold on to every hour. The battle will never stop until the war is won and that will keep us sane.'

Kemen put his hand on Luken's shoulder and they looked out over the plains.

Two armies rested on the horizon, or perhaps it was just one very large one. They could not tell and argued about it for some time before Kemen brought the argument home saying it was spread out so widely it looked like Luken's mother's backside when she sat down. Luken threw the first punch but Kemen blocked expertly having anticipated the blow. After a few minutes, bruised and a little bloodied, they sat on the grass opposite one another, breathing heavily.

'I saw Laila again today,' Luken said after a while.

Kemen laughed and said,

'Why you do not simply ask for her hand-in-marriage, I shall never know.'

Luken had fallen in love with the auburn-haired beauty the very first time he had laid eyes on her. She was a nobleman's daughter that had stolen away from home to join the war. She was as fine with a sword as any man and better than most. She had been found and brought before Kemen because she was Savari. Luken had been with him and had only needed to give Kemen one look for the Savari Prince to let her go with a mere warning. There were many women warriors, especially among the other tribes of the Four Stars, but the Royal House would be held accountable for commanding a noblewoman in war. They had decided that that could wait until after she had helped them win.

'We have spoken many times, she speaks with such honesty that it makes me afraid sometimes,' Luken said.

'Unlike common wenches who lie about the properties of your manhood,' Kemen snorted.

Luken made a swipe at the sniggering Kemen.

'I love her,' Luken said once the laughter had died, 'she knows my heart like no other.'

'And you know hers?' Kemen asked, straight-faced.

'I want to, like no other. I have already asked her,' Luken added slyly, 'you are the first to know.'

Kemen nodded. His closest friend was engaged and it was custom for him to arrange everything.

'We are at war, you are aware of that?' Kemen asked incredulously.

Luken broke into a wide grin and Kemen arranged for a feast, such as they could muster, to be held within the hour. Tents were strung together and soldiers drew their tiny traveling harps and flutes out of their tunics since the drums would perhaps scare the armies over the way.

Laila and Luken stood beneath the only tree that still survived, spring blossoms borne on the gentle wind, as they said their vows before the army and Kemen, who was as close to a priest that they would find at such short notice. The men drank the last of their wine and ale, merriment was had once again and for a while, tomorrow and yesterday were forgotten.

*

Luken led Laila shyly to his tent.

'I swear, you are blushing more than I,' she said, her hand cupping the side of his face.

'I have known…many women,' Luken began but Laila put her hand gently over his mouth. He did not need to explain to her what she could already see in his eyes.

'Lie with *me*,' she whispered. She stood back and slowly lifted the makeshift wedding dress that the other maiden warriors had made for her, up and over her head. Her hair fell down across her bare chest and shoulders like chocolate into milk, her dark eyes shone with intensity and Luken reached out with unsteady hands.

She let him take his time. He was like a child in the beginning, not knowing where to look, where to touch first. Then, he became the lover she knew he was, once his need for her had overcome his endearing anxiety, expert in all his strokes and satisfying her in so many ways he had to clamp her mouth shut with the palm of his hand for fear of startling the others. The fine silver chains he had placed around her neck at the ceremony tinkled against her skin like a charm.

She let him do that to her again and again. They had no rest that day, pausing only to drink water or stare at each other in awe. This was the first time that they had made love. This might just be the last and they both understood nothing else.

*

The next morning, just before the stars peaked over the plains, they could hear the horns of the neighboring army as the kuvuta descended first upon them.

'They will be here soon,' Luken said, pulling his leather pants on, 'I want you at the back of the line.'

Laila looked at him, mouth open indignantly.

'I will do no such thing! Just because I am your wife does not mean that I will not fight!' She was furiously pulling her armor on and pushing her hair back to fit under her helmet when Luken grabbed her by the arm and said carefully but sternly,

'Yes, but I am your general, and you will do as I say...please.'

'Kemen is my general!' she hurled back but at the smile upon Luken's face, realized her error, for she would be under his banner now and tried another tactic;

'I would that you let me fight as any other. You love all the people but you cannot put them all in the back line.'

Luken nearly shoved her out the tent before kissing her deeply on the lips. He held her to him tightly for the briefest of moments before sending her on her way and yelling after her,

'Stay on the back line!'

Minutes later, and the warriors were lined up, ready to do battle. Every Savari and Benat had horse and xanti now. So many had been killed and had left their clever steeds behind. They charged down the plain toward the other army being attacked relentlessly from above. Luken and Kemen led the charge as usual, all the soldiers hollering and howling behind them. Each one was fighting for something else today; for redemption, for revenge, for peace. They half clattered into the other army, a large host of humans.

The Men of Adam fought bitterly, Kemen reflected as he watched them hack long-time dead wraiths into even more bloody pieces. Kemen reached up and pulled the ankle of a kuvuta flying too low, yanked him hard to the ground, and put a sword through the belly of his off-balance beast. The human beside him on foot, slammed a hammer the size of a kikubwa fist into the wraith's head before spinning around and flame-throwing half a dozen kuvuta close enough to Kemen to singe his eyebrows.

The Savari Prince loved to watch the humans' illegal arms display. They had all sorts of weapons and most rang with the heavy, bulky equipment favored in the fifth human World War. Easy to fix, near unbreakable anyway, but difficult to carry and move around.

'If all else fails,' Luken roared from Kemen's right, mounted upon his frothing xanti, 'you can just smash them over the heads with it!'

Kemen laughed at Luken with his slender Benat bow, pretty leather whips and giant cannon. It had obviously been abandoned on the field and Luken was using it as a mace. Faces cracked open before him, blood spat in all directions and Luken laughed all the more.

The fight took them away from each other for a while. Kemen started to grow tired and dizzy. The stars were climbing higher; soon the wraiths would back off but not for another hour or so. He was thirsty, his limbs ached and he wanted to rest. This was when the most accidents happened. Sweat blurred your vision, sleep made you close your eyes for a second or two and spent adrenaline left you feeling like a puppet with no strings.

Kemen blocked a clawed arm just in time, severing the ugly limb and impaling the owner on his horse's horned helmet.

Bodies were being thrown from the sky now. Bloated and stinking carcasses of all race and creed. Fallen soldiers that the kuvuta had brought all this way! Kemen could have cried out with hatred. He could not help thinking that this was the worst battle they had fought yet.

His horse tried to climb over the dead that lay underfoot like a mountain of unstable, soft rocks and from the corner of his eye, he saw Luken. Blonde hair flying, blue eyes flashing, his leather armbands flapping in the wind like so many banners. Kemen was glad to see him, his heart lifted when the young prince met his gaze across the battlefield. Kemen only had one eye left but luckily it was his good one and even with Luken's *two* good eyes did he not see what Kemen did; a monster of a kuvuta came from behind, towering above the rest. He must be a commander of some kind, Kemen thought insanely. He urged his horse forward, through the masses of dead, his one arm outstretched and mouth open in a yell of warning. It was strange how war made the world silent; not as if you had gone deaf but as if the world refused to listen to what you were doing anymore.

Luken saw Kemen, regal and blood-stained on his shiny black horse. His eyes had been friendly at first glance, even relieved, but now they were wide open in fear, he was yelling something that Luken could only guess at but he would have bet that it was nothing good. He turned around just in time to see the bulky kuvuta that lunged toward him. It held a small, dull blade in its hand. It looked ancient; it looked cruel, like it had killed many more before him.

Luken reached for his long sword. He knew instinctively that keeping a circle around him until help came was the only way he would live through this encounter. All around him, the soldiers were doing so well, all their practiced moves going according to plan, and they were oblivious of him in the midst of their own little worlds.

The wraith lunged and Luken crouched low, thrusting his sword upward but the kuvuta shadow had already moved. It was beside him now and steel kissed as the blades met. Luken's arm shook with the effort of holding him back but he pushed the wraith off after two agonizing seconds. He was tiring very fast now, the sweat pouring from his head and arms. The creature moved with bestial grace and surrounded Luken in its swiftness. Luken hardly had time to see where the next thrust was coming from before he had to block it. He dropped his sword as the tiny blade thrummed against it and sent agonizing pain shooting up his arms and through his bones. His arms were broken, he realized then. No, shattered. Luken looked up at the monster before him and used his arm pads to deflect the next blow, pain cutting through him like a bolt of lightning. The boiled leather was no match for Savrek's demon blade and Luken's arm was cut clean off.

Kemen's face slackened in horror as he watched. He was mere paces away from his friend but it was going to be over before he got there. Savrek raised his fist and struck Luken through the face, teeth and torn skin flying. He plunged the blade down into his heart and swirled away to find his next victim.

Kemen leapt off his horse and onto his knees beside the dying prince.

'Luken!' he cried, brushing wafts of shadow and grit from Luken's face. Warm blood was soaking into his tunic from the artery in the arm and Luken was barely conscious any more. Kemen felt his heart wrench in such utter agony that no words could describe it and no sound could give life to it. His whole body shook in a silent tremor of dread and hatred and love too much for him to understand.

Luken looked up and focused on Kemen blearily for a second before going limp in his arms. Kemen could not move. He saw now all the warriors falling around him, all the faces painted with pain and horror, where before he could have sworn they portrayed fierce determination. The blood ran between the fallen like rivers. Kemen imagined that if he stayed there like that with his departed friend in his arms, the dead would perhaps bury him. They would fall upon him in all their multitudes and he would have to beg forgiveness from them, from their tortured faces and silent screams. That he had led them into this, that he could not lead them out. That they would die in a world of blood and shadow.

Just as he began to truly believe that not one would make it out of this battle alive and they would be condemned to lie forever on this rotting planet, a light broke out above him.

Fire, brilliant fire. It blazed across the sky like the mightiest flag he had ever seen and out of it flew a drey so large it could swallow his horse whole.

Kemen cried then. On his knees in blood and dirt. He cried.

*

While men were going mad, fighting amongst themselves as much as against the enemy, a new name started to rise that made them stop and take stock. Barbarian races had come together to form the powerful arm of guerrilla warfare among the sentinels. The warsaur and the cleya, it was whispered. Masked fiends screeching through the night. A sound that should have given hope but struck fear nonetheless when heard. The drums came first of course, that rhythmic beating that you thought was part of your heart's own until it started to gain pace and your fleshy pump leapt to keep up. The drums.

Faces painted with ash and chalk, eyes red blazes of fury with no mercy in the cold of night and the land held its breath for the first blood to spill...

Armies would walk past landscapes dying, choking on black plague as the corpses of long-dead kuvuta began to immerse themselves into the very ground they had been slain on, like some last act of cruelty. In places like these, the soldiers would find light-footed prints in the mud, like the owners had merely skimmed the surface; so eager were they for the kill. Those prints would lead to the sacred trees that the old elves had planted years ago when they found the planet. They blotted the sky if you stood close enough and could provide you with wood to build a boat for one hundred, if only you could cut it down. These trees were dying, slowly, and perhaps the cleya and warsaur felt pity for the trees and willed them to die faster, perhaps they felt the culprits should be held accountable, perhaps they even wanted to make a sacrifice of them to the mighty trees that had to watch the darkness infect all they had loved and watched over for thousands of years. Whatever the reason, these trees were now home to wraiths, nailed up still living and stripped of their shadows.

If the barbarians could do such things, reduce them to mere mortals again and not mythic beasts from the darkness, then were they really so terrible? Doubt started to form in the minds of all who gazed upon these monuments to reality and some even traveled with bands of others to see them. It represented something like hope only darker. Hope's ugly sister perhaps. All their magic disappeared when they hung like the scrawny pseudo-demons that they were. Hollow cheeks and sunken eyes, sallow skin covered in a thick black gruel that could be slaked off like mud.

This was what they fought; this was what they saw in the darkness. Truth gave them dark hope, fierce in its form and even fiercer in its retribution.

*

The kuvuta were strange creatures, biologically as well as metaphysically. They had no need of water; they thrived on flesh and blood and destruction alone. Some argued that they were much like the malachi, except the wraiths needed more than just the hemoglobin contained in human blood; they needed the act more than anything else to preserve some dark force within them.

The humans were preaching about demons while the cleya spoke of angry reincarnations of gods who had not received enough sacrifice from their followers. Everyone had a different theory. It seemed that killing them was the only thing they seemed to agree on and that fire usually worked best. But there were other methods too that worked just as well...

The kuvuta rarely ventured near the water. They did not fear it; they simply had no use for it. Few sentinel beings inhabited this watery realm and when they were done with the terrestrial inhabitants, they just created a dark star and everything else was taken care of. Now, they had to cross it. They had little choice left. The Blood Angels were hammering them from above so it was a great risk to fly. Moreover, simple river or ocean crossings that could be done on wing had become a difficult task since their beasts were falling ill at an alarming rate. The first signs had been excessive drooling, frothing at the mouth and blood leakage from all major orifices. Ragged breathing and weakness were often the prelude to their undoing. It took roughly four hours from initial symptoms to death and the kuvuta could not understand this new development. It usually happened just after a battle, when their beasts had finished feeding and were supposed to be at their strongest. Rivers now had to be crossed by foot.

A band of kuvuta, no more than fifty, with all of two beasts and a battalion leader with them, came to the great Falsho River. They were under orders from the remaining Lieutenant, Izyan, to find the fleshlings, who had begun nailing kuvuta to the trees, and obliterate them.

Esyago had been slain on the first day at the palace, Umar had been taken into the ground by the wyrms and Malik had been crushed by the fierce Drow General. All their Seers had been brain-damaged by the Telepathic wizards, drumming against their minds day and night. Left without eyes during the day, they were near blind to the raids that carved into their numbers.

Savrek was mounted on his ill steed, above the river, waiting for the first of the wraiths to begin crossing. They had become skittish of late. "Seeing things" they claimed and "smelling monkeys" in the trees. Most places they marched through contained some trace of battles fought where only the bodies of the enemy were strewn and others showed the signs of an ambush seen too late on their part. Whatever was happening, Savrek did not believe the water held any danger and neither, it seemed, did the others for they all charged into the river, eager for the sentinel flesh that awaited them not two miles away. They could be there in half an hour.

*

Kuvuta shadow merged with water at last. The zimun had been waiting patiently. They let them wade through for a little while, waited until every evil foot was wet before they leapt from their liquid world.

At first, the kuvuta were unsure of what was happening. Savrek, from his lofty position, saw what seemed like figures leaping out of the river itself, but they *were* the river, he realized. As soon as the first wraith was pulled down, the others followed in quick succession.

Savrek swooped down to try and avert disaster but he remembered watching others fall victim to the worm creatures in the ground. They had mounted their beasts thinking they would be safe only to fall victim to the wyrms that projected themselves far into the air, pulling them down anyway.

He steered his beast upward again and watched on as the dark disappeared beneath the water, foam and hissing bubbles the only marker for their departure.

Izyan would be most displeased.

*

The zimun groped at the skinny demon bodies beneath the shadow and clung on ferociously; dragging them down the tunnels with strength that was truly inconceivable. There was no room to hope. The kuvuta were unsure what fate awaited them down there for they needed air to breathe as much as they needed water to drink. The zimun dragged them on and on though, down through the tunnels they had labored at.

The pressure was mounting; the kuvuta could feel it in their bodies. Like walls closing in, but even that would probably not kill them. What then did these water-fayres have in mind? What lay in wait for them at the bottom of these dark holes?

Maji. The ones of water.

Aysel had not been able to talk before because for a maji to speak is to hear the sound of death come rushing to greet you. They boiled the very seas with their voices when lifted in song. What could such a voice do when raised in hatred?

Deeper and deeper the holes went, dug into the very ground beneath the rivers to keep the pressure on their precious maji lungs. And soon, the kuvuta could hear the sounds. Deep and rumbling, the water started to warm around them. Bubbles started to rise and escape to a surface they would never see again. Skin started to peel away, bone started to split. The sound of death came rushing.

Chapter 20

Old magic

The sixth day of the war had dawned. The day raids had gone well and the kuvuta were breaking into smaller bands instead of staying together, whereas the sentinels were amassing their armies for security. But perhaps the wraiths had a plan, Braenden thought darkly. In any event, the Alvar was assembling. He and Carrick had herded Izyan's scattered army toward the mid-belt and today, they would meet in the middle if all went to plan. As anticipated, the kuvuta had struck back hard after being terrorized through the day, and there had been casualties from all over last night. Was it worth it? Some had asked. Definitely, others had answered. The dark monsters had to learn that they were not invincible, no matter the consequences.

Kieran had come earlier on behalf of his mother and father, asking if the army needed anything.

'More sons,' came Brendan's reply to which Kieran had slyly remarked,

'Should we bring the camp-followers back?'

The army was rationed and the Adare' had brought the last of the water. It was do-or-die day and Mirian stood by Braenden's side on the front line as testament to this.

'Why have you waited till now to call me?' Mirian asked petulantly. Braenden sighed and replied,

'I felt like it,' mimicking her tone.

She flicked her hair haughtily over her shoulder and scoffed,

'Today you shall wish you did not wait.'

In truth, Braenden had waited to expose her because she would be a target for the kuvuta and if revealed earlier, would probably have been hunted down and slain by now. He hoped she had the power she claimed she did otherwise there could be a great defeat in store for them today. Reports were streaming in of reduced numbers everywhere, people having to burn their people faster because of infection and the wraith attacks increasing in violence and occurrence. It mattered not. Everyone knew what they had signed up for; he just wished they would save their energy for the battlefield.

Dawn tipped over the mountains that separated the two great Alvar and Braenden knew that Carrick had already been fighting, it was his turn now. He only hoped the High Elf General's men were fast enough to breach the gap in time.

The cloud rose from the ground like a thousand mounted riders galloping across desert terrain. It flew fast, swelling in size as he had seen it do for the past five mornings.

'HOLD THE LINE!' He called down the ranks. Every Drow was baying for blood, rooted only to the ground by their general's command. Braenden made to push Mirian back out of pure habit and met with a force that shook him out of his reverie. It felt like his hand was a magnet that had met with an opposing force, equal if not greater to his own. He looked down to find his hand pushing the air in front of Mirian's body. Her arms were folded and a serene smile graced her features. She was not even looking at him. He looked down again and the light played tricks with his eyes. A feathered hand, twice the size of his own flickered in and out of vision, gripping his hand gently it seemed. He looked up to face Mirian and saw the thing's outline towering protectively above her. Eyes like embers, feathers like an angel's.

He withdrew his hand and stepped away from his princess. He dared not look again and tried to focus on the approaching enemy.

'LOOSE!' came the automatic cry from his lips. Arrows sang through the air. Arrows that would seek their targets out and bury themselves deep in their skulls. Braenden was very fond of these. 'LOOSE, FIRE!' Each arrow was dipped into fire borrowed from the dreya themselves. It had been his idea to ask when the wandering band came to his camp, and he was ready to take full credit for it. Drey fire was extremely potent, clinging relentlessly to the victim, and some could not even be doused by water.

Braenden drew his long sword. Mirian was moving beside him, he could see her out of the corner of his eye. Her movements were more graceful than usual, as if some otherworldly force moved her. She walked past the front line as if meeting a lost love and the growls around him grew quiet as all eyes watched the Drow Princess. She was barefoot today on the still clean earth and her white robe billowed around her though no wind stirred the air. Her hands reached out to cup the face of her invisible lover and Braenden could feel the small hairs on his arms tingle. The air around him seemed to slow somehow and he watched as Mirian's body was blown back. Her feet remained planted on the ground but it looked like a strong wind had buffeted her backward for a brief instant. Then the particles of slow moving air seemed to collect themselves, drawing together like droplets of water. By now, the whole Alvar was silent, mesmerized by the feeling around them and the movements of their princess. The air sucked itself inward with painful sluggishness. The kuvuta were close enough to spear. Braenden could see each individual face leering at him, eager to see what his insides looked like, what they tasted like.

No one moved a muscle; it was like being frozen to the spot, though by your own madness and no other. Suddenly, just when Braenden thought that they were surely done for, a great thunderclap sounded in the sky above and it seemed that a white light leapt out of Mirian. It poured out of her like all the legions of the Worlds. Then he saw that it was not light, it was wings, feathered wings attached to great beings. Snowy white and deadly like a blizzard in the night. They fell upon the kuvuta with demonic force and Braenden gave the order to charge.

It was a good battle. The scales were tipped in favor of the Drows for once and the feathered men they fought side by side with. Over the mountain, just on its ridge, he could see the gold gleam of the High Elves. They had traveled hard, soon they would close in behind the kuvuta and a great victory would be had for the first time. It was a preternatural experience that Braenden would never forget. The Umanok tore wraiths apart with their bare hands like kindling. They stood so tall and so regal and there were so many, outnumbering his Alvar three-to-one. Braenden could hardly believe they had all come from a single entity. The tiny, lone figure on the hillside, her silvery-hair blowing in the winds of other worlds. They were here because of her.

*

It would later come to be described as the largest battle of the entire war against the darkness. The two mighty Alvars had managed to squeeze Izyan's great force between them. Umanok fought on the field in the world alongside the mortals who inhabited it and the Blood Angels arrived soon enough for their own piece of the glory.

Kai signaled to the others and they banked off to the left, breaking away from the main hold. They were exhausted. It was the longest single battle they had fought in so far. The kuvuta had been given no choice but stay and fight through high-noon and it was twenty-four hours since last he and his men had rested. They could not carry on like this for fear of losing more men to fatigue and unnecessary mistakes.

As Kai guided Valeo down to a quiet meadow, not yet blackened by the plague, he was saddened by those who had been killed under his command. The others had comforted him quietly, and each in their own way, saying that every war had its casualties and this was no mere flight-plan drill. Brenin had fallen, as well as Kern. Ionhar was badly wounded after today's battle and Owein was looking like he would collapse from the pure pace at any moment. Eiros had surprised him with his vigor and endurance. Nothing could beat Cahan. Lok was far too quick for any kuvuta, something dark driving him that Kai would talk to him about later. Delano was doing well even though he ate two food rations for every one they were supposed to.

Kai landed lightly on the faded green grass. The others did the same; all except Owein who's drey, Tuan, had been stabbed through the heart and killed. Owein was riding a fallen Blood Angel's drey, fierce things driven not by thought but by the need to kill. It plunged Owein into the heart of battles, only to bring him back out, bloodied and exhausted, hours later.

Delano chuckled as the new drey landed hard and unforgiving on the surface, his hind legs itching to fly again.

'I cannot...' Owein stammered, 'go any further. Let me go you deranged beast, go and fight by yourself for I am done for.' He rolled onto the ground dramatically, slapping the restless drey on the hindquarters.

'Food,' Delano mumbled as he threw packets of dried fruit to the others, keeping the sweetest flavor for himself. Eiros was too tired to argue with him about it and chewed in a subdued manner on his bitter oppanor.

Kai sat down on his haunches and called Lok over to him without the others seeing.

'Yes Captain,' Lok said. Kai tried not to flinch at the still unfamiliar sound of the title. Zach had left the hold to lead the Blood Angels, Llstar had gone to be by his side and Kai had been left in charge.

'You are able and well,' Zach had assured him. Kai had accepted and the others had too, without question, even though he was very young. It was their way.

'Sit with me for a moment.' Kai gestured at the space beside him and Lok sat heavily down on the grass, stretching his aching back and tired shoulders.

'I shall never know how they do it,' Lok said, referring to the Blood Angels. Kai smiled, looking down at the fruit paper he tore with his calloused fingers.

'They have trained,' he said.

'We have trained,' Lok countered.

'They have *only* trained. They know nothing else.'

'Or have forgotten everything else,' Lok muttered, 'like how to greet people…how to sleep perhaps.'

Kai frowned. 'Yes, I have thought upon that and I want you to imagine what it must have been like… You give up your life to fight an enemy that you do not know will ever come again for certain. Your life is bound to this task, your very soul. You must leave your people; leave all people for the secret must be kept. Solitude. Waiting. An eternity alone may stretch before you. You could choose to spend it with your comrades but who wants to be around reflections of themselves? It would be safer to split up anyway. A heavy burden. I think they have forgotten everything but what they must do and now that the chance to receive their lives back has come, they go mad with the need for it. They never sleep for it is time wasted and too much time has been wasted already.'

Lok nodded, once Kai had finished with his torrent of words.

'I did not think of it like that,' he admitted.

'I do not believe many do,' Kai said, 'and that is why we show face for them. They need never be understood but they need to be represented for who they once were.'

Lok smiled and nudged Kai in the ribs playfully, saying,

'And here I was thinking you just liked the attention!'

What was left of the Queen's Royal Guard had broken away from the Blood Angel army after the first battle over the palace district, when they realized that the Blood Angels had no intention of stopping and were headed due south. The small hold had landed on a bloodied and battle-ridden ground to the sound of tumulus roars of appreciation. They had been greeted like heroes by both Gau and star pirate alike. Extra food for the journey, mead to warm their weary bones. The Blood Angels were the salvation of the people and the soldiers wanted the chance to say thank you. The real Blood Angels had left amid a flurry of leathery wing and eager flame, not wanting praise, just wanting to fulfill their destinies. As the leader, Kai had paved the way for their white-lie by not denying the status the others so wanted them to have. These were the winged saviors and it gave the people hope to talk to them, touch them and know that the light was real. Kai's hold was more than happy to present a somewhat false front if it meant that the history books would do the Blood Angels the honor they so deserved, and not some misread interpretation of stony-faced madmen who cared as little for the people, it would seem, as the kuvuta.

When they had stopped over with an army for the night, helped them fend off the raids with fire and sweat and blood, they would fly again into the skies to find their hard-done-by brothers and join them in battle. They hung in-between; they breached the gap between hero and mortal.

Kai grew quiet and Lok waited for him to ask the question he had been called over for in the first place. Kai played with his fruit some more before saying,

'Lok, you worry me of late. Did something happen in that first battle, the one over the palace, for since then you fight with a ferocity I did not think you had.' Kai looked up and Lok did not lower his gaze, glad that someone was looking at him now. He could lie, give a story about the tragedy of so many dead and all the things that he had witnessed during the fight, but he did not. He wanted to tell the truth so that at least one soul who walked the Worlds with him would know.

'We broke atmosphere,' he began, 'we descended upon the darkness and my eyes scanned the many peoples.'

'Go on,' Kai said gently when Lok finally lowered his eyes.

'That was when I saw Ronan. He was flying alone…and he was singing,' Lok said quietly.

Kai leaned back and brought his hand to his face to do something but it seemed he had forgotten what. 'Our queen is dead, Kai.' Lok said it with such finality that Kai felt the weight of his words as if spoken from the gods themselves. He was silent for a while, wondering if Lok was crying or if he was simply concentrating really hard on his fruit. Kai noticed that he had a golden locket wrapped around his wrist and hand so tight that it bled in places. Bruises rose from beneath the links and Kai reached out to hold his hand.

'Your heart?' Kai asked softly.

Lok nodded, lips white against his teeth. 'I loved her, I love her still.'

Kai sat back again and his mind spilled over with how much was happening. So many had been lost, so many tears had been shed. Was it different to any other time in the Worlds? He did not think so. It was as if the same play was being presented time and time again and they were the actors. The Great Tragedy. Darkness against a collective smudge of grey where terrible things happened every day. Hearts were broken, lives were wasted, lovers lost, children abandoned. And in the same time and space, life was made, laughter shared, lovers taken, hearts made whole. What justification did any of them have? To say that they stood against blatant evil? For then they should all cut out pieces of their hearts. For love and peace? Never had either of these ruled the Worlds. No, they fought so that Lok could lose the woman he loved and cry on the grass before his captain. They fought so that Ionhar could tell Delano that he would arrange a woman for him in the next camp if only he could be sure that he was up to the task. They fought so that people could watch their children make the same mistakes they did, so that suffering could come again and temper the hearts of many. They fought for the bad poetry just as much as for the beautiful ballad, they fought for the tyrants as well as the benevolent, they fought for all things great and small, wicked hearts and gallant alike. They fought for themselves, for their right to live as flawed people and to learn that it was alright.

Kai gripped Lok by the shaking shoulder and embraced him like the brother.

'For what are we then if we are not all brothers and sisters.'

*

An older human soldier stood next in line under the giant blossom tree. It buzzed with the tiny stinger things and he wondered again why he was doing this.

Like organ donors, the volunteers lined up to give up their dead bodies when the time came, to a greater cause.

The man put one foot in front of the other, telling himself he had been through worse. The tiny enganya flitted up to him, level with his eyes and asked him if he understood the side-effects. He swallowed his dry saliva and nodded, looking over to the other madmen in the gardens staring at their hands and feet like they had found a lost prophet in the creases there.

'It works like a drug,' she crooned on, 'retinal irritation, tingling of the skin as well as a few hallucinations. The dose is light enough.'

He nodded again and decided not to look as she did it. Her stinger popped out like a claw from its skin casing and he felt the tiny prick. He felt light headed almost immediately and went to join the others by the water where they would cause no trouble and be left to themselves, until the bloodstream accepted the chemical and began to replicate it at no harm to the carrier.

What a strange notion, Ramroth thought, as he sat down to have a look at the procedure being done on one of his human Adare'. It had come about when an accidental sting of minute quantity had been inflicted on a human soldier. The man consequently had a severe talking-to by his captain where he had to explain why he was so heavily under the influence. The sting mark was discovered, the enganya responsible told to be more careful and at noon the next day, the soldier was slain by a wraith. A crow picking at his eyes on the battlefield, while the burning was underway, was reported to have keeled over instantly. A plan was hatched once all the pieces had been rapidly put together and experts were consulted on the matter.

'Perfectly harmless, High Adare',' the Chief Drow physician assured.

'Indeed,' Ramroth muttered as he watched the stinger insert itself into the epidermis of the wincing Wind Adare'. 'Is it only effective on human DNA?' Ramroth inquired, looking up at the overseeing physician questioningly.

'Yes. After much experimentation,' he added darkly, 'and therefore compatible with the High Elves and Drows too. Since they are dying by the thousands, I'd love to get a crack at them but they appear to be…busy.'

'Dying tends to take up a lot of your time,' Ramroth said absentmindedly, inspecting the tiny drop of blood that had raised its head in protest on the Adare's arm. The young man looked up at Ramroth; pale in the face at all this talk of death perhaps. He stroked Ramroth's face as if feeling for the one beneath it. Ramroth chuckled to himself and let the youth be led away.

'Long term affects?' he asked.

'None,' the doctor said, shaking his head, 'apparently the beasts fall like flies though so it's a miracle we found it so soon.'

'Fascinating,' Ramroth breathed as he watched the humans stare at the sky like children, picking flowers and smelling them as if for the first time.

'Truly,' the Drow agreed, 'the poison that flows through them is literally strong enough to kill a kuvuta beast but the human DNA seems to hold some ancient, disused strand, perhaps a defense mechanism against prehistoric insects, who knows!'

'I do hope they do not have to really die to kill the enemy though,' the Adare' added as an afterthought, wondering at the same time where his Arial was and if she was safe.

*

Naira was moving so quietly that she could not even hear herself. She had been told that the kuvuta see very well, especially in the dark, while the other senses were no better than average. It was going to be high-noon in a few moments. She was waiting for the signal. A band of humans, who called themselves the Rogues, were leading a day raid and in the chaos that followed, she would do her job. She was old; it was time for a new queen to take the hive. She had many, many daughters and had lived a full life. It was time to pay her dues.

The blue flare ignited in the sky and she hovered behind her rock waiting for the advance.

'Blue means in position and red means advancing,' she kept repeating over and over to herself until the meaning was lost and she made her way forward anyway. She could smell the kuvuta from where she was; smell their decay seeping into the land. They were not so far off now; the area where they stood waiting for further instruction verily stank of death and rot.

Another flare shot up, blazing against the stars that lit the sky once more. A chorus of shouts joined the cacophony of color and she knew it was time.

She flew forward, faster this time, praying that no one would see her, that no one would look down. She could see his looming figure from where she sat, crouched behind the dying clumps off grass. He was pointing and shouting orders in his vile tongue. She veritably itched to bring him down. Without him they would fall apart or the bigger fish would come swimming and then the war would really be won. They were close, she knew, but heavy losses made the struggle all the more desperate. Sacrifices had to be made. 'Double the effort,' she whispered to herself.

She was close now, close enough to smell the half-eaten sentinel flesh strewn around, taken from the battlefields that littered the planet like angry boils. They moved fast, she thought, as the kuvuta surged toward the approaching humans. She would have a minute, maybe less. She started to fly upward, mimicking the doomed seeds that blew on the wind to try and blend in.

A beast flapped its great wings from somewhere behind her and threw her off path. She could not correct herself though, it would arouse suspicion. 'Wasting time...'

Her new path took her around the front of roughly forty of the brutes, ready and waiting to leap forward after the first wave had been mowed down by the artillery and the humans were reloading. She panicked, knowing she had seconds to act. She drifted lazily past the snarling faces, suspended there for all to see. She tried to keep her expression blank but her heart was beating in a frenzy making her white "seed" face pink. A head turned, a tiny bead of sweat ran down her forehead. Agonizing seconds passed and then she was free. She quickened her pace; close enough to the target now to throw caution to the wind. Her little wings beat furiously against the stench that lay as heavy as a curtain drawn over the land. There he was, meters away from her. She gnashed her little teeth and flew full speed at the monster.

Impossibly, his head snapped in her direction and a clawed fist moved so fast through the air that it was merely a thought in her head by the time he had her in his grip.

'What have we here?' he hissed.

Naira tried not to struggle, some of her precious poison might leak out and she would need it all. 'A little assassin-fayre?' he sneered. Naira was surprised at how little these creatures knew of the Worlds they sought to devour. Fate playing tricks again, she thought, for if they had, then the war would be going very differently indeed.

She smiled a small smile, her last, and his face dropped. She died almost instantly. She had pierced his precious shadow, the lifeline to his black soul. The poison spread quickly. Izyan dropped to his knees, still holding the devious little enganya in his hand.

*

'He's dead,' Nyx panted, his hands on his knees as he struggled for breath. 'They are coming, I think they're angry.' He smiled and Corbin laughed out loud and said,
'We will be ready for them.'
'No, I don't think you understand - there are fucking thousands of them!'
Corbin frowned.
'We had to attack the whole bloody army to give the little one a fighting chance. A small raid would have drawn little or no attention from Izyan,' Cadeyrn explained on Nyx's behalf.

The four of them had landed on Emara with the Blood Angels and formed up with some amiable human allies but soon broke away when they realized they would be far better off on their own. These people had never seen any real action in the field, small-time mercenaries and some ex, old-school militia. Most of them had not seen battle in years. The Religion had them all under such strict regulations that they had been forced into some other career or had gone into exile after refusing to join the army. The quartet now standing in the face of many angry kuvuta after an assassination, were the only surviving Rogue combat agents, and they found that survival had become second nature. This is what they had trained to do after all.

Eira clung onto Corbin's arm, her brow creased with worry.
'What are we going to do?' she asked quietly.
'Whatever it is,' Nyx grinned with his wicked sense of humor, 'we had better do it fast.'

'What's that?' Cadeyrn asked, shading his eyes and staring at the opposite horizon.

'It can't be them can it?' Corbin asked, 'can't have circled us so quickly.'

'No,' Nyx agreed, 'looks like a storm is brewing...'

Eira frowned at the strange circle of clouds advancing on them.

'Maybe it's someone from our side?' she suggested hopefully.

'It never is,' Nyx grumbled.

*

When Renata emptied her lungs; veins burst, bone shattered, skin was blown away. She was just big enough to haul the mountains from their gravel beds and crush armies with them. She would die doing this, that much she knew. The war was going badly and she felt, against all her previous convictions, that she had to help. Vanora had taught her that much at least.

The fayre queen summoned all her magic; all her hoarded powers that could have made men weep at her feet and put their very eyes out at her beauty. She used it all to play her part and save the Worlds who would never love her. She towered over forests and slaughtered cruel men in black shadow for all of an hour. It was enough. Armies, close enough to hear her mournful wailing, bled from their ears and noses. She trampled whole battalions and crushed an army of near to four-thousand strong with three sweeps of her massive hands. She could feel the power ebbing from her and when all was done, and she lay on her back on the cold, hard grass, her fayres came for her and took her to the princess.

Through sand and stone they passed to find the elf maiden sleeping in a dim cavern. They woke her gently enough and she rubbed the sleep from her eyes saying her brother's name all the while.

'It is me,' Renata said. The other fayres lay her tiny figure down so that she lay sprawled in Vanora's cupped hands.

'What happened to you?' Vanora asked, little tears pricking at the corners of her eyes.

'I listened to you,' came the weary reply. Vanora smiled and a teardrop fell onto the queen. She drank it hungrily and sat up, revived a little from the precious magic of emotion.

'Thank you,' Vanora said, not knowing what else to say. 'Would you like more tears?' she asked hopefully. Renata laughed low and full.

'No tears can revive me now, sweet child.'

'Tears revived me,' Vanora said slowly, 'special tears.'

'How special?' Renata asked, pricking her pixie ears.

'I lost my heart and the drey queen gave me very special tears to grow a new one.'

'Maji tears,' Renata whispered to herself, knowing the Worlds owed Arial more than they knew.

Vanora stroked the soft wings of the fayre queen and said,

'But you are dying.'

'We all die,' Renata said. Her eyelids were struggling now.

'You should not have to die now,' Vanora choked. She was experiencing the strangest emotions, like a tidal wave had been released from someone else's soul and she was being swept along with it.

Renata smiled as she let her Worldly knowledge pass into Vanora, her last gift before she closed her eyes forever.

Vanora gasped as Renata was suddenly no longer in her hand but beside her, lying so gracefully in death, as though asleep despite her natural form. Her matted hair was caked with leaves and mud. Her opalescent skin once so soft now grew over with mold and moss. She was still beautiful Vanora decided.

*

A thousand little wings beat the air in the still room. The silk was lifted and Arial's body still lay beneath it.

The queen's last wish.

The body slowly lifted, the hair around her face flowing as if gravity had been stolen. Her stiffened limbs and greying skin becoming young again, fighting mother nature for her beauty. She vanished with the fayres, fair as the day she reached womanhood and no one was ever to know where her body finally lay.

*

Malachi, vampires, cheupe, najd, immortals. They lived as long as there was blood to drink and ground to lie down in and sleep, like the corpses they were. When they became very old, one of three things came to pass. They could become an Ancient, doing the bidding of the young, helping with rituals, signing the documents that would pave the way for future generations. They were the ones who remained behind to see that their children behaved and prospered. Living-dead, tired of blood and tired of the hunt. Not many let it get that far but just enough to keep the balance. Others died in their own way, many burying themselves deep within the ground to sleep forever. This was the respectable way to go. Quietly. When you'd had your fill and walked the Worlds a thousand times over. No one lived forever. Eternity would break your heart before the end. Sleep was a malachi's death if he survived long enough to embrace it. Large ceremonies were held in honor of the old ones when they decided to go down and once buried and gone, there was no returning. The Ancients made sure of that.

But some malachi were too strong, their hearts were too cold, they wanted everything but needed nothing. These were the dangerous ones, the ones who lived forever, the Daemons. Frightening creatures, banished from the Worlds for not wanting to rest when their time came. The Ancients had become good at spotting them. They became torrents of power, all the centuries of blood-lust feeding the parasite within until it mutated into something...*else*. Something not meant for this realm. Insatiable appetites, unstoppable powers. They were banished to some sanctum carved out of space and time for them alone. Who knew what went on there, what pain and suffering at the hands of the merciless and ever-hungry?

They could be summoned, these Daemons, by skilled weavers of malachi magic. Many usually banded together to share the burden although only three souls were essentially needed; one to protect, one to summon and one to channel. Walking with a Daemon was a task not to be taken lightly. Many had died trying. The Daemon was simply too strong, too eager to be back in this realm that it fed off your own body to such an extent that by the time it left you, you were already dead. The caller was no better off. The Daemon's soul could never truly leave its own sanctum and while the greater part of it was focused in the one who was channeling, the void it left was like an open doorway for others to come out too. They fought and ripped at the mind to get through and some had been driven mad by them. The protector must obviously provide shelter for the soul who was summoning but also, try to help him keep the other Daemons at bay. It was quite an effort, like fighting a small battle of body and mind all by yourself, and one that had been raging for six days now. A feat such as this had never before been undertaken. It would later be condemned by Ancients as ill-advised and impossible. Nevertheless, Damek, Kaleo, Tariq and Blain battled on.

Damek's mind had become a whirlpool of madness. He felt like a drunken man being kept alive and conscious by some unseen force, hell-bent on his punishment. Dehydration and thirst plagued him no matter how much he drank and he drained entire kuvuta armies dry to the bone. There was constant dizziness as if this place held lines and angles he could not understand. If it were not for Arial's essence, Kaleo's constant reassuring voice, he would have been lost to the Daemon inside.

The monster was thrilled with being alive again and Damek had to use every ounce of his energy on directing his feet to the enemy and the enemy alone. That was almost all he had to do, that - and respond to Kaleo - to prove that he was still there. His shared mind was almost at breaking point and he could hardly wait for the cool and calm of solitude. Perhaps he would sleep for a long time after this. He needed to rest. The Daemon drowned out his thoughts of sleep with its current needs. It said,

'Do not be selfish Damek'

Damek laughed at himself and the Daemon pushed his feet on. There was a kuvuta army nearby. Damek had the Daemon trained well enough, kept threatening to kill himself if the Daemon took anything else. It had roared with mirth inside his head for what felt like hours but had conceded to this nagging vessel like a madman in a prison cell fed steak, medium rare, when he would in fact have liked it any way at all.

Damek's flushed mind swung in the direction of the five-thousand souls who would feed his Daemon today. He moved in erratically frenzied movements as if he had never eaten before or would never again. He tried to close his eyes but the Daemon snapped them open, focusing on the seething horizon of fresh meat, coiling around his tired mind like a great serpent that could be felt but not seen.

One foot in front of the next, Damek thought wearily, his eyes rolling back into his head as the Daemon shot him a bemused glare.

*

Kaleo was more than a little worried. He had watched this thing take possession of his friend's body slowly but surely over the past few days. At first, a mere manic glint and dark aura were the only markings of the monster. Damek could still speak coherently, still plotted and planned, still grieved. Then, as the hours wore on and the Daemon devoured more of the shadow, Damek started to recede into the shell of his own mind, relenting his body to the blood-hungry beast within. They tracked the kuvuta armies like the hunters they were. It seemed Damek had managed to hold some sway over the Daemon but there had been one frightening moment on the third night where Kaleo thought they were done for…

'So you are the creature of the night that feeds on the darkness?' It was a scouting convoy of heavily-armed Drows. Kaleo tried to do all the speaking; explaining what was happening and how they should come no closer to Damek than they already were. The Drow captain had laughed him off, wanting to see for himself this ancient piece of malachi craft.

Damek's body was seated on the overhanging branch of a tree, like a skulking bird of prey. It was not uncommon for malachi to be seen in positions that seemed odd to the other sentinels. Something strange powered their limbs and they could do things that others could not, so the Drow was not alarmed at first, until he stepped closer still and realized that Damek had his back to him but his head had twisted around completely and was staring right at him with eyes that looked like the windows to some dark place he wished never to go. Black and glittering yet empty and dead. The Drow thought he could see fire racing across the retina, his private nightmares reflected by the pools of night in that inanimate face.

'I have seen so much,' the thing said to him without moving its lips, 'shall I SHHOOOWWWW YOU?'

The Drow had fallen over his own feet trying to run away from the figure that swooped down from the tree like some giant soul-eating bat. Kaleo would have laughed if it were not so frightening.

'I hope you were not seriously going to feed off them, Damek,' Kaleo reprimanded, 'it is a high crime, they will have us hunted like dogs and put down with less kindness.'

The creature in his friend's body just looked at him, blinked once and ran off into the darkness, on the hunt for his next kuvuta meal. Kaleo had torn after it, using flight several times just to keep up which was extremely dangerous unless you were moving from one World to another. It moved in such erratic paths that Kaleo just had to guess and hope he did not plunge headlong into a mountain range or end up drifting aimlessly in an ocean somewhere. By the time he caught up with it, it stood in the middle of a mass killing-ground, offering laughter up into the night air, holding mangled limbs that glistened in the light of the moons like pieces of torn magic.

Kaleo would have to approach it slowly on such occasions, hearing its guttural growls and snatches of language so old; Kaleo could not even place its origins. He would talk soothingly; he would speak of the other Shadow Brothers and of Arial. Damek's voice would surface, distorted by the Daemon's will to suppress it. They would argue for a few moments before the body would slump to the ground and Damek would hold up his blackened and bloody hands, choking the words,

'I am here Kaleo, take me somewhere quiet.'

Kaleo knew they were doing much to help the war effort, so much so that he swore Damek had eaten half the race and nothing the kuvuta tried to do could stop him, but at what cost he wondered? Damek would mutter things under his breath like a deranged man and then burst out into erratic laughter that sounded like it was echoing off a different landscape than the one they stood in. When he was not acting like a senseless person, which were the stages that Damek struggled for a foothold Kaleo guessed, then he was behaving like some sort of god that could neither see nor hear Kaleo at all. He would walk upright again, collecting pretty rocks with thought alone and making them swirl around him like debris orbiting a planet. Dark storm clouds would hang over his head, threatening to release untold power. Violet and emerald lightning glazing the air above them so that Kaleo felt he was being pulled into the dream-world along with his friend. Static energy would prick at his skin and play havoc with his senses. If the Daemon did not feel like walking around something on their way to the next hunting ground, the object would simply disintegrate, bursting into tiny pieces of itself like a shattered mirror. Trees, massive boulders, anything. Kaleo was trying not to feel like he was alone. He had to remember that Damek needed him near, was buried somewhere inside his former body, and would perish if left to himself.

*

Damek was shivering with cold. It seemed the Daemon had decided it no longer liked the feel of clothes against his skin. Damek hoped that Kaleo had picked up his discarded cloak in the sands and not run far away by now. It was so strange being inside this creature's head or having this creature inside his...he could no longer remember. It did whatever if felt like doing, whatever impulse besieged it. Time for this being had spanned too long for any reason to prevail except the selfish need to live on, take what it wanted regardless. All social frameworks had become useless. Damek felt as though he had been trapped inside this place forever. A dreamscape of macabre nothing. Every now and again, he would be plucked out from under the surface of this strange insanity by the voice of Kaleo or Arial's face swimming before him. It was the only way he did not fall under the spell permanently. He longed to know what was happening with his body but he could no longer say.

They crested the hill and the Daemon let him see through his own eyes briefly. Four small figures stood in the valley. Humans. Damek shuddered.

'Help...me,' he murmured quietly. Kaleo grabbed hold of his cold hand and said,

'I will call to you when it is safe.'

'Hurry...' Damek slurred; the Daemon was whipping itself up into a frenzy. They had been lucky so far not to stray into an army of humans. Kaleo doing careful guide-work to prevent such a disaster for no blood tasted as sweet. A guttural roar sounded from somewhere deep within Damek's throat, perhaps anguish, perhaps restraint, two creatures would battle it out now.

Kaleo had seen the look in the Daemon's eyes and had heard the strange muffled voice of an anxious Damek. He had run flat-out down the sandy hill, waving his arms in the air and shutting his ears out to the sound of beating human hearts. He reached the four people with hands still in the air. Strangely, they only had eyes for the monster on the hilltop.

'You HAVE to get out of here,' he fairly cried at them, yanking at the big man's sleeve and practically sending him flying. The wind from the Daemon's soul was starting to howl and Kaleo was desperate.

*

'WHAT THE FUCK!' Nyx yelled. Dust was flaying their eyes, Cadeyrn was lying in a crumpled heap ten feet away and all this had happened in mere seconds.

Corbin could see a figure moving among them, so fast that it flitted in and out of his vision like an apparition. He pushed Eira behind him protectively and called out to Cadeyrn,

'ARE YOU ALRIGHT?'

Cadeyrn was running back toward them through the ever-worsening sandstorm, waving his arms about wildly. Corbin looked over at Nyx, the whites of his eyes showing his fear and confusion.

'DO I HIT IT?' Nyx cried over the noise of the wind.

'JUST RUN,' Corbin shouted in reply. Whatever was happening, they would have no part in it.

Corbin glanced back up at the hilltop expecting to see the figure they had seen so briefly before the sudden storm had started. Instead, he was looking right at its face, five inches away, black eyes looked at him with a hunger only lovers can give. Its face was pale and twisted as if it were uncomfortable in there, whatever it was. It was naked. Corbin tried to cry out as the creature reached out to embrace him but no sound would escape his lips. He felt the heat-wave blow over his head as Nyx let off a round from their blaster but nothing happened. The firearm Nyx had used was an anti-spacecraft weapon and it just did nothing, as if it were never fired. The creature stood steadfast, gazing lovingly at them all like the sand-man from their nightmares.

'FUCKING VAMPIRES!' Nyx yelled, pulling at Corbin's sleeve and pushing Eira into the dusty wasteland where she would hopefully not be seen. The monster grabbed hold of Corbin's shoulder and pulled him away from a struggling Nyx with ease. It drew his body toward it like a lullaby and Corbin knew that it was death that wanted him. Out of nowhere, something charged headlong into the vampire holding Corbin and he was released. His feet hit the ground like a revelation, he grabbed Nyx and they ran, following the silhouettes of Eira and Cadeyrn through the dust.

*

Kaleo was holding on to Damek's body with all the force he could muster and eventually he could feel the monster being subdued; the muscles relaxed and the shoulders slumped against his. He had risked his life but if he had not, he would have risked everything. No matter how many kuvuta Damek killed, if he took but one human life, the death penalty awaited them all.

Damek was slowly coming to and the dust storm was clearing, the dark clouds receding to the atmosphere where they belonged. The landscape had looked preternatural only moments before. The horizon had looked as if it were on fire, smoke rising and an eerie red glow penetrating the dust. When Kaleo looked again, he was looking into the eyes of an angry but tethered Daemon. He backed away and let the creature stand up. After all, it had kuvuta to kill.

*

Corbin, Nyx, Eira and Cadeyrn had reached the relative safety of a small oasis in the scrubby wasteland. Cadeyrn was busy rubbing his arm where he had been grabbed by the smaller vampire, Nyx was busy running his fingers through his sand-strewn hair, gabbling quietly to himself, and Corbin was just standing there with his hand over his neck in a trance.

Eira looked at these three men so troubled by their childhood nightmares, failing to see the greater picture.

'Fucking vampires man,' Nyx muttered.

'I could *feel* it…singing…in my head,' Corbin added.

'It flung me – ME – clean off my feet!' Cadeyrn yelled.

Eira said, 'Will you focus for one second!' They all stared at her and waited for her to tell them what was worse than vampires on the loose. 'The kuvuta are right over there!' she cried, her finger pointing to the army that had chased them and now stood quiet and silent like death itself. 'There are only two vampires against all of them! They will never make it!'

Nyx shrugged and said, 'I say let them try,' before he began walking off. Eira grabbed hold of his arm and spun him around angrily;

'They wanted to bite us and they didn't, is that not proof enough that they are on our side?'

'Of course they are on our side, without us they can't live,' he scowled. 'I have to give blood once a year so that my best friend can be attacked in the middle of a war we are trying to win? If you want to call that friendly fire then go ahead.'

Eira shook her head, 'They are only trying to help.'

'Look guys,' Corbin said, pointing to where the lone vampire who had grabbed him stood facing the army, one hand still covering his neck. The vampire was laughing at the sea of kuvuta faces and no one could understand what was happening.

It was like watching magic then; the dark type. The kind that they never want you to know exists. The kuvuta came at the vampire and he braced himself. When they hit him, he carved a whole right through their ranks with his mere presence. They flew left and right, high into the air. Some were trodden underfoot but most were ripped from themselves in such gruesome ways that Eira vomited all over the sand beside her. It was like all the laws of physics had been neatly swept aside and a new order was reigning supreme. So much power packed into one single body. It made no sense at all and Nyx held on to Corbin for support as they watched the carnage below with transfixed horror. It was over in minutes and when it was, Corbin could feel the air release, like it had been holding its breath and now it had exhaled.

The creature was sitting on a blanket of dead and dying wraiths. Their blood drenched him and he scooped it up with both hands, pouring the black liquid into his mouth. It seemed the shadow had lifted from the sky, like the scales had finally been tipped and this figure was celebrating it with the flesh of others.

'Maybe we should...' Eira began.

'You'll stay right here,' Corbin said darkly. He was not going to watch his wife fall victim to the same fate.

'I think we should leave,' Nyx remarked, a small note of hysteria in his voice. Cadeyrn laughed quietly at his deftly hidden tone of panic and got elbowed in the ribs for his efforts.

'Shh,' Corbin hissed and they did as they were told.

Another figure was approaching now, the vampire from before, the one who had saved Corbin. He walked slowly toward his comrade, kneeling in the middle of his slaughterhouse. A hand was tentatively stretched out and the kneeling vampire started convulsing violently. The other one held on so gently and with so much care that Eira's heart nearly broke. She ran forward, ignoring the cries of alarm behind her. When she reached the pair, she could see that something was wrong with the mass-killer of the kuvuta. His whole body shook, his eyes rolled backward and forward and strange words were pouring out of its mouth. His skin was darkened in patches and his hair was wild, streaked with blood, his face distorted by nameless forces. The other vampire looked so different that Eira could have sworn they were not of the same race. He was stroking the hair of his friend, guiding his head onto his lap and crooning softly to him in old Osrillese. He appeared not to have noticed Eira until she spoke;

'What happened to him?'

Kaleo frowned and looked up at this brave Woman of Eve, hoping the Daemon was far enough gone by now to not be brought back by her strong human voice.

'He has been possessed for some time now.' His Udaranese was strange and thick but she could understand.

'Oh,' Eira said, reaching out slowly to help him calm the other with soothing strokes.

'We did it to help the best way we knew how but it has been hard for us all,' he continued. Eira nodded and then her crewmates were with her. Nyx stood back a little, still wary of the predators. Cadeyrn was looking on in fascination and Corbin was on his knees, looking like a field medic taking charge.

'He will swallow his tongue,' he explained to the still vampire who let him take the other. Corbin turned the shuddering vampire onto his side and ran through a full body-check. Kaleo's reproachful look softened.

'Umm...' Corbin began, not knowing what to do next.

'He will be fine. The Daemon is leaving him now,' the vampire said, resting a clawed hand on Corbin's shoulder. Corbin could only nod, his hands holding the now calming vampire still.

'Thanks,' Cadeyrn said, surveying the destruction of an army that would have flattened them in an instant.

'Thank him,' Kaleo said, moving backward and gesturing for Corbin to do the same.

*

Damek needed space, he needed air. He lay on his back, gasping in pain and choking on all the blood the Daemon had devoured. His head swam, spun once around and he was hurling it all up. It felt like a black river had found its source within him and it just kept flowing. He was faintly aware of Kaleo's voice and of other people around him but he did not care. It felt like dying this, and he wanted to do it in peace.

*

That night, the six unlikely companions moved over to the shelter of the oasis from earlier. Cadeyrn made a fire while Nyx sulked about sharing camp with vampires and Eira and Corbin huddled beneath the stars like the lovers they had almost forgotten to be. Kaleo had gone to fetch them food and he came back with two wild hares. Nyx almost forgave him everything.

'Have you eaten?' Eira asked carefully, much later that evening. How hard it was to speak to these beings. Kaleo smiled darkly and drew a blood bag out of his cloak pocket. He tore it open and sucked on it quietly while the rest ate their roast hare with fingers dripping with fat.

The vampire, Damek, was still lying on his side although he had stopped throwing up now. Eira was grateful for that much. Kaleo was staring into the fire, reflecting on things that Eira could only guess at. How could you breach such a forbidden gap?

'Are you alright?' she asked feebly. She did not think he heard her for he made no reply. She opened her mouth to repeat the question but he held up his hand to silence her and then looked over at the motionless Damek.

'I do not believe he will make it.'

Eira was struck by the emotion with which he spoke these words. Perhaps what the radicals said was true. Her people were but children of time, where the immortals mastered it. They had had so much longer to conquer and to understand the emotions that all others simply blaze through in a lifetime. What is loneliness when felt one-thousand-fold? What did it become then? What was love? She shuddered to think.

'Can I help?' she asked in the same feeble tone. Kaleo met her eyes briefly for the first time that day and her breath was taken away by the strange beauty in these creatures. They were by no means pretty; jutting jaws, sallow skin and movements that were entirely preternatural but it lay in their eyes then, the seduction, the magic. He lowered his eyes immediately and Eira got the feeling that he was deliberately trying to ignore them all. Human blood. She moved closer to the unconscious Damek and double-checked that everyone was sleeping. 'If...if I give...will he wake up?'

Kaleo stared at her, dumb-struck by her blatant offer. Eira did not wait for a reply. She shuffled over to Damek and turned him over onto his back. She looped her hands behind his neck and heaved, sliding her fingers around his shoulders and hauling him up into a sitting position.

They were so strong. She could feel his contours beneath his tattered cloak and tried not to look at his naked form beneath it. 'How do I do this?' she asked Kaleo.

'He will wake for you,' Kaleo whispered, drawing nearer as if witnessing a miracle event. He wondered silently if this was how it was in the times before when malachi had roamed among humans. They had lived like gods it was said, blood given freely and without question. What made them fear you one moment and then want to give themselves to you the next? Power? Immortality? Kaleo was unsure but here was this woman, this beautiful, warm woman, on her knees for a malachi.

Eira sat like that for a while, feeling ridiculous. Limp vampire hanging in her tiring arms and another, rapt with attention, staring straight at her. Soon though, she felt warm breath on her neck. She closed her eyes with the feel of it. It felt like every fantasy she had ever had where she was the only one who mattered. Goosebumps ran down her back and arms and by the time the not-so-lifeless arms began to draw her in like something precious never to be lost, Eira's neck was arched back and exposed. His hands were searching her hair, he was naked beneath his cloak, moving beneath her and she wanted to give herself to him in some way she had never given before. She felt almost nothing when he bit down, the flood of ecstasy only coming when he took his first drink. The feeling was over almost as soon as it had begun, leaving her light-headed. She was aware of being laid down softly on the sand.

Kaleo rushed over to Damek and they stopped before they embraced, stopped to look at one another. They looked like they were studying each other's faces in case they would never see each other again.

Eira woke the others to watch and explained what she had done. Nyx gasped like a little girl but Corbin told him to be quiet again. The night stalkers were speaking fast Osrillese, the words pouring out in great gushes. Damek was silent then as Kaleo drew something out of his pocket; a lock of hair, spun gold. Damek's shoulders shook as he cried and the humans gave them space to talk and cry for a while. Unaware that anything other than savagery could come of these hunters until now.

Eventually, Damek looked up at them and walked over.

'Thank you,' he said. His voice was deep and sincere and Eira was still feeling the aftermath of her gift. He toyed with the hair for a little while before he pocketed it and sat down in front of them. 'You have done much,' he began, 'I was nearly gone. Our ancestors are strong,' he smiled darkly, 'but I saw the others before I came back.'

'Others?' Corbin asked, 'there are more of you channeling demons?'

'Daemons,' Damek corrected, 'and no, only me. But others helped and they are dying too. Tariq and Blain lie wasted. They have had nothing for six days and they have given everything. I understand it might be much to ask, but know that we would not seek to do you harm. Would you give again?'

'Yes,' Eira said, without hesitation.

'Alright,' Corbin agreed.

'Why not?' Cadeyrn shrugged.

Only Nyx remained silent. 'I'll navigate,' he said finally.

*

Mirian had a strong spirit, Maya could tell that much from a mere glance. Good posture, strong hands, straightforward attitude but not overly confident. She was born to wield great power. It would come almost effortlessly because she believed it was hers to wield. Maya envied her that. Magic was like living in a cavern full of asps and every year the torches burnt lower. Maya had been bitten young and she had not been quite strong enough to recover; now they wanted her to help save the Worlds. How ironic.

'Remember always that you are in control,' Maya said firmly.

'Yes,' Mirian said, a hint of mock-boredom to her voice. Maya grabbed the willful student by the sides of her face and pulled her closer, willing her to see all that she was still blind to and would see in time. The limitlessness of it all.

'Remember always that you are in control.'

Mirian had nodded like a frightened child but as soon as Maya had let her go, her composure had returned. Maya turned to the ward, Dunkan, and gave him an appraising once-over with her liquid eyes. 'You did well. She is ready,' she said. The Drow bowed low and Maya was summoned. It was time to leave. She was too precious to leave on this doomed planet.

A light elvin battle-cruiser, the Paladin, would take her far away, to the darkness that she had to sew together. She was sorry to leave it all behind, all the excitement, the potential. They broke atmosphere and Maya turned around in her seat to look back at the planet Emara.

'It is beautiful is it not?' the High Elf pilot asked.

'Oh yes,' she breathed.

'We will be the last to see it like that,' he said coldly. Maya frowned and turned around again to see what looked like a black waterfall pouring into the planet. It was the most powerful sight she had ever seen. The attack had begun and she watched black melt out of black and onto that pretty little place teeming with life.

Her heart caught in her throat and she looked back at the pilot. He was concentrating on the path ahead, or so it seemed, and Maya sat back in her seat trying to erase that sight from her memory. Flashes, instead, of her youth, came unbidden and she squeezed her eyelids tightly shut in an effort to erase them. "Antimatter", the scientist called it. She had ripped a whole through her house at the tender age of twelve in a stormy tantrum. Her entire family lay dead and in pieces at her feet while she still lived. She had only tried it once again after that at Taigo's gentle insistence. It had been a controlled environment but she had still felt skittish. It had gone well; her body and mind knew naturally how to guide it as she matured. That did not matter though, like the one person not shot dead in a massacre, it seemed to fade in comparison to the death of so many.

They were slowing down, nearing the first of the dark stars. Maya peered out the window and to her surprise, she could see it! Not just the event horizon or perhaps the idea of where it was by the movement of things around it. It shone like a star except not with light. It was hard to explain.

'They told me you would be able to see it,' the pilot called over his shoulder as if he had read her thoughts and Maya nodded, realizing finally that she was not some untouchable anomaly. The people close to her knew her for who she was and she had been surrounded with friends all throughout her solitude. She smiled and opened the hatch to the door. The pilot howled out something to her about a protective suit but she was beyond listening. Walking out there was like being in a dream, anything was possible. She was untouchable but could grasp everything in the palm of her hands.

She faced the black hole like it represented all her childhood fears, sucking all her love and belief into it like some endless motif. She closed her eyes, threw back her head and screamed out in pure elation, freedom. The tears ran down her face as she let go and forgave herself at last, white light streaming from her mouth and fingertips. The dark star shrunk like a beaten dog before her awesome power and soon it was just a whisper of what it once was. A black flame clinging to the wick. Maya sighed deeply and the flame blew out.

*

He stood alone, darkness his only friend and comfort at this bleak hour. No news. It had been twenty-four hours since the last report and there was this gaping hole inside him now like someone had pulled the plug on his soul.

Nothing and no one could have heard Uriool coming; it was Sirena's footsteps that betrayed their silence. Uriool wanted it that way. First the father for the sin and then the wayward child. He slipped away to find the one they called Lord Nagesh and left her to walk into the arms of the other.

Soren turned his head. That sound, something from long ago… someone. Footsteps. Sirena. Unmistakable. How much of himself had he lost already? He waited until she thought she had him before he spun around and grabbed her by the throat, lifting her clear off her feet and watching her choke. Her eyes widened in fear that he could smell. Her little feet twitching, her throat fighting against his strong hands, her eyes watching him.

He released his grip ever so slightly and lowered her to the floor again. He stared at her for a long time, trying to remember, battling with what was left inside his heart.

'Sirena,' he breathed, in simple Udaranese. It felt strange on his tongue to say such things even after such a short time. He began to remember this woman, beautiful and cruel; she had been his only refuge. What was he doing? Her lips were flecked with red droplets now and he bent to lick them off.

Sirena squeezed her eyes shut and felt the creature taste her. He was stroking her closed eyelids now, like a child inspecting a lost but beloved toy.

'It's too late for you, you know,' she hissed, 'for me too.'

Soren cocked his head to one side, listening to the words form in her mouth and reach his ears.

'Why did you come here?' he asked and he let her go, reluctantly it seemed. She staggered backward and fell down. Getting up with all the dignity she could muster beneath the pain and straightening her skirts. Soren smiled. He remembered now.

'I have come back to etch the image of your face in my memory so that when we go to hell I can point out the beast, and all the other lost souls who you led there will know who you are,' she said defiantly.

Soren hissed and some of his shadow fell away. Sirena forced herself not to look away. This is what she had fallen in love with; her whole life was represented by this foul thing that looked suddenly so sad. Tears rolled down her flawless round face as he came closer to her and reached out to cup her cheek. He was naked now, his disgusting skin so close to her own. Hollow cheeks and empty eyes that saw right through her. Torrents of feelings passed between their gazes but it was too late for them now.

A masked face was floating in the room behind Soren's disfigured body, moonlit and perfect.

'Do it,' she whispered into the night, 'do it now.'

Epilogue

"Statues of Arial and Ronan stand upon every planet in the Worlds, all those who owe their lives to her and her angels." She paused, as if in thought, 'they say that on the celebration of the Seventh day, she cries tears of blood for her drey and for her malachi...how sweet,' the woman remarked. It was supposed to sound sarcastic but it came out a little nostalgic.

Damek sat motionless behind his borrowed desk, eyes fixed on this woman he had found.

She carelessly placed the book back on the shelf in the wrong place deliberately, ashen eyes smoldering beneath long lashes, skirt riding up her thighs.

Her arms were bruised from where they had grabbed her and her head still ached dully from the questioning but then *he* had come. Damek. She moved closer to the vampire, hips swaying, and swung herself up to sit half-way on the polished wood, one leg dangling as it rested over the other.

'You must have really loved her,' she said, testing the waters. Something dark passed briefly over the vampire's features and it made the small hairs on her neck stand on end. He then sighed deeply and the spell was broken. She was not afraid of him. She had seen too much.

A knock sounded at the door and another night stalker was inside the room and beside them, before her ears had even registered the sound. This one looked rougher than the smooth figure seated calmly before her.

'Are we ready Blain?' Damek asked, barely masking the weariness in his voice. Blain smiled a strained smile and nodded.

About the Author

Chantelle Roberts studied environmental management at the University of South Africa. She works for a large printing company and enjoys reading, writing, and persuading people not to eat tuna. She was born in South Africa and lives with her chameleon and three cats on a quiet farm in Pretoria.